How to Read a Book

Also by Monica Wood

The One-in-a-Million Boy

When We Were the Kennedys

Any Bitter Thing

Ernie's Ark

My Only Story

Secret Language

How to Read a Book

a novel

Monica Wood

MARINER BOOKS
New York Boston

This is a work of fiction. Names, characters, places, and incidents are products of the author's imagination or are used fictitiously and are not to be construed as real. Any resemblance to actual events, locales, organizations, or persons, living or dead, is entirely coincidental.

HarperCollins books may be purchased for educational, business, or sales promotional use. For information, please email the Special Markets Department at SPsales@harpercollins.com.

FIRST EDITION

Designed by Emily Snyder

Library of Congress Cataloging-in-Publication Data has been applied for.

ISBN 978-0-06-324367-5 (hardcover)
ISBN 978-0-06-341088-6 (international edition)

24 25 26 27 28 LBC 9 8 7 6 5

For my beloved band:
Sarah Braunstein, Kate Christensen,
Lewis Robinson, Bill Roorbach

and for incarcerated women everywhere

How to Read a Book

1

Violet

THE VISITORS' ROOM IS EXACTLY the functional, state-designed space you'd expect. A bland, boring rectangle, solid wall at each end and a bank of windows along both sides. One bank of windows opens to the Outs, a skeleton of barbed wire where goldfinches sometimes light, and beyond that a bumpy, sloping field, tufts-of-this and thickets-of-that whose colors change all year long. On this day I'm thinking of, I am twenty-two years old, on short time that still feels long, and the field is snow covered, bluish, with dead stalks sticking out here and there like cries for help.

The walls are naked except for a poster that shows you what to do in case of choking. No furniture except for a table and thirteen armless, ass-pinching chairs. Two tables, actually, arranged head-to-head, holding nothing but our paper, our pens, and our copy of the book under discussion. What color there is runs from putty to Band-Aid, but when we're all here, the room feels warmish, lived-in.

The other bank of windows runs along the main corridor, and across that corridor another bank of windows looks into the chow hall, not a wall in the place without a window in it. Doors too. Everything here is designed to murder your privacy.

I can still see us so clearly: twelve women dressed in our blues, our dry hands folded or spread or drumming, and the Book Lady at the head of the table, sensible button-up blouse patterned with smiley green bees, helping us discuss a book we hate. I feel the way I always feel in Book Club. The way I believe we all feel. Safe.

The book is called *Scar Tissue*, a so-called true story about a famous cardiac surgeon who grew up eating dirt. Actual, literal dirt from a junky front yard in East Texas. Dirt sprinkled on her Cheerios, punishment for reading the newspaper.

Dawna-Lynn goes first, as usual. She swipes her stringy hair behind her ears. "What do we care about a rich lady doctor whose biggest tragedy is winter in New York City?"

"It's snow, lady," says Renee. "Get over yourself."

Like most of us, Renee and Dawna-Lynn grew up in Maine and take great exception to a famous cardiac surgeon's whining about two inches of slush as she pushes a double stroller across Fifth fucking Avenue.

Kitten says, "Nobody eats dirt for sixteen years and gets to be a famous cardiac surgeon."

Then Shayna: "Nobody eats dirt for sixteen years and gets adorable twins with matching dimples."

Then Jacynta: "I wouldn't walk across the street to spit on her."

And Marielle: "No way her lowlife parents were secretly educated and talented."

And Dorothy: "What a liar."

And Jenny Big: "You can't hide talent."

Automatically, we look at Dawna-Lynn. At my first Town Meeting, she belted all the comic songs from her high school's long-ago production of *Guys and Dolls*, and even the COs broke up laughing. Dorothy, who has six kids and bladder prolapse, literally peed her pants. I was new and scared, and the show made me laugh so hard I suddenly believed I could stand the next twenty-eight months without dying of despair. It was also sad, though, because Dawna-Lynn, whose nickname is Showtime, has a Broadway voice that should have given her a different life. A choice here, a choice there, she could be posing in a ball gown with her Tony award instead of hamming it up at Town Meeting in her blues.

"I understand your point," the Book Lady says. She always understands our point, because she's a retired English teacher who enjoys "lively" discussion. Plus, she likes us. "However," she adds, which she always does, "in order for reading to become an exercise in empathy, it helps to think of all the characters in all the books as fellow creatures."

"Even the ones we don't understand," says Brittie, who's got the pointy face and eye circles of a tame raccoon.

Jenny Big adds, on cue, "Even the ones we don't like."

Desiree finishes up: "Even the ones we hate with the fiery shitballs of hell."

The Book Lady, who is older-lady pretty, with a sweet peachy face and wavy, ash-colored hair and soft jowls, opens her hands. "There you go. It's not that hard."

Her idea about fellow creatures is okay in theory—the Book Lady has tons of theories, especially about compassion—but all the same we find it quite the stretch to invite the famous and successful cardiac surgeon into our family of fellow creatures.

In the year and a half since we've been coming to Book Club, the Book Lady has tried out all kinds of authors, from Virginia Woolf to Zadie Smith, and we've complained about them all. We love complaining. It's weirdly empowering. The Book Lady hasn't figured that out yet.

Not that we don't have preferences. Our favorite stretch started last fall, when we asked for the classics most of us had read in high school and remembered from before. *To Kill a Mockingbird, Of Mice and Men, The Great Gatsby*.

Those books felt like family. Those books took us through the worst of winter—a heartless one, too much snow, too many days without yard time.

Ethan Frome was the last of the batch, and this time around I read it with different eyes. Beautiful Mattie turns into a "querulous" hag after a sledding accident with Ethan. It's basically about how life sucks and nobody who deserves love ever gets it.

Before prison, I was a more forgiving reader.

"The author should've called it *Ethan Frome, God Hates Your Guts*," Dawna-Lynn said at the time. So the Book Lady, of course, asked us what we thought about God, a question that lasted us through the remainder of that session.

Every Friday, two hours, books, books, books. We get to keep them after we're done, and that's no small thing, a stack of triumphs under the bed.

Today we're at the end of that dismal winter, discussing a flashback to where the famous cardiac surgeon first meets her gorgeous financial-manager husband in the elevator of their apartment building. We already know this guy, whose obnoxiousness through twenty-seven chapters goes right over the author's head, but she's circling back to their first meeting to show us that life has a shape but you don't see the shape until later.

Good point. I'll give her that.

Then Shayna pipes up, out of the blue, that one time her boyfriend threw her clothes out the window of their second-floor apartment because she wouldn't give him a blow job before she left for work. This is Book Club, this out-of-the-blueness, because reading books, even annoying books about lucky people who think they grew up tragically, gets us talking.

"My boyfriend did that," Desiree says. Her hair, despite being done up in a layer cake of braids, looks dull and flat. Eyes, too: dull and flat. "Third floor, my clothes, plus my purse, plus my elephant figurines, everything smashed on the street."

Jacynta goes next: "Fourth floor: my clothes, my purse, my mom's jewelry."

"Me too," says Renee. "Fifth floor. Plus my cat." Renee is short and dark and pretty, and I really, really hate that her cat got tossed.

But this happens a lot. A game called Who Got It Worst, and most of it's true.

Then Aimee. Little Aimee, who looks about twelve, a shivering little field mouse. She says, "My husband threw my baby. He threw my baby out the window. I didn't really care about the clothes."

The Book Lady just listens. Which I guess is what makes these things come out. She'll ask a "leading question," like the God one, and then it's yak-yak-yak till she "winds us down" and asks another.

Usually by the time somebody gets sent up, even if the Reason is of the sort that makes the news, it's months or more since the coverage, so we either don't remember or don't care. But when the Reason is throwing a baby into the street (the baby didn't make it, and Aimee cries all the time), it sticks. So: sometimes we know. Either way, we don't talk about our Reasons. We talk about Before: our families, boyfriends or girlfriends, husbands or wives or kids if we have them. Job and hobbies. The people and things we miss on the Outs (endless endless endless list). What we ate. Where we lived. Old TV shows. Who we loved and hated. Never about our Reason, even if everybody knows what it is. They know mine.

As for Aimee, her Reason was actually the husband's Reason. He's the one who did the baby throwing. A jury of her so-called peers did not believe this. Imagine the courtroom: Husband, a good-looking civil engineer. Wife (Aimee), a pitifully young mother with depression so bad her lawyers can't get her to comb her hair. Which is how she lands on the inside, crying for her baby at Book Club, and he winds up on the Outs, managing a bridge project. Maybe someday he'll have another baby to toss out a different window and then Aimee will get a second trial and her hair will stop falling out. That's what we all kind of hope, because Aimee is so tiny and delicate, little sparrow bones. If she was an acne-scarred monster with a bald patch and giant swinging boobs—I won't name names—then we'd believe the jury just like everybody else. That's just how people are.

The Book Lady has gone super quiet. Desiree, sitting across from me, catches my eye: *Uh-oh.*

We call her Bookie. Bookie the Book Lady. On her first day she introduced herself as Harriet. First name only, of course—millions of rules—but within a month we knew her last name (Larson) and the name of her street (Belmont) and the make of her car (Toyota Corolla, marine blue). And by now, a year and a half later, we know she has daughters, Annie and Ellen, who live in London with their families. Also a niece, her dead sister's child, who's headed for grad school in California, which hurts the Book Lady's heart a little. Her house is a Queen Anne with deep windowsills loved by Tabsy, the Book Lady's black-and-white, overweight, indoor-only, prone-to-vomiting cat.

We're not supposed to know these things. The math guy, a slab of beef from the community college, wouldn't even tell us his real first name, made a lame joke about aliases. But the Book Lady, for all her methodical handouts and typed lesson plans, treats us like a bunch of girls just talking.

The Book Lady is thinking. From her chairback hangs a crisp canvas bag that says EAT SLEEP READ. Behind her, the dull back wall of the Visitors' Room. To her left, sunlight flooding in from the Outs, catching a starburst of wrinkles on her hands, which she sets on the table, palms down.

Everybody quits sooner or later—mostly sooner—and if I were the Book Lady the last thing I'd do is come here once a week to hang out with ingrates who complain about my reading choices. Of the fifteen books she's brought in by now, not one has met with unanimous approval.

In the stillness of the Book Lady's gaze, which is sort of tender and mysterious, I'm glad to have read those fifteen books. The library here, oh my God, nothing but romance and double agents. I can't say I loved *The Great Gatsby*, but sometimes a sparkling sentence can really rip you up.

So we drove on toward death through the cooling twilight.

A sentence like that can put you someplace other than the shithole where you happen to be reading it. Or it's an ambush that puts you exactly in the shithole where you happen to be reading it.

The Book Lady contemplates her hands. Maybe she's considering a kindly, diplomatic way to say she's just about had it. But no. Instead, she takes off her reading glasses and says, "Not once, not in my entire sixty-four years, has a man thrown my things out a window."

You can almost hear the room relax, like a let-go balloon.

"You're lucky, Bookie," says Jacynta, who has close-set features that make you think she's eternally pissed-off and scowly, which she is not.

The Book Lady says, "That's right, Jacynta. I am lucky."

"Not everybody's lucky," Kitten says.

"Kitten, I married a man who loved me."

"That would be Lou," says Renee. *Dat*, she says, French-Canadian Maine through and through. *Dat would be Lou.*

"Yes, Renee. Dear Lou."

"He died, though," says Marielle. Marielle, a mill-hand's kid, beefy and tender.

"Well, yes, Marielle. But we had a good run."

Shayna says, "When your niece leaves for California all you'll have left is Tabsy."

"Oh, but, Shayna, Tabsy makes for a wonderful husband," the Book Lady says, and then we're all laughing, because we've sort of fallen for Tabsy ourselves. And the Book Lady's clearly not leaving us.

Then we're back on track, talking about luck, and books, and life, and why the *Scar Tissue* author's flawless twins don't deserve a forty-thousand-per-kid preschool.

"Oh, darn," the Book Lady says. She frowns at the wall clock like its sole purpose is to ruin fun. "Quitting time already."

This moment always catches me unaware. The door opens, and real life thunders in. A howl from 4-Walk. The iron echo of a CO coming in one door or going out another. The metallic clatter of the chow hall.

"Wait, wait, before we go I have a surprise," the Book Lady says, which always means a new book. She slumps her satchel on the table and removes the stack. "It was written in the forties, but you'll find it feels quite contemporary. People call it a novel, but in fact it's two novellas."

A little murmur of approval: "novella" sounds kind of swanky, or at least short.

"It's about a brother and sister at a crossroad in their lives. Separate but related crossroads. The sister is experiencing either a crisis of faith, or a nervous breakdown. Won't it be fun to discuss which it is?" She passes out copies of the book: *Franny and Zooey* by J. D. Salinger.

A burst of energy zings around the room, because some of us already know this author. As I said, we like familiar things. "Before" things. The Book Lady knows this.

I pick up my copy and hold it. I like the weight of a book, any book, in my hand. This one's pretty. Small and slim, plain white cover with stocky black letters.

"Thanks, Bookie," we say.

"And remember," the Book Lady says, "if the characters aren't quite what we wish they could be . . ."

"Fellow creatures," Dorothy says.

We all get up to leave, holding two books now, the one we hated on the bottom and a fresh start on the top.

"I read *Catcher in the Rye* in eighth grade," I tell the Book Lady.

Brittie says, "So did I."

"*Catcher in the Rye* is for innocents," the Book Lady says as Roberts, the ugliest CO in the place, looms outside the door, because God forbid we get two extra seconds of Book Club. "This one's for people with some life behind them."

We like the sound of that. We are women with some life behind us. We know some things.

The feeling lasts till I get out to the corridor and then there I am. I should say there *we* are. And by *we*, I include not only the other women, but the souls who came here with us, invisible but present, like hovering ghosts. Some of them are alive, somewhere on the Outs, greatly altered, maybe forever, by something we did. And some of them are dead, also because of something we did. On certain days—the quieter days, when nobody gets written up or lugged or dragged to the Fishbowl, the days when the place feels not like a dementia unit on Mars but like an animal shelter filled with calm dogs, I can almost see them, our Reasons, small smoky thicknesses in the air. Like guardian angels, in a way. Guarding our memory of them. They float among us, quiet and uncomplaining, and they refuse to disappear.

Come dark, in the quiet of your cot, you can taste them, like ash after fire.

We don't talk about this. But we know. We know this about each other.

Our Reasons meet us in the morning and whisper to us at night. Mine is an innocent, unsuspecting, eternally sixty-one-year-old woman named Lorraine Daigle. She is part of me now, a sliver of bone knitted to one of my bones.

At night, locked down, prayers said, I murmur, "Night, Brittie," and Brittie whispers, "Night, Violet." After that, in the blessed privacy of my own head, I think-whisper, *Night, Lorraine*. Every night I think-whisper this. At the age of twenty-two, I do not yet know how many more days God will give me, but I know this: I will think-whisper *Night, Lorraine,* at the end of every single one.

2

Frank

After the torment of the trial—pitying glances from the jury box, merciless renditions of Lorraine's final moments—Frank Daigle had sequestered himself for over a year, a jury of one, enduring daily calls from his daughter, Kristy, who believed her father paralyzed with grief. *Take a walk, Dad*, she advised him. *You're a mess. Put one foot in front of the other, literally. She would want you to.*

Eventually, if only to avoid her calls, he'd taken to walking two miles each morning to Portland's artsy downtown peninsula, where he'd rarely ventured in his former life. At Coffee by Design, he ordered a macchiato (Lorraine would have called this "airs") and took it into Wadsworth Books, where he bought the morning paper and settled into a well-loved leather sofa to watch the day unfasten: Jake tapping book orders into a keyboard; Robin feeding the latest in a rotation of cats up for adoption; Marnie, the store manager, dragging the rickety book cart to the sidewalk.

This new ritual pleased him unexpectedly. Frank had been a reader as a boy, and damned if the place didn't smell just like his childhood library, with the same tottering shelves and thick-legged tables laden with books.

About a month in, the book cart lost a caster. "I hate this thing," Marnie growled. The ill-made contraption had three tiers of two-sided shelves, slightly skewed and crammed with bargains.

Frank lowered his paper. "Flimsy stem mounts," he said. "No surprise there."

"Well, I hate it." Marnie had exquisite deep-brown skin; kind, daughterly eyes; and dark, springy hair shot through with streaks of gold.

"Door needs work, too," he said.

She regarded the door with suspicion. "What's wrong with it?"

"Closes slow. Cat could get out." In fact, this had happened, two cats previous, a Siamese with half a tail and a death wish. It was Frank who'd sprung from the sofa and wheedled the creature back inside.

"I thought doors closed at, like, their own pace," Marnie said. "Like they come with their own speed."

Frank shook his head. These kids didn't own so much as a hammer among them.

"Also," he ventured, "the carpet by the back door could use tacking."

"I was gonna tape it."

"No," he said. "It needs tacking. And the walls want paint."

They agreed on twenty-five hours, minimum wage, and only when they shook hands did Frank realize that getting hired as the store handyman had been his aim all along.

He was often late to revelations of this sort. As a teenager he'd talked himself into football because his father, whom he loved, wanted him to play. He was sized for the D-line but in body only; every hit gave him pause, every sozzling crack, because Frank Daigle was not born to hurt people. Lorraine fell for Frank the defensive lineman, but he was a team chaplain at heart. He'd given her love, patience, stability, and her only child. These gifts had turned out to be the wrong gifts.

The new job became a salve for such thoughts; he regained a sense of purpose he'd been unaware of losing. He took up reading again and stocked an endcap with favorites: Lee Child, Patricia Cornwell, Paul Doiron, damn good storytellers in his opinion. He also took charge of the cats, shelter animals who showed well in public and had the run of the place despite the cage with its (newly repaired) gate. The store had a way of tidying the pitch-and-lurch of his feelings, forcing the past to recede, bracketing his days with the zeal of youth.

His daughter had been right—he *was* a mess—though wrong about the reasons.

Today he was on his knees, painting a boot-scuffed stretch of molding near Magazines and Periodicals. Behind him, he heard a polite throat clearing, a dainty ahem from Robin, the freckled Faulkner-lover who managed the used books. "Frank," she said. "We have a situation."

His heart hiccupped. "What is it?"

"Nobody wants Boris." She pointed dramatically to the window, where the current cat, a faded female tortoiseshell, spent its days curled like a Russian hat in a plank of sunlight. "She's been here two weeks without so much as a nibble."

"What's wrong with her?" Frank asked. "Aside from her name."

Robin wrinkled her nose in sympathy and consternation. "She's sort of stinky."

Frank laid his paintbrush along the top of the open can, wiped off his hands, and stood up. "I could give her a bath after I'm done here."

"Oh, Frank, could you?" Marnie was here now, arms crossed, as if Boris's hygiene were a problem, like scuffed molding, that only Frank could solve.

"Cats hate water," Robin reminded one and all.

"The sink in the basement is sizable," Frank said, glancing at the unsuspecting Boris. "Plenty of room to tango."

Robin clapped her hands like a child. "Thank you, Frank!"

"While I've got you here," Frank said to Marnie, "we'll have to replace that." He pointed to one of the store's many quirks, a neat square of glass, age-pocked and cloudy, inexplicably mounted above the entryway to the children's room, too high to clean or to see through. "Tinted glass, I was thinking, in a pretty color. Pane's about two-foot square. That's a one-man job."

"Blue," Robin said. "I love blue."

Marnie agreed, as she agreed with all of Frank's suggestions, and as the young women returned to their own tasks, Robin called back, "This place looks great!"

The youngsters, of course, didn't understand that he was overqualified. He'd spent his working life at Pierce Machine Company, forty-four years, retiring as a toolmaker with a good pension, prickly feet, and a cranky back. He'd made jigs and fixtures for all manner of ship and tank and jet-engine parts; the modern world boomed with the fruit of his labor, and his hands bore marks of that work. The one time he'd returned to visit—just after the accident, a homing instinct—the place had been washed clean, everything computer controlled now, immaculate sheets of plexiglass covering the vivid mess of production. The floors shone. It was like visiting Oz, and he'd felt like the horse of a different color.

But these kids, who had acres of poetry committed to memory and the mechanical skills of an aardvark, they needed him. His demotion to handyman felt like cool air whooshing through his body. By the end of day one, he'd transformed the balky book cart into a gliding triumph.

You need a therapist, Dad.

You need more exercise, Dad.

You need a dog, Dad.

What he needed was work. And so Frank Daigle, who'd labored all his life amid the roar of a machine shop, spent twenty-five hours a week in the scholarly quiet of a bookstore. What an "air," and that air felt great. He knelt once again, the open paint can smelling of a fresh start. He picked up his brush, grateful.

The bell over the door jingled. Frank raised his head. But no.

He might as well admit it: he was looking for her.

The youngsters loved the jingling bell and thought he'd installed it on behalf of escapees, though in truth few of the cats posed a flight risk. Boris slept so soundly people thought she was a toy.

No, the bell was not for Boris. It was for him. And her.

3

Harriet

In retirement Harriet had expected to plant masses of flowers, but so far she'd managed only a few potted succulents that didn't mind neglect. Who had the time? So much of her post-teaching life revolved around Book Club, reading and rereading, researching authors, and preparing questions to plump up their discussions. She'd fully committed to exposing the women to the open air of literature, to the sunshine of fresh ideas—an endeavor not unlike gardening after all. The sowing and reaping. The fruitful mistakes. The tang of expectation.

> DISCUSSION STARTER: If you were God, would you alter the facts for these characters?

> DISCUSSION STARTER: Do books change depending on when and where we read them?

> DISCUSSION STARTER: Why do people tell stories?

Harriet spent many pleasant hours on these questions, and on warm-up prompts to which the women's written answers ranged from bafflement to mutiny.

> Please write a sentence (10 words) to describe your reading experience.

JENNY BIG: I don't get why Franny's mother puts up with it.

JACYNTA: Shit happens get over your own pussy whip self Ethin!!!!!!!!

AIMEE: [redacted]

DAWNA-LYNN: Loved this book in high school, when I was happy.

MARIELLE: I flet sorry for lennys mouse so it ruined everything

RENEE: If I was God I would let the mouse live.

KITTEN: I wish Atticus was my Father and Scout was me.

DESIREE: Why are the females always the crazy ones??????

DOROTHY: Moral of the story: Lord, what fools these mortals be.

SHAYNA: sory

VIOLET: Ethan reminds us that life is treacherous, like winter weather.

BRITTIE: sucked sucked sucked sucked sucked sucked sucked sucked sucked sucked.

Despite Harriet's selections, the women came to Book Club anyway, never missed a Friday morning, week after week, in part because they had nothing else to do and in part, Harriet hoped, because being together in a room discussing even the most unacceptable book made the prison disappear.

They were small-town girls, mostly. Like Harriet herself. They came from up north, potato country, they came from the dead and dying mill towns along the state's churning rivers, they came from drug-plagued counties Down East, where monstrous waves smashed into cliffs in God-fearing images that wound up on postcards sold in gift shops from Madawaska to York. The women knew these natural views firsthand, and also the less lovely scenes of an out-of-work boyfriend gutting a poached deer, a midnight drug deal in a bedroom smelling of shit from a howling baby, a Glock 19 pointed across a kitchen table laid with brand-new dishes from Walmart.

And worse. Far worse. Harriet knew nothing beyond what they sometimes revealed during discussions. She preferred to meet the women where they were, on the given day. Every week, they began with an invocation:

I am a reader. I am intelligent. I have something worthy to contribute.

Did they ever. The women of Book Club had no patience with "pussies" like Ethan Frome or "douchebags" like Curley's wife (what a thing to call a woman!) and yet they brimmed with opinions, psychological analyses, judgments, and, on occasion, approval of their fictional comrades.

She was thinking of them now, with her usual measure of warmth and bemusement, as she pushed open the door to Wadsworth Books, met by the steadying aroma of old carpeting. She spotted a new clerk at the counter, an androgynous teenager whose enormous black-framed eyeglasses took up most of a genial, fine-boned face. Shiny dark hair fell in crinkly waves over one ear, and a stringent buzz cut exposed the other.

Harriet approached. "Is Tyler working today?"

"Tyler left for acting school!" the clerk said. "In Paris!"

Oh, no. After the disaster of *Franny and Zooey* (Harriet's attempt at a corrective for *Scar Tissue*), she was hoping that Tyler might help. He'd tried to warn her off Salinger, but she'd insisted that twelve incarcerated women from Maine would delight in New Yorkers from the forties who spoke in erudite, elliptical, finely turned sentences. Only Violet seemed to appreciate the spiritual howl in both novellas, possibly because she'd been raised by ferocious Baptists.

"You just missed him," the clerk said, pushing up the unwieldy eyeglasses. "He came by to see everyone before he left."

Harriet felt unreasonably sorry to have missed saying goodbye. Theirs had been a pleasant, circumscribed relationship, clerk and patron; Harriet believed these small connections made the world go round.

"And you are?" Harriet said.

"Baker. I'm filling in part-time. I'm a visual artist, actually."

Harriet paused. "Is Baker your first name or your last name?"

"Both."

"Your name is Baker Baker?"

"No," the clerk said, with a tenderness normally reserved for small, helpless animals. "It's one name."

She would have to ask her niece, who knew about such things, if one-name people were now a trend and what this trend might signify. Was Baker shucking the chains of patriarchy, or emulating a pop singer? Harriet genuinely wanted to know.

"I'm looking for a book," Harriet said.

"Oh, totally."

"It's for a book club. Tyler was the one I always worked with."

"I'm way better read than Tyler," Baker said. "What was your last book?"

"*Franny and Zooey*."

"How'd it go over?"

"Mixed," Harriet said, an understatement. They were still plodding through the final pages, Brittie and Jacynta pronouncing Franny and Zooey spoiled rotten, Dawna-Lynn deciding that Franny had a breakdown only because she could afford one. These left-field opinions pleased and surprised her: Harriet had never thought of existential crisis as a luxury, but now she did.

"I think I need something a little less Yale-and-tennis-racketish," she said now. "Maybe a family saga. With farm people, perhaps."

The surefooted Baker trotted down from behind the high counter. The poor thing's ears had been stabbed—deliberately, Harriet surmised—with multiple hoops and rattling pins. "This one's popular," Baker said, plucking a volume from New and Noteworthy.

Scar Tissue: A Memoir.

"We already read this," Harriet said. "'The narrator is a liar I wouldn't cross the street to spit on'—that's a direct quote from my book club."

"I saw it on Netflix. The evil dad makes the kid eat dirt. It's a pretty depressing movie."

"The book is also depressing," Harriet said, "but in far more stimulating fashion." She took a dramatic pause. "Because it's a book."

"Oh, totally," Baker said, undaunted, selecting a novel about entomologists in Manitoba, which, according to Baker, used the paradigm of metafiction in a traditional structure.

"I'll check the stacks," Harriet said.

"Just give a holler."

Harriet loved the stacks—those narrow channels crammed with possibility. She navigated slowly, already hearing the women's voices, for they loved to read chapters aloud, like plays, taking votes on who took which part. Voting meant something to these women who decided nothing, and Harriet relished offering them a bone of autonomy, however meatless, though she'd been warned at volunteer orientation not to "let them con you."

As she reached for a bright-red spine, her bag slipped from her arm and knocked a book to the floor.

"Oh, hello!" came a voice, overloud, from nowhere.

Harriet let go a little squeak and turned to find a man looming nearby. She'd seen him here before—a tall, good-looking older man with hazel-brown eyes and a silver crew cut. He carried an unopened can of paint, which he set down in order to scoop up the book.

"Allow me," he said. The book all but disappeared in his hand—the man had huge, appealing hands, callused and work-reddened and spider-cracked with fresh scratches. He noticed her noticing.

"Cats hate water," he said.

Harriet made note of the scratches, swallowed a laugh. He looked so serious, handing her the book. It wasn't hers, but she accepted it anyway. After a moment, long enough for his face to go crimson, he asked, "Are you shopping?" his voice too low now.

"Pardon?" Harriet asked.

"Are you shopping?"

Harriet gestured to the shelves. What else would she be doing?

"Good, then," the man said. His bobbing Adam's apple put her in mind of a heron swallowing a frog. "Happy shopping, all right, there you go." Then he darted away with his paint.

She regarded the book she'd knocked over: *Spoon River Anthology* by Edgar Lee Masters, a collection of brief life stories spoken by the dead in a fictionalized Illinois graveyard. She'd read it herself in college, grateful to have finished college in her forties, because the little tales—epitaphs, really—asked the reader to understand regret. She could already hear the women, experts in regret, channeling these voices from the grave. Violet's choirgirl timbre, Renee's starched consonants, Jenny Big's throaty grit. Dawna-Lynn would blindside them somehow: her rendition of Zooey's "fat lady" speech had brought them all to tears. Shayna, who could barely read, would opt to be the audience, holding her book like a butterfly she feared to harm.

Book in hand, decision made, Harriet rounded the end of the aisle and once again met the loud-soft man, who was now carrying a short length of board.

"Oh," Harriet said. "Pardon me."

"My fault," he said, stepping elaborately aside to let her pass.

She held up the book. "Happy accident." As she reached the counter she heard him call, "That's good, yes, wonderful."

"Oh, hey," Baker said, taking the book. "Success."

"Let's hope," Harriet said. "I'll need to order the rest."

Baker examined the cover. "Dead people talking?"

"It's a classic," Harriet said. "Denizens of a graveyard accounting for their lives." As Baker frowned at the jacket copy, Harriet added, "Useful fodder for reflection."

She sounded more schoolmarmish than she intended, which happened a lot. All her life people had misjudged her age, and it didn't help that she'd been named for her grandmother. And now, as time would have it, she was indeed the old lady she'd long resembled, moving through the world as Harriet Larson, retiree. She was sixty-four, looked every day of it, tried not to mind.

"Oh, totally," Baker said. "I just thought—you know, dead people talking. You might want to bring extra wine to the meeting." The youngster had a cuddly laugh; if hamsters could laugh, they would sound this way.

"Believe me," Harriet said, "I would love to bring extra wine to the meeting."

Baker leaned on the counter, shirt gapping to reveal an accidental eyeful—small, pretty breasts tattooed with a giant spiderweb. Did this mean something? She'd have to ask Sophie. The whims of youth moved at the speed of light. Not all youth: the waitresses at her favorite diner, the young mother who worked at the 7-Eleven, and the young mechanics at Arlo's Auto Repair reminded Harriet of herself at that age, and she never felt old when she was with them. Same with Book Club, she realized. It was odd, how at home Harriet felt at the prison. "At home" wasn't quite right. Useful? Needed? Here on the outside—"on the Outs," as the women put it—she felt misplaced and out of sync much of the time.

"Who is that man?" Harriet said, lowering her voice.

Baker leaned in again. "What man?"

"The one with the paint."

"Oh, that's Frank. Frank Daigle. He's like our handyman?" Baker's eyes glinted, and what glorious eyes, long lashes and shiny dark irises. "We think he's really cute."

"I see." Good grief, didn't these people have better things to do than make toys out of old folks? "May I order the books, please?"

Baker removed the cumbersome eyeglasses and read the jacket copy more carefully.

"Not a single soul in that graveyard went to Yale," Harriet said.

Baker clicked at the computer. "I can't get them for another week." Leaning in again, voice lowered: "It's two days, tops, if you go through Amazon."

"Amazon is the devil," Harriet informed not only Baker but whoever might be listening. She slid her credit card across the counter. "The Nazis worked with more subtlety."

"Oh, totally."

Harriet took the bus home, already planning her questions. *What is the purpose of an epitaph? Whom would you trust to write yours? Is it possible to sum up a human life?*

At home she took the yowling Tabsy into her lap—he was needier than her children had ever been, her self-governing girls who called Book Club a hobby. The cat's lawn-mower purring felt like affirmation. After a year and a half, Harriet had learned to second-guess her Book Club choices, but this one, which had almost literally dropped into her lap, looked like a winner. She relaxed, leafing through the laments, protests, and exultations of the departed souls of Spoon River, Illinois.

I was a gun-smith in Odessa. . . .
I was the Widow McFarlane. . . .
I was the daughter of Lambert Hutchins. . . .

Harriet clicked her pen, reading, choosing, underlining, gone from the present-day world.

I saw myself as a good machine
That Life had never used.

She could already hear the women reading the plaints and praises of ghosts compelled to speak—Dawna-Lynn's actressy confidence, Violet's clean-water purity, Desiree's juicy fervor, each woman an instrument unto herself. Hard to believe that on Harriet's first day as volunteer Book Club leader, these same twelve women had struck her as nearly identical. Of course that was the point of uniforms, to render the women interchangeable. The better for the COs to herd them like a single species of cow. But anyone who'd ever known two cows, as Harriet had as a girl, understood that even identically marked cows made sure you knew who was who.

I thirsted so for love!
I hungered so for life!

She could hear the women now, channeling voices dying to be heard.

4

Violet

Every day: same, same, same. The boredom feels like lice and you itch all over. Day after day, broken up sometimes by a job in Industry or Laundry. But even with a job, Monday feels pretty much like Thursday. February feels like June.

Until it doesn't. One random day, between Noon Chow and Town Meeting, your roommate might vanish and nobody will say why. Maybe she got lugged for spitting on a guard and until she comes back, you're on your own, surprise, 144 square feet to yourself. For how long you don't know, you just pray that if your old roomie doesn't come back, the new roomie will be someone who, at the least—at the very, very least—brushes her teeth every day. Washes her pits. Won't twist your thumb for being a high-and-mighty who likes vocabulary.

Sometimes when your roomie disappears, she goes for good. Out-of-state prison, maybe, closer to a family that doesn't want her. Off to serve out time in a county jail or prerelease. Or just plain sprung, to clear space for an overcrowd.

As you get closer to your time, you hope it'll be you. You'll be the disappeared roommate, CO summoning you from the dayroom or the yard or chow or Book Club or College Math or the library or Industry. It'll be your name they call, and next thing you know you're walking out the gate wearing the stuff they stripped off you back on day one. It won't look anything like your stuff anymore. You'll be on the Outs wearing a stranger's clothes.

Which is where I am, right now, on the Outs, or almost there, almost, confused as hell. At first I thought I didn't hear him right—Murphy, a CO with bad acne on his face and on his soul—but it turns out I did. *Powell*, he yelled. *You're up*.

I don't get to say goodbye to my roomie, Brittie, or anybody else really. Dawna-Lynn and Jenny Big happen to be in the dayroom crocheting this huge blanket for Jenny Big's grandson. They say bye. And Renee, coming out of Industry as Murphy's unlocking the first door. She drops a tower of sheets and bearhugs me (against the rules) and I don't even know what to feel. It's too soon to be happy (Murphy could be messing with me) but too late to go back and say my goodbyes or grab the books I saved from Book Club, which I keep under my bed, and anyway nothing really registers until the door unbolts and I walk straight through, and behind me Renee hollers to the dayroom, *Violet's out!*

It takes a while to walk all the way to the front gate. Murphy herds me through the prison's grimy guts, to a room that looks like the room they took me to when I first got here. Some paperwork, a change of clothes, my brain on fire, then I'm walking with Murphy again, partly inside and partly outside, snaking through the yards and into the buildings, door after locked door, gate after locked gate, Murphy clanking with keys and his gun belt and his tin heart. And then all of a sudden, within spitting distance, there's the final gate and my sister, Vicki, in the parking lot, leaning on her car.

Murphy pretends to lose the key. Messing with me now for real. He jingles and jangles, taking his sweet time. Asshole. I just wait. My heart feels like peeling paint. I made friends here. I did. But I will not miss this place. I wouldn't mind knowing how *Spoon River Anthology* ended, but oh well.

Finally, a great unlocking, same hell-rattle as when I came in, except this time it's the sound of hallelujah.

"Good luck," says Murphy. "See you soon." That's supposed to be a joke, hilarious. He thinks I'll tell this oh-so-funny joke till my dying day, which'll be plenty long after *his* dying day, considering he's a wheezy blob of hate on borrowed time.

Vicki waits in the lemony light of April, dressy slacks and a snappy blazer, neat gold earrings, hair a super-deep red, expensive salon job—all that and a bag of chips, as we say up home. The gate clanks a final fuck-you behind me. Murphy lumbers back across the yard, keys hitting against his ugly butt (my first week I thought it was dogs jangling through the halls), and I take my first full breath in twenty-two months.

I open my arms to the fresh air. "Holy shit."

"Mouth," Vicki says.

"Sorry."

Vicki used to be the wild one, the one you'd have expected to wind up inside, but now she's got the buttoned-up air of a real-estate agent. I run to her, hug her hard, hoping to feel, you know, homecoming-ish, but no. She just kind of sticks there, stiff and judgy. Might as well hug a phone pole. "Congratulations," she says, like I won something. My freedom, I guess. Good behavior, six months early. I won that.

Most likely it's nothing I did, though; it's just the fickle system. One minute it's the dregs of winter, you're in Book Club listening to Dorothy read the words of Mrs. Merritt from *Spoon River Anthology*, channeling this passionate woman who died in prison, everybody fellow-creaturing like mad, sniffling and not hiding it, because to feel pity in a pitiless place is no small thing. Next minute it's early springtime, brightness all over, the field outside deer-tramped but waking up, you can smell it. And I am suddenly, somehow, miraculously gawking at this waking-up field in the free open air.

"Get in," Vicki says, so I do.

"Nice car, Vick. Smells new."

"It *is* new."

How do you make conversation on the Outs? I can't remember. Even with my sister. Especially with my sister.

"How'd you rate this?" I ask her.

"Got married."

"Who to?"

"Billy Wingate. We're redoing our house."

"You have a house?"

"The Jordan place. We bought it last year."

"Wow," I say. "Guess you made out."

"Guess I did."

Billy Wingate owns a dealership on Route 2 just outside of Abbott Falls because his dad, who owned it before him, died of a heart attack at forty-six. Billy was in Vicki's class in high school, but I never thought she even liked him much. Money talks.

"You could've told me," I say to her, meaning the wedding. "I would've been happy for you."

"I'm telling you now."

"Because I asked."

Vicki puts the car in gear, and out of the lot we go. It's so pretty out here, the field a vast hill-and-dale sloping upward till it crashes into the ugliest manmade hulk you've ever seen. From inside you can't see more than the field's upper rise, a sweep of grass and wild shrubs and bushes. We've seen turkeys out there. Deer. A moose one time, on Thanksgiving, which turned a crap day into something we talked about for weeks.

I stick my head out the window of Vicki's shiny new Buick because I've never seen the prison from this angle. I arrived in the dark of night, for starters, in no mood to drink in the scenery. The prison looms at the top of the rise, low brick blocks and ugly add-ons and of course the chain-link and barbed wire. The only part I can see from here is Men's. Women's is way back—separate from the hollering stink of Men's—a "progressive" model that we were supposed to appreciate every minute of every lice-boring day.

Well, I did appreciate it, actually. I got lugged once—which means off you go, not to the Fishbowl but to the Pod, a cellblock in what used to be part of Men's for when you need a lesson about "living in community." It was early on, when I was so depressed I couldn't haul myself out of bed for the six a.m. head count. We called it "felony sleeping." Three times, you go to the Fishbowl for a day or two, a cell just off the dayroom, solitary but not really. Four times, and you get lugged, and the lesson about "living in community" is two hundred ants swarming your toilet. No wonder the men holler all day long; their building is an ugly, crumbling disaster. We hear them in their yard, which is near our yard soundwise but not sightwise. You get lugged once, the alternative looks pretty damn good.

I did appreciate it. The progressive model. It wasn't awful. We laughed a lot. There was a weirdness about our laughter, though, always a tick or two short of hysterics. I had this little group—Brittie, Marielle, Shayna, Desiree, and Kitten, all from Book Club. We invented this game called When I Get Out First Thing I Do. Imagine us in the dayroom, knitting—you might take us for a houseful of prairie ladies, minus the gingham. The first round is always sex-sex-sex.

Brittie: "When I Get Out First Thing I Do I blow my sweet, sweet baby while he drives me to a fancy-ass hotel."

Shayna: "When I Get Out First Thing I Do I fuck my man so hard he calls for Jesus." (Shayna has a way with filth.)

Jenny Big is a lifer, but she goes anyway: "When I Get Out First Thing I Do I dig him up and kill him again twice over." She's serious: that little muscle along her jaw, twitchy and all-business. As I said, we don't generally talk about our Reasons, but Jenny Big's is a doozy that made the news. She poured kerosene on her goat-faced husband while he was passed out and snoring, huge piss stain on the couch she'd just brought home after four months on layaway. Her only regret, aside from the ruined couch and forty years, is that her dog, Elmo, a twelve-pound terrier mutt, went down in the fire.

Elmo comes up a lot in Book Club. A *lot*. Everything reminds Jenny Big of Elmo, because no one else has ever loved her.

Dawna-Lynn, who's got four years left on a fifteen, goes next: "When I Get Out First Thing I Do I stand outside this fucken chicken wire and sing the score of *Les Miz* and then the score of *Rent* and then I keep on singing till they open the gate and let the rest of you bitches out." This one gets applause because we can imagine her doing it.

Renee: "When I Get Out First Thing I Do I tell my mémère I'm sorry." This is the closest we ever get to talking about our Reasons. The people you owe apologies to.

Then Kitten: "When I Get Out First Thing I Do I kiss my baby girl fourteen times." Kitten is big and soft and fluffy, but her voice squeezes shut when she plays this game.

And Dorothy, old and round and pink-cheeked, not exactly playing but within hearing: "When I Get Out First Thing I Do I buy my grandson seven birthday presents."

The numbers are about the years gone, and that's when everything gets blue and quiet and not at all fun. Kitten's baby girl, Princess, is fourteen now and living with a family out in Oregon.

Anyway. Here we are, the knitting prairie ladies, big, high-ceiling dayroom, corridors radiating out. I live in 2-Walk, where mostly the women are nice. Not Crazyville, at least. 4-Walk is nothing *but* Crazyville.

And then, somehow, I'm out of 2-Walk, out of the dayroom, out of Book Club, out of Industry, a free woman riding in the passenger seat of my sister's car that smells like a dealership. I breathe and breathe, oh my God, pure relief. And there's this odd, achy twist of longing inside my relief, as I follow the wavy field and the prison above and understand that never again will I sit in the dayroom and hear Brittie start a round of When I Get Out First Thing I Do.

"Pastor Rick says to tell you he prayed for your redemption," Vicki says, checking her eye makeup in the rearview, which makes me realize how bad I must look after twenty-two months of neglect. Maybe that's why she's doing it. "He still considers you part of the flock, Violet, despite the obvious. He says to remind you that no matter who forsakes you, Jesus shall not forsake you."

"You're going to church again?"

"I had to. Mama needed me. And I'm glad I did."

"Can you send a message back to Pastor Rick? From me?"

Vicki's mouth does that thing it does when she's suspicious, which is much of the time. "What's the message?"

"The message is Pastor Rick can shove Jesus straight up his ass, okay? Not partway. The whole way. The whole way up his lechy old-man hypocrite ass."

Vicki won't dignify this with a response except for her hands tightening on the wheel. The rings are quite the show, a sparkling band and a diamond cluster the size of a newborn's fist.

"Vicki, pull over."

She pulls over.

"Thank you."

"You're welcome."

This is Vicki fulfilling a deathbed promise and not one thing else. Our mother wrote me every single day until she died, and Vicki didn't write once.

"Don't leave," I tell her.

"Hurry up."

I get out to scan the field for a meadowlark, not that I know what a meadowlark looks like. The social worker said there was one here last spring. I check out the field, which as I said is huge, the prison pretty much ruining the view. Off with my shoes, off with my socks, and the roadside sand feels good. And the grass, oh my God. I forgot how sweet the feeling. It's not green yet, still that wintry yellow-going-toward-lime, but you can tell it's already tipped over to unstoppable. You can tell it wants to be alive. If a meadowlark shows up, I think I will know it. Or it will know me.

"What are you doing?" my sister yells from the car. "I don't have all day, Violet, Billy's waiting, we have an appointment at the tile store at three."

"Fuck you, Vicki. Fuck your tiles."

"Mouth!"

"Our shit library ran out of etiquette books," I yell back. "Do you know what a meadowlark looks like?"

From inside the car she shoots me a look: *Our mother died of a broken heart and it's all your fault, so fuck your stupid meadowwhat.*

"You never wrote," I mutter, getting back in.

Vicki steadies her eyes on the road.

"Troy never wrote, either," I say. "I thought he would."

Troy was my boyfriend-slash-fiancé-slash-future-slash-everything, long story, never threw my stuff out second-story windows, but. There was something. He played rough. I admit I was a tiny bit afraid of him.

Vicki grips the wheel, the show-offy diamonds pinging with light. "He's with Becca Frye. Took him five minutes."

"I figured." My only good friend. She visited me one time only, I guess so she could brag for the rest of her life about visiting someone in the slammer. The joint. The crowbar hotel.

"You sure know how to pick 'em," Vicki says, glancing over, some pity maybe. She seems older in a way I can't name. She always looked like a schoolgirl, but now she resembles one of those married ladies on TV who drink wine at lunch.

"Mama wrote," I remind her. "Every day, just about."

Vicki nods. "Mothers can't help it."

She drives for a while, not talking, until we reach Portland, trafficky and loud, and even though prison was also trafficky and loud, this is not what I'm used to. Abbott Falls has one stoplight, but Vicki's doing pretty well, and I realize as we drive straight into the city that she's done a dry run already. My heart does a little fish-flip, but I don't dare ask where she's taking me. I thought that by day's end I'd be in the boring, familiar nothing of Abbott Falls, where I could sit by the water in my old spot and watch the river spill over the boulders and listen to the sigh of the paper mill and think and think and think. And then I'd get up and face it, I'd just *face it*, because my hometown is burning with people who watched my mother slowly die through my trial and incarceration, and I would really, really like to be done feeling ashamed.

"This is the best I can do," Vicki says, turning onto a street with lots of trees, and cars parked bumper to bumper down both sides. She slows down in front of a three-story apartment building, double parks with her flashers on.

"Here." She gives me a key, a number for the landlord, and inexplicably, our mother's engagement ring.

"She wanted you to have it. I didn't need it, obviously. She would've given it to me instead. I'm the firstborn."

The ring is gold with a tiny stone and it won't fit right. My mother was a hefty lady, an easy laugher, and I am not.

Vicki says, "Mama didn't raise us to be criminals."

"I know that, Vicki."

"She raised us right."

What can I say? My mother raised us right, and what she got for her trouble was a manslaughterer child who killed her with grief.

"Third floor," Vicki says. "Three B. Your rent is paid for a year." She hands me an envelope, a fat, lumpy business envelope all sealed up. She reaches into the back seat and hauls out an overnight bag, really nice, tapestry with many zippers, bulging full. She gives me that, too.

"You're just leaving me here?"

"You're better off. Believe me."

"I mean, it's a big city."

"The social worker said Portland would be best. The most opportunity." She looks a little bit sorry but also extremely Vicki. We used to be close, before high school. She loaned me her cutest sweater for my first day, but after that we kind of drifted. I figure we would've found our way back eventually if not for this.

"Vicki. I don't know where anything is."

"Nobody wants you back home, Violet," she says. "Not Aunt Pammy, not Aunt Linda, not Uncle Eddie, not the cousins. Nobody. I'm sorry. But that's how it is."

Vicki attended every second of the trial—not for me, for our mother, who could barely walk for the grief. Vicki held her up as she tottered into a seat behind me. I could hear every breath my mother took, little saw blades shredding my insides, cut by cut. Maybe she had cancer already; maybe it wasn't all me.

"I didn't mean it." I'm talking about the woman in the other car, Lorraine Daigle, but the way it comes out, it could be Mama.

"Well, she's dead whether you meant it or not," Vicki says. "And that poor man sitting there, day after day."

She means the husband. The nicest, nicest man. Frank Daigle. On the second day of the trial, I felt the back of my head heat up, and when I turned around, there he was, just across the way, first row behind the prosecution, his eyes watery and bloodshot. He did not hate me. I could see that he did not hate me. Frank Daigle had a kind face and he did not hate me.

I put down the tapestry bag, giving Vicki a chance to hug me good-bye, which she does not do. Instead, she gets back into the car and the passenger window slides down. I lean in.

"I thought the sentence was fair," she says, implying that the rest of the family didn't. Did they think I deserved more, or less? "You might as well know I'm pregnant. I'm going back to live my life, Violet. I'm sorry."

A car squeezes past us, a man at the wheel blatting his horn. Vicki puts the car into gear, and I notice her fancy manicure, shiny pink polish with appliqués of tiny Easter eggs. It's Easter week, I realize. As little girls we dyed eggs on the sunporch with our mother, Mama singing in a way that resounded, as certain music will, inside my own body. Her voice built a shelter around us, and I miss it still.

"What was it like?" I ask. "When Mama died?"

"Awful." Vicki shuts her eyes. "Be lucky you missed it."

"I don't feel lucky."

"She weighed eighty pounds."

My pillowy mother, eighty pounds. My throat freezes over. "I wish I'd been there," I manage. "That's what I'm saying."

"If you'd been there," Vicki says, swiping at her salon hair, "she wouldn't've gotten sick at all."

I say nothing. I believe this.

"I wish it wasn't this way, Violet," Vicki says. She might be crying. "Please don't call us. You'll be all right."

And then my only sister—the firstborn named for a queen—pulls away in her big, bright car. I stand on the brick sidewalk of Grant Street in Portland, Maine, where I know not even one person out of sixty-five thousand people, and watch my sister drive away to her husband, and her new tiles, and her future children who will never know their aunt Violet, a woman who would have loved them despite everything they will hear.

5

Harriet

HARRIET'S HOUSE FELT ESPECIALLY QUIET tonight. In the halo of a single lamp in the parlor, she planned tomorrow's questions, her pen scuffing dutifully against her notepad. It was late, nearly one. She laid down her pen, the air soft with absence, and listened. Once Sophie left for good, this—this dusty quiet—would once again become the sound of evening.

As if on cue, Sophie hurtled through the back door, a sudden, cyclonic presence: snapping lights, clinking keys, then the cup-and-kettle sounds of tea being made. "I brought you a crème brûlée!" she shouted into the parlor. "But don't get your hopes up, it's avocado-basil!" Sophie bartended twice a week at Danube, a snooty wine bar in the Old Port, and often brought her aunt a hifalutin treat.

"I've some book-club questions to try out on you," Harriet called. She liked to practice on Sophie, who could be blunt and graceless. Perfect dry run.

"You want whipped cream?"

"I'm fat enough, thank you very much."

"Never stopped me."

The kettle whistled, and after a few minutes Sophie appeared, wearing a filmy purple top with black jeans and blaze-orange cowboy boots pulled from a closet that resembled an exploding yard sale. "You're gonna hate this," she said, setting down the desserts, which she'd avalanched with whipped cream. She took hers and melted into Lou's slouchy lounger, the cat hopping into her lap like the fickle hussy he was.

"That poor creature will die of missing you," Harriet said. Sophie had moved back in temporarily, and nobody was happier than Tabsy.

"He's a cat, Aunt Harrie," she said, chowing down. "You're projecting."

"There's a perfectly good university not a mile from this house."

"I know. I work there."

"You could keep your day job while getting your master's, is what I'm saying."

"I hate my day job. I swear Petrov's former KGB." She meant her boss, Dr. Mikhail Petrov, a Russian behavioral scientist studying cognition in animals—African grey parrots, specifically. But Sophie wasn't an animal person, Tabsy the sole exception.

"It would be so much easier to stay, honey. Don't you think? So much less . . . transition." For weeks now, time had felt wavering and dangerous, her life a swift gust of years in which she had somehow raised a family, outlived her husband, returned to college in her forties, and taught for fifteen years. She was sixty-four, an inconceivable number.

"I'm moving to Berkeley, Aunt Harrie," Sophie said. "Not Mars." The program was set to begin in July. Today was the first day of May, and Harriet was already counting.

"This dessert is god-awful," she said.

"Told ya." Sophie reclined the chair all the way, as Lou once had. "I gave my two weeks' notice today and Petrov's on tilt."

"Is he ever not on tilt?"

"Nyet."

"Well, it's good, honest work," Harriet said, one of Corinne's expressions, rest her soul. "Your mother would be proud."

Sophie laughed—her mother's joyful, fire-engine laugh. "I clean bird cages *so* honestly. My mother would be over the moon."

"Don't joke. I'm not in the mood."

Sophie got up, spilling the cat, to snap on a few more lights. "Master of social work, Aunt Harrie. I'll be a *master*. I'll be *insufferable*."

Harriet smiled in spite of herself. "I feel sorry for the cat, that's all."

"Poor kitty," Sophie murmured, "poor little kitty," and Harriet opened her arms to receive a big, sweet armful of niece. She inhaled

Sophie's sweaty hair—Sophie always smelled this wonderful way after a restaurant shift.

Sophie kissed her aunt—a noisy, extravagant smack—then swiped the dessert for herself and returned to the deep chair she claimed to remember with Uncle Lou in it, though she'd been a toddler when he died. Annie and Ellen had carted their baby cousin everywhere, their living doll. "I'll be back for Thanksgiving," she said, mouth full. "And Christmas. I'll force you to get a live tree and you'll be picking needles off the rug till February. I'll sing 'Jingle Bell Rock' till your ears bleed. You'll be so sick of me."

Oh, that girl, the spit of her mother. Same impish dimple, same shiny-dark eyes. Hardy and unbeautiful and irresistible. Same hair, too: a comical mess of tight, untamable curls. These physical reminders could knock Harriet clean off her pins.

"What's in this tea?" Harriet asked. "Mulch?"

"Chinese herbs," Sophie said. "I want you to live forever. Oh, and guess what, Luis said he'd move to Berkeley with me." *Guess what* was Sophie's favorite question—her life, despite the scar of tragedy, was a perpetual looking forward. "He's already online, looking for a gig."

"I'm glad you'll have the company," Harriet said, and meant it. Luis—a long-waisted sous chef with a passion for Adele—liked to laugh, even at himself. Sophie could do worse, and she seemed to love him. Even more, she liked him, better for the long haul. Harriet had loved Lou, but at times he'd been hard to like.

"He's got a hundred aunts out there," Sophie said. "We'll never have to cook a meal." She dispatched the rest of her dessert in one lusty gulp. "That's me. What've you got?"

"One of the women got released early. No notice. Just—poof, gone." Harriet set down her cup. "She was so smart. I'll miss her terribly."

Sophie's eyes flew open. "Transition! Oh, no! Run!"

"Don't make fun."

"Don't make it easy."

"You are a cruel and terrible girl."

That laugh again—a joyful clanging. "Life goes on, Aunt Harrie, you have to adjust."

But hadn't she done enough adjusting? Husband, gone; sister, gone; daughters, gone in their way. Another blink, and she'd be seeing Sophie off at the airport. She picked up her notepad and read, "Is it possible to sum up a human life?"

"What?"

"We're finishing *Spoon River Anthology*. Is it possible—"

"No way," Sophie said. "People are too complicated, and nobody is just one thing." She sat up. "Let me see."

Harriet gave the book over. "Normally we'd be on to the next one, but this met with shocking enthusiasm, so I gave it an extension."

"I read this in high school," Sophie said. She thumbed briskly through it, the type of reader who tortured the pages. "Mercifully short chapters."

"They're not chapters exactly. More like poems. Epitaphs, really." Harriet checked her notepad and read, "Whom would you choose to write your epitaph?"

"Hmm." Sophie flopped back into Lou's chair, rumpling her clothes, legs crossed at the ankles.

"Poor question?" Harriet asked.

"No, I'm thinking," Sophie said. "I guess I'd choose you."

"Your life wouldn't fit on a headstone."

"Then don't try for the whole thing. Pick one part." She slid Harriet a look. "Here lies Sophia Jane Martin, who ate crème brûlée with her aunt."

Harriet laughed. "I can think of worse epitaphs."

"Hey, I remember this one," Sophie said, flattening a page. "Mrs. Merritt. It was my turn to read aloud, and I did it with an Irish accent."

"Dorothy read that one a couple of weeks ago. Not a dry eye in the house. We had no idea she could act."

"Well," Sophie said, "you'd kinda have to be an actor to embezzle eighty grand."

Silence.

"Sophie?"

Sophie uncrossed her legs and casually straightened her flouncy sleeves, no stranger to theatrics herself.

"Sophie. Did you google her?"

"Yup." She took out her phone and started tapping the screen.

"Are you googling her now?"

"Nope."

Harriet sat up. "Unless they choose to tell me, I know nothing about their crimes. Unless *they* choose to tell me."

"Well, *they* know way more than nothing about *you*. Whatever googling I did was out of concern."

"You did it out of morbid curiosity, and I hope you're ashamed of yourself."

"I'm not," she said, still tapping. "We think you're too trusting."

"We?"

"Annie and Ellen. We all agree."

"Oh, I see. The three of you in cahoots." Her daughters, who'd fallen in love with a couple of Brits during a trek through Europe, lived next door to each other in London. "Grown women with families," Harriet muttered. "You'd think they'd have better things to do."

"Concern is not cahoots, Aunt Harrie."

"So, what, they sent you on a spy mission?" Harriet asked. "They got their baby cousin to do their bidding?" She heard her own phone pinging in the kitchen just as Sophie's phone made a *cheep-cheep* sound. "For heaven's sake, are you girls texting right now?" Harriet despised email, loathed texting, and was the last to know everything.

"We're not saying you should quit or anything."

"Oh, what a relief. Thank you very much for that permission."

"Just don't tell stuff to the inmates," Sophie said, tapping away.

"What 'stuff'? I don't call them inmates. Will you stop texting, please? It's infuriating."

"Stuff like how old you are."

"What's wrong with that?"

"They could steal your identity." Sophie had been arguing this way since toddlerhood. *Look at this, Corinne,* Harriet thought. *Remember our ruthless little prosecutor?*

"That's absurd," Harriet said, "and in any case, they don't know how old I am."

Ping went her phone in the kitchen, as Sophie's phone cheeped again. She checked the screen, then held it up, showing a long blue box of text. "Desiree said you looked older than sixty-four, and Renee told Desiree to shut her big fat yawp."

"And here I thought I had an amusing little story Ellen would enjoy," Harriet said. "I guess I'll think twice before opening my own big fat yawp." She marched into the kitchen, which was littered with Sophie's belongings, empty dessert cartons, and spilled tea bags.

Within seconds, Sophie clanked into the kitchen. What was on those boots—spurs?

"Don't be mad, Aunt Harrie." In her frilly top, she resembled a cactus flower.

Harriet crossed her arms, reaching for an authority she didn't quite feel. "What you did, young lady, was a gross invasion of Dorothy's privacy."

"It's public information."

"*My* privacy, then."

Sophie had the grace to look chastened, though not nearly chastened enough. Was this the fate of adults on the threshold of their dotage? To be turned into children by children? The new store clerk had called the handyman "cute"—a strong, capable adult man! The thought of it riled her all over again. "And when exactly would Dorothy do all this identity stealing, Sophia Jane? Between Supper Chow and Lock-down?"

"People get *out* of prison, Aunt Harrie. One of them just got released early, you yourself told me that."

Exasperated, Harriet turned her back on Sophie. She gripped the lip of the sink, facing the window and her safe, leafing-out neighborhood. Relentless moonlight silvered the trunks of trees. "Who else did you look up?"

"Nobody, Auntie."

"Don't 'Auntie' me."

"You Sophia-Janed me first."

"Who else, Sophie?"

"Just two, I swear. All I had was first names."

"I'm so sorry. How inconvenient."

"One of them set her husband on fire."

"Enough!" Harriet snapped. She took a long breath, accosted by a vision of Jenny Big talking about her dog, Elmo, her small eyes welling. As Sophie waited in the heavy silence, Harriet spotted a fox fleeting through the neighbor's yard, furtive and low to the ground, here and gone.

A ping, a cheep, another cheep.

"Annie thinks one of them might show up here," Sophie said. "Ellen's afraid you'll get all auntie-mom and take them in."

"Now you're being ridiculous."

"You took *me* in." Harriet felt Sophie's arms slide around her from behind, twining her waist. "I was a twelve-year-old orphan, Auntie, and you took me in." She laid her cheek on Harriet's back.

"I know exactly what you're doing, Sophia Jane, and it isn't working." Though it was. Of course it was. She loved Sophie, Corinne's only child, fierce and affectionate; she loved that warm body against hers. "It stands to reason I'd have murderers in Book Club," she said quietly. "It's a prison."

A pause, then: "Possibly I overstepped."

Harriet took another cleansing breath, and Sophie's body moved with her, arms tightening around her waist, reminding her of the toddler who'd fought sleep, night after night, forcing Corinne to peel the mewling child from her body, limb by limb.

"When we gather to talk about books, Sophie," Harriet said, "we're readers." She stared out at the moonlit grass. "Not embezzlers. Not murderers. Readers."

She felt Sophie nod. "Readers who murder people."

In spite of everything, Harriet laughed. "Murder's underrated. When I was teaching I considered it more than once. I'm considering it now, in fact."

Sophie tightened her grip. "I bet you were a great teacher."

"If that's an apology, I accept."

Sophie's arms slid away, and now she was standing very close, waiting, drenching Harriet in the bittersweet heat of her attention. "I wasn't a great teacher, in fact," Harriet said. "I was diligent and organized and taught them what they needed to know. I did not organize field trips or direct the school plays. I was not *beloved*." She took in Sophie's pained expression. "But in Book Club," she added, "I feel like the teacher they want." This simple truth, spoken aloud, left her a little breathless. "It's the only classroom, if you can call it that, where I feel time moving the way it ought, when it's just us, discussing a book, existing exactly as we wish to. Of course, the women have their own ideas about how time moves, but for those two hours . . . Are you texting again?"

"I'm telling the cousins to back off." Sophie tapped her phone one last time. "I'm sorry, Aunt Harrie. Really." She smiled. "*I* belove you."

"Then don't treat me like a doddering old tizz."

"It's so hard not to when you talk like a Victorian."

They both laughed now, and Harriet shooed Sophie off to bed.

Outside, crocuses glinted in the dark, another spring in the making. How had all this time, decades and decades of it, piled up with so little resistance? How had Sophie, that clinging, headstrong child, become a woman leaving? The fox reappeared, a quick-moving smudge in the moonlight. As it vanished anew, Harriet felt a vast and mystifying gratitude. She and the women had passed the winter reading books they hadn't cracked since age fifteen, books with recollected plots, books with well-trod furrows of discussion, books understood best in retrospect. She was glad to have honored their request to revisit the past, for the future—theirs; hers—felt shadowy, and immense, and beyond discussion.

6

Violet

INSIDE THE ENVELOPE: FOUR HUNDRED bucks cash, plus a bank check for a lot more. Not enough to buy a house. Maybe a car. A lot of money, to me. My mother was a saver.

The apartment's okay. Furnished and everything. Vicki's husband probably carried the couch up three flights one-handed. Or maybe one of his brothers. Those Wingates, there's no end of them and they all look alike, short and burly; at the dealership they're all in the service center except for Billy, who's got the personality for sales. I secretly liked him in high school, but when Vicki wants something there's no Off button.

The furniture smells new. They stocked the fridge with the basics: eggs, juice, milk—Oakhurst, the brand Vicki knows I like. I check the drawers and cupboards. Again, the basics: canned soups, not-plastic plates, not-plastic glasses, knives that cut. Vicki went to a lot of trouble to set me up here. Mama must've made Vicki promise, and Vicki, for all her Vicki-ness, was never one to go back on her word.

In the bathroom I find fluffy towels, whitening toothpaste, and an expensive shampoo, Paul Mitchell. I pick it up, open it, smell it. Almond, which reminds me of my mother.

This is Vicki saying I'm sorry I can't be your sister anymore.

They might have let me out for the funeral, I think they might have, just a couple hours, but I didn't find out till my mother was in the ground, unreachable. Nobody wanted to see me. Not Vicki, not the aunts, nobody. Their world collapsed when Mama died. I understand.

On the dresser, a framed photo of me and Vicki with our parents back when we were happy. At least, according to Vicki we were happy—I was too young to know. Vicki's the taller one with the dripping Popsicle; my Popsicle looks frozen stiff, my sundress clean and pressed. On the frame's top edge, a single word in curly letters: FAMILY. It's a sad picture, really, my mother all shiny and in love and not widowed. I don't remember my father—according to Aunt Pammy he drove a motorcycle and was quite the looker—and only sometimes do I wonder what it would be like to have one. I turn the frame facedown, gently, and sit on my new bed, trying to feel free. The bed, oh my God, fresh sheets and a decent mattress. Thank you, Vicki. Thank you, Mama.

I lie on top of the bone-white bedspread and cry. For a good twenty-four hours. Crying for my mother. Crying for my old life before prison. Also, and this is crazy, crying for my old life *in* prison, where I had people to talk to and stuff to do once in a while. I monogrammed tee shirts. Three mornings a week in Industry, eighty cents an hour. Commissary money. Our commissary was two vending machines, one of them with a Ding Dong permanently stuck in the chute.

The thought comes to me that all the crying might not be just for Mama but also for a tiny, idiot part of me that expected Troy to be waiting outside those gates. Even though he didn't call once or visit once or write once. Even though he hooked up with Becca Frye, my former friend. That idiot gene or cell thought he'd be out there, shining in the light.

For three days, maybe five, I don't so much as open the door. After two years in the company of divas and wailers and men with guns, it's here, in this city I don't know, where I feel unsafe. I drink a lot of water, since it's free and I'm scared to run out of orange juice. There's a microwave, some Lean Cuisines and a gallon of Gifford's mint chocolate chip in the freezer, a few vegetables, some apples and bananas, ten cans of chicken-noodle soup, packages of spaghetti and instant rice and ramen noodles. I could live inside these three rooms for quite some time, but I barely touch the food.

The phone Vicki left for me is a pay-by-the-minute burner, and she prepaid quite a bit. I check the contacts first: none. Not even Vicki. I hoped maybe my aunt Linda, but no. Aunt Pammy, definitely no. Mama died slow and hard, and grief does weird things to people.

The apartment has no TV. Not one book. Vicki was never a reader, which pained Mama, who read to me at night well into high school while the before-Billy Vicki was out "raising the dead," as she liked to say. Hard to imagine now, Vicki with her salon hair and Easter manicure.

It's quiet except for creepy noises from the bathroom pipes and the constant hum from the street. From the window I watch people scurrying to and from work, little kids riding tricycles with mothers on phones trotting behind, a few bright knots of African people in flowery clothes carrying big pocketbooks (the women) or net sacks (the men) filled with I don't know what. I wonder if Vicki set me up in Portland, the exact place where my romantic new life was to begin, as one last fuck-you for clobbering our mother's heart.

Among Vicki's five thousand refrigerator magnets (JESUS LOVES YOU; LET GO AND LET GOD; HEAVEN KNOWS; LOVE IS A 4-LETTER WORD) I find a dirty sticker with a Wi-Fi code on it. All at once it feels like I've got company, and I can breathe a little better, googling everything, making up for lost time. I'm talking hours on YouTube, days of this, falling asleep to videos of Prince Harry and Megan Markle's baby; Hurricane Dorian pillaging the Bahamas; new (to me) songs by Rhianna, Lady Gaga, all my old loves; then a Lean Cuisine, a big glass of water, and back at it.

I take forever to wash my dishes, trying to make time mean something. I track down the highlights of Superbowl LIII, which I missed because Jenny Big started gum-flapping about Tom Brady being a pussy-whipped girlyman cheater, her dog Elmo had better footwork, Rams rule, Rams rule, Rams rule, over and over, really loud, no matter who told her to shut the fuck up, and just short of halftime the COs said okay ladies that's it.

Which is how Tom Brady got his sixth ring while we sat in lockdown. We sulked for over a month, and to be honest, I never got over it. Troy was a football player, a wideout with long arms and sticky hands, repeat state champion Class C, and it's because of him I came to love the game.

On day five, or maybe eight, I wake up with that sick-stomach feeling of too much scrolling. In front of me, a whole day to fill, and more beyond, and it feels like time has a color and that color is beige. I can smell myself, still in the clothes I came in. As I strip them off, I wonder what took me so long. Why hold on to the smell of prison? And yet I did. But it's time, so I take a shower, half-surprised not to disintegrate. The water is shockingly hot, and the shampoo feels like first prize in a beauty contest. I stash my smelly clothes and open the tapestry bag.

Everything is the wrong size. In prison there's six sizes: massive, fat, normal, skinny, skeleton, and ghost. I went in normal and came out skeleton, because even the apples tasted like paper. I pick out a pink button-up shirt (pink's my worst color, which Vicki knows) and a pair of black jeans. Nothing blue, thank you, baby Jesus. Never will I put on blue again. There's another shirt in there, also pink. And another one, also pink. Also Vicki's black denim jacket from high school; it used to reek of boy-of-the-month cigarette smoke but doesn't anymore. No undies, no shoes, so I wear what I have, week-old undies and sweaty socks and shoes from before I went in. Shoes from my former life. A pair of New Balance running shoes that I never ran in.

"I'm a runner, Violet," my sister used to joke as she trotted off to meet this boy or that one, to roar up and down the back roads, to go drinking at the sand pit, as Mama sat up praying for her firstborn to return to Jesus. But I was the one, in the end. I fell in love—a hard fall, all the way down. "You can't go, Violet," Vicki whispered to me the night before, the two of us in our pj's, side-by-side beds, as I confessed my plan with Troy. "You can't go. *I'm* the runner." I ran anyway, straight into disaster, and after that Vicki had to be the good daughter, the one who sat next to Mama at the trial, the one who had to hold her dwindling hands. The one who married a boring man with money. Maybe Vicki doesn't like her real-estate clothes. Maybe that's why she filled my tapestry bag with pink.

I put on the pink clothes because it's time to go outside, breathe all that free air. Vicki wouldn't be scared of Portland, one-way this and stoplight that, but I am. Stores and restaurants and museums and hip, good-looking people all over the streets, the opposite of Abbott Falls, which is quiet and sits on a river, and aside from the new Dunkin' Donuts (where I met Troy), and religion, and high school sports, the town doesn't have much to say for itself since the paper mill cut back.

So I make it only to the end of the block before chickening out. I don't own many things, but I want them now, barreling back up the stairs and unlocking my door and breathing hard and touching everything that's mine. Chair, table, coat, fork, towel, Paul Mitchell shampoo, mine mine mine. Then I take Mama's ring and squeeze it in my fist, hard, harder, my mother's diamond a little barb of comfort and blame.

Two days later, I try again, creeping downstairs past the two other apartments. Nobody ever seems to be home, although at night the building fogs up with the odor of cooked onions. Which isn't as bad as it sounds. Outside, I stand on the stoop for a while like it's a diving board and the street is a twenty-foot pool. The doorbells have stickers above them: Amouzou, Stewart/Driscoll, Slater, Rugaba, Twombly/Harris, Abdi. 3B is blank; that's me.

Along the street, both sides, old trees are beginning to bud, a sweet spring green that always makes me weirdly sad. The trees' wide arms pull some of the shabby from the buildings. In Book Club the Book Lady gave us a mantra that we chanted together, which was kind of lame but we all did it, and I whisper it now: "I am a reader. I am intelligent. I have something worthy to contribute."

Finally I step off and start walking. Two blocks, then right, onto a busier street, lots of morning traffic and a couple of angry horns but also a cobblestone square and a plaza with benches and a low wall. Across from there, an art museum with an ugly sculpture out front. A squat, rusted seven. The number seven. It looks famous.

When Troy and I were driving to Portland, singing loud enough to break glass, we were headed into a life that would include this art museum. We would visit this grand museum and fall hard, together, for one special painting. Something small and shimmering and not famous. We alone would recognize its greatness. That painting would forever after be "our" painting, that artist "our" artist.

This is how my mind worked then.

People everywhere, not a single one remotely familiar, some of them in a show-off hurry, briefcases and satchels filled with crucial papers. Also lots of artsy types with nose rings and meaningful tattoos. Troy had six tatts but I hate needles. *Has*. Troy, wherever he is, *has* six tatts but he is past tense to me.

I move along with the other people, worried one of them might grab my cashier's check, which I'm gripping hard while memorizing my route so I can get back, what if I can't find my way back? It turns out I live in a part of the city called the peninsula. Which means the downtown. Which is, I guess, a peninsula. You can smell the ocean. I pass a Renys, a discount chain I know from home—*Renys: A Maine adventure!*—and my heart does this little wing-lift as I about-face and barge through the door. The lady at the counter startles, gives me the once-over, then dismisses me as harmless. I'm glad to know I look harmless.

I take a cart, and then a minute just to breathe. I pick out a wallet, then some undies—two six-packs with lacy leg holes. Goodbye, cotton saggy-ass grannypants. I add a three-pack of socks with rabbits on them, rabbits wearing eyeglasses, and two long-sleeve tee shirts in my new size, skeleton, one green and one black with thin purple stripes. And a purse, a small, cheap one that I hope looks non-discount. In Closeout I find a skirt and a pair of flats in case I ever go someplace nice. There's also a blouse with ruffly sleeves, but it's a dead-ringer shade of prison blue. So, no.

I bring my cart to the front, digging cash out of my pocket and handing it over left-handed because I won't let go of the check. Not for one nanosecond. Spending money feels dangerous. I don't even know how much my rent is. Or who would hire me. At the last minute I grab a bottle of Woolite for handwashing everything I just bought. The laundromat in Abbott Falls was kind of expensive, and I can't even imagine what it costs here.

Down the block I find a bank, where a woman with beaded cornrows and plum-colored lipstick helps me open an account, checking and savings, with the cashier's check from my envelope. First I have to explain my situation.

"We all start over from somewhere, Ms. Powell," she says. Her name is Lillian; she's smiling at me even though I've admitted I'm a manslaughterer, and her generous face just about upends me. She has a light accent; maybe she knows about starting over.

"My sister left me here on my own," I tell her. "I watched her car disappear." My hands are shaking so bad I can't get the flap loose on my envelope.

"Here you go," Lillian says, taking the envelope and parting the flap with a letter opener. "You see? Not everything will be hard."

I tell Lillian that all I have left of my mother is a ring that doesn't fit and this check, so is there a way to make a copy of the check so I can keep the original?

"Oh, no," she says, looking genuinely hurt on my behalf. "I can give you a copy, but not the original." She smooths the check on her clean desk. "Do this," she says, running her finger over Mama's signature. "Go ahead."

So I swipe my finger across my mother's name—*Eleanor V. Powell*, in curly letters—pretending I can feel the heat of her hand.

"There," Lillian says. "You see?"

I nod, ridiculously grateful for this kind woman, who tells me I can't write a check or use my debit card for five business days. They have to double-check everything, and who can blame them? For a PIN she says to pick something easy to remember, so I pick the last four digits of my inmate number. But then I'm instantly heartshocked. What a stupid-stupid-stupid pin number.

"It's okay, honey," Lillian says, "we can redo it," but I can't face the whole bank-card thing all over again, so I let it go.

As I exit the bank I'm crying a little, big surprise, because Lillian was so nice and I picked a stupid pin number and my mother died of grief and my boyfriend-slash-fiancé-slash-future-slash-everything didn't come to my trial or visit me even once and I could die right here and not a single person on the face of the earth would hear about it.

Troy and I had been heading for Portland, the city of our dreams. His mother was all *Oh, no you don't, young man, you're going back up north*. That means college. But he didn't go back up north. Because of me.

Also, he'd been cut from the football team for violating alcohol policy. This was a big red flag, but I wasn't the type to see it. The only flag I saw had butterflies on it. Bluebirds and daisies.

I would see now. I would know a red flag in a hot minute.

We stopped in Freeport to go to L.L. Bean; Troy wanted a thick lumberjack shirt, and boots with craggy soles, his warning to Portlanders: real man in town. But after that we lost our bearings and wound up on Route 88, a mistake, and it was okay, we were almost there, just a few miles from our "destination"—we laughingly called Portland our "destination." Because it was our true destiny. We were so happy, headed to our true destiny in Troy's rehabbed Camry to start a joined life where Troy would play in a metal band and I would work at Dunkin' Donuts (I had experience) to save up money for college. We planned to get married at City Hall as soon as we arrived. Our mothers would forgive us later. My mother thought Troy was a bad influence. Troy's mother thought the bad influence was me.

Before we left Abbott Falls that day, Troy bought a "good" bottle of whiskey to celebrate (I found out later from Renee that Jim Beam is crap) and also a little stash of pills that I didn't quite trust. But *destiny* was the most electrifying word. Life was fluffy clouds parting just for us, the two of us, living on love and sunshine. So we celebrated a little bit, cheers to this and cheers to that, then we lost our sense of time and celebrated a lot, and then Troy put one of the pills on my tongue and I licked his salty finger, and then we pulled into a woodsy road in broad daylight to make love, wonderful, beautiful, marriage-day love. He didn't call it that. He called it something else. And afterward he said, *Babe, I better not drive, you better drive, they won't arrest a girl.*

So I did. I drove.

Here in Portland, everything is suddenly too much. The sun, the people, the freedom, the buildings. I'm still retracing my steps in my head as I pass a cute restaurant with tables on the sidewalk, maybe a job in there. Maybe I can leave the felony question blank and they won't notice. Then another cute restaurant and a coffee shop, maybe a job in there. Then a parking garage, automated, no job there. And then just when I'm ready to retrace, fast-fast, scared out of my wits in my too-big pink blouse and too-big jeans and my sweaty socks and my running shoes and my Renys bag, my breathing goes wonky and I stop right here on the street to look at my pathetic loser self in a store window.

But instead of my own self, I find a tortoiseshell cat napping in a slant of sunlight. A serene, spreading swirl of cat, conked out atop the book about the famous and successful cardiac surgeon who ate dirt as a child. I hated that book, but it looks to me now like an old friend.

The cat's whiskers jitter as it sleeps. Paws, too, a little bit. Dreaming of a fat mouse, yum. It's got a pale-pink collar—a girl?—that has lettering all the way around. All I can make out is NIMAL REF. The collar matches her pinkish spots on mostly gray. A sign on the window says ADOPT ME. And oh my God, here I go again, a full-on blubberfest, standing here on a Portland sidewalk looking into a bookstore window, crying like a baby because the cat lifts its head and widens its eyes as if to say, *Violet Powell, where the heck have you been?* and all of a sudden I know the First Thing I Do.

7

Frank

He was standing on a ladder, hijacked by happiness, tapping nails into a frame he'd built for the perfect pane of glass, snapped up at Marden's for a song. He'd barked with glee when he found it: discounted surplus, tempered, tinted blue, eighteen inches square. With luck it would slide right in.

"Looking good, Frank," called Baker from behind the counter, a raised wooden colossus that he referred to as "On High" for its formidable design: you had to look up to buy a book. Look up from your phone. Look up from your thoughts. This seemed good and right.

"Shouldn't be long," Frank called back, and Baker gave him a passionate thumbs-up.

The bell jingled.

By habit, Frank turned to check, and oh, my, there she was, standing just inside the door. The youngsters called her the "book-club lady," which made her sound stuffy, but no sir, she was not, she was brisk and plump and brightly pretty. Her lively gaze traveled the distance of the main room, up the ladder, and rested on him.

Since the botched hello—the one he'd spent weeks rehearsing—Frank had been planning a less risky gambit, and now was his chance: a friendly wave, that's all. Casual, inviting. He lifted his hand, realizing too late that he was gripping a hammer and had ten minutes' worth of finish nails clamped between his lips.

"Are you planning a massacre, Mr. Daigle?" the book-club lady asked.

He lowered the hammer, face ablaze. "Just a minor one." As he spoke, the nails spilled to the floor in a tinkling cascade, chiming against the blue pane propped against the wall.

"Ah. Good to know." Her eyes swept briefly over the fallen nails. "Carry on."

Her smile creased the skin near her eyes, and Frank melted straight into his shoes. He watched her approach the counter, her ashy hair lifting like cinders as she moved.

What the hell was Baker grinning about? Mortified, he glanced away, only to catch Marnie grinning from the window, where she was replacing Winter Reads with Spring Flings, an assortment of books about gardening, home repair, and romance. They were *all* grinning at him—Jake from his computer cubby, Robin from where she was restocking Used Fiction.

He retrieved the nails, remounted the ladder, and finished the frame as the book-club lady—who knew his name; she knew his name—discussed with Baker a book that had "worked out" better than expected. What did that mean? You liked a book or you didn't. She began to browse, thrillingly nearby, hovering over the New Fiction table. Though she was no ballerina, she moved with grace; her earrings glimmered. After a little while, she heaved a light, feminine sigh.

He climbed down again. "Can I help you?" he asked, which was not his job.

"Would that you could," she said. "But I run a rather fussy book club."

"Oh. A book club. Wonderful." He all but shouted over the thundering in his ears.

"They have unpredictable tastes."

The youngsters had gone suspiciously quiet, and suddenly this felt like an audition for a different job. He said, "What type of book are you looking for?"

She thought a minute, the scent of soap wafting. She said, "Something literary but not intimidating."

"Aha." Already he was out of his depth.

"Something with a positive message," she added, "but not for nitwits." She had large, kind eyes. Big smile. A woman of size in every way.

Lorraine had been slim, a relentless weight watcher who bargained with food, but here was a woman who clearly enjoyed her meals.

"This table's popular," he said. He pointed to the sign, then read it helpfully: "New Nonfiction."

"Oh, lord no. If I never pick another memoir it'll be too soon." She sounded like a certain type of hard-to-please customer, but the merriment in her face instructed him otherwise.

Down from On High came Baker's voice in a stage whisper: "Try the bestsellers."

"We have all the bestsellers," he said. His cheeks burned, and he hoped it didn't show.

The book-club lady made a little face. "The bestsellers are all mysteries."

"You don't like mysteries?"

"I love mysteries. But, again, it's a book club. Mysteries are . . ." She waved toward the endcap packed with his favorites. "Once you find out who killed whom, there isn't much left to discuss, I find."

"I take your point," he said. His heart made a sparrow-flutter that hurt, but not in a bad way.

She continued, "We've read fiction and nonfiction, classical and contemporary, but I still never know what's going to land." She laid her purse on the table, and a beige bag that said EAT SLEEP READ in blue lettering. Frank's knowledge of women's fashion couldn't fill a thimble, but he did notice that everything the book-club lady wore seemed to match, which wasn't the style, judging from the shapeless, multicolor getups other women wore into the store. Not to mention the epidemic of pink hair stripes, even on women the book-club lady's age, which he estimated at someplace within his own vintage. She could be younger—the clothes aged her some. She had a youthful spirit, he thought, and her shiny hair flashed in the light.

"What about poetry?" he asked. Sweet Mary Magdalene, what did he know about poetry?

"Poetry," she said. She frowned mightily.

"Sorry."

Robin actually laughed out loud.

"Poetry," the book-club lady repeated. "Why did I not think of poetry?"

"I . . . don't know."

"The last book we read was poetry of sorts, and they loved it," she said, brightening. "Do you know *Spoon River Anthology*?"

"I believe that's the book you dropped," he said. "I mean the last time I saw you. And I picked it up. Not that I'm taking credit." The sparrow in his chest was going berserk now. "I'm just saying, it was on the floor. Right over there. And I . . . gave it back to you."

"Indeed you did. A fortuitous occasion."

"And your book club liked it?" he asked.

"It's set in a graveyard, which served as an apt metaphor."

"Sounds like a tough crowd."

She observed him, frowning, tapping her lip. Her hands looked young. She said, "Most poetry is designed to be read aloud, don't you agree?"

"Yes, I, yes," he said, though not once in his life had he read a poem aloud. The tattooed busybodies watched him from On High, and he knew just what they were thinking: *Isn't Frank adorable! The book-club lady sounds like a poet, and Frank sounds like a talking dog!* Well, he was not adorable. He was a grown man in his late sixties who was in no way through with living.

"Mr. Daigle," she said, gathering her things, "you have given me hope. I shall hie off to Poetry."

Before she could "hie," he blurted, "You must be a schoolteacher."

"Is it that obvious? I'm retired."

"Yes. I mean no. I mean I'm retired too. Machinist."

"My uncle was a machinist." She observed him more closely now. "Stinson Machine in South Portland: 'Precision tolerances, repetitive quality, and quick delivery.'"

A jangle of joy, and he said, "I was at Pierce Machine in Gorham."

"Oh, of course." A pause. "What did you do there?"

"Tool room."

"Ah," she said. "Smarty-pants."

"Oh, now." In Frank's entire life, he had not once met a person outside his work life who understood what it meant to work in the tool room, that shop-within-a-shop where creative, versatile, old-school machinists created jigs, fixtures, and dies that kept the glamor machinery humming. Tool and die makers kept the world spinning.

"My poor uncle Chesley could barely stand at the end," the book-club lady said. "Those concrete floors aren't very forgiving."

"My back's all right," he said, scrambling. "I'm only sixty-eight."

A squawk of laughter came loose from On High, and Frank suddenly hated all young people, who thought they knew all things and in fact knew only some things. Then he felt a waft of affection from that same infuriating source, and loved them again.

The bell over the door jingled, a great mercy, and in walked four customers at once, three of them regulars and one a skinny, washed-out young woman who looked oddly familiar. Before he could place her, Harriet was offering her hand, which felt like—well, it felt like . . . He couldn't think what. Like a memory.

"I'll leave you to your massacre, Mr. Daigle," she said.

"It's Frank."

"Harriet," she said. "Harriet Larson."

He had nothing else to tell her or show her, so he watched her disappear into Poetry. He shot the youngsters a malevolent glance, which they thought hilarious. Then he picked up the pane of blue glass and gingerly remounted the ladder, wishing she were still on scene to witness the muscular flex of his forearms.

The pane was not precisely square, a challenge that put him in mind of the life's work Harriet had so readily recognized: the geometric puzzles, the inspired solutions, the hum of invention, no two days the same. How he had loved his tools—the pleasing heft of a micrometer; the fluid swivel of a bench vise; the sleek beauty of his favorite surface plate, a one-foot-square slab of speckled pink granite. He called it Pinky, like a pet. Surface plates of all sizes lived at Pierce Machine, but Pinky was Frank's go-to, sixty pounds, smoothed to a tolerance of a tenth of a thousandth of an inch, one-thirtieth of a human hair. On retirement day Mr. Pierce had gathered everyone into the tool room, including the office ladies and the custodial crew, everyone beaming. Mr. Pierce announced, with misty pride, that Pinky would be going home to Frank's garage workshop with the good wishes of every soul at Pierce Machine. Frank welled up despite a titanic effort not to, back aching, feet prickling, teardrops plopping onto Pinky's gorgeous surface until Mr. Pierce said, *That's all right, Frank,* and again, *That's all right,* until somehow Frank recovered and somehow Frank retired.

He was jiggering the pane into place when he registered a small commotion at the counter. A girl was holding Boris, the tortoiseshell cat. Same girl who'd seemed familiar but not. Best he could make out, there was a confusion about references, and addresses—the girl either didn't have one or couldn't remember it or didn't care to provide it. From behind she resembled a young boy: narrow, rickety shoulders, lank, collar-length, no-color hair, troublingly thin. Boris squinted smugly over the girl's shoulder and Frank felt a twinkle of gladness: the cat had found its person.

The pane wouldn't quite set into the upper corner, so he joggled it out again, studying the corner, half his attention on the girl. He still couldn't place her, until she turned to profile and the twinkling vaporized, something heavier moving in, a cloudy reckoning just beneath his ken. It shimmered there, trying to form, as Harriet rounded the corner past Puzzles and Games, balancing a stack of slim volumes against her chest. "My goodness, what a surprise," she trilled, for she appeared to know the girl, if only in some awkward way. There followed an additional back-and-forth between Baker and Harriet, and then Marnie arrived to right whatever had gone wrong, and then Harriet said, "I'd be delighted to offer a reference," and as he craned his body, already knowing without yet knowing, an involuntary *no* already forming in his throat, the pane tapped the metal top of the ladder, a ping of sound.

The girl turned and looked up, full face: large, haunted, amber eyes.

Violet Powell.

And just like that, he plummeted into the ditch of memory.

8

Harriet

SHE HEARD A SOUND BEFORE the sound, a soft lowing, like pain, just outside her consciousness, but it registered only as the bookstore's usual murmur. A glitch in the sound system, perhaps; a book slipping from a crammed shelf; a muffled complaint from the children's room.

The sound barely signified, for it was Violet who had her attention. Violet, of all people, in a pretty pink shirt and a denim jacket that looked old and loved. She was trying to adopt a cat, the one that had been sleeping in the window for weeks now, a homely, slow-moving female with a ridiculous name—Bruno or some such.

Harriet took a huge, delighted breath. "My goodness, what a surprise."

Violet's face washed over with relief, her hair tucked behind her small ears. "Bookie," she said.

Never, not since her first baby had found her gaze and held it, had a human face met Harriet's in such incandescent need.

"We have a problem," Baker said, presiding over a clipboard.

Harriet set her books on the counter. "And what problem would that be?" Instinctively, she rested a hand on Violet's meatless shoulder, a knob of bone beneath the denim. As she did so, the spidery brush of the cat's whiskers grazed her thumb and she realized that, for all her time conducting Book Club, she had not once had occasion to touch Violet Powell.

At the moment, Baker put Harriet in mind of a border guard with sympathy for the immigrants but greater fealty to the law. "The form has to be complete," Baker said.

"What form?"

"The adoption form." Baker lifted the clipboard, form facing out, as if helping the legally blind.

"You have to fill out an adoption form?" Harriet had rescued Tabsy from a box at a yard sale, no forms required.

Baker's kohl-lined eyes swept nervously over the stack of books Harriet had yet to purchase. "You have to follow certain steps."

"*She* doesn't think so." Harriet pointed at the cat waiting politely in Violet's arms as if it had lived there, just there, for years.

Baker looked bureaucratically pained. "There's rules about it, though."

"It's a *cat*," Harriet said. "A lovely young person is here right now, offering it a home."

"Oh, totally," Baker said, "but the rules are to make sure the cat goes to a responsible party."

"I'm responsible," Violet said. She glanced at Harriet to confirm.

"She's very responsible," Harriet said. "A former student."

"It's not personal, though. It's everyone." Baker leaned forward with a now-familiar air of conspiracy. "There's like these rings of psychopaths who grab cats and dogs for unspeakable experiments."

Violet tucked the cat closer. "I never heard of that."

"Because it's claptrap," Harriet said, yanking the clipboard toward her. "Now, what is it that your mighty form requires?"

Violet's expression changed then, a twinge of humor, and Harriet got the message in a single, kindred sparkle of comprehension: here they were, together again, sidelining authority.

"You have to have the same address for six months," Baker explained, reaching across, tapping the relevant line with one short, black-lacquered fingernail.

"For heaven's sake," Harriet said, "she just moved here, what do you expect?"

"It's okay, Bookie," Violet said. "I can wait." She looked self-conscious now, stranded. She swallowed, a barely perceptible lizard gulp. The cat shifted in her arms.

An ocean of feeling overpowered Harriet now, a dislocating tide of affection for this girl who had done nothing but wait for a very long time. The cat, too, had waited. Harriet rested her eyes on Violet and the cat, their unguarded patience, and went briefly light-headed with a feeling akin to motherly love. She was still cupping Violet's shoulder, she realized. Harriet believed only conditionally in God, but she couldn't shake an outlandish, jangling notion that Violet had been sent to her.

Now Marnie was here, sensible Marnie, the store manager, confident and can-do. "If I can get a waterproof reference," she said to Harriet, smiling, "from, say, our most reliable customer."

"I'd be delighted to offer a reference," Harriet said, letting go of Violet at last and digging in her purse for a pen.

That lowing again, and a metallic *ping* as Frank Daigle turned, the glass turning with him. It was this sound—a small oops—that called her to look up, and there he was, frozen atop the ladder. His eyes had shocked open, goggling at Violet, his mouth ajar, his body canted with the glass, his whole face askew in a way impossible to decode. And there again was the earlier sound, the one she'd heard without hearing, a sludgy *lowing*, like something thick and lethal bubbling up from the ground.

This sound was not the store's usual murmur, this sound was not a glitch in the sound system, this sound was not a book slipping from a crammed shelf, this sound was not a muffled complaint from the children's room.

This sound was a man unraveling.

A man with a pane of glass between his hands, its tinted face making a prism of the ceiling. A man with a mud of sound in his throat. A frozen man with wide-open eyes trained on Violet, who froze in turn, keeping his gaze.

Frank Daigle, the store handyman, hinged between some before-and-after that Harriet did not wish to investigate. Lifting the glass to stare through it, he suddenly looked dangerous. Then he began to move.

Was he coming for Violet? The cat thought so. It bolted from Violet's arms as the frozen man, eyes unswerving, descended one rung, and another, releasing wheezy huffs of breath, crying out, "Nnnn"—*no? was he saying, "No"?*—as everything else let go.

"Oh my God," Marnie shouted, as a slow-motion domino-falling commenced, a silvery racketing rain of spilled nails, spilled tools, spill of books grazed by the spilling ladder, and finally the man himself spilling, gripping the blue glass, breathing hard, stumbling down the spilling rungs.

Time hovered in that way of disbelief, and in that hovering Harriet caught something in Frank Daigle's eyes—some pleading, intricate sorrow. *What is this?* she thought, but by then the glass, too, was spilling, sailing, and Harriet was hustling Violet through the door, beneath a jingling bell put together by a man who was flying apart.

9

Violet

PEOPLE WANT TO KNOW ABOUT sex in prison, mainly because they watch too many movies. It's true you can go a little flooey on the inside. You're lonely, you're scared. Human touch is a thing, a real thing that humans need or else they die, or want to. Sometimes we hugged, which isn't allowed, but a lot of girls did it anyway. The COs let it go unless it was a super-obvious sex hug and they shut that shit right down. "Get a room," they'd say, which was funny until you had to remember what "a room" really meant: reinforced window, metal door with another reinforced window. Cot with a crap mattress. Sheets that felt like a day-old beard, sheets that reeked of All Pine, sheets that got mixed with Men's over in Laundry, sheets that came back with disgusting, can't-wash-out man stains. Every single week at Town Meeting, we asked: *Please separate Men's from Women's—towels and sheets and oh-my-God facecloths, pleeease.* But they never did. It wouldn't be "time-efficient." Anybody who doesn't think men are hopeless, revolting pigs should take a good long look inside a prison laundry.

The reason I bring up sex in prison—I did not have sex in prison, not with a girl and not with a CO—is because of what happens after I see Frank Daigle in the bookstore. At first I'm shaking so bad I can't even run, everything goes tilted and bright, and I forget which direction is home, and "home" is not the right word for the apartment Vicki put me in on Grant Street, and I can't remember the number of the building, which is either 520 or 250, what if I can't find it again, those buildings all look alike, then all of a sudden here is the Book Lady—

The Book Lady. She sat me down on this wooden bench, and now she's back, her peaceful hand on my back.

"He's gone, Violet," she says. "Whatever that was, it's over." She sits down next to me and murmurs, "There, there."

I'm not kidding. "There, there," like a kindly godmother in a children's story. So here I go, ugly-face heave-ho bawling. Snot and drool, the works. As the Book Lady pats my back and whispers "there, there" and other generally soothing mother-hen fairy-godmother words, I can't help it, I turn into a human geyser, Old Faithful sobbing on a cute bench in front of a cute bookstore in cute Portland, Maine. *Don't leave*, I pray, *please don't leave*.

A miracle: she doesn't leave. She stays, in her crisp white blouse patterned with tiny dots. Slacks, too: crisp, beige. And the same functional beige shoes I know from Book Club. I always figured she dressed this way for us, like a grandma who never broke the law herself but forgave other people who did. But I guess these grandma clothes are her real clothes and her real self is there-there and a soft back-patting hand.

I keep seeing Mr. Daigle's face at the top of that ladder. Everyone must have thought him angry, or vengeful, or crazy, or worse. But I know what I saw. I'd watched him through the endless days of my trial—our trial, maybe I should say—and I came to understand that he was not angry, or vengeful, or crazy, or worse. He never hated me. I know this.

I hear a new sound, a whimpering that seems to be coming from far away, like a stabbed-up fawn staggering into a clearing and watching its deer family leap away and melt into the forest forever.

But it's not a stabbed-up fawn. It's me.

"There-there," the Book Lady says, patting and patting. "It's over, you're all right." She's whispering sympathetically and I'm hiccupping nonstop and her hair is graying in gentle waves and her whole self is easy and tender and kind of blooming and I want to hide myself in her large, soft body.

Which is what I mean about your instincts going flooey. Even the biggest girl on the inside—Florence, six-three in sock feet and built like a snowplow—had something tender about her, a cottony presence that made you want to draw near.

The Book Lady has that. I lay my head on her bosom, and I wish she was my mother, my aunts, my sister, my grandma, every woman now dead or dead-to-me who ever loved me. The Book Lady knows I did wrong, and here she is anyway, patting and cooing, in a public place where she knows people and doesn't care who sees.

"Just breathe, Violet," the Book Lady says. The city drones around me, the city where I was headed with Troy until the universe said, *Think again*. Nobody pays us the slightest attention, a nice lady patting the back of a weeping girl. "Whatever came over that poor deranged creature," she says, "it has nothing to do with you."

"He's not deranged."

"The *sound* coming from that man."

The cat is back in the window, sitting up now, staring at us. Her name is Boris, and I would rename her something obvious, the most obvious name imaginable: Fluffy or Mittens, something normal-normal-normal.

"We can go back in," Harriet says. "The form won't take a minute."

"No," I tell her, "I can't go back in there." Boris needs a better person than me, is what I'm thinking. Someone who didn't kill a teacher.

"Breathe," the Book Lady says. "There you go."

Somehow I pull myself together and find my way back "home" with the Book Lady walking me up the stairs, her hand cupping my elbow like I'm the old lady and she's the stupid girl instead of the other way around. My hands shake so bad I can't work the key.

"Let me," the Book Lady says, and then we're in.

She works up a stir-fry with my softening vegetables. She boils some rice and spices it up with a bottle of something Vicki put in the door of the fridge.

"Thank you, Bookie," I say.

"Call me Harriet, dear. We're on the Outs now."

She does up the few dishes, rinsing them and then stacking them in the dishwasher, which I don't know how to work, but she shows me, very patient.

"You need books," she says, looking around. No rugs, no curtains, no posters or prints, worst of all no books.

"I didn't get to take them with me," I tell her. "I was going to buy *Spoon River Anthology* at the store so I could finish it."

"They don't come back from the dead, if that's what you were hoping."

"I wasn't," I say. "They seemed okay with being dead as long as they got their say."

Harriet smiles at this, which makes me feel like I've said something right.

"We miss you in Book Club, Violet."

She says "we," but she means "I." Nobody inside ever mentions the ones who leave.

I miss me in Book Club, too. I miss how Harriet was forever showing us how to read. How to look for shapes and layers. How to see that stories have a "meanwhile"—an important thing that's happening while the rest of the story moves along.

Three bears strolling in the forest: story. Goldilocks wrecking their house: meanwhile.

Heartbroken Cinderella sweeping and scrubbing: story. Handsome prince searching far and wide: meanwhile.

Felon from Abbott Falls on the terrifying Outs: story. Book Lady plinking dishes at the felon's sink: meanwhile.

I jam my fists into my eyes, wiping them hard. "Do you know who that man was, Harriet?"

"His name is Frank Daigle. The handyman." She studies me with her kind eyes. "They like him very much, and until today he appeared harmless. I can't imagine what came over him."

"I can," I say. "I can imagine exactly what came over him."

So I tell her the story. Not just the accident and the trial but also Troy and Vicki and my mother, and even Pastor Rick. I tell her how bad I miss home even though there's no home, not really, left to miss.

Harriet sits with my story for a few moments, the way she sometimes did in Book Club. *Let it settle first*, she'd tell us. *Let it settle before deciding what it's about.* Finally, she says, "I remember that accident. The woman was a teacher, as I recall?"

"Kindergarten."

"Oh, my."

"Twenty-two little kids."

"Three or four years ago now?" she asks me.

"Three."

"How old are you, Violet?"

"Twenty-two."

She's close enough that I can smell her own expensive shampoo. "You were just a baby," she says.

"I took a life, Harriet. That's a fact."

"Facts are facts," she says, like facts are harmless as daisies. She checks out my kitchen counter. "Did your sister leave you some tea?"

"I don't know. We can look." I'm sitting in one of the two chairs in the kitchenette, which seems small now. In a good way. Harriet takes up room. She lands on some tea—ginger peach, which Vicki and I drank at night in our bedroom to feel grown up when we were middle-schoolers. No kettle, but Harriet finds a saucepan and uses that. Something about her bustling about in my kitchen—no other word for it: *bustling*—makes the world stop veering all over the place.

"You had the loveliest voice in Book Club, Violet," she says, opening a cupboard. "Such a loveliness. Not only your physical voice, but your opinions, too. A clarion resonance that was pleasant to the ear." She *bustles* as she speaks, choosing two cups, keeping her distance, in a way, while offering comfort. Maybe volunteer rules apply on the Outs. "In fact, Violet," she says, "I suspect you could read the dictionary under a tree and birds would cease their singing in order to listen."

I can't help it, the crying just happens. Most newbies cry all night long the first night. Sometimes two nights. Rarely three. Then nothing. I didn't cry at all, not the first night or any night after, because my mother was crying plenty enough for the two of us. Maybe tears hide away in the body until such time as they can spout safely. Freely. In the clear.

I guess I'm in the clear.

Harriet assesses my no-rugs no-curtains no-pictures no-books apartment as the water boils. "We'll have to get you something to read." Her own voice is a loveliness to me. A clarion whatever.

"Books won't solve my problems, Harriet."

"No, but they give your problems perspective. They allow your problems to breathe."

"I can't go back to the bookstore."

"You most certainly can, and you will." She pours the water. "But not today." The ginger scent reminds me of Vicki. Of Mama. Of our house on Stickney Street. "Also," Harriet adds, "you'll get a library card. Portland has a marvelous library, and you're six blocks from the main branch."

I take one sip. "Thank you for helping me, Harriet."

"Well, Violet, I was also motherless at your age."

This is supposed to make me feel better, but it doesn't. I imagine Harriet young and alone.

"My mother became ill," she tells me. "My sister was in college, my father had a farm to run, so it was left to me to nurse her. And nurse my father, too, as it turned out." She shakes her head. "He wasn't good at being a widower."

"Your father died too?"

"It didn't take very long. My sister helped out when she could, but she was already out there inhaling the world, and it was too much to ask her to come back." Harriet takes a sip of tea. Her cup has hot-pink lettering: FOLLOW YOUR BLISS. Mine says BE YOURSELF, EVERYONE ELSE IS TAKEN. "It was also left to me to dispose of the farm," she continues, "and when a kerfuffle ensued over the abutter's fence lines, Lou Larson cruised into my life like a rescue ship on a cold black sea."

"Wow."

"Property lawyer. He solved all my problems, so I married him." She smiles quickly. "Romeo and Juliet we were not, but I loved him enough to be happy enough. I had two babies, one after the other, and a good life. We were good to each other. Faithful."

"But he died, Harriet. You told us in Book Club that Lou died."

"Yes, and then I went to college, and I became a teacher, and if I hadn't done those things, I would not be sitting here with you right now." She lifts her cup in a toast. "Life is full of surprises, Violet. Drink up, you'll feel better."

I obey, and she's right, I do feel better. But when she readies to leave, I feel worse. She looks at me like I'm a coat she might buy. My mind starts ticking: *Pick me*.

"I live on Belmont," she says, "not far. It's on the bus route, but you can walk if you feel ambitious."

"I do feel ambitious." A total lie; I feel like digging myself a six-foot hole.

"Then why don't you come to my house for dinner on Thursday, say six o'clock? I've got Book Club on Friday, and maybe I can run some questions past you." She writes the address on the magnetic pad Vicki stuck to my fridge. It says BRIGHT IDEAS. "Any food restrictions?"

I laugh, and after a beat she laughs too, because in prison we ate whatever they gave us, and this is a prison joke.

"I'll be there, Harriet," I say, hoping not to sound overeager when in truth I'm brimming.

She digs a schedule out of her purse and gives it to me. "You'll want to walk over to Congress. It's the number four."

"How much is it?"

"I buy monthly passes. Parking is a trial, and the bus is quite relaxing. I believe a single ride is a dollar fifty. Do you have exact change?"

"I think so. I bought some underwear at Renys today."

"A Maine adventure," she says, which is the Renys tagline, and wow does it feel weird to hear myself laugh, twice in two minutes. If I dropped dead this very second, it would be okay. I would put this laughter in my epitaph.

"Harriet?"

"Yes, Violet."

"Do I tell the bus driver where I'm going, or what?"

All at once it seems to hit her that I'm not a prison-hardened felon filthy with street smarts. I'm a Baptist draggle-tail from Abbott Falls, Maine, who's never once taken a city bus. On the inside, a few of the girls called me Cindy-Lou Who. But I wasn't the only Cindy-Lou Who. Kitten cooked meth in Caribou, but the farthest south she ever traveled was to Bar Harbor for a high school band concert.

"Tell you what," Harriet says. "I'll swing by here at quarter to six and pick you up. That way I can show you the route."

"Okay." I heave a way bigger sigh than I intend.

"And on the way back, we'll retrace, for practice." This sounds like future invitations, not just one dinner at Harriet's but maybe more.

"I wanted the cat," I confess. "More than I wanted the book."

"I know."

"I was kind of looking for a fellow creature."

"Of course you were," Harriet says. "I'm sorry that poor man scared you."

"He didn't scare me," I say.

"I suppose we can attribute his appalling behavior to shock." She takes up her purse and pats my shoulder one last time. "You have paid your debt, Violet, and now you have every right to live your life."

After she goes, my no-rugs no-curtains no-pictures no-books apartment holds the feeling of another person for the rest of the day. But then it fades, and it's just me again. Me and Lorraine Daigle. And now her husband, that nice man, who did not try to scare me. He did not.

Why was that not obvious to everyone who saw? *I* scared *him*.

10

Frank

He little remembered fleeing through the back door, chased by his own scorching memories, finding his car, driving himself home. Only now, in his garage workshop, in the forgiving company of his machines, did he begin to recover his breath.

He took a consoling inventory: grinder, belt sander, bench lathe, drill press; and when his eyes came to rest on the surface plate—Pinky, his old friend Pinky, her faultless tolerances, her smooth, speckled beauty—it came to him what Harriet's hand had reminded him of. His own hands quivered, a wreck of old cuts and calluses; he could see this, how badly they quivered. He pressed his palms to the cool granite, and with the word *tolerances* loose in the room, he rested his forehead on this slab of stone as old as Earth itself, thinking, *Sweet Jesus, what a world.*

When at last he could breathe, he found he could not work. He went into the house, fixed himself a ham sandwich, and found he could not eat. He poured a glass of water from Lorraine's beloved farm sink, and found he could not drink. Finally he left the house, stood on the back steps, and found he could not stand.

So he sat, woozy with shame. Of all the bookstores in all the world. He should have been more prepared; he'd known she was getting out early. The victim advocate, a young woman named Felicia, had called to inform him.

"If you have any questions, Mr. Daigle, any at all!" Fix-it-all Felicia, the woman with the answers. She'd been assigned to him from the get-go, and the part of him that could stand outside himself admired her follow-through.

"Not at the moment," he'd assured her. "But thank you."

"Are you sure? No question is too minor, Mr. Daigle! Usually when the perpetrator gets out early—"

"No questions. Not at this time."

"It would be entirely natural, Mr. Daigle, to experience feelings of—"

"That's all in the past," he said, and when he said it, he believed it. The remote, irrelevant past.

"Oh, Mr. Daigle!" said Felicia, who loved her "survivors" and resolved to soothe them even if she had to lash them to a train track to do it. "You are entitled to your feelings."

"Fully aware," he said, and after that, what more could Felicia ask?

Now he could hear himself groaning just as he had in the store. Seeing Violet Powell—her face clean as an apple, exactly as it had looked in the courtroom—had ignited a fire of memory that rained down on him when he least expected it, all those dormant recollections descending like flaming shards, starting with the cruiser pulling up at his house. *Instantaneous*, they said. *Your wife did not suffer.* For that, Frank had felt grateful—he knows this, counts on this—but even as he'd staggered to a chair, numbed and gasping, the trooper's military bearing making the news nearly instructional, even then, in that surreal *your wife did not suffer* moment, he recognized an unseemly shock of relief.

There it was, ugly and undeniable: relief.

And telling Kristy: the screaming, good God, the screaming, not that he blamed her, she adored her mother and emulated her in all ways. But holy mother of Moses, the screaming. Finally, his son-in-law, the gentle and forbearing Tom Streit, took the line and Frank was able at last to repeat the words all in a row and in the correct order.

There followed the business of planning the wake and funeral, a packed affair, friends and colleagues shoulder to shoulder, the church smelling of mold and incense, Lorraine's longtime lover skulking into a back pew. Handsome enough, faintly disheveled, fighting tears, finally divorced and free at last, which was how Lorraine, exactly one month before the accident, had come to confess. *This is your fault, Frank, you're completely oblivious, you could have headed this off and you didn't.* The man was a know-it-all dog breeder who'd sold them a neurotic and short-lived spaniel years back. *He's strong, he knows what he wants, don't I deserve to be happy?* And now here the man was, a shadow returning, struggling to control his face as the casket rolled down the aisle.

For her part, Kristy sobbed through her eulogy, requiring Tom and the boys to stand at the pulpit with her—the three of them tall and wan and weak-looking as they petted her shoulders, held her arms and hands. For his absence in this spectacle (*Dad! I need you up there with me!*), Frank had never been fully forgiven.

And just when he thought he'd survived the worst of it, free to return to his wifeless house and remake his life, the prosecutor asked for a meeting. Three years gone now, and Frank could still hardly bear to remember: John Sheeran in his featureless office, his sea-blue eyes, big round face, an Irish cop. He sat behind a badly made desk freighted with paper. To Frank's right, his worked-up daughter; to his left, thank God, the ever-calm Tom.

"I'm going to need you, Mr. Daigle," Sheeran said, leaning back in his chair. His belly had outgrown his jacket, giving him the air of an out-of-work Santa.

Frank girded his loins, as they say. "I don't know that I can help you, Mr. Sheeran," he said. "Under the circumstances."

"What kind of *answer* is that, Dad?" Kristy said. They'd gone over this already, back at the house. She spread both hands on the prosecutor's desk, her tanned, ropy arms flexing with the effort.

"Kristy," Tom murmured, petting the back of his wife's knotted neck. "Easy."

"Do you believe in justice, Mr. Daigle?" Sheeran asked. He crossed his arms, and Frank felt suddenly like a perpetrator.

Kristy pounced. "The right answer is *yes*, Dad. *Yes*, Mr. Sheeran, I believe in justice." This was Kristy at her worst; like her mother, she also had a best—a helpful, charming best—but Frank despaired of seeing that Kristy anytime soon. Surely not today.

"Yes," Frank said. What else could he say? "I believe in justice."

"That's very good news," Sheeran said, "because an injustice has been done to your family, and I intend to make it right."

"He understands," Kristy said. "Thank you, Mr. Sheeran."

"In fact it's biblical," Sheeran continued, "the agony that a remorseless woman named Violet Powell has wreaked upon your family. Not to mention upon twenty-two kindergarteners who have lost their beloved teacher. Not to mention upon the law-abiding citizens of the great state of Maine."

"With all due respect, Mr. Sheeran," Frank said, "the girl didn't seem remorseless." He wished he could unsee the arraignment: the crying girl, her ashy, red-eyed mother struggling to breathe while a woman—young but not as young as the girl—held her fast. Daughter, he guessed, and the way she gripped the mother, tender and desperate, gave Frank to believe that the mother was not only brokenhearted but ill. At the mother's other side, two more women, probably the girl's aunts, faces bunched with outrage, the girl seeming to feel it, glancing back at them only once during the entire span of the trial.

"She cried for *herself*, Dad," Kristy said, with a twinge of hysteria a tick or two beyond the average person's hearing but alarmingly audible to him. Kristy had her mother's build and obsession with fitness and otherworldly ability to not hear what hit her ears as unacceptable. "That girl *killed* Mommy. Don't you give her one *iota* of pity." She dabbed her face with a tissue plucked from the detritus of Sheeran's desk. Tom, bless his heart, caught Frank's eye: *You're doing fine, Frank.*

"I've prosecuted all manner of Oscar contenders," Sheeran said, "and this one makes Meryl Streep look like Shepherd Number Three in the first-grade Christmas show at St. Patrick's."

Frank closed his eyes and deeply imagined a freshly milled cube of steel, a nearly sentient thing, an entity that hummed in his hands, that knew its own properties, its possibilities, its limitations. Metal comforted him, always had.

"*Dad*," Kristy said. "Pay *attention*." Even on good days she spoke in italics.

"Honey." That was Tom; thank God he was here, his reassuring son-in-law, a neutral party.

"Mr. Sheeran," Frank said. "If I understand correctly, you're asking me to sit through the trial as some sort of exhibit."

"The 'exhibit,' Mr. Daigle, will be Violet Powell, a one-hundred-thirty-pound female with a blood-alcohol level of point-one-eight. Translation: blotto, plastered, shitfaced. Pardon me, Mrs. Streit." He tented his meaty hands, an exaggeration of calm. "Violet Powell selfishly chose to take the wheel of her boyfriend's car. She chose that. With a little help from an as-yet-undetermined dose of Oxy, about which you will hear much more at trial, she crossed the center line heading south on Route 88 at the same moment that your law-abiding wife was headed north on Route 88 to L.L. Bean to return a pair of size-two classic-fit jeans. Violet Powell committed these acts of her own free will, and any decent person might ask why." He paused. "Why?" Then his hands flew apart, the big finale: "Because she *felt* like it, Mr. Daigle." His pale eyes bulged. "She *felt* like it."

Sheeran reminded Frank of an actor, one of those character actors who did the same character in a hundred movies, and as he tried to place the name of the actor, he realized that Sheeran himself was acting. This was a performance, and he expected applause, or whatever the equivalent of applause might turn out to be in this event.

"Dad, are you *listening*?" He could feel Kristy's sniffling at his right ear, the heartbreaking heat of it.

"I loved your mother, Kristy," he said, and dropped his face into his hands.

Despite everything, this was true. He'd married a headlong woman from a yappy clan of scrappers. She wanted five children. Five! Sure, he'd said to her, you bet, and meant it—"father of five" appealed to him—but it was not to be, and Lorraine blamed him. Not in words, but in the way she mothered Kristy so fervidly, in the way she'd hardened over the years, her ardor cooling in an alchemy not unlike what he saw in the materials he worked with every day. She'd begun their marriage as lead, soft and pliable, elastic and forgiving, but over the years she'd transformed herself into a high-carbon steel, strong and hard and resistant to wear.

But Frank was not one to dwell. He'd loved Lorraine as she was, in her changing form over their years together. From the start he'd seen traces of a hard, wiry woman in the soft, loving girl he married. And if he could sense the hard woman in the soft girl, didn't it stand to reason he could also, if he tried enough, find the soft girl in the hard woman? And if he could find that soft girl now, would that not break his heart?

He stayed put for a few ticks of the clock, hiding inside the cup of privacy made by his hands over his face.

"Dad?"

"Mr. Daigle?" Sheeran's chair scraped back, casters squealing. It wanted oiling. "Mr. Daigle."

"We don't know that she was returning a pair of jeans," Frank said, looking up. "Just to be clear."

Kristy whirled to face him. She had Lorraine's face, chiseled and fierce. "The jeans were on the seat *next* to her, with the *receipt* in the bag, Mommy told me they didn't *fit* right, they made her *hips* look funny! L.L.Bean jeans aren't *cut* for slim women!" She turned to her husband. "What is he *doing*?"

What Frank wanted to say: *You're forty years old, Kristy. You have two big boys. Please stop calling her Mommy.* What he said: "If I have to sit in a courtroom being gawked at for days on end, I want the details to be accurate. That's all."

"Violet Powell was driving on the *wrong side of the road*, Dad. Is that *accurate* enough for you? Mommy swerved to avoid hurting *her*!" Kristy turned again to John Sheeran, who appeared momentarily off his game. Frank felt an unwelcome twinge of triumph. Lorraine had routinely accused him of ceding his ground, but really that was only with her.

"Let's just listen to your dad, Kristy," Tom said quietly. Frank felt his son-in-law's steadying hand on his shoulder.

"*Listen?*" Kristy shrieked. "Listen to *what*? He's talking like a *crazy* man!"

He understood, against his will, that before the trial commenced, his daughter would be out shopping for exactly the right clothes. Her grief was genuine—savage and bone-rocking—and she'd give anything to drag her mother back from the dead. But there remained a jot in her character that would warm to the courtroom spotlight. Kristy would want to be thought beautiful in her sorrow.

"I'm sorry, Kristy," Frank said. "It's nothing against your mother."

"Mr. Daigle," Sheeran said, unconvincingly, "we won't ask you to make an impact statement if you're not up to it. Many survivors find themselves unable to speak in court."

"He'll do whatever you need," Kristy said. "We all will. My dad doesn't know what he's *talking* about, he's in shock."

Sheeran put up his hands. "Juries respond to stories," he said. "I don't care if your wife was returning a pair of jeans or on her way to a barn dance. The point is that a human being, a kindergarten teacher innocently engaged in the quotidian business of life, was taken from her loved ones without so much as a fare-thee-well by the craven actions of Violet Powell, who deserves the fullest punishment that the law allows."

As Kristy fireballed her father with Lorraine's trademark stare, Frank understood that Sheeran was attempting some sort of hypnosis by repeating "Violet Powell" in sentences containing synonyms for human depravity. At the arraignment, though, the word that had come to Frank was not *craven*. The word that came was *young*.

"Mr. Sheeran," he said, exhausted now. "You can make that point without telling a courtroom full of people that my wife was returning a pair of jeans to L.L. Bean when you don't know that for a fact." Why had he agreed to this meeting? He'd expected a prosecutor more like Tom, precise and unflappable, not a jackrabbit gloryhound that made Kristy and Lorraine look like amateurs. He felt outnumbered, outmaneuvered, and outranked, a déjà vu from his experience of Kristy's girlhood.

Kristy stood up. "I can't *listen* to this!" She held up one finger, the nail painted Dracula red; she and Lorraine bought the same beauty products. "I need a minute," she said, whirling out of her chair—as much as 104 pounds of sinew can be said to whirl. Tom gave Frank's shoulder an encouraging squeeze, then followed his wife from the room.

The door shut behind them. This was Sheeran's moment.

"Are you glad your wife died, Frank?"

Frank's mouth opened. He tried to say no but found he could not, and a hot shame roared through his body and smoldered there, a painful burning that he accepted as his due.

"It's not going to come to light that you beat her?"

"What? No!"

"You didn't pop her on the jaw from time to time, slam her head against a wall?"

"No! Of course not! What in the world—"

"Then what is your problem with the goddamn jeans?"

"I like accuracy. That's all."

"All right," Sheeran said, recovering his balance. "How about I say your wife was driving to Freeport with an L.L. Bean bag on the seat, and in the bag was a size-two pair of L.L. Bean classic-fit jeans. Make of that what they will. I'm not trying to turn you, or Lorraine, or anybody else into a liar."

"Thank you. I wanted to make that clear."

"Clear as a bell." Brian Dennehy, that was the actor's name, a natural. "I'm trying to establish a picture, Frank. I'm trying to tell a story, a certain type of story for an audience of twelve. Little details create a story, a person, a tragedy people can relate to. We want the jury to imagine a size-two kindergarten teacher being crushed by four thousand pounds of metal. And we want them to imagine you in your empty house."

Frank covered his mouth against a spasm of bile. Poor Lorraine, his Lorraine, tanned and taut and fearless, his ropy little jackrabbit obliterated in seconds.

And yet. Lorraine had not, in fact, been on her way to L.L. Bean. Lorraine had been on her way to see a divorce lawyer. Her "soul mate" was free now: let the games begin.

Since the day she confessed, he'd urged her to recall the ways in which they'd been happy—hadn't they been happy?—but the affair had run too long, they were past hope, their daughter long grown, nothing to hold them. And it was Frank's fault for "not revealing his full self," whatever that might mean; by default Lorraine skated, blameless. Her oafish brothers had taught her to lead with her chin; in her world, the winner was completely right, the loser completely wrong.

As his stomach convulsed, he endured a monstrous, confusing stew of feeling for this woman who'd so recently ravaged him without mercy, this woman whose awful death had delivered him from the coming mudslide of it's-your-fault and I-deserve-happiness and half-your-pension-is-mine and I'm-taking-the-house and don't-even-think-about-it-Frank-you're-no-match-for-me.

He'd decided to fight. Now he wouldn't have to.

She's better off, people sometimes said of the dead—the old and sick. Lorraine, tackled while rushing for the future she wanted, was not better off.

But *he* was.

And he knew it. And his relief shamed him, try as he might to feel otherwise.

That was his problem with the goddamn jeans.

Sheeran offered Frank a Kleenex. "You all right, Frank?"

"I'm good," he said, wiping his mouth. "I'm good."

Sheeran nodded. "We'll want you in the courtroom every day," he said, solicitous now. "The defense attorney, Dean Weingarten, is a belly-crawling snake in the grass who'll portray Miss Violet Powell as a fragile, unworldly, small-town first offender, a little lamb who got lost in the woods."

Frank had always loved that song: *I'm a little lamb who's lost in the woods . . .*

"Dean Weingarten, who claims a three handicap when in reality he's a goddamn eighteen, will paint a Technicolor sad-face picture of Miss Violet Powell as the innocent flower corrupted by a pretty-boy jock, and we're not gonna let them do that to Lorraine."

What the hell was Sheeran talking about? Frank had never so much as touched a golf club.

"Are we, Frank?"

"Are we what?"

"Are we going to let a blowhard golf cheater do that to Lorraine?"

Having decided to simply float along this wave-crash of someone else's making, Frank shook his head.

"Damn straight, no," Sheeran said. "Violet Powell drank her weight in booze and chose to get behind the wheel. She chose that, Frank, and we're not gonna let Dean Weingarten bullshit a jury of Violet Powell's peers."

Frank had stopped listening. The song was in his head now. Sometimes he'd hum it for most of a day as he stood at a grinder, feet aching. *Someone to watch over me . . .* Lorraine had also loved that song; they'd danced to it at their wedding. Of course the lyrics suggested the delicate yearning of a woman, but Frank felt them in his own yearning, a yearning he had not, it now appeared, sufficiently conveyed to his wife over their years together.

I know I could
always be good
to one who'll watch over me . . .

Kristy was back. Tom was holding her purse, which looked like a small pink bucket. Lorraine had one in green.

"Your father and I had a talk," Sheeran said, acting again. Or maybe not. The job probably meant something to him, tossing bad apples into the clink. "Violet Powell took your mother, and we're gonna make her pay."

"Dad, let's make her *pay*," Kristy said, her face crumpling. Frank gave up then, gave in, gave over. "Oh, sweetheart," he said, taking her into his arms, comforting her as she cried and cried, which was all she'd wanted anyway, his fatherly arms around the cold rack of her body. Why had it been so hard for him to give her what she wanted?

That day in Sheeran's office had mercifully faded over the course of three years. Now here it was again, raw and vivid.

Are you glad your wife died, Frank?

Three years: Kristy and Tom now renovating their house in New Hampshire, their once chatty boys now glum teenagers, Frank now left to his retirement, all that water now under the bridge.

Are you glad your wife died, Frank?

All that murky water, under the bridge.

Until Violet Powell reappeared and asked to adopt a cat.

Who was that man in the bookstore? Who in God's name *was* that? How had he been so brutally ambushed by his own shame, the courtroom rising up before him, the jurors and their softening mouths, his sobbing daughter, the girl's tremoring mother, his dry eyes taken for a widower's dignity?

Are you glad your wife died, Frank?

He covered his face now, reliving not the past, but the present. To the kids in the bookstore he must have resembled the villain from those horror movies they were always going on about, crashing their innocence with a rain of flying tools, the blue pane sharp and lethal. And dear God Almighty, Harriet Larson—who knew his name, she knew his name—her lovely mouth forming a horrified O. Had she thought he was lunging at the girl? Is that what she thought? He was not lunging; he was fending. Fending off the knives of memory, holding the blue pane in front of his heart, hoping she could not see through it.

He spent the rest of the day in the garage cleaning his tools, micrometers and calipers and files and scales, busywork that quieted his mind. As dusk crept in, his eye came to rest on a box fashioned from Popsicle sticks and glitter from one of Lorraine's kindergarteners. He used it to store nails. It came to him then that the garage was the only place on the premises not saturated with Lorraine. He still saw the house through her eyes—the paint she'd chosen, the arrangement of vases and chairs. He kept it that way for Kristy. The garage, by contrast, was now and always had been only his.

Wherever his wife had gone, whatever mote of creation she now inhabited, he wished her peace, even if, God forgive him, he had not wished her back in the world, all that grief and tumult. *I was faithful to the end, though,* he thought. *I sat there day after day, Lorraine, knowing what I knew. They pitied me, as they were meant to, they exacted a price I did not ask for, and the girl paid.*

11

Harriet

"WAIT," SOPHIE SAID. "WAIT JUST one second." She tossed her bag, missing the chair, and approached Harriet, who was stirring a risotto at the stove. "You invited an inmate to dinner?"

"I did, yes," Harriet said. The risotto smelled divine: rosemary and mushroom, Lou's favorite. It had taken most of their twenty years to expand the palate of her meat-and-potatoes man. Now she regretted all his never-to-be surprises: he'd died before trying goat cheese, sun-dried tomatoes, tapenade. His late middle age would have been a wonder.

"You promised to be careful, Aunt Harrie."

"I promised no such thing." Harriet moved her niece aside to get the salt. "And she's not an inmate."

"Ex, then." Sophie hovered at Harriet's elbow, all perfume and hair mousse, until her phone dinged and she glanced at it.

"Don't tell your cousins," Harriet said.

"It's Luis," she said. "We're going to a movie." She was dressed in one of her crinkled, flibbety tops in a cloudburst of color, plus the orange boots she'd been traipsing around in for months.

"Have fun," Harriet said, stirring. As Sophie edged closer, Harriet said, "You're going to burn your sleeve."

Sophie stepped back, tapping at her phone. "I thought there were rules."

"I thought we settled this."

"I called off the cousins. You should be thanking me."

The girls weren't in cahoots at all, Harriet realized. Sophie was the one who'd sounded the alarm, who'd badgered the girls into worrying over their mother's "trusting" nature. They called once a week to say I love you, to extract advice about toddlers and husbands, to grumble about work and each other and the "bloody" English weather. Annie and Ellen expected their mother to worry about *them*, insisting, from three thousand miles away, on remaining her baby girls. They had yet to work out how to love her in a grown-up way.

Cahoots had been wishful thinking.

"Can I stay for dinner?" Sophie asked.

"You have plans."

Sophie waved her phone. "I just canceled."

"I didn't invite you."

"I live here."

Harriet laughed. "You can stay if you promise to behave."

"What makes you think I won't?"

"Because you are your mother's daughter." She lifted the wooden spoon and pointed it. "I do not need to be safeguarded from my dinner guest. *She* is the one in need of safeguarding. From the world." Harriet tapped the spoon against the lip of the pan, then handed it over. "Stir."

Sophie laid down her phone and took up stirring, eyes narrowed in thought. "You know what I think?"

"Oh, I'll miss this."

"What?"

"Your pesky perseverance. You have not altered one atom of your character since you were three."

Sophie gave a little snort. "Speaking of unchanging character, I think your dinner guest is Plan B for the empty nest."

"Keep stirring," Harriet said.

"I was Plan A."

"I take your point, Sophie." Harriet ransacked the silverware drawer more noisily than necessary. "Your point is ludicrous."

"How old is she?"

"A baby. Younger than you. Stir."

"Do you know what she was in for?"

Harriet handed her a fistful of cutlery. "If you can't stir, then please set the table."

"So you *do* know." Sophie trotted off, then called from the dining room, "If she's younger than me, she couldn't have been in for long. Was it drugs?"

Harriet listened to the haphazard clink of knives and forks. Sophie set a table like a bad juggler: yet one more sound she would miss.

"Should I open some wine?" Sophie asked, returning to the kitchen. Clever girl.

"No wine," Harriet said.

"So . . . multiple DUIs?" She yanked open the linen drawer. "Something more or less victimless?" She scooped up some napkins and rambled back to the dining room. "You can tell me, Aunt Harrie," she called. "I won't judge. I'm not judgy."

Sophie's judgments could in fact fill an oil tanker; her temperament suited her less to social work and more to tax law, or quality-control inspection, or window number seven at the DMV. She was also kind-hearted, and Harriet hoped her love of the underdog would see her safely down the wrong chosen path. People chose wrong paths all the time and turned out all right.

Back in the kitchen again, Sophie said, "I promise to be good."

"Glad to know it." Harriet passed the spoon to Sophie and gathered up her keys.

"Where are you going?"

"I'm picking up our guest, whose name is Violet Powell." Harriet pointed at her niece's phone lying among the herbs. "Look it up on your binky, you know you're dying to." Giving Tabsy a pat on her way out the door, she called over her shoulder, "And for God's sake watch the risotto. I'll be back in fifteen."

"I won't look it up, Aunt Harrie," Sophie called as Harriet reached the steps. "I would never do that!"

Harriet found Violet waiting on the street in front of her building, dressed in a blouse and skirt and ballet flats, clutching a jar of gourmet jam. "I didn't know what to bring you," she said, getting into the car. "I hope you like blueberry."

"This is perfect, Violet," Harriet said, "and entirely unnecessary."

"I thought about knitting you a bird."

Harriet laughed, and they chatted easily on the drive to the house. When they arrived, Violet sat up, lips parted. "Wow, Bookie," she said as they pulled into the driveway. "It's exactly how you described it."

"Is it?" Harriet showed Violet into the foyer of what suddenly struck her as a ridiculous house. Ceilings too high, rooms too deep, rugs too thick, memories too real. Stocky sideboards and credenzas took the weight of framed photographs, cumbersome mementos of a life she no longer lived.

"There's the grandfather clock," Violet said, clearly awed. "With the faces of the moon. Oh, and the lion's-head doorknob." She took it all in, ceiling to floor, landing on a framed photo of Lou on a fishing boat. "Is that Lou?"

"Good guess," Harriet said, though she did recall discussing Lou's crazy pompadour hair when they'd read *The Great Gatsby*.

"Hi," Sophie said, clanking in from the kitchen in her orange boots. Her eyes glittered with suspicion.

"Hi, Sophie," Violet said. After a measuring beat, in which she appeared to accept Sophie's suspicion and pretend to not mind, she added, "Congratulations on grad school."

"Okay, wow," Sophie said, "is there anything you didn't tell them?"

"I'm not them," Violet said. "I'm me."

It was like watching rivals setting up for a duel. From there the dinner party proceeded in fits and starts: Sophie made only flickering stabs at small talk; Harriet kept pouring water into nearly full glasses. Harriet and Violet spoke of Book Club—what else had they to speak of?—sometimes in lingo that recalled prison. Sophie asked no questions, and though she observed each exchange with hawklike interest, she did not pounce.

"Is there something you care to add, Sophie?" Harriet asked. She sounded spiky. She was.

"Nope," Sophie said. "The risotto's really good."

"Best I've ever had," Violet said, "not that I've ever had it." Her colossal effort to enjoy herself was a kindness to Harriet and a defiance to Sophie, whose thorny attention was like having a CO at the table.

As Harriet moved the girls to the parlor for dessert, she noted how vaporous Violet seemed next to Sophie. Women left prison physically diminished, but in Violet that diminishment seemed of a different order, as if the part of God that is said to dwell in all creatures had flown from her, only to perch somewhere nearby, awaiting reentry.

"How are the questions going for Book Club?" Violet asked. "Do you need help?"

"That's my job, usually," Sophie said from Lou's recliner. She'd made haste in claiming it, her boots crossed at the ankles.

"I decided we'll just read aloud tomorrow," Harriet said. "I'm trying out poetry. Leading questions might be a bridge too far." She passed out decorative cups of ice cream—Gifford's mint chocolate chip, a flavor Violet had once pined for in a Book Club round of When I Get Out First Thing I Do. "You all loved *Spoon River* so much, anything else is going to feel like an insult." She shook her head. "I still can't fathom why that book was such a hit."

"Maybe because we feel like the talking dead," Violet said. "Desiree started writing her epitaph."

Sophie shifted in Lou's chair, a leathery groan. "Is she on death row or something?"

"Nobody in Maine is on death row," Harriet said, a tad snappier than she intended.

Violet waited for Harriet to take a spoonful of ice cream, then did the same, precisely, which broke Harriet's heart a little. "Anyway," Violet said, "Desiree said it would take a whole book, so then Dawna-Lynn said hers would take up two books, so then Renee said hers would take three books."

"Who's tomorrow's poet?" Sophie asked.

Harriet reached beneath a pile of books and pulled out a sheaf of papers stapled together. "I bought several books and chose a few things from all of them. Something's bound to hit." She hoped that was true. "I printed a set for you, Violet."

"Really?" Violet took the sheaf, admired it, and said, "You'll have to take the staples out."

"Ah," Harriet said. "Good catch."

"Did you print me one?" Sophie asked. Her chin lifted just a stitch.

"Sophie, for goodness' sake, since when do you read poetry?"

"Since now."

"You can have mine," Violet offered.

"No, it's okay," Sophie said. "I'll just borrow Aunt Harrie's when she's not using it."

"Are you sure?"

"Keep it," Sophie insisted, as if offering it as her own gift. Oh, that girl.

"Sara Teasdale," Violet read, leafing through the pages, "Wanda Coleman, William Butler Yeats, Elizabeth Bishop . . ."

"Never heard of them," Sophie said.

Violet looked up shyly. "I've heard of Yeats."

Sophie set down her empty ice cream cup. "I studied psychology. We didn't have time for poetry."

"You have to *make* time for poetry," Harriet said.

After a cheerless pause, Violet asked Harriet, "How is everyone?"

"Marielle got lugged for felony sleeping," Harriet said. "Dorothy's daughter had twins."

"Tell them hi for me."

"Is that allowed?" Sophie asked, settling deeper into Lou's chair, a pecking-order signal so transparent that Harriet nearly laughed. She hadn't the slightest doubt that Sophie knew plenty about their dinner guest. Throughout the effortful dinner and now dessert, Violet had suffered the cool waterfall of Sophie's appraisal. Sophie had her phone out; perhaps she was googling "felony sleeping."

"Being an animal lover, Violet," Harriet said, "you may be interested to know that Sophie works with a parrot who has acquired a vocabulary of one hundred thirty-five words."

"I don't work *with* a parrot," Sophie clarified. "I work *for* a Russian lunatic."

"Dr. Petrov is an animal behaviorist," Harriet continued. "According to Google," she said, side-eyeing her niece, "he emigrated from Moscow.

Master's from MIT in chemistry. PhD from Princeton in biology, another PhD from Harvard in behavioral psychology. Quite a lettered personage." She took a dainty spoonful of ice cream. "Sophie thinks I live in the nineteenth century."

"Only because she does," Sophie said, easing up a bit; she'd been out-googled.

Violet set down her own dish. "In Book Club we teased her about that sometimes."

Then, a miracle, they both smiled, a little. Sometimes cahoots could work out just right. "Your job sounds pretty great," Violet said then.

An idea jingled into Harriet's head, sudden as the bell over the bookstore door. She said, "That job will be vacant soon."

"It's a terrible job," Sophie said. "I'd way rather tend bar at Danube."

"Classy, right?" Violet said.

"The tips are pretty classy."

"Sophie's been Dr. Petrov's lab assistant for two years," Harriet said. "That's a lot of clout, isn't it?"

"Aunt Harrie, I'm a glorified chambermaid."

But Violet, it seemed, was enthralled. "The parrot knows a hundred thirty-five words?"

"*Knows* is the key," Harriet said. "Lots of birds can imitate human speech, but Charlotte understands what the words mean."

Violet looked up cautiously, as if afraid of being made fun of.

"No. it's true," Harriet insisted. "Charlotte's in the news from time to time."

"I love animals," Violet said. "I didn't know parrot research was a thing."

"It's a thing if you have grant money and a university willing to host you," Sophie said.

"It was quite a coup for our university," Harriet added, "which is an excellent institution, Violet—"

"And not a mile from this house," Sophie said, a cahootish triumph.

"I was saving up to go," Violet said.

The air went leaden again, so Harriet made another stab: "Dr. Petrov will be lost without you, Sophie."

"Ha," Sophie said, sitting up, hair spangling in the lamplight. "No he won't."

"I bet he will," Violet said. She sounded like a child trying to please another child.

"Well," Sophie said, "you don't know him, and I do, so . . ."

"You underestimate yourself, Sophia Jane," Harriet said, a warning. She should have urged them both to the sofa, side by side; in the current setup she had to ignore one to address the other. "Sophie plans to become a social worker," she said to Violet. "That's why she's leaving her current job." Of course Violet already knew this; everyone in Book Club knew.

Sophie and Violet exchanged a look that communicated a human wrangling as old as Eden:

Your aunt is really nice.

You can't have her.

Harriet shifted in her chair, a plush swivel in a whimsical print that she'd bought in the hope of hosting a dinner party just like this one. She'd imagined an easier flow of conversation. More guests. *Older* guests. More laughter. *Some* laughter.

"We had a social worker on the inside," Violet said. "She pretty much sucked, but nobody cared. She only came once a month anyway."

"How?" Sophie asked.

"What?"

"How did she pretty much suck?"

Dear Lord, Harriet prayed, why didn't I sneak some wine in the kitchen?

"She didn't believe us when we said things," Violet said quietly. "She thought we were liars because they told her we were liars."

Sophie tilted her head, innocent as the moon. "There are no liars in prison?"

"Oh," Harriet said. "Sophie."

"Plenty of liars in prison," Violet said. "Plenty of liars everywhere."

Sophie and Violet locked eyes as Harriet felt herself disappear.

"The social worker was there to help us," Violet said, "but if somebody thinks you're a liar, it's hard to feel helped."

Oh, how Harriet missed Lou right now, her blustery people-lover who gloried in the shenanigans of property law. He'd have these two singing the same song, probably literally, lickety-split.

"If I was a social worker," Violet said, "I wouldn't be the kind that makes my person feel like a liar." Her eyes appeared enormous in her delicate face.

"I won't be that kind." Sophie was sitting fully upright now, a blot of ice cream on her chin. All at once Harriet wanted to cry.

"Bookie always believed us," Violet said. "Harriet, I mean."

Something shifted in the emotional air exactly as the sun dropped from view and the room dulled and the cat beelined into the room, hurdled the ottoman, and landed directly in Violet's lap. "Hello, Tabsy." Violet laughed, a genuine gurgle of pleasure. "We meet at last." She seemed beguiled, and so did the cat.

The recliner popped upright. "I believe in respecting the client, no matter their circumstances," Sophie said.

"Good," Violet said. "That's good." She chanced a quick, darting smile.

"Getting back to my point," Harriet said, "Sophie's job will soon be open."

"I wasn't asking for approval," Sophie said. "I was just informing you that all social workers aren't like the one you had."

"She wasn't really mine," Violet said, scratching the euphoric cat behind the ears. "She was for all of us. Eighty-eight of us."

"Well, there's the obvious problem," Sophie said.

"I think the obvious problem was she hated being a social worker." Violet said this as a matter of fact, but the truth tumbled into the room like an unpinned grenade. The precise cant of Sophie's chin recalled little-girl Sophie hoarding toys. The traitorous cat didn't help. Harriet didn't know whether to laugh or cry.

Violet gently removed the cat from her lap. "Well, I guess I should go."

Harriet rose to get her keys.

"It's okay, Harriet. I can walk."

Before Harriet could further protest, Violet was at the door. As Harriet returned her jacket—a denim thing that might have come from a church bin—Sophie reappeared. "It was nice to meet you," she said. Speaking of liars.

"You too."

They looked so different, these girls—women, she had to admit. One in her neat little skirt and spiritless hair, the other a bomb-blast of color and curl.

Violet snapped the jacket all the way closed. "That was the best meal I've ever had, Harriet. Like, in my whole life."

She wanted to hug Violet but didn't. Not a few days ago, this child had soaked Harriet's blouse, literally crying on her shoulder, but here, now, everything felt more precarious, less free, as if the COs had them in their sights. But it was Sophie who had them in her sights, and Harriet felt suddenly bound by volunteer-inmate rules.

ACCEPT NOTHING FROM INMATES; GIVE NOTHING TO INMATES.

DO NOT SHARE PERSONAL INFORMATION WITH INMATES.

DO NOT INITIATE OR ACCEPT PHYSICAL CONTACT WITH INMATES.

DO NOT RELAY INFORMATION FROM AN INMATE TO ANY OUTSIDE PERSON.

DO NOT RELAY INFORMATION TO AN INMATE FROM ANY OUTSIDE PERSON.

"Don't be a stranger," Harriet said, shaking Violet's hand. "You have my number."

Violet turned to Sophie. "Could I have yours?"

"My number?"

"You don't have to."

"No, it's—I guess it's fine." Sophie took Violet's phone and let it rest in her hand, just long enough to telegraph that she was doing all and sundry a big fat favor. Corinne again: a wonderful person who enjoyed demonstrating her wonderfulness. Maybe Sophie had chosen Berkeley only so it could be understood that her commitment to social work required a round-trip journey of six thousand miles. These flaws made Harriet love her more, not less, because Sophie had fought all her life against her own nature. To be loved by prickly Sophie was to truly be loved.

"There you go," Sophie said, handing the phone back.

"I'm not gonna call," Violet said. "I just want to put some people in here."

"Oh. Okay." All the edge had drained from Sophie's voice. "But you can text if you want."

"I won't, though," Violet said. "Well. Thanks, Bookie." She stepped onto the porch.

"Violet, wait," Harriet said, "let me wrap some leftovers." She trotted back inside, quickly put together a second meal, and when she turned, it was Sophie there waiting. Violet was still outside, like a dog unused to house privileges.

"Oh my God," Sophie said, "I don't know why I was so mean."

"I'm disappointed in you, Sophie," Harriet said. "You could have made this easy, and instead you made it hard."

"I know." Her eyes welled. "I'm sorry."

"Your mother was the same way," Harriet said, snapping shut a plastic tub. "Protective as a junkyard dog." She joggled the tub into a paper bag with rest of the leftovers. "And she still managed to be my favorite person."

"Tell you what," Sophie said, grabbing the leftovers. "I'll drive her home."

Minutes later, Harriet watched the two of them get into Sophie's car, Violet stashed against the passenger-side window like wet laundry, Sophie stolid and take-charge at the wheel, backing out with her blinker on. Two jaunty beeps as they eased away. Was that an apology?

Oh, Corinne, she thought. *I did the best I could.* Well, that's what social-work school was for, to teach what her niece would learn soon enough: People set their husbands afire, they nurse their dying mothers, they rob demented old men, they sing songs that bring listeners to tears, they kill a woman while drunk on love and 86-proof. The line between this and that, you and her, us and them, the line is thin.

12

Violet

THE NIECE IS A PIECE of work. No mother, no father either, which might be why she acts like Harriet is four hundred years old and through with life and in dire need of protecting from people like me.

If only Sophie could see her aunt at Book Club, fearing nothing, including Jenny Big, who looks like a Sasquatch with worse hair. And Dawna-Lynn: when she asked to sing a number from some ancient Broadway musical, Harriet summoned the nerve to hum along. That was day *one.*

In other words, Harriet doesn't need protecting. From anybody. But Sophie doesn't know this enormous fact about her aunt, so she gives me the devil eyes all through dinner. I chow down anyway, cleaning my plate not only because the food is mind-blowing but because Harriet made it. My mother cooked every day but couldn't put her heart in it. *Since your father died, I can't put my heart in it.* That's what she said about everything: cooking, her job at the library, our schoolwork, shoe shopping, walking down the street on a sunny day. *Since your father died, I can't put my heart in it.*

Well, I put my heart all the way into the beautiful meal Harriet cooked for me.

Then, after staring at me all night like I'm a house rat with plans, Sophie suddenly decides it would be a crime against humanity to let me walk home a mile and a half on a beautiful springtime evening. Which is how I end up in her car, straining for conversation.

"I like your shirt."

"Thanks."

"My sister used to wear stuff like that."

"You have a sister?"

"Not anymore."

"She died?"

"No. Sort of."

After that, silence falls like ice from a rooftop. We drive without speaking until she stops at a light.

"My aunt wants me to give you my job with Dr. Petrov," she says. "In case you missed it."

"I didn't."

"It wouldn't be my call. I mean, even if I put in a word, it wouldn't be my call."

"I'm not qualified anyway."

"A trained woodchuck is qualified." She has this crazy hair, cork-screw curls flying every which way, and a round, honest face that doesn't really match the loudmouth hair. It's hard to tell if she's a wolf in sheep's clothing, or the reverse. Brittie was the same way, and she turned out to be a lamb.

"I applied at three Dunkin' Donuts, but they didn't call back," I tell her, tightening my grip on Harriet's leftovers for courage. "I need a job, and I'm really good at working."

At the next stoplight, she says, still staring ahead, "If I put in a word, it's only because my aunt wants me to and I hate to refuse her anything."

A twitter of hope whirs in my chest. "Are you saying you *will* put in a word?"

She pauses. "It's the worst job in Portland."

"I think I'd like it, though."

"You won't. Petrov'll give you your own key so he can call you day or night to run in and check on the birds. Just say no. Mrs. Rocha will back you."

"Who's Mrs. Rocha?"

"The lab manager. She can handle him. Don't call her Maria."

"I wouldn't mind checking on the birds."

"Also, the birds could die on your watch. Oliver's fifty-four and on borrowed time. Petrov will collapse with grief and blame it on you."

You wouldn't call her beautiful, exactly, but she's got a presence about her. Like a healthier, cleaner, more confident version of Dawna-Lynn. The kind of person who would either throw herself in front of a train to save you or throw *you* in front of a train just because.

"How long do parrots live?" I ask her.

"African greys? Sixtyish. Sometimes longer."

All goes quiet again. As she rounds the corner near the park, she says, "The birds are jerks, by the way. They scream all day long. It's unbelievably annoying, but the pay is good. He doesn't pay the students at all. You'll get all of it." She keeps driving, and her expression doesn't change.

More silence; maybe she's thinking. Maybe she wants me to feel beholden. The only person who ever put in a word was my aunt Linda, who went to high school with the manager of the Abbott Falls Dunkin' Donuts; I was sixteen, and her word-putting made me feel loved and lucky. What word would she put in now, *guilty*?

Sophie says, "My aunt is a generous person." She stops at another light. "It would be easy to take advantage." Her voice has this alluring roundness to it, like maybe she sang in her high school choir. Like Dawna-Lynn's voice—quite the decoy. I find myself wishing for a chance to like her; if I were Harriet's niece, I'd hope to be exactly this fierce.

"You could give your aunt a little credit."

"Oh?" she says. "You know her that well, do you?"

"I would never take advantage. I know *that*."

"Like you knew you would never do time?"

As she moves the car through the intersection, I catch the tiniest flinch in her jaw, enough to make me think those words flew off her tongue, that if she'd taken one second to think it over, she'd have said something else instead. One thing I learned in prison is that sometimes rotten things fly off people's tongues because they're mean, but mostly it's because they're scared.

Sophie is scared of me. And I'm glad. Because she ruined dinner and made Harriet feel bad. She rounds the corner to Deering Avenue. Two more minutes, tops. I wouldn't mind jumping out now.

"Can I tell you something, Sophie? I mean in all honesty?"

"Shoot."

"You're gonna be a shit social worker."

These words do not fly off my tongue. These words step out one by one, wearing shoes.

"You're right," she says. "But that's the track I laid out, and it's hard to get off a moving train," and all of a sudden she's bawling her eyes out, her whole face drizzling.

People. Oh my God.

"Uh, maybe you wanna pull over?"

She obeys, a few yards short of Grant Street. The car idles quietly; it's a good car. I wait like a hostage while she tries to recover.

I open my leftovers bag—a stiff paper grocery bag—and there's the whole meal tucked into plastic containers: the risotto, the salad with nuts and raisins, the squishy bread, even a little tub of Gifford's mint-chocolate-chip ice cream, my favorite, which maybe Harriet remembered from Book Club. Hand-churned, or hand-packed. Hand-somethinged. I dig out a paper napkin; of course Harriet thought of a paper napkin, the expensive thick kind.

Sophie presses the entire thing to her face, wet splotches shredding the paper. "You see what's happening here, right?" she says. It comes out muffled and weepy.

"Yup. You ruined dinner, embarrassed your aunt, and now you're crying but probably not about that."

She balls up the napkin though she's a messy crier and nowhere near done. "She gave her kids everything, and they moved to fucking *London*, but then my mother died and I landed in her lap, and she gave it all to me." She tosses the napkin into the back seat. "And now I'm leaving, and her nest is empty again, and you look like a baby bird with its mouth open."

I check my grocery bag, and sure enough, there's an extra napkin—of course Harriet included an extra napkin. "Here."

"Thanks." She mops her face. "The only thing I know about you is that you just got out of prison."

I glance at her phone, which has basically been glued to her body since I walked into Harriet's house. "I guess you know a little more than that."

To this she says nothing.

"Your aunt is lucky you love her."

Again, nothing.

"You have nothing to fear from me."

Again: nothing.

I grab my door handle. "Do you think I'm not sorry?"

"I don't think anything. I don't know you."

"The woman I killed taught kindergarten," I say, angry now. "Her daughter cried through every single second of the trial. Her husband was the sweetest, sweetest man." I shove the door open. "I'm plenty fucking sorry, and I don't deserve even the worst job in Portland, but I need it."

"Wait, no. Violet."

I pause only because for the first time all night she's called me by name.

"I'll put in a word," she says.

"Don't do me any favors."

"It's for my aunt. I love her, she likes you, and so."

She puts the car into gear and drives me to my building. I don't get out right away, I don't know why.

"Anyway," she says, "no guarantees. Petrov might decide he wants a lab assistant with a degree in chemical physics. Or landscape design. Or French theater."

"I don't have any of those."

"The birds bite," she says. "Don't wear earrings. Prepare for autocracy, mind-numbing routine, and soul-crushing futility."

"Considering my most recent address, that should not be a problem."

She looks startled, then laughs. A little. So I laugh. A little. Maybe she's all right; being related to Harriet is one for the plus column.

"Don't screw it up," she says. "I'll be across the country by then, and I couldn't care less about Petrov, but I don't want my aunt to be disappointed."

"I won't screw it up," I say, shoving the door open. I get out, lean into the window. "Sophie," I tell her, "I'm just a person."

As she drives away, I can't help thinking of Vicki doing that exact thing. What I wanted to say—to Vicki then, to Sophie now: I'm just a person, who hopes to become a *good* person. If they didn't agree this was possible, I could not bear to hear it, so I just stood there with my unfinished sentence and let them go.

My apartment looks almost cheery as I flip on the lights. A long, humming flood of adrenaline comes out of nowhere. You get that a lot in prison, but this time I think it's just gladness—gladness that two people besides Vicki know where I live. Instead of storing the leftovers, I decide to eat them.

The food tastes even better the second time. I haven't eaten like this not just since before prison but since before ever. I gobble every last crumb of dinner all over again, with my table set to look as close to Harriet's as possible, which is not remotely close. How long does it take to cook a meal like this? Imagine her thinking of me all that time. Through all that bread baking and salad making and risotto cooking.

I can see why Sophie wouldn't want to loosen her clutches.

Why she might think I'm trouble.

But I'm not trouble. I am not trouble. I am a baby bird.

13

Harriet

THE WOMEN ASSEMBLED IN THE usual disorder that somehow righted itself within seconds. They'd been shuttled to the empty chow hall, the unit managers having taken over the Visitors' Room for a meeting.

"Chow hall," Brittie groused. "Fuck this."

"Watch your mouth," Jenny Big warned. "This ain't ladies' night at the Strip Palace."

"I worked there," Kitten said.

Shayna: "Me too. Sucky tips."

"For *you*."

"Shut it."

"Shall we begin?" Harriet said.

Jenny Big made a fancy-lady gesture. "Why, yes, we shall."

They made frequent fun of her, but Harriet always felt in on the joke. "Can I read something first?" Dawna-Lynn asked. "I wrote it last night."

A unison of "yes," and Dawna-Lynn began, loud, bold syllables: *Hup-one, hup-two.* A poem about hiking. Over hill and dale. Not because she liked it—she hated hiking—but because she could. *Hup-two*, the poem concluded, *to anywhere but here*.

The women applauded. Volunteers were advised to keep up their guard by reserving their opinions, but Harriet preferred her guard unkept. "I never much cared for exercise," she said, "but Lou, bless his heart, wouldn't hear of it." The women leaned in; they liked Lou stories.

"There he'd be, forty paces ahead in a *monsoon*, dragging me and the girls on one of his bracing hikes meant to build character."

"Hiking sucks out loud," Renee said, and everyone laughed.

"And I'm a fraidy-cat in the great outdoors," Harriet said, pulling the poetry sheaves out of her bag, "but oh my goodness, there he was, dear, windburned Lou, hup-one, hup-two."

"Asshole move," said Desiree.

"Oh, he couldn't help it," Harriet said. "Type A attorney, forward-march was his default. I turned the girls around and let him finish the hike himself." They were all nodding, as if they, too, had married type A attorneys. As so often happened in Book Club, Harriet felt a stirring of belonging, her foibles fitted to a more forgiving spectrum of human striving. What did the outdoors matter inside these walls, where "nature" appeared as a songbird chancing to light on the barbed wire? "Dad kept them entertained," she said. "Mom kept them alive."

"Preach," said Dorothy, who'd raised six kids, and the rest, mothers all, lifted a hand in testimony. Harriet lifted her own hand in motherly solidarity.

"Now," she said, "who's ready for some poetry?"

She passed out the sheaves, which were not exactly allowed, staples or no. Books got shipped straight from the bookstore, but hand deliveries had to be preapproved. She'd taken too long in her selections, though, so she'd brought them herself, cruising through a security detail so used to her that she sometimes had to remind them to take her keys.

"Some of the poems are old, some are new," she said. "I thought we'd try a bit of everything, then choose a poet whose work we'd like to study further."

All at once, the women looked skeptical. Reluctant to move on from *Spoon River Anthology,* they'd brought their copies just in case.

Harriet scraped her chair forward, all business. "Where should we start?"

"Old," Dawna-Lynn said, brooking no argument.

"Then we'll begin with William Butler Yeats," Harriet said. "He was Irish."

"I'm Irish," Kitten said.

"All right, then, Kitten, you start."

After Kitten read one of the short poems, which met with grudging approval, Harriet directed them to a second poem, called "When You Are Old."

"It's a man speaking to the woman he loves," she said. "Unlike his rivals, who are taken with the woman's youth and beauty, the poet vows to love her into her old age."

Renee gave a little snort. "Like that'll happen."

By way of introduction, Harriet chanced an explanation of iambic pentameter and its romantic properties. "Five beats to a line," she instructed them, and together they chanted the beats: *Da-DAH, da-DAH, da-DAH, da-DAH, da-DAH.* Now they were laughing again.

"That's it exactly," Harriet said. "Jenny, will you read?"

Jenny Big cleared her throat daintily, squared her beefy shoulders, and held the sheaf in both hands, away from the table. Over time they'd all begun to take performance cues from Dawna-Lynn. "*When you are old and gray and full of sleep,*" Jenny Big began. "*And nodding by the fire, take down this book,*" and now here they all were, once again transported to another time and place. "*And slowly read, and dream of the soft look / Your eyes had once, and of their shadows deep. . . .*" The reading was hypnotic, beautifully paced; Jenny Big's voice had a raspy lushness that could make poetry of an oil bill.

When she finished, the women fell silent—perhaps, like Harriet, wondering whether they'd ever been loved for themselves alone.

"Holy shit," Jacynta said.

Marielle's mouth dropped open. "Right? Like, *right*?"

Harriet laughed with relief. "The Irish pretty much cornered the market on beautiful writing."

Jenny Big said, "Iambic pentameter doesn't hurt."

Then Dawna-Lynn: "When he says he loves the, the—"

"The *sorrows*," Brittie sighed. "The *sorrows* of your changing face, oh my God."

"He makes the old lady sound beautiful," Jacynta said. "Like if you love somebody, it's their whole self, not their face." Her own whole self shone.

"So good, Jacynta!" Dorothy said. They often celebrated their smallest agreements, which made Harriet wonder about the daily struggle to stay civil.

"It's the words," Jacynta crooned, "it's the fucken words." She quoted the dead Irish poet as if he were her current boyfriend: "*But one man loved the pilgrim soul in you . . .*"

"That is so *romantic*," Marielle agreed, followed by a muted ripple of affirmation.

Brittie heaved another gurgling sigh. "I'd do that guy in a hot second."

"It's *poetry*," Jenny Big growled. "Don't talk like a whore."

"It's not like I'd make him pay," Brittie said. This was how it went in Book Club: offense rarely taken, humor easily earned, even though outside of Book Club the air often reeked with offense.

"I wish Violet was here," Marielle said. "She'd love these."

How odd to hear Violet's name. Disarmed, Harriet blurted, "I already gave her a copy."

Everyone looked up.

"You've seen her?" Renee asked.

"I—ran into her as I was doing errands."

"Violet's in Portland?"

Harriet hesitated. "They sent her to a city, is all I can say."

Jenny Big laughed. "Wow, Bookie, you'd make a sucky criminal."

"The worst," Renee agreed.

Jacynta laid down her pen. "Tell her I turned into a real poet."

"If I see her again," Harriet said.

"I bet you will," Aimee said in her mouse voice. She slid a sheet of paper from the stack on the table. "Are you gonna ask us to write in iambic pentagram?"

"Pentameter," Dorothy said.

Thrilled, Harriet opened her hands. "I can't think of a reason not to."

"Let's try it," said Dorothy, who was fifty-one, looked seventy-five, and had once studied literature at Barnard. She, too, was old and gray and full of sleep. After a knee surgery that went south, she'd fallen for opioids, and that had been that.

"Thank you, Dorothy," Harriet said. Prepared for just this eventuality, she passed out eleven notebooks, old-fashioned grade-school copy books she'd found at Wadsworth Books. Spiral bindings were forbidden; but so were these if she brought them herself. A baby-faced CO with bright cheeks had seen them and let her sail through.

The women admired their notebooks, a step up from the recycled loose pages they'd been using from the unit office. "I wish they came with locks," Aimee said.

"Alas, they do not," Harriet said. She'd bought twelve, one for herself, which she opened flat. "Now. Does everyone recall—"

"Five beats to a line," Jenny Big said. "When YOU are OLD and GRAY and FULL of SLEEP."

"I don't like to rhyme," Jacynta announced. "It stifles my voice."

"Your voice is plenty strong enough to survive, Jacynta," Harriet said. "Let's just try it."

"But I don't want to write a poem like that." Jacynta put on her pouty face. "I like my own style."

"Could you repeat that, Jacynta?" Harriet asked, delighted.

"I like my own style."

"No, the first part, beginning with 'But.'"

Jacynta crossed her arms. "But I don't want to write a poem like that."

"Once more, please," Harriet said. "Exactly those words."

Jacynta's glitter-black eyes narrowed, but she complied.

"Anyone?" Harriet waited, looked around. Dorothy got it first, then Marielle. Then Dawna-Lynn, who laughed out loud.

"What?" Jacynta said.

"You answered in iambic pentameter, J."

"No effin' way, Showtime."

Dawna-Lynn laughed again. "But *I* don't *WANT* to *WRITE* a *POEM* like *THAT*."

Now everybody got it. Shayna said, "And *BOOK*ie *WINS* the *TEA*cher *PRIZE* to*DAY*."

Indeed, Harriet felt like a winner, for everyone was cross-talking, cackling, one-upping, all in varyingly accurate attempts at the most elegant meter in the English language. It was on.

The women bent over their notebooks, writing. They'd been moved all over the place lately, chow hall the worst so far, fish smell and lunch-prep clatter. But the women wrote wherever they landed.

Eleven notebooks, eleven bent heads, eleven pens moving across eleven pages in iambic pentameter. Twelve, including Harriet herself, and Violet, too, for all she knew, reading the same page in her apartment, this very minute, all of them connected by a dead Irishman.

Poetry, of all things. Thanks to Frank Daigle, of all people.

She suddenly wished them all into her parlor, a feeling as shocking and urgent as love. She wished them into comfy chairs, *her* chairs, surrounded by paintings and rugs and the scent of tea. Everyone safe, and free, enjoying their best selves. Violet's actual presence in her house had made this vision possible, and Harriet regretted it a little. Book Club had always felt like a cocoon, impervious to the Outs. And now it didn't. Jacynta. Marielle. Dorothy. Aimee. Dawna-Lynn. Renee. Brittie. Kitten. Shayna. Jenny Big. Desiree. As one by one she imagined them into the outside world, *her* outside world, the notion collapsed. This was not a cocoon; this was prison, where they were not safe, not free, not their best selves.

For fifteen minutes the women wrote, the sound of scraping pens, intermittent sighs, a shifting chair. They came to the end more or less together; this had begun to happen with regularity.

"My youngest is graduating next week," Dorothy said, looking up from her poem. Perhaps she'd been writing about him.

"Welding school," Marielle explained. "Proud mama."

"I'm putting in for a furlough," Dorothy said. "It's within fifty miles."

Shayna clicked her tongue. "You won't get it."

"Might. I'm on short time."

"You don't get furloughed unless it's your kid's funeral," Desiree muttered.

A cloud descended on the group squeezed too tightly around the table. Harriet could not save the moment because there was too much she didn't, couldn't, know. It was Aimee—meek little Aimee—who tried. "If you get furlough," she offered, "you might get to dress."

"To the *nines*," Dorothy said.

"When I Get Out First Thing I Do I buy six little black dresses," Desiree said, and Jenny Big instantly tagged on: "When I Get Out First Thing I Do I buy a Baby Dior sports coat for my new dog, which I shall call Elmo Two."

"That'll be cute," Kitten said, and they all agreed, pretending now, pretending that Dorothy would see her son graduate from welding school, that Jenny Big would get a second chance with a dog. And because no CO occupied the room, having pegged Harriet as a harmless volunteer lady who loved books, and because good news arrived as sharp, skinny icicles in this frozen place of bad news, Harriet turned in her seat, said, "Congrats to your son," and threw her arms around Dorothy, who returned the pressure tenfold.

The cloud persisted, though, and with nearly an hour left in the session, nobody offered to read what they'd written. Harriet turned to the sheaf of poems, tried out a few by living writers, who suddenly struck her as reaching too hard for meaning. She imagined these poets, women with herb gardens and advanced degrees, in a sunny alcove writing about pain.

Near session's end, Harriet sensed another shift in mood, an invisible message that zigzagged around the table. Dawna-Lynn stood up. "I almost forgot," she said. "We have a surprise for you." Harriet smiled, because this was what she said to them before passing out a new book.

"It's not much," Dawna-Lynn said.

Shayna shook her head. "Don't say that. It's what we've got."

Out of nowhere—where? her underpants?—Dawna-Lynn produced a small knitted bird. Most of the inmates, sooner or later, learned to knit and crochet, and here was a colorful bauble, purple and gray, crafted from sparkly yarn.

"Oh, it's lovely," Harriet said, and it was, bright with whimsy and beautifully made.

"It was mostly Dawna-Lynn," Jenny Big said, "but we all did at least one loop."

"I knitted the tail," Marielle offered.

Jacynta said, "We wanted it to be from all of us."

"Thank you," Harriet said. "I'm touched. Honestly." She petted the bird. "You know I'll have to ask permission."

A collective groan.

"He'll say no," Shayna said. "He hates Book Club."

"Why on earth would Mr. Flinders hate Book Club?"

Brittie said, "Because we love it."

What little Harriet brought *in*, though rarely vetted by Security these days, occasionally got the once-over from Mr. Flinders, the unit manager, an officious stickler with long, skeletal hands. In her head she called him Mr. Fingers. "You're clean," he liked to say, returning her bag. A perfectly innocuous remark delivered as if he'd just removed her clothes.

She'd never had occasion to bring anything *out*.

In any case, Harriet understood the rule: "Accept nothing from inmates" meant *nothing*: not a candy bar, not a thank-you note, not a harmless knitted bird.

She placed it on the table, the better to admire it.

"It would look pretty on your windowsill," Aimee suggested.

"Not there," Brittie said. "Tabsy'll get it."

"She means the little window," Renee said. "The one in the hall. Pay attention."

"Rest assured," Harriet said, petting the bird, "I'll find the ideal spot."

Harriet watched them shuffle out, back to the dayroom to line up for Noon Chow. The little bird sat orphaned on the table. She scooped it up, quick as a cat, and slipped it into her satchel's interior pocket.

She drove home, already planning a unit devoted to Yeats. The women were sentimentalists, preferred poetry to prose, and enjoyed writing. It had taken her too long to discover all this, but at least she had a map for the way forward. She pulled into her driveway, waylaid by a memory of Corinne standing on the hood of Lou's Escalade singing "La Bamba" while Lou and the girls, including tiny Sophie, danced on the sidewalk. In the snow. Dear Lou.

As she got out of the car, still inside that memory, the knitted bird fell from her bag and bounced on the ground. She gathered it up, held it in her palm. *Look at me, Lou,* she thought, *Your fraidy-cat turned into a rebel.* She'd taken the little prize for one reason, plain and simple: she wanted it.

14

Violet

SOPHIE DOESN'T CALL ME BACK about the bird job, big surprise, so after reapplying to the three Dunkin' Donuts I could reasonably walk to, plus one on the bus route, I'm forced to diversify. Congress Street is lined with possibilities, but it's not like I'm carrying a briefcase full of qualifications, just my on-sale Renys purse with nothing in it but a wallet and a key. I browse the whole length of Congress Street, filling out applications for the places that don't turn me down outright: six coffee shops, two bagel stores, a copy center, a Thai restaurant, and a weird store that sells only hats. I skip the art galleries. The high-end restaurants. The bookstore (obviously). And Renys, I skip that. Renys reminds me of home, and I couldn't bear being turned down there.

On all the applications, the same line: *Have you ever been convicted of a felony?*

Around noon I wind up at the public library, not to apply for a job but to ask for a library card. Because Harriet suggested it. And it's free. Also I want to finish *Spoon River Anthology* so that if Harriet asks me back to dinner, I can make conversation.

The librarian looks exactly like a librarian, glasses and everything. "Not only *can* you get a library card," he says, "we're delighted to give you one."

He is delighted. I swear to God, the light in the place turns up a tick.

From a slim, silent drawer he pulls a white form, one page. "I'll need a photo ID with your address on it. A driver's license should do it."

"I don't drive."

"Or a state ID, something with your photo and address."

This is what happened at the bookstore, exactly. My most recent ID isn't the sort you present to law-abiding booksellers. Or librarians. So I just stand there at the circulation desk with nothing but my worthless word.

The librarian beams at me. "No worries." The gap between his front teeth makes him look sweet and defenseless. "You can use a piece of mail," he offers. "A utility bill, a letter. A little something-or-other to prove you live here."

"I don't have anything like that. I just moved here."

"Ah, then welcome to Portland." He beams again, probably doesn't have a normal-temperature smile. "I'm sure we can solve this."

Because he looks like a librarian, because he wants me to use his library, because his teeth aren't right, and because he thought I might have a letter in my possession, a letter somebody wrote to my current address, to me, to me personally, I start blinking back hot dumb tears. Again.

This librarian, though. He is so polite, so respectful and kind. Instead of dropping dead of shame I tell him my story. Not all of it. Some. Not as much as I told Lillian the bank lady, but enough. Not only does he process a card based on my word that I live here, he finds *Spoon River Anthology* deep in the stacks, then walks me over to New Fiction and makes a few recommendations.

I croak out a thank-you.

"My pleasure," he says. "Happy reading."

Troy predicted that Portland would be heartless, that we'd have to scratch and claw to get anywhere, that traffic would be soul-crushing and the rents so high we'd sleep in a park for a while. At the time this sounded blindingly romantic. Nobody cares about you in a city, Troy said. In the city, you're a number. Nobody will care but me.

Wrong again, asshole, I think, stepping back into the street with four books pressed to my heart, one of them so new the spine will crack when I open it later. The sunshine feels tart and clean, the city buildings look sharp and bright, and I am suddenly the sort of person librarians recommend books to.

I cross the square to sneak a look at the bookstore. Different cat in the window. Big guy, marmalade tabby, flattish ears. Maybe the other one remembers me, wherever she went. I'm the one who wanted her first. For a second—literally, one second—I consider going in there and applying for a job. I glance up the street and down, kind of hoping to see Harriet strolling along with her canvas book bag. But no.

Something about the quality of the sunlight puts me in mind of the prison yard, so I say a prayer that Brittie and Dawna-Lynn and Kitten and Shayna and everyone else are out there right now feeling this healing sunshine on their own heads. I feel happy, imagining this.

Then I remember that today is Wednesday, Town Meeting day, and into my happiness God pours sadness in exactly the same amount, like he's measuring it out in a Pyrex cup. I have to picture everyone stuck in the dayroom, asking for the same stuff they asked for last week, and the week before that, et cetera, no sunshine for them. For me, either, suddenly. My family disappeared me. My mother is dead. So is Lorraine Daigle, her kindergarteners now in third grade, haunted by that dimming loss.

But in the other half of God's Pyrex cup, Harriet invites me back to dinner right away, and Sophie shows up, extra nice, all smiles, for dessert with Luis, her cute boyfriend (who's gay, but whatever), and when Luis and I turn out to have the same favorite song—"Rolling in the Deep" by Adele—he sings for us, and he's really good, and it's the kind of evening I never dreamed for myself even back when I was a big dreamer. The only not-perfect thing is that Sophie, who's leaving shortly for California, says not one single word about the parrot job.

Three weeks on the Outs, and no work for me.

The coffee shops don't call.

The bagel stores don't call.

The copy center doesn't call.

Dunkin' Donuts doesn't call.

The Thai restaurant doesn't call.

The weird store that sells only hats doesn't call.

But then, guess who calls? Mikhail Petrov, PhD twice over, Sophie's Russian lunatic. Person #3 in my Contacts. He wishes to "bring me in" for an interview, which sounds a little too law-and-order.

"When?" I ask.

"Now, if you please."

I tear through my dresser looking for something to wear, breathing at the back of my throat like there's a live, pulsing frog sitting there. The one thing that looks at all science-interviewish is a pink blouse from Vicki. Too big, but it's got a dressy, pointed collar and stiff cuffs. So I put it on, with the skirt and flats I bought at Renys. I look like someone at a costume party who nobody can guess what they're supposed to be.

It takes a long frantic while to find Huntington Hall, just as long to find the unmarked bird lab within Huntington Hall, and when I finally make it there I'm sweating through my Vicki blouse, expecting to get fired before getting hired. I walk into reception, and there is Dr. Petrov, tall and solemn, waiting for me.

"You're Violet Powell," he says.

My name sounds like a mouthful of water, but even without the accent, you wouldn't take him for American. Everything about him seems foreign.

"I'm so sorry, Dr. Petrov, I couldn't find you."

He slashes my face with his eyes. "Am I not standing before you at this moment, Violet Powell?"

"No, I just meant . . ." I don't want to say *I'm late*, so I just stand there like a dub.

Dr. Petrov's face, long and angular, does a thing that I will discover passes for smiling.

"You look like a Violet," he says.

"Oh. Okay."

"An observation merely."

Just then, Mrs. Rocha, the lab manager, gusts through the door and snaps it shut behind her. "Is this the new assistant?"

"You ask me as if it were my decision, Mrs. Rocha," Dr. Petrov says. To me, he adds, "Mrs. Rocha is the boss."

I have no idea how to respond. He could be joking. Who knows what ten months of snow does to the Russian sense of humor? For her part, Mrs. Rocha just ignores him. "Come with me," she says, and I trail her into one of three rooms—of wildly varying sizes—located just off reception. The design of the place is all afterthought.

"Sit," she says. I guess this is her office, tiny and overstuffed and too hot, upholstered with afghans in blinding colors and patterns. At least one draped on every chair; on her desk is another in progress. You can't see the walls for all the photos and posters of darling children and naughty puppies. The posters have jolly, hugely uninspiring sayings. One of them I recognize from the prison library: LIFE IS TOUGH AND SO ARE YOU.

Mrs. Rocha is round and twitchy and sort of light brown all over, hair, skin, eyes, clothes, like a giant hamster. I spend quite some time in her office, filling out forms. One of them has the usual question, and I decide to leave it blank.

"Now, then." Mrs. Rocha reads all the forms; this takes time. Then she slides her glasses down her nose and studies me for a long, humid, demoralizing amount of time.

"You need this job, Ms. Powell?" she asks.

"I do."

"You have looked elsewhere?"

"Many elsewheres."

"Without success?" She knows. Maybe Sophie told her.

"So far."

The glasses slide back up. "Sophie put in a word for you," she says. "Until you prove yourself, however, I'll have one eye on you."

"Okay."

"No more than I'd have one eye on anyone else."

She definitely knows.

"To prove yourself," she goes on, "you must show up every day. On time. Ready to work. That's not too much to expect?"

"I couldn't find the lab, Mrs. Rocha." My insides feel like cold oatmeal. "I got to campus super early but then I couldn't find the lab and not one person I asked knew where it was."

"Of course you couldn't find the lab. Nobody can find the lab. They put the lab on the dark side of the moon." She folds her soft arms, appraising me. "And yet you managed to arrive on time anyway. Because you planned ahead."

"I was one minute late." Might as well admit it; I can see she's the type to keep track.

"I interviewed two people yesterday," she says. "They were also late. Far later than you, and do you know why?"

"They didn't plan ahead."

"Precisely," she says, giving the hem of her powder-brown sweater a tug, maybe to cover her hips, but it rides up again. "You should know that we also use students as assistants. Psych and bio majors, mainly, but not always." Her nose twitches, hamsterish. "The English majors look like Victorian poets dying of consumption. They work for extra credit, bragging rights, and a good recommendation when the time comes for grad school." Still talking, Mrs. Rocha puts on her lab coat, a big, square, starched thing with lollipops on it—beige lollipops wearing pale-peach bowties. "In other words, the student volunteers, with few exceptions, are a trial. Their work experience consists of résumé-building junkets to Guatemala, where they built houses for the unsuspecting poor."

Mrs. Rocha is blunt and allergic to screwups and reminds me of Jenny Big. Those are the exact reasons why I instantly love her. Plus, I like how she snaps something shut the second she's done with it: door, notebook, file folder, desk drawer, like she believes in spies.

"Your three years with Dunkin' Donuts will come in handy here," she says.

"I started when I was sixteen."

"You have suffered your share of whiners and complainers? Coffee too hot? Donuts not round enough?"

"I liked it, though."

Her eyebrows, painfully tweezed, shoot up. "Then you're in for a real treat here."

I think I'm supposed to laugh, but I don't just in case. I love her fog of hair and pointy glasses, like a lady in a cartoon. And her puffy bosom. Not a chance she missed the blank line in my application, but she's letting it go. For now. That's our pact. She wants me because I'm a punctual person who needs this job like nobody knows. And also, I guess, because I didn't build a house in Guatemala.

She runs briefly through my responsibilities: Keep track of inventory; maintain the phone logs; keep the lab clean; monitor the students and do their work when they don't show up, which happens a lot. But my main job is to make sure the birds are clean and safe and fed and happy.

"You'll want this," she says, giving me my own lab coat—my own lab coat, a thousand times more thrilling than my Dunkin' Donuts uniform, which was also thrilling at the time. She leads me to an even smaller room and assigns me one of six gigantic lockers. Then it's back to reception, where she unlocks a metal door that opens into a short hallway with another, key-coded metal door at the opposite end. In between, on the right-hand side of the hallway, there's an old-fashioned wooden door flanked by showstopping photographs of parrots. On that door hangs a sign: PETROV.

Locked doors and hallways. For one blinding second, it's prison all over again, but Mrs. Rocha, says, "Come along, Ms. Powell," opens the PETROV door, and then I'm in the mahogany splendor of Dr. Petrov's office. I've never seen such rugs, thick and richly patterned. And the couch—a gigantic suede thing with swoopy rolled arms, like something borrowed from Buckingham Palace. Except for one of Mrs. Rocha's corny, multicolor afghans draped over a matching chair, the office is classy and lavish and possibly designed to scare people.

He looks up from his overloaded desk. "Well?"

"She'll do." Mrs. Rocha gives me another once-over, not in a bad way. "If you want one that fits, you'll have to buy it yourself," she says, meaning my lab coat. The sleeves come to my fingertips. "Which is a shame, but the budget here is a disgrace and certain people don't seem to get that you put yourself out there to attract donations or you end up on the street. You have to make an effort once in a blue moon. You can't assume you're the ruler of all creation and that all creation joyfully bends to your will."

Dr. Petrov puffs out a sound, something between exhausted boyfriend and prison guard.

To me, Mrs. Rocha says, "See if you can convince the Great Oz to put the birds on YouTube."

"Mrs. Rocha," Dr. Petrov mutters, returning to his papers, "you are the sound of one hand clapping."

"So I hear," she says. "All day long."

"I am not running a circus."

"Actually," she says, "you are."

I envy their back-and-forth, like they know exactly their place with one another, who's who and what's what, all in balance. As Dr. Petrov gets up, I realize anew how tall he is, ballplayer tall, with large, graceful hands that could palm a basketball. For a tick or two he says nothing, just observes me. Science-observes me. Mrs. Rocha has vanished back to reception.

"So," he says. "We meet the birds." He waits, allowing me to go first. But where do I go? The door to reception is locked and the door to the lab is locked, so I just stand there like a stranded prisoner.

"I'm really sorry I was late," I tell him, thinking he's about to change his mind.

He says nothing as he punches in the key code. The door opens into the Bird Lounge, the avian equivalent of a rec room. There's a full-size fridge, a long countertop with a double sink and a microwave. Two upholstered armchairs, well shredded in spots. A cubby or bin or shelf or closet for absolutely everything, from drop cloths to bird mash to nail clippers to cuttlebones, which reminds me treacherously of prison.

Among all this bounty, three African grey parrots greet us in a racket of peeps and gurgles and shrieks. As Dr. Petrov closes the door behind us, they go quiet, heads atilt. In the corner, a student in an oversize hoodie is transferring a gargantuan bag of bird treats into smaller plastic tubs. Dr. Petrov barely gives him a glance.

One of the parrots lifts off from a rope swing and flutters down to land on Dr. Petrov's shoulder. The other two, sitting together, stare at me from atop a gigantic cage. The other cages are equally roomy, furnished with toys and ladders and mirrors and ropes. The birds are shockingly pretty, whitish faces framed by a bonnet of light-gray feathers with cream edging, a scalloped look that blends to darker grays on the back, lighter again on the belly, like creatures dressed in shadows. Thick black beaks; pale, glossy eyes; show-off tails the exact shade of cayenne pepper.

Dr. Petrov introduces me first to the one on his shoulder: Oliver, fifty-four years old. Oliver can speak in phrases—*See you later! What time is it? Whew, that was close!*—words in the correct order but not always in the correct context. If you say, *Hello, Oliver,* instead of helloing back, he might say, *We hold these truths to be self-evident.*

"I took him as a kindness," Dr. Petrov says. "It's too late to teach him anything."

"*Whoopity-doo!*" Oliver yells.

I laugh. "Whoopity-doo to you."

Dr. Petrov kisses Oliver on the beak. "Who's my stupid bird?" Right on the beak. The kissed parrot looks honored.

Next I meet Bob and Alan, twelve years old. They share a cage because they're bonded. Bob and Alan are adept at "labeling," a science word for calling things what they are—"block," "nut," "key," "grape"—and getting it right almost one hundred percent of the time.

"Say hello," Dr. Petrov tells them.

Alan says, "*Hello, dear.*"

Then Bob lifts his foot, a greeting. "*Hello, dear.*"

"Oh," I whisper. "Oh my goodness."

"Alan learned that from a student," Dr. Petrov explains. "Bob picked it up from Alan." He tickles Alan under what passes for a chin. "These birds," he says. "They came with ridiculous names."

Bob is still waving his foot. "May I pet him?" I ask.

"Go ahead."

As I reach out for Bob's silky head, Alan heads me off, a lightning snap that tweezes a shred of skin at the base of my thumb.

"You will learn," Dr. Petrov says, plucking a square of gauze from a huge box kept suspiciously handy. He presses it to the bleeding nick and holds it there.

"All animal species suffer from jealousy," he says. "Not just *Homo sapiens.*" His English is better than mine, but formal. After Sophie's description, I'd expected him to talk like Boris and Natasha in those old cartoons. "With time," he adds, "you come to know them, just as you come to know humans."

He studies my palm for a long moment, still applying pressure, then looks up. "African greys are emotional animals," he says, releasing my hand. "You will learn this." He tosses the bloodied gauze into a metal can and leads me to the Observation Room, holding the door as I pass in front of him, courtly and old-fashioned.

The Observation Room is a large, airy, glassed-in space, a parrot playground decked out with rings and perches and potted trees and plastic swings in sunset colors. If I were a parrot, I'd love it in here. At the center of the room, a Formica table—the "session table," where most of the studies take place. Beneath it, a set of plastic bins filled with random objects like toy keys and plastic rings and squares of cloth and kids' blocks in different colors and sizes.

A feeling comes over me, that itchy feeling you get when you think you're being watched, and sure enough, I look up to find a parrot eyeballing me from a high-up perch.

"*What name?*" it says, looking sweetly at me, and I have this crazy urge to say I love you.

Dr. Petrov sort-of smiles. "This is Charlotte."

"*What name?*"

"Tell her," Dr. Petrov says. "She will learn."

I shift a little on my feet. "It's, uh, Violet."

"*What name?*"

"Violet."

"Say again," Dr. Petrov says.

I don't know if he means me or the bird. I figure it's me, so I repeat: "Violet."

"Again."

By now I'm starting to feel like one of the birds, not in a bad way. I repeat my name, one, two, ten times, more. And again. This goes on for about five minutes, until my name sounds like somebody else's. The world tilts a bit as Charlotte makes her way down to me, perch to perch, then she faces me, eye to eye, from a living branch of a potted tree.

"*What name?*" she says.

"I told you. It's Violet."

"*Hmmm,*" Charlotte says.

I have to laugh, pinwheeled by sudden happiness, wondering if all the hurt of the past three years has been leading straight to this. On purpose. God works in mysterious ways, my mother always said.

This is some mystery. It is.

"Is she a little smaller than the others?" I ask.

"An observer," Dr. Petrov says. Again, he looks at me, and I feel studied. "The other girl observed nothing. No affinity."

I can't wait to tell Harriet that Dr. Petrov isn't at all the ogre Sophie described; it's just that his natural voice comes out like bullets and his height is intimidating.

Also, I'm glad to know Sophie had no affinity and I do.

"Perhaps," Dr. Petrov says, "in prison you trained yourself to notice everything."

This is the one and only time he will acknowledge hiring an ex-con to assist him in a lab loaned to him by a university and funded by grants from esteemed foundations and institutes.

"Come here, darling." For one panicky second, I think he's talking to me, then Charlotte steps daintily onto his forearm, sidles down to the crook of his wrist, and nibbles gently at his irresistible ring, a brilliant gold band. "Tut," he says, and she stops, sidles all the way back up.

On this first day in the lab of Mikhail Petrov, I don't yet understand how special these birds are. How could I? What I do know is there is nowhere else I want to be right now, no person I would rather be than me. It's been a long time since I felt this way, and the realization pours down, cool and refreshing, as I experience the watchful consideration of a scholarly African grey parrot.

Even in retrospect, the moment shimmers.

"*Want nut,*" Charlotte says. The birds sound generally alike, but not exactly, and even at first I can see that. Charlotte sounds like a Russian behavioral scientist with a cold.

"Want plum?" Dr. Petrov asks.

"*Not plum,*" Charlotte says. "*Want nut.*"

"Want banana?"

"*I. Want. Nut.*"

Dr. Petrov takes a shelled walnut—a big fave—from his lab-coat pocket and hands it to me. "Make friends," he says. Everything sounds like an instruction because it is.

I'm scared to get bitten, but Charlotte is polite. I love her black tongue, her thick, dappled feet. Something humble in her, and shy, except for the surprise of her bright tail. Within days, I'll wonder how I ever thought the birds identical.

"How old is she?"

"Twenty-two."

"That's my age," I say. "Maybe we're meant for each other." I lift my hand, hoping to pet those soft-looking feathers, but Charlotte inches farther up Dr. Petrov's arm, just beyond my reach.

"She is sizing you up," Dr. Petrov says. "Sing to her."

"You mean, like, a song?"

"Unless you prefer to sing lab notes." I don't yet know how rarely he jokes, this serious man. "Charlotte loves singing."

They're both waiting to see what I'll do. A harmless challenge, I guess, so I sing the chorus of "In the Garden," a Baptist hymn my mother used to sing to me and Vicki before bed. *"Oh, he walks with me, and he talks with me, and he tells me I am his own. . . ."* My face burns but not distressingly.

"Like an angel," Dr. Petrov says. "The other girl refused. I can only conclude that she possessed the voice of a bullfrog."

He moves toward me, lowers his shoulder, and allows Charlotte to step onto my forearm. She lifts first one foot, then the other, like an empress stepping over a puddle. You really can't imagine how sweet. Dr. Petrov says nothing for a minute, then withdraws a few feet away to "observe." I will learn soon enough this is his favorite word.

Charlotte sidles up and down my arm, finds a spot she likes in the crook of my elbow, and waits there like I'm the bus stop and Dr. Petrov is the bus. I love the one pound of her, the faint pressure.

"Can she really learn my name?" I ask quietly, afraid to move, to jostle her, to break the spell.

"Do you not believe me?" he snaps.

"No, yes, of course."

He's a touchy man, I can see this already. As he stares at me, I feel momentarily weightless. "When I was a boy of four," he says, "I watched the KGB drag my father from my screaming mother's arms."

After a paralyzing pause, I say, "Oh."

"Life is short. I have no use for the niceties." Then, as if nothing happened, he turns to Charlotte. "She will learn. You must introduce yourself each time. The other girl could not be bothered."

Charlotte hops off my arm and onto his. "*Want nut,*" she says, and he gives her one.

"Her right foot looks funny." A scar knots the dappled surface of one toe, a healed-over scar, dainty but not small.

"A skirmish, perhaps, with another bird," he says, placing Charlotte back on a perch. "Or with a human who I hope is dead, and suffered in the going. I bought her from a private owner when she was eight." He bends to me, his eyes clear and cold and curious. "We all have scars, yes?"

What can I say? We all have scars. So I say yes.

"And also our secrets?"

He doesn't seem to expect an answer, and I don't have one, so I reach up to pet Charlotte. She leans into my touch. I skritch the back of her neck, which feels so strange, not at all like skritching a dog or a cat. You can feel the quills where the feathers attach, hard and not cuddly. I prefer petting her velvety head and back because the feathers feel smooth and soothing, but Charlotte keeps twisting around, her intentions clear. So I keep skritching, already helpless.

"Say your name," Dr. Petrov says.

"Violet," I say. "I'm Violet."

And then another of his observing silences, long enough for my insides to heat up, long enough for me to remember I'm an ex-con, long enough to think who would hire an ex-con to work at a job that requires trust and confidence, at a *university*, with a brilliant scientist, two PhDs. I wonder if maybe I've misunderstood, and that something I want very much is about to be taken from me.

I'm standing before him in a way that feels dangerously like court. "Dr. Petrov," I ask, "did I get the job?"

He waits a long time to answer. I scroll through all the ways in my short, dumb life that I failed the people who thought they loved me. For one sickening second, I consider dropping to my knees. But I don't want to disturb Charlotte, who's back on my shoulder, settled beneath my hair and making a bird sound that's not unlike a cat purring.

"Dr. Petrov—"

"Was I not clear?"

"No, yes, of course, you were."

"I thought I was clear."

"You were. Definitely." I wait another ridiculous second. "So, in other words, you're hiring me?"

"I am."

"As your lab assistant?"

He heaves a great, humiliating sigh, maybe second-guessing. "Yes, you are hired."

I'm hired. I am hired. "When do I start?"

"Now, if you please," he says. "Violet."

Do you hear that? That pause before my name? Everything I'm made of goes still—blood, water, skin, bone—perfectly still, and it takes one second, two seconds, three seconds for me to understand.

You look like a Violet.

He doesn't mean capital-*V* Violet: a person.

He means small-*v* violet: a flower.

15

Frank

HE'D LEFT HIS TOOLBOX AT the bookstore and could no longer stand to be without it. His best level was in there, and his grandfather's claw hammer, and his favorite micrometer, and his sense of meaning. When he finally mustered the courage to return to the store and retrieve it, he chose early morning, two weeks to the day, so he could clear out and get gently fired with the fewest possible bystanders.

"Oh-my-God-he's-here!" Robin squealed, all but vaulting the counter. "Everyone! Hey! It's Frank!"

The youngsters set upon him like a pack of kittens. Only Jake held back, allowing a fellow male his dignity.

"We called you and called you," Robin said, throwing her arms around him.

"No, no," he said, stepping back. "I'll just pick up my things."

"Frank," Baker said, "we know the whole story. Jake looked it up online."

Jake cast his eyes down. "Righteous anger is a tool of justice," he said, quoting lord knows what.

Marnie stepped in then, her dark eyes glittering with worry. "Frank, we had no idea."

Oh, their faces, so young and willing, unmarked by loss or uncertainty. But who was to say? Who knew what things they carried?

"I made a terrible scene in this good place," he said to them. "And I'm very, very sorry."

"She's the one who should be sorry," said Marnie, her pink lips pursed in concern. "After what she did."

"To think we almost gave her a cat," Robin said.

"I trained on a hotline last year," Baker said, pushing up those huge, absurd eyeglasses. "I believe you had, like, a flashback? Like a temporary psychosis?"

"Oh. I, no, I don't . . ."

The others nodded solemnly, the store gone eerily quiet, a single puzzled customer peering out from Puzzles and Games. The youngsters crowded together, their faces reminiscent of the jury, all that unwanted sympathy.

"I didn't mean to scare anyone," he murmured. They leaned in to hear him. "I'll get my tools and go." His mouth was so dry he had trouble forming words. "The girl paid for her crime. She's a decent person. That's all."

They gaped at him, awestruck.

Baker spoke first: "Frank, that's so totally beautiful."

"No. Please."

Then Jake, in his CAUTION: LIVE WRITER! tee shirt: "I wish my dad was that forgiving."

Marnie laid her hand on Frank's arm. "Frank's our store dad."

"Totally," Baker agreed, "Frank's our store dad."

And Robin, her clasped hands bright with rings: "We love you, Frank!"

Did they love him? Who exactly did they think he was? Certainly they loved their creation—good old Frank, father figure from a bygone time when fathers checked your oil and put air in your tires. That was all right. He didn't mind. He, too, loved what they'd created.

"You're not quitting," Jake said. "We won't let you."

"Say you'll stay!"

He wanted to come back, even though they'd be eyeing him now, in a different way, protecting him from further upset, poor old widower Frank and his tragedy. He deserved that indignity after the disruption he'd caused, and would bear it if only for their easy forgiveness, their instinct for seeing his best light.

"I'll stay," he said.

A collective cheer erupted from the pack, as if it were his birthday, and in fact it *was* his birthday, May 14. Kristy would be calling him tonight with a litany of the inventive and wifely things Lorraine would be doing, were she still alive, to prepare for a party she wanted and he didn't.

A stab of memory: Lorraine in her yellow silk pajamas, reading the paper at their kitchen table as he makes her coffee and toast. He puts it in front of her and she looks up, untouched by the ravages of sleep, her hair somehow in place though she has yet to take her morning shower. *Thank you, honey*, she says. *I love your coffee.* She said this to him every morning. *I love your coffee.* He'd given her at least that. She'd loved at least that.

"How can we help?" Marnie asked sweetly.

"Pretend this never happened," he said. "That would be my druthers."

So everyone went extravagantly back to normal, applying themselves to the letter, if not the spirit, of Frank's request. As he listened to the pleasing thud of books being shelved, the clickety-clack of books being ordered or reordered or searched for, the rattle of the jumbo-size cat-food bag, he felt himself being followed, predictably, their group gaze warm and deeply interested and too much, too much. No longer would he be the handyman who did well with cats and flirted adorably with their most reliable customer. Now he was visible to them in a different way entirely. And so, for the first time in this haven of usefulness, he felt unseen.

In the downstairs storeroom, among teetering stacks of books, he found the blue pane, cracked but not shattered. He'd have to find another, no small search. The spilled tools had been secured in a grocery bag next to his toolbox, which was still open. He imagined one of the youngsters—Marnie, most likely—carrying the open toolbox downstairs as if it were a soufflé, careful not to spill or jostle anything that hadn't already spilled, as the others fetched the remaining tools, cautiously, one by one, fearing to be accidentally pierced or scratched or sawn in half. The vision amused him, his first lightness since setting eyes on the startling specter of Violet Powell.

He carried everything back upstairs to resume the job he'd left undone. Over and again the bell tinkled, but Harriet, thankfully, did not appear. After touching up the window frame—the pane he'd replace later—he spent the remains of the day fitting new baseboard into place in Biography, cutting, trimming, nailing, painting. On most days he enjoyed such projects, the mindful repetition, but on this day his scuttling thoughts kept landing in the same place: forgiven by the youngsters, he had two apologies yet to give and could see no way to give them.

As he packed up at noon, he was again aware of being watched, of having been watched. He shut his toolbox and stood to face them. "It's been three years," he assured them. "I'm all right now." Marnie and Jake nodded vigorously. Robin had tears in her eyes.

At the back door, he found Baker waiting for him. "Frank, a second?" A furtive glance back into the store. "I can help."

"What?"

"I'm an artist, Frank. I see light. Your light is gone." Baker's own light shone fetchingly.

"My light is gone?"

"Uh-huh."

"What light?"

"You have one of those lighted-up faces. We all thought so. But after, like, your breakdown . . ."

"My breakdown?" Oh, lord. *Was* it a breakdown? Out of the clear blue, a sudden crack in a memory he'd so carefully sealed over?

A soulful head tilt now from Baker. "Frank, you look like a snuffed-out candle."

"I didn't know that."

"Oh yes, Frank."

How he envied this bejeweled bookseller, who brimmed with a brand of self-assurance found mainly in this generation of the young. He himself had never felt confident, outside of his work. Baker filled the doorway, blocking his escape, studying him; Frank felt both repelled and flattered to be so duly scrutinized, to have this dear young person pay him the rare compliment of curiosity.

"As long as you're armed with so much training," he said now, "there *is* something I'd like to ask."

Baker glowed. "Sure, Frank. Anything."

"I would like to make an apology to someone. Would you recommend sending flowers?"

"Are you talking about the killer?"

"Let's not call her the killer."

"Oh, totally." Baker looked serious, as if on the other end of the hotline, talking a stranger off a ledge.

"I frightened that poor girl. Harriet, too. The book-club lady."

"It totally wasn't that bad. The glass didn't explode or anything."

"Tempered," Frank said. "Less likely to shatter."

"Wow," Baker said. "Lucky."

In truth, he'd forgotten the details. Psychosis, lord! He might well have dreamed the whole thing.

"It wasn't *good*," Baker amended. "I'm not saying it was *good*. But when people, like, know the whole story—"

"There used to be an ad everywhere," he said. "'Say It with Flowers.' I guess you're too young to remember."

"Flowers are the *worst*, Frank," Baker said. "The carbon footprint required to get them here is obscene, and they're dripping with pesticides. The children of Ecuadorian flower workers are two hundred percent more likely to experience—"

"I had no idea. Sorry."

"Why don't you, like, make something? With your machinist machines?"

"I'm not artistic."

"You made those wheelie things for the book cart."

"Casters," he said. He'd made a custom set—with plate mounts, not stem mounts, he wasn't fooling around. The work had been a balm, a statement, his answer to the junk flooding in from overseas, that affront to the trade.

Baker nodded. "In my opinion, those count as art."

Say it with casters.

"You could make metal earrings, or an ankle bracelet, totally therapeutic," Baker went on, afire with helpfulness, and as Frank listened to one loony idea after another, a notion began to form.

"You've been very helpful, Baker," he said.

"Well," Baker demurred. "I'm totally trained."

Instead of heading home, he swung by his old workplace, thunderbolted by nostalgia as he pulled into the expanded lot. He'd been a family man here, a family man earning his pay by keeping jets in the air and ships on the sea.

His phone buzzed in the cup holder, where he'd tossed it days ago. A string of text messages:

Happy birthday, daddy! Present in the mail!
call me now
where are you????
Dad please call. IMPORTANT.
DAD!!!!! VERY IMPORTANT!!!! CALL ME!!!!

Because his phone was nearly out of juice, and because Kristy's very-importants were never—not ever—very important, he left the phone where it was, walked across the newly paved parking lot, through a sparkling set of glass doors, and greeted Mary Jane at a front desk as sleek and uncluttered as the woman herself.

Mr. Pierce wasn't in, but the shop foreman, Curtis Jackson, came out to slap him on the back and shake his hand, hard.

"Frank Daigle! Damn! How you been, man?"

"Been good, Curtis."

"You *look* good."

"I pray for you every night, Frank," Mary Jane said. "You and that daughter of yours." Svelte and silver-haired, Mary Jane had arrived at Pierce Machine looking like somebody's cool grandma, and twenty-five years had not changed that perception. Her age had long been an object of some speculation, though only a madman would chance asking.

"Thank you, Mary Jane," Frank said. After the accident he'd received a flurry of cards from workmates he hadn't seen in years. Mary Jane's doing, undoubtedly. Everyone here had come to the wake.

"I'll tell Kristy you asked after her."

"You do that, Frank. God bless you."

He could feel the sugary warmth of her goodwill at his back as he followed Curtis to the shop floor, a vast expanse that looked freshly washed and waxed. Another stab of longing for the old days, the grime-and-oil days. The current machines—all computer-controlled now—gleamed with the arrogance of hospital equipment, their operations protected by plexiglass casings awash with coolant. But they still made lots of noise. Frank turned down his hearing aids.

"You could let a baby loose in here," Curtis said, hand sweeping up to show it all.

Frank remembered that feeling: propriety and pride. Nothing like it.

"Where's Mr. Pierce?" Frank asked. He'd been fond of his old boss, a man of heart.

"We don't see much of him lately." Curtis lowered his voice. "Cancer."

"Aw, no."

"He'll beat it," Curtis said. "Stubborn as a nanny goat, that one. Hey, we never see you, Frank. You gotta come out for a beer one of these times."

"I will," Frank said.

"No, I mean it," Curtis said. He was a cushiony Black man with kind, deep-set eyes that had seen their share of sorrow. After his teenage son, Marcus, died of meningitis at a sports camp, Lorraine had brought dinner to the Jackson house once a week for months; she was thoughtful that way.

Looking around, he missed the guys—and Audrey, big wave from across the shop floor. He stood there awhile, watching his old crew move between machines and stations, carrying stock, checking specs, moving cutters of all sizes in containers of all sizes. The smallest cutters resembled fine, foil-wrapped candy, their tips anodized with bright alloys in shades of silver and copper and gold. The largest ones looked like warheads.

"These new machines'll blow your mind," Curtis said. He led Frank deeper onto the floor, where Frank was pelted by backslaps from men he hadn't seen in years now. There were fewer remaining than he expected, most of the machine tenders now young folks fresh out of tech school.

"Look at this, Frank," Curtis said, stopping at a machine so new it still shone. "Five-axis. Turn and cut without resetting."

Frank observed with an insider's reverence as the machine went about its mission, fashioning a giant valve from a hunk of steel. "Boeing?" Frank asked.

"Lockheed," Curtis said. "New customer."

"Not too shabby."

Curtis laughed. "Not shabby at all."

Frank had made a few good friends at Pierce Machine, but realized after retirement how much those friendships depended on the daily connections of the workplace. He'd been more naturally drawn to men his own age, and like him they were retired now. Jack and Russ had moved to Florida; Leonard sent handwritten postcards from the road; Mitch was dead.

"So. You lookin' for scrap?"

"Yup."

"What for?"

"Bookends," Frank said. He would show Harriet that he was a man who made amends. Who knew his way around a milling machine. A man with manners, and sense. As opposed to a demented, window-wielding swamp thing. "If you don't mind, I'll look through the bin," he said. "I'm thinking stainless steel, separate parts, maybe do some brazing."

"Aww, that'll shine up nice," Curtis said. "Lady friend?"

Before he could answer, Audrey barreled over to body-slam him with her outsize warmth. "Frankeeeee!" she squealed. "My Frankie-Frank!" She'd always made him smile, this husky, effervescent, supremely talented machinist. Mr. Pierce had installed a ladies' bathroom, but she was still the only woman in the place.

"I'm getting hitched," she said, wiggling her bare fingers. "The ring's a looker, and it kills me not to wear it in the daytime."

"Hate to see it pull your finger off."

"A full caret, Frankie-Frank, my baby's *loaded*."

She was joshing now, in their old way, and Frank wished himself back among this noisy, genial fold. If not for his touchy back, his cranky feet, his failing eyes. Oh, how he missed being a working man. Not just saying it; being it.

"Frank's got a lady friend," Curtis said, and Audrey let loose one of her famous owl-shrieks. After a fruitless hunt for details, she switched tactics, a blow-by-blow of her coming nuptials, possibly hoping to inspire him. "The dress has an eight-foot train, Frank," she gushed. "*Eight* feet, and we're doing the vows in my grandma's pasture." Frank chuckled, picturing Audrey floating across a field, dragging a length of satin dotted with deer ticks. She concluded with a juicy kiss on Frank's cheek before jogging back to her station.

"Goddamn ring turned her into Snow fuckin' White." Curtis laughed, and Frank, too, was smiling. He'd always enjoyed Audrey. He'd enjoyed all of it.

He got home at midafternoon with some beautiful steel and bronze, enough to fashion a sincere apology. Harriet would turn up at the store eventually, but he did not expect to see the girl again. Still, he planned to make two sets of bookends, if only to complete the intention.

The phone was ringing inside the house. *It's Harriet*, he thought rashly, sprinting inside, picking up just as he realized, of course, that Harriet did not have his number and wouldn't call if she did.

"Oh my God," Kristy huffed. "*Finally*. I called both phones, I texted you a million times!"

"What is it, sweetheart?"

"It was going to be your birthday call," she said. "But. Are you sitting down?"

"Yes."

"I mean it. Sit."

He didn't. "All right, I'm sitting."

"Okay. Dad. Listen. Violet Powell is back on the street."

He should have thought to head this off, but with all the clamor in his skull he'd missed the fact that at some point the marvelous

Felicia, gold-medal victim advocate, would have called the victim's daughter.

"I know that, sweetheart."

"You *know*? And you didn't *call* me? Six months *early*, Dad. Six *months*!"

"For good behavior, I presume."

"She didn't pay her full *debt*, Dad." Her voice quavered toward a higher register—her Lorraine register—that reliably foretold trouble. "How good was her *behavior* when she decided of her own free will to drink half a bottle of—"

"Kristy? Breathe."

"I can't believe you didn't *call* me. Imagine if Mommy could have those six months instead of her."

Now he did sit. He closed his eyes. This would simply have to be gotten through.

"Violet Powell gets to cavort around after twenty-two measly months in prison?" Kristy said, steaming ahead. "While Mommy *doesn't* get to help me pick a new color for my den, or snuggle on the couch with me to binge-watch *Say Yes to the Dress*, or go to the boys' robotics tournament next month?"

He could see Lorraine leaping on the sidelines, yelling her head off and wearing the team shirt. A good grandmother, better than most.

"I doubt the girl's cavorting, sweetheart."

"Are you—Daddy, are you *defending* her?" He could hear her frown; his daughter had fully audible facial expressions, always had.

"There's nothing to be done, Kristy."

Shockingly, she quieted. He could hear her breath slacken. He'd always been better than Lorraine at calming their daughter, even in babyhood when she keened for hours like an injured rabbit, Lorraine swaying and cooing her, the baby inconsolable until all at once she looked straight into Frank's eyes, recognized him as her besotted father, and drifted off to sleep.

"She's somewhere in Portland. That's where she ended up."

"It's a big city, Kristy."

"New *York* is a big city, Dad. Portland's barely a *town*. You might run into her at the dentist's office."

"I don't even run into people I know." He'd lived in this city for ten years now—Lorraine had "needed" to be nearer some urgent and unspecified "action." Ten years, no close ties. Like many men of his vintage, he'd let his wife manage the friendships.

"It's not that big, is what I'm saying," Kristy insisted, "and bumping into her might bring up stuff you don't want to face."

Then she went bone quiet.

"Kristy?"

"Was it Felicia who called you?"

"Oh, yes. Efficient Felicia."

"So, she probably . . . She told you Violet Powell's mother died while she was in prison?"

Frank felt a jolt of pity. "The girl's mother died?"

"Felicia didn't mention it?"

"No. What a shame."

"That's exactly why I hoped she didn't tell you, but I figured she did." She cleared her throat as if to sing. "I know what you're going to say."

"I wasn't going to say anything."

"I'm sure Osama bin Laden missed *his* mother," she said. "And Hitler. And *Stalin*."

"Kristy," Frank said. "Why don't we say a prayer for the girl and call it quits."

"I wish you could hear yourself, Dad. That girl robbed you of your *wife*, who would be baking a Black Forest cake for your birthday this very minute."

Violet Powell had robbed him; this was true. A luckless girl joyriding with her blockhead boyfriend had stolen something vital and inexpressible: the natural ending of his marriage. Lorraine had died before "closure," her favorite word. Surely they'd have reached some measure of grace after the raging mess of divorce; some hard-earned dignity. Eventually. Instead, he'd landed in a courtroom, a phony widower hiding his relief.

"How did your choir problem turn out?" he asked.

Kristy heaved a great, surrendering sigh. Good: they were done. "Luther gave the solo to Stephanie Bowman," she said. "An *alto*, Dad, with the pitch of a *crow*." She paused. "I have a beautiful soprano voice. Nobody else will say it, but I will."

"I'll say it," he said. "Why don't you sing the solo for your old dad?"

"What? You mean now?"

"Sure."

"Right now on the phone?"

"Why not?"

His daughter had a clear, slight, pleasant soprano voice. The alto likely sang with more power. But this was Kristy, his child, and therefore her voice pleased him as no other, and she sang for him now:

"*Depth of mercy, can there be,*" sang his only child. "*Mercy still reserved for me . . .*"

He saw her standing in her clean, well-appointed kitchen, unself-conscious, eyes closed as if singing the solo in church.

Now incline me to repent,
Let me now my sins lament . . .

A hymn about forgiveness. Asking for it, hoping for it. He laid down the phone and placed his elbows on the table, resting his forehead on his clasped fists as if in prayer.

16

Violet

RENYS, THANK GOD, SELLS LAB coats that fit. I buy two: one for me, one for my locker. Deep pockets, good length, arctic white—no lollipops for me.

Every morning, eight sharp, Mrs. Rocha looks me over. "Very good," she says. Her pointy eyeglasses wink in the light. She slides the reception log over. I sign, slide it back. Signature: check. Date: check. Time: check.

Today, though, eight days in, she stops me at the front door. "He wants you in the Ob Room today," she informs me.

My hearts starts up. "What?"

"Masuda left a month ago, better offer. That's three inside of a year. He thought he could manage alone, of course, but even the Great Oz sometimes accepts his limitations."

"Wait. Mrs. Rocha. I'm going to assist with the studies?"

"It's the ol' bait and switch."

I blink at her like a stunned goat. "You mean with the actual studies? Who's Masuda?"

"Egyptian postgrad," she says, "finishing up his psychiatry training. Brilliant, easy on the eyes." She gives her hair a little pouf. "Boy, oh boy, between the two of them, you could choke on the testosterone."

"I'm replacing a brilliant Egyptian psychiatrist? Mrs. Rocha, it's my second week."

"You won't get coauthorship," she says. "I can guarantee you that."

"But I'm not qualified."

"Oh, close enough. He doesn't let them do much, which is why they leave." She signs me in quickly, then shoos me to the locker room, where I store my lunch—a peanut butter sandwich and a Coke—and when I return she's holding a short stack of articles she's printed out. "Read these," she says. "He's not patient."

Seven articles in all, packed with charts and footnotes in tiny print. But guess what, except for one on "sentinel behavior in psittacine birds," I've already read them, having spent my first week of employment looking up anything written not only by Dr. Petrov but by other scientists, not many, working with African greys.

I don't tell this to Mrs. Rocha, who wants to help me. Who put some thought into what I ought to read. Who spent time printing out these articles. Who thought of me the whole time she was doing it. I thank her for the papers and spend the next couple of hours with them at the reception desk. It's pretty heavy going. Even having read them already, I'm learning plenty more besides. What a feeling in my brain: a vast, windy newness. I hope college will be like this.

Dr. Petrov pops out of the inner sanctum only once, around nine, to get coffee. He glances over at me. "Ten o'clock," he says.

"Mrs. Rocha told me." I straighten up, trying to look ready.

"It's your big day," he says, which sounds so fake-American I want to laugh. But as usual he's not joking. He gets his coffee and goes back to his office, leaving two closed doors between us.

At quarter to ten, I open the door to the hallway, pass the PETROV door, then punch the numbers to the Bird Lounge.

Oliver's alone, and goes nuts when he sees me. "*Who's a good bird!*" he shouts. "*Jiminy cricket!*" He might be dancing.

"Hi, Ollie," I say, giving him a little kiss, just as I've seen Dr. Petrov do. Ollie makes a kitten sound and tugs at my hair; nothing mean, just a little pull to say hi. I've known Ollie for only a few days, and already I love him more than I loved Troy.

"Are you lonesome, little boo?" I ask him, at the same moment I realize there's a student sitting in the corner, reading.

"You the new lab assistant?" he asks, still reading.

"Yeah."

"I'm Jamal. Thursday-Friday, eight to twelve." He's slight and cute, short dreadlocks and old-fashioned horn-rim glasses. Mrs. Rocha is the students' official supervisor; she keys them in at eight, twelve, and four o'clock, but otherwise doesn't spend much time in the Bird Lounge. The birds are okay one at a time, but together, apparently, they give her the creeps.

"Cages are done," Jamal says, back to his reading. "If you wondered."

Then I realize: this is one of my tasks, to make sure the students do what they're asked to do.

"Did Ollie get his physical therapy?"

Jamal looks up. "Not yet."

"He should have it right after breakfast," I remind him. "The others can go later, but Ollie gets bored."

Jamal closes his book and goes straight to Ollie, where I see the physical therapy already set up: a series of small, spongy balls that Ollie walks on to exercise his hobbly feet. Jamal scratches the back of Ollie's neck. "Boss Lady called you a bore, my man."

"No I didn't. Oh. Joke."

"*Whew, that was close!*" Ollie calls, and Jamal and I both laugh. Nice people everywhere. Ollie whistles the opening guitar riff to "Smoke on the Water" as I open the door to the Observation Room.

"You are early," Dr. Petrov says. "Very promising."

Before I can so much as say hello, he's got me paging through daunting binders of lab notes logged by hand, organized by year, by bird, by study: "Probabilistic Reasoning," "Invisible Displacement," "Mutual Exclusivity," "Liquid Conservation." One is about "Delayed Gratification"; that, I've heard of.

He explains that at least two studies will be going at any given time, sometimes with guest scientists from other labs using our birds, testing for various aspects of bird intelligence and communication. It takes time and patience; by design, the birds spend far more time at play than at work. Charlotte, especially, will give wrong answers on purpose if a session goes too long. The notes are entered into spreadsheets: right/wrong answers, time of day, mood of bird—who knew birds had moods? It will be my job to make these notes during sessions and then transfer them to a computer.

I ask, "Why not record straight to a laptop?"

"Because," he says, suddenly frosty, "like most human beings in the twenty-first century, the birds cannot keep their eyes off a screen."

I'm sorry I asked, but he gets over it quickly. I haven't seen much of him since my interview; he's been denned up in his office working on a grant, which Mrs. Rocha describes as "tragically past deadline." He looks a little tired, seated at the session table, plucking small objects from a plastic tub. All the objects are bright, though the colors vary between and within each category. Bob and Alan home right in, laser focused, maybe looking for a favorite toy, but Charlotte's more interested in me.

"*What name?*" she asks, a chain-smoker's rasp.

I can't help but laugh. "Violet. I've told you a hundred times."

"Violet."

"That's right. Good bird," Dr. Petrov says. "Come here."

I assume he means the bird. But he doesn't. I do as I'm told and sit across from him at the session table. A minute later, Charlotte works her way over, standing between us.

"This one likes to work," he says, "don't you, good birdie?" He picks her up, pets her, puts her down. "Not like those idlers up there." He means Bob and Alan, who take no offense from their perch on top of a file cabinet.

"Hi, guys," I say. They do not reply, though Bob does wave his foot.

"Lazy gigolos," Dr. Petrov says, and I'm not sure if he's kidding. He has a face that's hard to read: beautiful, with a hint of something else that's . . . well, the opposite of beauty, whatever that is. I saw a lot of faces like this over the last two years, a guarded stillness that implies Keep Out. "And so," he says. "Violet. We begin our work together."

He tends to speak in present tense, which might be a language thing despite all his Americanisms, but it gives you the idea that you and he exist alone in the moment, especially when he steadies you with his eyes, which are either ice blue or ice green, depending on the light.

Everything about him has a not-quite quality that can be a little unnerving.

On the session table he arranges fifteen random objects: blocks, keys, swatches of paper and wool cut into shapes, and pompoms. In all, three shapes, four materials, five colors, all mixed up.

He says, "You will be responsible for setting up each session."

"Okay." I look hard at the objects—how many, what color, how much space between them.

"Not now," he says. "This is the overview." He picks up a block. "Charlotte, look. What toy?"

"Block."

"That's right. Block. Good bird." He shows her a pompom. "Charlotte, look. What color?"

"Orange."

"That's right. Orange. Good bird." He selects a square of paper. "Charlotte, look. What material?"

"Paper."

I spent hours reading the studies, but I guess part of me didn't quite believe. I'm speechless. Thrilled. "Wow."

"Not *wow*," Dr. Petrov warns me. "We observe; we record what we observe. That is all."

I nod obediently, nerves jangling. "Observe and record."

"*Wow* skews the study," he explains. "*Wow* creates expectation. We observe what is. Not what we hope. Not what we suppose. Not what pleases us."

"Okay."

"We leave *wow* to those who believe parrots are circus animals. Silly pets. Entertainers." As he resets the tray, he adds, "Leave *wow* to stupid people who do not understand science."

"I will," I tell him.

But. Oh my God. Wow.

He mixes the order of the objects, takes some away, adds others. Of all the objects, only one is green—a small, flat triangle of felted wool. "Charlotte, look. What shape green?"

Charlotte eyes the tray. "*Three corner.*"

"That's right. Three corner. Good bird." To me, he says, "She means triangle. Certain sounds are hard to make without lips, so we offer words they can more likely pronounce." He glances so quickly at my own lips that later I'll think I imagined it.

He taps the tray. "Charlotte, look. How many yellow?"

"Want nut."

"No. Charlotte. Look. How many yellow?"

She eyes the tray for a moment, performs a modest feather fluff, then says, "*Four.*" It takes most of my willpower to swallow a *wow*, because Charlotte is dead right: one yellow pompom; one yellow key; two yellow blocks. This bird can count.

A bubble of pain forms in my gut, the bubble that contains my mother, who taught me to count using gumdrops. Right answer, I got a kiss; wrong answer, same; my first memory. I want her to be alive. I want to have not driven to Portland with Troy. I want to have listened when she cupped my face and said, *Not him, he'll hurt you.* I want to have come here the way I originally thought I might, as a college student. Maybe I would have met Dr. Petrov anyway. Maybe I'd be right here, right now, my living mother waiting at home in Abbott Falls to hear about my first day in the Ob Room. Somewhere in this city, Lorraine Daigle would be teaching twenty-two kindergarteners their ABCs. If a parrot can tell me my name, then why can't three years drop through a hole in the universe? What's one more miracle?

"*Want nut,*" Charlotte says, and this time Dr. Petrov gives her one.

As Charlotte chisels at a juicy walnut, Dr. Petrov fills me in on the progress of the other birds: Oliver is sweet but useless (unfair), and Bob and Alan are coming along despite Bob's problems with focus. They've learned some shapes and colors, can label forty-eight objects, and despite not yet mastering the art of counting, they're being tested for other concepts of a higher order.

"Like what?" I ask.

Dr. Petrov picks up two keys—red and yellow, large and small. "Charlotte," he says, his voice suddenly gentle, confiding. "Which key bigger?"

The suspense doesn't last long. "*Red,*" she says, correctly. "*Want nut.*"

"Bob and Alan will succeed soon enough," he says. "Charlotte is their example."

Sure enough, Bob and Alan seem transfixed, watching their colleague earning treats. My head fills with *wow*. I want to believe in these marvels, this work, this man. I don't want to ask, but I have to: "Is there a trick?"

Sometimes you can feel the air-shift of a person's rage, and now is one of those times. "You insult me with such a question?" he says. His mouth moves, but the rest of him goes rigid. He stands up, which sounds benign enough, but when you're that much over six feet it makes a statement. I remain sitting because I sense I'm supposed to.

"Go," he says, pointing to the door.

"I'm sorry, Dr. Petrov."

"I said go. Let me think."

So it's back to the Bird Lounge with me, quaking and breathless. Jamal looks up from the counter, where he's giving Ollie a shower, misting him with water from a pink spray bottle. "*That's the ticket!*" Ollie yells. "*Okey-dokey!*" His previous owner must have been an eighty-year-old man. Or maybe Harriet.

"He fired you, right?" Jamal says.

"No. Maybe."

But Jamal looks sure. A plunging dread takes me over, because this is the only job on offer, and it comes with an icy, hard-to-please scientist who believes me an *observer*. Who saw my *affinity*.

Instinctively, I clutch the front of my lab coat. *Mine mine mine*. "I don't understand what's going on."

"Petrov's an egotistical asshat, that's what's going on," he informs me. He continues to mist Ollie, who shudders his feathers in glee. "Good recommendations, though."

"*Bada-bing bada-boom!*" Ollie shouts, and I can't help but laugh a little even though my insides feel like wet paper.

"Mr. Funnyman," Jamal says.

Just then the door to the Ob Room swings open and Dr. Petrov shoots Jamal a look, icicle-sharp. "Less pressure," he snaps. "It's a shower, not a drowning." To me, he says, "In."

So I go back in. And sit where I sat. And wait to be fired. I have never been fired. I've had only the one job, and they liked me. I restocked the napkin holders without being asked; I kept the drive-through station clean, which wasn't my job. I remembered everybody's name, not just the regulars'.

Charlotte senses my panic, I think. She hops to a perch nearer Bob and Alan. I hold my breath as Dr. Petrov opens his mouth to speak.

"Violet," he says, "I have spent decades of my life defending my work against lesser researchers who believe I must be cueing the birds. Or starving them. Or torturing them. Or performing some sort of prestidigitation."

I'm having trouble hearing him over the deafening heart-thump in my ears.

"I spend sixty percent of my precious time writing grants," he says, "to barely maintain a functioning laboratory in Maine." He says "Maine" like Maine has fleas. "Do you understand?"

I don't, actually. What do I know about the high-stakes, knife-in-the-back competition for grant money? About the scratch-and-claw world of scientific research? "No" doesn't seem like an option, so I say yes. Yes, I understand.

"This work is not a curiosity." His voice is deep, with a hint of static, as if the birds taught him to speak rather than the other way around.

"No, of course." Like the birds, I find myself desperate to please him.

"What we do here matters to the greater scientific community."

I just nod, waiting for the worst.

"Through intelligently conceived studies and impeccably executed experiments," he says, "we have revealed previously unknown avian cognitive abilities." He says *we*, but I'm pretty sure he means *I*. "These birds communicate. They think. They count. They solve. They decide. Most significantly, they say what they mean, and mean what they say; a skill with which human animals struggle profoundly." His whole face—keen and fearsome—tightens. "This is my life's work, to demonstrate higher-order cognition in animals once dismissed as birdbrains." He pauses. "Look at them."

Too panicked by now to move so much as an eyelash, I don't actually look.

"Violet. Look at them."

Bob and Alan are preening each other, ignoring us. As for Charlotte, she has inched down a series of perches as if listening for her name to come up.

"African greys are more intelligent than we ever imagined." His lips—thin but soft-looking—purse. "'So what?' you ask. 'So what?'"

"I'm—not asking that."

"I will tell you 'so what,'" he says. "'So what' is not merely *that* they learn, but *how* they learn. The methods we use here have been replicated with human children. Children with difficulties."

"I didn't know that," I say. "That's—very, uh, noble."

His face slackens a little, and his voice. "The 'so what' is significant. The 'so what' can relieve suffering in this world. The 'so what' is my sole purpose in this miserable, fleeting life."

I figure this is over, so I get up. "I didn't ask 'so what,' Dr. Petrov. Just to be clear."

"Didn't you?"

"No. I didn't." I plunge my hands into the pockets of my snowy, perfectly ironed lab coat, balling my fists; I've sworn off crying, as a first step—to where, I don't know. "This is a job I can do. I want to do it. I have affinity."

At that very second, Charlotte—my ally, my champion, my savior—launches herself from the table and lands on my shoulder. Wouldn't most people laugh? Even a humorless Russian behavioral scientist condemned to an underfunded lab in flea-bitten Maine?

But no. Instead, he sits down. Because we're in an animal lab, and because Dr. Petrov doesn't seem to differentiate much between human animals and animal animals, I take this as a sign of trust. He sits, I stand; he has allowed himself to be smaller. This I "observe." Charlotte settles deeper into my shoulder, her feet relaxing.

"I left my homeland," he says. "My brothers and sisters, my beloved uncles. I did not do so to waste my professional life performing tricks."

I just nod, blinking hard, Charlotte leaning against my neck. She's surprisingly warm; African greys have a body temperature of one hundred six. She leans a little harder, as if to say, *There, there.*

"I ask one thing of you, Violet," he says, nearly gentle now.

I nod: yes, anything. Charlotte nods, too: a motion in my peripheral vision.

"Do not deny what is right in front of you," he tells me. "You have beautiful eyes. Believe them."

What is right in front of me, I believe, is a two-PhD scientist who I have already disappointed. Who thinks I have beautiful eyes.

"So . . . ?" My voice comes out meek and mousy, like Aimee the baby-thrower. "I'm not fired?"

"Fired?" He looks genuinely shocked. "What gives you that idea?"

"I just—thought."

"Again you conclude before evidence," he says. "Do not conclude. Observe."

What I "observed" was him kicking me out of the Ob Room, which led to a pretty obvious conclusion, but I keep that to myself as he collects Bob and Alan from atop the file cabinet.

He glances at me, then takes two keys from the tray, a big red one and a small yellow one. He shows Bob the big red key. "Bob, look. What color?"

"*Red.*"

Alan, I notice, is rapt.

Then Dr. Petrov holds up both keys for Bob, showing them side by side. "Bob, look. Which key bigger?"

Bob looks and looks. Poor guy.

"Little kids have trouble with bigger and smaller," I say, defending Bob. "I mean, I've observed that. They teach it on *Sesame Street.*"

"That's right," he says to me. "Very good." He widens his arms. "We teach the children." He gives all three birds a walnut, and they take their time, rolling the treat on their leathery tongues. These are creatures who appreciate pleasure.

"Masuda betrayed me, and the undergraduates cannot be counted on," he says. "You, Violet, will fully participate in our educational endeavor."

"I'd be honored," I say, but in truth I'm not yet sure what he means. And I "observe" that he doesn't mention the other postgrads who left. I "conclude" that turnover here is epic, and that Dr. Petrov might be the reason.

Though he disappears into his office for the rest of the day, by quitting time I'm still brimming with knowledge and moving with a prickly, glittering electricity. I was hoping to say goodbye, to maybe hear a good word about my work ethic or my promise, but he doesn't look up as I pass his door.

In reception, Mrs. Rocha is also getting ready to leave. "Your big day." Her smile, like her, is big and quick.

"I'm not fired. That's one thing."

"Pay no attention to him," she says. "Listen, third shift canceled for tomorrow. Can you do supper and bedtime?"

"Sure." Tomorrow is Saturday, but I have nothing else to do.

She makes a note on one of her many sheets. Then, in case of a further emergency, we exchange numbers, and I'm officially official. I realize this week was a test, and I passed.

When I get outside, the soft air hits me, and I nearly cry out with shock and joy. Big fluffy sky, trees leafing out, daylight well past supper-time. I got out at the stick-colored end of April, and thanks to Harriet, I've made it all the way to the fully flowering now.

17

Frank

Frank spent the morning suspending a wooden sign over Staff Picks, careful work despite his murmuring dread: Kristy was due in town. Newly solicitous since learning of Violet's release, she was coming to "check on him." In person. To "talk it through." "Lest you run into her unexpectedly." Lest. Oh, Kristy. Not only had he already run into Violet Powell unexpectedly, he had fashioned an apology to her in three dimensions.

The bell jingled: no. There had been a book-club lady sighting on Thursday, according to Baker, while Frank was across town having his teeth cleaned. For this week, at least, he'd likely missed his chance.

At noon, as he rounded the corner for home, he found Kristy's car already ill-parked in his driveway. He grunted, parking half on the lawn, since she'd left him so little room. "*Dad*," she wailed, steaming from his own front door and then stopping abruptly, arms akimbo, a skinny column of righteousness in black tights (or leggings, or whatever she called them), short little boots too heavy for the day, and some sort of tunic hemmed with pompoms.

"Sweetheart, I didn't expect you for another hour."

"Where have you *been*?" The pompoms shivered when she moved.

"Out minding my own business," he said.

Her arms dropped. "Be glad someone cares enough to *worry*, Dad. Stephanie Bowman calls her father twice a year, and she thinks she should be *canonized*."

"I was at work."

"Oh." He took in the pell-mell of confusion, impatience, and thwarted plans on her face. "You're still doing that?"

"Sweetheart, when did you get here?"

"*Hours* ago," she fumed. "The boys have a robotics meet in Conway at three and of *course* didn't tell us till this morning." She'd slicked her hair into a violent bun at the top of her head, like an ice skater or synchronized swimmer. It made his own hair hurt to look at her.

"It was good of you to come anyway." He lifted his arms. "I'm glad to see you."

She surrendered then, her shoulders dropping, and marched straight into his hug. "Oh, Daddy," she said. There was so little to her, really; small bones encased by a resolute sleeve of gym muscle.

"Come in," he said. "I'll make some lunch."

"I already made myself a smoothie."

"Then I'll eat and you can watch." He shepherded her inside, where she'd already made herself at home, one of Lorraine's twizzly gadgets unearthed from beneath the counter and now dripping with kale and lord knew what else she'd toted from New Hampshire. He made himself a roast beef sandwich, enjoying his daughter's silent judgments about the welfare of cows.

"The twins tell us *nothing*," she was saying, slumped in Lorraine's chair as he joined her at the table.

"That's kids, Kristy," he said. "They don't think ahead."

"Well, I'm sorry for all the times I last-minuted you, Dad." She shocked him with a grin. "What goes around comes around."

He chuckled. "Forgiven." This was the Kristy he loved most.

"It's not like they're *invaluable*," she said, getting up to rinse the smoothie gadget. "They're on the *pit* crew, Dad, while the glamor spot goes to Stephanie Bowman's obnoxious little psychopath who thinks he's the next Elon Musk."

His daughter looked the way she felt: tired and unappreciated. She was aging, he realized with a jolt. Bluish pockets under the eyes, a softness around the mouth. The tightly wrung hairdo didn't help.

"That sandwich looks toxic," she said. She was still at the sink, washing his few dishes—no sense protesting, and anyway Frank liked these kitchen sounds.

"Do you remember cooking with me?" he asked. "When you were little?"

She frowned. "I thought it was Mommy I cooked with."

"Nope. It was me." He and Lorraine had always divvied up the meals—Lorraine loved cooking but preferred to swap roles on principle.

"I remember that red apron," she said, grinning, and he could imagine her at five, swamped by an apron that went to her ankles, cooking with Daddy as Lorraine sat at the table, writing lesson plans and sipping wine. They'd had some beautiful times as a family.

"Luther sent me flowers," she said. "Did I tell you? Like *that* can make up for it."

"Who's Luther?"

"The choir director, Dad. I *told* you. The one who gave my *solo* to Stephanie Bowman." She was rummaging in the lower cupboard, returning the gadget to its rightful spot, which involved much clinking and clanking.

He said, "I was told sending flowers was no longer done."

Kristy stood up. "Who told you that?"

He sensed an ambush but walked in: "Someone at the bookstore."

The pompoms went still. "You're sending flowers to someone at the bookstore?"

"No," he said patiently, "someone at the bookstore told me sending flowers is no longer done, which is the sort of thing I don't know much about anymore, so I'm asking you."

Kristy picked up half his roast beef sandwich and took a bite. As she chewed, studying him, he saw Lorraine in the working of her jaw, her small, even teeth. *You're too soft, Frank,* Lorraine had told him, defiantly confessing her betrayal, standing in exactly the spot Kristy occupied now. *You give in too quick. Who can respect a man like that?*

Kristy set the sandwich back on his plate, leaving a neat, round bite mark in the bread. "I'm just gonna put it out there, Dad, okay? My therapist thinks I have PTSD from the shock of Mommy's death, the *horror* of it, the completely unanticipated—" She broke off, collecting herself. "Is this 'someone' at the store, this 'someone' who erroneously told you sending flowers is no longer done, is this 'someone' a woman?"

"What?"

"A woman, Dad. A female human."

"Kristy, I'm talking about a youngster. A kid who works there."

She backed away from him, all the way to the kitchen door, then stopped, folded her arms, her eyes large and scared. "Tom says I should prepare myself, but I'm not prepared. If you have something to tell me, Daddy, I'm not prepared, and I need you to know that."

I need you to know that. This phrase was all Lorraine.

"I have nothing to tell," he said.

"Fine," Kristy said, then left the room, as she often did on these visits, to racket around the house laying hands on Lorraine's things.

You gave me no choice, Frank. I need you to know that.

He'd wept for weeks—consigned to the guest room as Lorraine's dog breeder "got his ducks in a row"—until one night he found himself wrestling not with grief, or fury, or outlandish hope. He was passing into another stage, could feel it happening, awful and inevitable and right. The new feeling was not, as he might have expected, hatred. No. It was dislike. Dislike, plain and simple, without passion. He did not like his wife.

He got out of bed, strolled down the hall, and entered his rightful bedroom, where Lorraine slept. On her bedstand—*his* bedstand; she'd bizarrely moved to his side—he found the appointment card, a divorce attorney in Freeport, near L.L. Bean. She slept deeply, easeful as a child. He lifted the blankets from her body—coolly, matter-of-fact, as if by prior arrangement.

"What the hell, Frank!" Even in the best of times she hated being woken.

"Out," he said. A simple command. He pointed down the hall to the inferior room, the inferior bed. "Get out. I'm sleeping here."

He was calm, certain, unmovable. She saw this, and he saw her seeing this, spellbound, a little afraid, and he was glad. She sat up, snatched up the card, gathered her pillow—some foolish "beauty pillow" she'd bought online—and did as he said. Before leaving him there, she turned around, lovely in the moonlight, her hair tossed and glinting.

"Well, well," she said. "Where have you been all this time?" Then she padded down the hall and shut the guest room door behind her. Within hours, she'd be dead.

Kristy was back, holding one of Lorraine's figurines, breathing audibly, a bad sign. She said, "Is the 'someone' you're sending flowers to the same 'someone' you were seeing behind Mommy's back?"

Her words dropped into the room before he could grasp their meaning. They merely landed, like an unaddressed package on a doorstep. Could be anything inside.

He squinted at her, trying to comprehend. "What?"

"You know." She tightened her crossed arms. "Dad, you *know*."

"Kristy," he said. "I don't." But he was beginning to. Oh, he was beginning to—a cold, slippery knowledge eeling through him. The implication seized all his breath.

"The *woman*, Dad. I know about it. I *know*. Okay?" She hugged the figurine, a cherubic angel with spread wings. "I know why you were so weird about the trial, I know why you never visit her grave. Okay? Dad? She *told* me. I know now and I knew then, but she died before I could confront you, so what choice did I have but to forgive? You were all I had left."

She was crying now, in the kitchen doorway, defenseless. As for Frank, his heart went ragged, raging; it took all he had to fully hear her words, let alone absorb them.

"So," she said. "We can stop pretending." She wiped her eyes with the heel of one hand, smearing her makeup. "The truth shall set us free, right?"

The truth wanted out, a physical pressure raging beneath his breastbone. But what was he to do now with the truth? Tell his grief-stricken child that her mother was not only a cheat but the worst kind of liar? He thought about getting up but couldn't move.

"Kristy," he said. "That is not true."

"That's what she said you'd say." She stared at the floor. "I figured you ended it after the accident. I mean, what kind of person could keep it going after that?"

"It's not true," he repeated.

"So, we're not gonna do this?"

"Do what?"

"Fix it," she said.

"How?"

"Admit it, for starters. Say you're sorry for hurting her."

"I didn't hurt her."

"You see this shoulder, Dad?" She patted herself just above her heart, the angel in her fist clicking against her collarbone. "This shoulder was wet with her tears. With her *tears*, Dad."

Her voice did not rise, despite the dramatics; he understood how wounded she was, how gutted on her mother's behalf. Of course she was; she worshipped her mother. What choice did she have but to believe Lorraine? He understood this. At least Lorraine had shed some tears; for him, he hoped.

"Please say the flowers woman isn't the same woman," Kristy said. "I mean, I get that people move on, I get that, but Dad, it can't be *that* woman."

"There's no woman," Frank said. "There *was* no woman." What could Lorraine have been thinking? She planned to marry the dog breeder the moment both divorces came through. How long had she thought she could forestall telling Kristy the truth? Now she would never have to.

"So," Kristy said. "What now? We just forget it? Pretend it never happened? Pretend Mommy died not knowing?"

"Your mother . . ." he began, and in the moment resolved to spare her the rest. He could say no more. He ran his hands hard down his face, a physical stay against rage. "I love you, Kristy. I loved her. Please know that. Believe me or don't, but the subject is closed."

She shook her head. "I never even told Tom. He thinks you walk on water, and I didn't want to deny him that."

"Oh," Frank said. "Sweetheart." *You think your mother walks on water, and I don't want to deny you that.*

"Fine," Kristy muttered. "Your marriage, your business. I just need you to know that I know. And now that I've put it out there"—she gestured as if she'd vomited on the kitchen floor—"I have to forgive you all over again."

Kristy began to gather her things where she'd dumped them on the counter—a red purse, keys dangling from a foam disc that read SAINT CATHERINE'S ROBOTICS TEAM, another bag packed with her special foods—she carried so much wherever she went. She tore a paper towel off the holder, wrapped the figurine, and dropped it in with the rest. Taking leave, even in a huff, took time. He wanted to go to her, undo the ruthless bun, release the softness he knew was there, for she was his daughter too.

"Oh, Kristy," he said. "I'm sorry for your loss."

"Oh, Daddy. I know you are." Then she was gone.

The next morning a bouquet of tulips arrived at his door—apparently sending flowers *was* still done. They came with a note: *Give me time.* Like her mother before her, Kristy had a knack for upsiding him when he least expected it. For one fleeting, bewildering moment, he missed them both.

18

Violet

THE BIRD LAB TAKES UP half the second floor of Huntington Hall, so wouldn't you think Dr. Petrov would be grateful, but no. He's a guest of the university, a five-year renewable post by way of a truckload of grant money and a ton of good publicity about his work with African greys; he has no teaching duties or any other university duties as far as I can tell; and yet he complains constantly about the aged building, the cleaning staff, and the every-other-Thursday visitors to the lab: *Same idiot questions, such idiots!*

But receiving visitors is part of the deal, so the job of leading the grand tour has already fallen to me. I like it. I like leading trios of academic deans or rafts of local fourth graders to the Ob Room and watching the *wow*.

"Don't let him exploit you," Harriet warned me last night, mistaking my enthusiasm for desperation. "Not three weeks gone, and you're swimming in unpaid overtime." We were sitting on her front porch, a Sunday evening mild in every way: pleasant conversation, dinner cooking, porch windows wide open, summer on the way, Tabsy listening to us from the sill.

"He's not the dictator Sophie thinks he is, Harriet," I said. "She didn't like the job, that's all. But I do. I love it."

"That's all well and good, Violet," Harriet said, "but make sure you stick to your guns. You're a free, independent woman now."

That's exactly how I feel these days, like a woman, in a new life that includes Harriet and her blooming yard. Sophie's in California now, so I get Harriet to myself.

"I'm glad to have guns to stick to," I said. "The work feels worth defending."

"From whom?"

"Detractors. Disbelievers." I took a self-conscious sip of lemonade—real lemons, homemade. "I sound like him now."

"Just remember, you're being paid for forty hours, not fifty."

"It's not that many," I tell her, though it is. Fifty-five hours this week, in the strange, happy company of warm birds and the chilly scientist who loves them.

A hummingbird rockets past us, backs up, hovers in front of my pink blouse from Vicki, then buzzes away. We both laugh. Harriet's yard is full of hummingbirds, which reminds me of our house on Stickney Street in Abbott Falls. Last summer I saw one hummingbird only, a tiny jewel that zipped through the razor wire and never appeared again.

"Where were we?" Harriet asked.

We'd been discussing *Spoon River Anthology*—a womanly discussion about life and legacy and the bottomless currents that burble beneath even the simplest existence. That's Harriet's word: *burble*. We'd been reading aloud, back and forth, remarking how the characters chose to record their brief time in this ever-moving stream. A few tried to capture the whole winding length of it, but most settled on the rocks and ripples—a moment, a day, an especially fraught or tender time. Some recalled their death, some their life. Some relived their worst, some their best. All of them, though (Harriet and I both noticed this), seemed compelled to make some sort of accounting, convincing those still living that they, too, had lived, and not in vain.

Harriet's a good reader, which I didn't realize until last night; in Book Club she preferred to hear us. Reading the epitaph of Tom Merritt, who died at the hands of his wife's young lover, her voice went thick with feeling:

And all I could say was, "Don't, Don't, Don't,"
as he aimed and fired at my heart.

"Wow, Harriet. So many of these are tragic."

"The things we do for love," she said. "Your turn."

The next speaker was Mrs. Merritt, who took the fall for her young lover. I tried to copy how Dorothy had acted it out during what turned out to be my final Book Club session, how she'd captured Mrs. Merritt's forbearance:

Silent for thirty years in prison! And the iron gates of Joliet
Swung as the gray and silent trusties
Carried me out in a coffin.

"Poor Mrs. Merritt." My shoulders tightened, imagining thirty years.

Harriet tapped the page. "Read the next one."

Elmer Karr: the murdering lover. Nineteen years old. He, too, went to prison, and when he got out, all of Spoon River forgave him. I read, *Oh, loving hearts that took me in again. . . .* I looked up at Harriet. "Everybody just forgave him, like that?"

"It's based on a real case," Harriet told me. "The law wouldn't believe the boy acted alone, so they convicted the woman as an accessory and gave her more than twice the lover's prison time."

"I bet Dawna-Lynn had something to say about that."

She laughed. "You bet correctly."

I said, "Why did they forgive him and not her? He's the one who pulled the trigger. She wasn't even there."

Harriet thought it over. She always took our questions as if the future of literature depended on them. "Perhaps it's an oddity of human nature to judge women more harshly. Or maybe we expect so little of men, their transgressions don't register the same."

For a second I tried to imagine all of Abbott Falls as loving hearts who took me in again. Lucky Elmer Karr. *Oh, helping hands that in the church received me . . .* Nineteen when he took a life, just like me.

Harriet closed her book. "Beautifully read, Violet." But she was looking at me funny. "You know, I've been wondering about something." She looked out over her tulips, white with red centers, like half-filled cups of wine. "Something that has troubled me from time to time." She paused again. "Is it possible that . . ."

Where was she going with this? She did look troubled. She turned to me on her pretty porch, in her bright porch chair, hugging the book to her chest. "Could it be, Violet, that someone besides you was driving the car?"

All at once, Lorraine Daigle crashed unbidden into our peaceful evening: Lorraine Daigle, and the white-bright sunlight of an ordinary day. A rise in the road, a spasm of denial, *oh-no-no-no*, shrieking brakes ripping a hole in that day. A near miss, whiff of relief, shock of living breath, then the concurrent bone-shatter of Lorraine Daigle's clean blue Chevy Impala cracking a hundred-year-old tree, slow-motion bedlam of metal and more metal and popping airbags and scorched rubber and raining glass.

After that: silence. Even the birds. The grass. The trees.

"Does it matter now?" I asked Harriet. "Who was driving, I mean?"

"It does if you took the fall for your young man."

Car doors creaking open, our feet on the pavement, the machinelike hissing of Lorraine Daigle's car, yards away in a shelter of trees. Our footsteps, faster now, toward the wet gurgle of a badly damaged human, then silence again, like no silence ever, then the high, unhinged yowling of my boyfriend-slash-fiancé-slash-future-slash-everything, *Jesus fucking Christ, Violet, what did you do what the fuck did you do*?

We couldn't have gotten her out. She hit the tree so hard, the car like a crushed candy wrapper, front nearly fused with the back, a bloody thing somewhere between, a thing I now know to be Lorraine Daigle, an innocent woman with a husband, daughter, twenty-two kindergarteners. Doors canted, roof caved in, chrome flung all over the road, tree already scarred beyond repair—we couldn't have gotten her out if we tried.

The point is: we didn't try.

The fuck, Violet! The fuck! We stared at Lorraine Daigle, what was left of Lorraine Daigle. All three of us had our mouths open. Troy's car was idling not far away, perfectly whole, as if waiting for someone to dash into a store for a pint of ice cream. *The fuck!* He gripped me by the arm, bruises for days. *What the fuck did you do?* And then we were running.

I was running. I speak for myself. As Lorraine Daigle died alone, I was running to Troy's waiting car, the getaway car, but already other people were pulling over, good Samaritans running and yelling, and the world woke up, too late now for us to do the wrong thing.

For *me*. Too late for *me* to do the wrong thing. Good Samaritans everywhere, doing the right thing.

"I didn't take the fall for my young man, Harriet. I was in the wrong lane, and she swerved to avoid me."

"That's a trouble off my mind, then," she said. I caught a polished sequin of disappointment in her face before she could hide it.

The kitchen timer inside the house went off—lasagna with sausage, which I'd been so looking forward to. "I shouldn't have asked," she said as we got up to go inside. "It's none of my business." She nudged the screen door open; the kitchen smelled heavenly. "I suppose I'm just trying to look after you, Violet."

I should have felt happy to hear this; I hadn't felt "looked after" in quite some time. But Harriet wanted Troy to have been behind the wheel, and it made a difference to her that he wasn't. A small difference, but a difference nonetheless.

In Book Club I was just like everybody else, a person being punished for a crime, and in that setting, she could more easily see me as "a human continuum." That's how she put it one day—we were reading *The House on Mango Street*—and at the time it made sense. We are a continuum of human experience, neither the worst nor the best thing we have ever done. Or, more exactly, we are *both* the best thing and the worst thing we've ever done. We are all of it, all at once, all the time.

But here on the Outs, I've rejoined the good people, the people who have not done wrong. Who can blame Harriet for preferring that I be one of them?

I want to be one of them, and at work I can pretend I am. That's the thing about a good job: you get up every day looking forward, not back. The next morning, I iron my lab coat and walk to work feeling bad about Harriet but good about Ollie, who's learning the words to "In the Garden," my mother's song. We had a couple of PhD candidates from NYU here last week running trials, so I spent most of my time in the Bird Lounge with him, and the song is just between us.

Dr. Petrov is a man of his word: he's made me a full participant, every minute in the lab a thrill. Even the chambermaid tasks feel critical—mixing bird mash, changing the mats, wiping down the Ob Room after sessions. Dr. Petrov once lost a bird to a virus, and now he can't keep everything clean enough. I should say *I* can't keep everything clean enough. For him.

But I try. I try to be indispensable.

Today we're drilling Bob on new labels, and it's not going great. We've got a new toy—a batch of wine corks painted in colors the birds know. New objects are always motivating, and cork-shredding turns out to be a huge hit, but Bob can't, or won't, say "cork"—not for a walnut, not for yummy plum, not even for the cork itself.

"All right, Bob," Dr. Petrov says. "Good bird." Big, beleaguered sigh, as if he himself is personally responsible for Bob's limitations. I record Bob's last wrong answer and close the logbook. As Dr. Petrov lifts Bob to a perch near the window, his wedding band catches the light and I squint briefly into the thought of a wife somewhere: tall, clenched, scientific, like him.

He gives Bob the plum anyway and leaves him to it.

"Let's see how Alan does today," he says, lifting Alan from his perch. Charlotte's back in the bird lounge with Ollie, having earned the morning off. She learned "cork" in two days, and as a reward she's spending her break joyfully shredding a hot-pink cork. Ollie, too; he gets all the same toys, though he's basically a loafer, like a great-grandpa the family takes in out of love or obligation.

"Ready?" Dr. Petrov says to me.

Am I ever. Dr. Petrov takes everything personally, I've noticed, which is why pleasing him makes me feel such a sense of accomplishment. I switch logbooks, note the date-time-circumstances, and wait for Dr. Petrov to begin. These are official sessions, not warm-ups, not demos, and they make me feel like a scientist.

Dr. Petrov picks up a cork and shows it to Alan, who looks overjoyed, remembering it from yesterday and the day before. Dr. Petrov allows him to test it with his beak, then takes it back.

"Alan, look. What toy?"

Alan thinks a minute, a sad puddle of yearning. "Blue," he says meekly. He did this yesterday, too. The cork is blue, but that's not what we're going for, and he knows it. I record his wrong answer.

It's like nothing else I've ever experienced, seeing a bird understand. So much intelligence and desire in that one square inch: eye, eye ring, a patch of feathers. Alan knows what Dr. Petrov wants; Alan knows also what he himself wants. How painful it must be to lack the words.

"No, Alan," Dr. Petrov says. "That is wrong. Cork. This is cork."

Then Dr. Petrov turns to me, and the show begins. He lifts the irresistible cork to the light, in front of my face.

"Violet, look. What toy?"

The method is called Model/Rival, based on the work of a German scientist and perfected by an American who Dr. Petrov calls "that woman in Cambridge." I play the "model" for the behavior Dr. Petrov wants the birds to imitate, and by doing it correctly, I become the "rival" for Dr. Petrov's attention, which ups the ante for the birds, who hate being ignored. Especially by him.

My job as the "model" is to slowly, enthusiastically, and clearly say, "Cork."

"That's right, Violet!" Dr. Petrov says. "Cork! Good job!"

I know it sounds stupid, but this fills me with joy. Dr. Petrov hands me the cork—my reward for answering correctly—and now my task is to act out a big crazy deal over the cork, make it as tempting and delectable as I can. Which is harder than it sounds. I mean, it's a cork.

Alan fans his feathers—he wants that cork something fierce. I coo over the cork for another few seconds, then it's time to switch roles. I hold up the cork to Dr. Petrov's face. "Dr. Petrov, look. What toy?"

"Cork," he says.

"That's right, Dr. Petrov! Cork! Good job!" Even more than when he praises me, I love when I get to praise him.

"What a wonderful cork," he says when I hand it over, "what a splendid, magnificent cork . . ." The gyrations he goes through make me laugh out loud—like the cork's a cross between Godiva chocolate and uncut heroin—but he's dead serious, and Alan is all in.

We swap roles again. "Violet, what toy?"

"Grrrch," I say. This is part of the deal.

"No, Violet. That is wrong." He turns his back on me for two excruciating seconds, as if I've gravely disappointed him. I feel the way Alan must, longing for Dr. Petrov's attention to return, which it does. "Try again, Violet. What toy?"

I make another nonsense bird noise, and Dr. Petrov scolds me again, turns his back. This part never goes the other way.

After three seconds, he turns and says, "Try again, Violet. What toy?"

"Cork."

"That's right, Violet! Cork! Good job!" And back and forth we go, over and over, until he finally turns again to the riveted Alan.

"Alan, look. What toy?"

Alan pauses, afire with yearning, poor guy. "Cuh," he says.

It will take a while for Alan to get the whole word, but "cuh" is a treatworthy start. "That's right, Alan!" Dr. Petrov says. "Cork! Good job!" And it *is* a good job: Alan knows the label now, though he can't quite say it. It takes practice, like learning a word in, say, Russian. The tongue must learn new ways to move.

Dr. Petrov surrenders the prize to Alan, who goes to town, shredding with gusto. As I note Alan's partially correct answer in the logbook, Dr. Petrov sits back like a man after a good meal. "He will have the whole label by the end of the week."

"I agree," I say. I'm ridiculously happy for Alan, for Dr. Petrov. For me. It's the little things; birds teach you that.

"Violet," Dr. Petrov says, "I meant to tell you. Mrs. Rocha is leaving us."

This is big news. Mrs. Rocha has been here so long that bits of yarn fluff turn up everywhere—on the bathroom sink, in the birds' toy box, squished between the pages of the reception log.

"She would like to do some grandmothering, apparently," he explains. "And to soak her bones in the Arizona sun." He makes bone-soaking sound like boot camp.

"She didn't say anything to me."

"Mrs. Rocha is a locked vault. Do you know what is inside that vault?"

"No."

"Yarn." He shakes his head. "You communicate well. You follow directions. Moreover, you understand the birds." He does not smile. "I wish to offer you her job."

I've been here just long enough to know what I don't know, which is everything. "I like *this* job," I tell him.

"You will continue to do this job."

"Plus hers?"

"What do you think Mrs. Rocha does all day?" he asks. "She keeps the schedule. She takes care of the finances, which are hardly worth noting. Occasionally she forces me into appearances and interviews. Otherwise, she occupies herself with blankets."

"She does a lot more than that, Dr. Petrov," I say. In fact, now that I think about it, she's been giving me more responsibility daily, tasks she claims to be too busy for.

"Mrs. Rocha provides steady ground beneath my feet," Dr. Petrov continues. "A trustworthy female who does not thwart me."

This all sounds weird and coded and maybe directed to somebody not on the premises. I know nothing about his personal life except that despite his wedding band, he can't have much of one—he's always here. He looks a bit stranded now, possibly misty-eyed, though it's hard to tell, since his eyes glint no matter his mood.

"Dr. Petrov," I say. "I didn't go to college."

"Neither did he," he says, meaning Alan. "But he's a good learner."

"Oh," I say. "Ha."

But he's not joking. "Do you like the birds, Violet?"

All I've done since getting out, it seems, is cry, and now I want to cry again. "Dr. Petrov," I tell him. "I kind of love them."

"Love." He shakes his head: wrong answer. "Ah, well," he says. "People must be people. Mrs. Rocha leaves in two weeks."

I got promoted to shift leader at Dunkin' Donuts when I was seventeen, which felt like a really big deal. But this.

"My name is Mikhail," he says. "Friends call me Misha."

You know how some men undress your body with their eyes? Misha undresses my face, and it takes some time, and believe me, it hits the target.

Alan has me deep in his sights. He looks relaxed, feathers smoothed, so handsome. *Don't be afraid, Violet*, he seems to say. *He's with me.*

"Misha," I say at last.

"That's right."

His name feels like chocolate on my tongue, and I taste it all day.

Around three-fifteen he comes into the Bird Lounge where I'm showering Ollie and waiting for the four-to-eight, a psych major who's always late. The noon-to-four left early with a headache, a.k.a. hangover.

"I'm going out," Misha informs me, car keys rattling. He takes a lot of meetings, all of them reluctantly. This the first I've set up, with a marketing professor. My idea: get the students to design a publicity campaign for the lab.

"Silly idea," he says.

"*Yummy*," Ollie croaks.

"Ollie thinks it's a yummy idea." I turn my back on Misha, giving Ollie a good spritz.

"Do not call him Ollie. He is your colleague, not your pet."

Ollie chortles and chirps, a signal that Misha has drawn nearer. I sense him as a humid warmth at my back. He says nothing, just hovers there, a humming presence so intense that Ollie senses my distraction and knocks the mister out of my hand with his beak. It clatters to the floor, and as I bend to retrieve it, Misha withdraws.

"Tomorrow, then," he says.

I turn once again to tend Ollie, hiding what must clearly show on my heating face.

"*Bye-bye,*" Ollie calls as Misha retreats from the Bird Lounge, shutting the door behind him with a soft click. I listen, my breath coming in short little gasps, as his footsteps move through the hallway and out to reception and disappear altogether. A minute later, I hear the loud clank of the outside door below me, and I rush into the Ob Room, where I find him below in the glorious sunlight, walking briskly to his car. Before he gets in he looks up. Fifty yards and a pane of glass between us, but our eyes meet in a shock of lightning. He's joggling his keys, lingering, as if to say, *Should I come back?*

Yes, I think, *come back,* but he gets into his car and drives away, leaving me fully ignited, my pulse in my ears. Of course I believe I've imagined it all. He has left me here in a state of helpless, sopping desire, which I don't yet understand might be the point.

At the end of the day, Mrs. Rocha comes into the locker room as I'm getting my things. She's got an afghan scrunched under one arm.

"Two weeks, Mrs. Rocha?"

She purses her bright lips. "I didn't tell you before because I don't want any boo-hooing."

Not until she says this do I realize how much I'll miss her. "You could've told me. I'm not a crier." This is the whoppiest lie I've told in my life.

"I don't like a fuss," she says. "We come, we go. This is life."

Mrs. Rocha is short and squat; she sits on a little stool near the door, and all I can think of is a fairy-tale animal, a hedgehog, maybe, imparting wisdom to the younger hedgehog learning the ways of the forest. "Dr. Petrov is helpless, as you no doubt have noticed," she says. "This place needs a woman to keep it afloat, always has."

"I'll miss you," I tell her. She's taught me a lot, Mrs. Rocha has, including how to knit and purl, a skill I never got the hang of in prison.

"Now, that's very sweet," she says, getting up. "I was going to wait until my last day, but again—tears."

"Again—not a crier."

"Good, then. Here you go." She hands over the afghan. "Think of me next winter when I'm soaking my bones in the Arizona sun."

Oh, it's a beauty: reds and golds with black edging, soft enough to have been knitted from clouds, like something you'd give a queen on her wedding day.

"Now, Violet," Mrs. Rocha says, snapping a Kleenex from a knitted box. "What did I just say?"

By the time I get outside, I'm still sniffling a bit. The afghan weighs enough that I decide to take the bus home, so I cross the street to wait. A woman who looks like a professor smiles at me.

"Promotion gift," I tell her.

The campus has livened up; it's the last week of May, summer sessions already starting. Everywhere I look, students of all ages cross greens and walkways with great purpose. Newly promoted, I can imagine myself someday among them, taking classes at night, studying weekends, maybe earning credit from my day job with Dr. Petrov. As this thought drifts through my head, one of the not-hurrying students catches my notice and brings a sound to my throat so alarming that the woman waiting with me subtly moves away.

He's crossing the grass between walkways, headed toward the building I just came from, his walk gut-punchingly familiar. *It's not him it's not him,* I whisper, and when the bus pulls up, I scramble to a seat near the back, *it's not him it's not him*, and at the last possible second, the bus cruising through the green light, I chance another look.

It's him. Troy. My ex-boyfriend ex-fiancé ex-future ex-everything. A feeling I can't name bends me over. Literally. I ride three stops with my face in Mrs. Rocha's afghan, and when I get off, I walk to my apartment, spread the afghan on my bed, and gaze down on this thing of beauty, this thing that is mine now, and like a bird learning a label, I repeat over and over, touching the colorful squares as if they composed the map of my life: You are here. You are here. You are here.

19

Harriet

As harriet rounded the corner of River Road, her phone rang. She pulled over next to the field, now purpled with tiny flowers, barbed wire sculpting the top of the rise.

"I have two minutes, Sophie," she said. "Book Club starts in a bit."

"Tell me what you're looking at."

"A flowery field in the first breath of summer. Which sounds poetic, but there's a prison on it."

"Ha." The line went quiet, then: "Tell me a Corinne story."

"Oh, that woman," Harriet said. "Sophie? Are you crying?"

"Luis left."

"Oh, honey."

"A hairdresser named Todd, Auntie. It couldn't be a worse cliché."

"You'll land on your feet, Sophie. You're exactly like your mother that way."

"Tell me again."

"You're exactly like your mother. Who would not have recommended a sexless union."

Sophie half laughed, a good sign. "It wasn't sexless, for your information." She sniffled. "Or a union."

"You can do better, Sophia Jane. That's from your mother." She checked her watch. "I'll call you later with however many Corinne stories you need." A good Corinne story—Harriet had hundreds—usually did the trick. For Harriet too. "And just for the record," she added, "I never liked him. His taste in music was appalling."

"Liar," Sophie said. "I love you."

Harriet was thoroughly searched on the way in—not a full pat-down, but close enough—which never happened. As she arrived at the unit, Sophie still on her mind, she found the Visitors' Room unavailable. Inside was a pale man in a blue suit, briefcase opened on the table, talking to Dawna-Lynn.

"Down the hall," barked the CO she privately called Stoneface. He directed her to the "computer room," a large, windowless supply closet made smaller by towers of storage boxes and defunct monitors.

The women had already assembled, wearing badges in three colors: green, yellow, red.

"Our status," Jacynta explained, flicking her green badge. "Minimum, medium, or maximum."

Harriet did not ask which was which, though she could guess. "You can remove them for Book Club, if you want."

"Not today," said Renee. "Big Balls in the house."

Just outside the thick glass door, Stoneface stood rigid as a totem. A flotilla of state officials, grim males in dark suits, were being led through the unit, an evaluation of some sort underway, everybody on edge.

"Gonna be ass-tight around here for a while," Shayna said. Her left eye was bruised and swollen. She and Jenny Big had red badges. Everyone else wore either yellow or green.

The women settled into the too-small space, and Harriet glanced around. "Well, it's a good day for Yeats," she told them. "My niece got her heart broken."

"Aw," Aimee said. "The gay guy?"

"How—"

Renee laughed. "Bookie, he listens to Adele."

Stoneface was watching her. Could he hear through the door? "Is Dawna-Lynn coming?" she asked.

"Lawyer meeting," Desiree said. "Motion for new trial."

A joyless snort from Marielle. "You know how many girls in here get new trials?"

"Desperation move," said Jenny Big. "Last couple years of a long haul, you get antsy."

"Motion denied," Shayna muttered, swiping at her bad eye. "Let's read."

Read they did. After experimenting with a few contemporary poets, they'd returned in a big way to the romantic lyricism of William Butler Yeats. From her years in the classroom, Harriet understood that any group, no matter how diverse, eventually acquired a personality; Book Club had decided they were misunderstood souls born to the wrong era, and William Butler Yeats was their proof.

As the officials moved in and out of eyeshot, following the warden in a parody of a college tour, Harriet introduced the day's first poem, "A Prayer for My Daughter," long but accessible, inviting murmurs of motherly understanding.

"*I have walked and prayed for this young child an hour,*" Dorothy read. "*And heard the sea-wind scream upon the tower . . .*"

Around the table they went, a reading relay, Shayna and Aimee declining to read by raising a finger, a pattern now agreed to and well established. One reader intuitively knew when to stop, the next when to resume, and whenever Shayna's or Aimee's turn arrived, whoever was next unconsciously paused a beat or two, as if acknowledging Shayna's and Aimee's presence in the reading of the poem.

"*May she become a flourishing hidden tree,*" Jacynta read. "*That all her thoughts may like the linnet be . . .*"

They nodded, soft-eyed, speaking and hearing a litany of wishes from parent to child. Even the world outside the door seemed to hush, nothing much beyond a low male rumble from the visiting officials.

She can, though every face should scowl
And every windy quarter howl
Or every bellows burst, be happy still.

In the final stanza, the women read more quietly, swapping off more quickly, and Harriet imagined their motherless children waiting at home, or in foster care, or, in Aimee's case, in the sweet hereafter.

Marielle asked, "What's a linnet?"

"It's a European songbird." The illustration Harriet had brought, from Lou's collection, was presently stuck in Security. "Lou knew a lot about birds," she said. "He knew a lot about everything. I just went along for the tick-infested hikes up one mountain and down another."

Desiree said, "He was trying to break you, Bookie."

"Hey, no dissing Lou," Jenny Big said. "Not his fault he liked fresh air."

"He was otherwise without flaw," Harriet said, but her joke felt hollow. She couldn't fathom the men these women had loved, and loved still, the type that threw cats and babies out of windows. How could that many bad men live in the world? How could so few have crossed her own path?

"You know what?" Kitten said, squinting down at the poem. "It kinda seems like Yeats wants his daughter to not have opinions."

"He doesn't want her to be *hurt* by her opinions," Dorothy countered, just as the door opened and in swaggered Dawna-Lynn, pink-cheeked and brimming. Red badge. Everyone looked up.

"My uncle Pete got me a decent lawyer," she announced. "He says felony murder was the wrong charge."

"Wait, wait, *who* says?" Brittie asked. "Uncle Pete, or the new lawyer?"

"The new lawyer," Dawna-Lynn crowed. "Who, unlike the old lawyer, is not an incompetent scum-sucking dickwad." There followed a murmur of assent from the women, most of whom believed they, too, had been wrongly convicted and poorly defended by incompetent scum-sucking dickwads.

"Heads up, Showtime," Kitten said as Dawna-Lynn sat next to her. "A linnet is a songbird, and Yeats might be a sexist."

"Shall we write?" Harriet said.

"We shall," Renee said, and in the remainder of their time, they wrote wishes for their own children—a life of ease and beauty—and read them aloud.

As Book Club ended and the women dispersed, Harriet flinched as she caught sight of Stoneface observing her from the door. Behind him stood Mr. Flinders, who asked to search her book bag. She waited, idly watching the women lining up for Noon Chow, Big Balls emerging from a tour of 3-Walk, everyone on edge.

"Prison," Flinders said, "is not a sorority." Then he let her go.

Harriet drove away in a gloom. *Prison is not a sorority*. But Harriet kept forgetting. Her small, accumulating transgressions made her not more wary but less, thwarting the very point of the rules, which was to force volunteers to keep retuning their radar. Wasn't that how every woman in Book Club got there, including her? Bit by bit, choice by choice? But really, where was the harm in the women knowing that she owned a cat? Named Tabsy? Who liked the east-facing sill?

Downtown, she found a parking space on the street, which improved her mood, and as she got out to feed the meter, she spotted Violet coming out of a bank.

"Harriet!"

Violet's obvious delight erased all the melancholy of the morning—the suits, the badges, the extra search.

"Hello, stranger," Harriet said. It had been a while—lately Violet spent all her time at work—but she looked shockingly well, her face alight.

"I've got the afternoon off," she said. "Dr. Petrov's at a conference."

"Then come with me to the bookstore," Harriet said. "I'm weaning them off Yeats."

"I don't . . ." She brushed back her hair as if it embarrassed her.

"You have nothing to be ashamed of," Harriet insisted. "You're not the one who lunged at a stranger like a deranged kangaroo."

"He didn't lunge," Violet said, "and he had his reasons." She wore well-fitted jeans and a bright, lime-green shirt with a scalloped neckline that cheered Harriet immensely.

"We all have our reasons. For everything. Come on." She cupped Violet's elbow, and Violet allowed herself to be walked to the store, where they found a whiskery cat in the window, gray and shaggy with fluffy white boots.

"Get a load of old fattypants," Harriet said. "If you want him, I'll vouch for you."

"I'm always at the lab. He'd be lonely." Violet tapped the window. The cat struggled to its feet and touched its nose to her finger. Violet smiled, and all at once Harriet saw what had changed: she no longer looked like an inmate. Harriet couldn't place why, exactly—likely a pileup of many things, beginning with a private place to sleep and ending with a good haircut. Surely the other women as well—Dawna-Lynn with her neck tattoos, stoop-shouldered Shayna, Dorothy with her brittle hair—would move through the world quite differently on the Outs. Violet had put on weight but moved so much more lightly.

She turned to Harriet now. "Bookie? Can a person get cancer from a broken heart?"

"Of course not. Where did you get that idea?"

Violet had large eyes, and every so often Harriet felt slightly thrown looking into them, a sensation not unlike standing at the top of a building and fighting an urge to jump. "There's a thing called broken-heart syndrome," she said, "when a person is so stressed by sorrow their heart blows up. And sometimes they get cancer."

Dear God. "I should think that would be rare, Violet. Extraordinarily rare."

"Rare isn't never," Violet said. "You said your father died right after your mother."

"Violet, my father was a chain smoker."

The cat jumped down and disappeared. Violet kept her eyes on the empty space.

"You belong among books, Violet," Harriet said, "and it's a free country." She pushed the door open, and to her relief, Violet followed. After a quick check for any sign of Frank Daigle, Harriet went to the counter, where Baker noted Violet's presence with an alarm so fleeting nobody but Harriet—and Violet, alas—could have caught it.

"This is my friend Violet," Harriet said. "She'll be helping me with my book selections today."

"Oh, totally," Baker said, lip ring wincing in the light. "If you need anything, give a holler."

Harriet made a beeline to Poetry, trailed by Violet, who was breathing so loud Harriet turned to make sure she wasn't fainting. "I'm sorry you left Book Club before we discovered poetry, Violet. It changed everything." She made a quick scan of the titles, pulling several volumes from the shelf for inspection. "I think the ladies like Book Club better now."

"We always liked Book Club," Violet said. "But we also liked being jerks about the books. Fake anger was part of the fun."

"Beats real anger."

"That was the whole point, Bookie." She turned her serious eyes on Harriet. "Ethan Frome wasn't gonna bite back."

The volumes in Poetry were slim- to medium-size for the most part, except for the occasional "collected works" of someone prolific and long-lived: Eliot, Frost, Pound.

"I don't see many women," Violet observed.

"The women were home, ironing shirts." Harriet paused. "That was a joke, Violet. Sort of."

"Oh. Ha."

Despite her twenty-two months, her talent for subtext, her occasional profanity, Violet struck Harriet as unskilled in the work of the world. Her time in prison had not quite released the religious chokehold in which she'd been raised. Harriet herself had led an unadventurous life, but you didn't reach the age of sixty-four without learning a few unhappy truths.

The cat appeared, waddling down the aisle toward them. "Look," Harriet said, "a tumbleweed."

"Hey, handsome," Violet said, an instant lightness rinsing her voice. She scooped up the cat with a little *oof* of effort. The cat swooned, and Violet buried her face in its fur.

Harriet picked out a book of sonnets, contemporary poems in an old-fashioned form. "My method," she explained, "is to leaf through lots of books until I find something that might crack Dawna-Lynn. She's the toughest nut."

"Good plan," Violet said, still holding the cat. "How are they?"

"Wearing badges."

Violet nodded. "Inspection. After a few weeks they kinda forget about it."

"Why don't they just *brand* them and be done with it?" Harriet said. "By the way, Jacynta would like you to know she's writing in iambic pentameter."

Violet let the cat go. "They know you saw me?"

"I hope that's all right."

"It's just . . . It's pretty crappy to hear about life on the Outs when you're still inside."

Point taken. Harriet said, "You're a kind person, Violet."

Violet looked startled. "It's just that I know how it feels."

Harriet turned to a book of poems by a contemporary woman poet, but the poems went for pages, speckled with crimes of punctuation and words like *interstitial* and *exigent*. The women preferred shorter poems. In comprehensible English.

Violet was paging through a book of poetic quotations, each of them ornately printed, one to a page. She said, "My badge was green."

"Well, you have a minimum-security heart."

"Does that mean good?"

"It means I don't want Dr. Parrot to hurt you."

"Misha would never hurt me," she said, flushing fiercely, and all at once Harriet knew.

Misha. Oh boy. She decided not to push it. Instead, she peered over Violet's shoulder to see the page. Maya Angelou: *You alone are enough*. Violet snapped shut the book, as if caught at something.

"Excuse me?" came a voice at the end of the aisle, and there was Frank Daigle.

"Mr. Daigle," Harriet said. It had been a month since she last saw him, that fleeting impression of sorrow amid the chaos of spilling tools and glass. It was still there, that sorrow, and something else, too, something warmer, reassuring; in any case, not at all frightening.

"It's Frank, please," he said. "Stay." He spread out his hands. "Stay right here. Please."

He disappeared, leaving empty air at the end of the stacks, Harriet unsure what to do. "Should we leave?" she said.

Violet set down the book. "No."

Before Harriet could make a move, back he came, carrying two cardboard boxes, one atop the other. They looked heavy. Harriet took a step back, bumping into Violet, who had not moved.

"Please," he said. He set the boxes on a Savor the Summer display.

Harriet recalled his age as sixty-eight, not terribly old, not these days. Silvery hair tamed into a thick crew cut, and a lean, almost boyish build. But he had the face of an old man, heavily etched with experience. She'd puzzled over his behavior in the weeks since, had turned it around and around, recalling that lowing sound as he held the glass, come to think, like a shield. She could only conclude that, after losing his wife in so gruesome a fashion, seeing Violet had kindled a fight response. Or was it flight?

"I've been apprised of your circumstances, Mr. Daigle, and I'm very sorry," she said, drawing herself up and shielding Violet, whose silence felt like a piece of furniture at her back. An armoire-sized shame.

"I can't imagine what you must think," he said. "It wasn't at all what it seemed."

"Nevertheless," Harriet said.

"No, it's all right," Violet broke in. "I understand."

"Please accept my apology," he said, patting one of the boxes. "I was told flowers are bad for Ecuadorean schoolchildren." The moment was drenched in paradox, for this same window-wielding creature had soft, deep-set eyes that emanated kindness, and a placid voice, pleasing to the ear.

Violet stepped into Harriet's way, seized one of the boxes, opened the flaps, and lifted the contents. "Oh my God," she breathed.

They were, in a word, exquisite. Each bookend was a perfectly proportioned, beautifully made silhouette of a cat, long and regal and burnished to a spiritual shine. The metal looked both hard and soft, heavy and light, a disorienting trick. This whole exchange was disorienting.

Violet opened the second box, tipping it to show Harriet her own gift, an identical set of shimmering cats.

"I made them myself," Frank said.

"How?" Violet asked.

"In my garage."

"No," Violet said. "I mean *how.*"

Quietly, he described the process. Because her uncle had been a machinist, Harriet knew what Frank meant by milling and boring and turning and brazing, but Violet clearly did not. She listened with parted lips.

As for Harriet, her reluctance loosened. He'd chosen the metal, drawn up plans, roughed out the shapes, coaxed a thing of beauty into being. There were worse ways to say I'm sorry.

"They certainly are beautiful," she heard herself say, "but I think it best not to accept."

"I accept," Violet said. She gave Harriet an unreadable look, gripping the bookends tightly enough to leave dents in her skin. "I want them."

Frank Daigle was a blusher and seemed to know it, which only made the moment more excruciating. Surely this man was harmless, a mild fellow who'd gone briefly berserk when confronted with his wife's—well, with her killer.

"Thank you, Mr. Daigle," Violet said.

They stood there, all three, for another awkward moment. Something happened in the air, a change so palpable that Harriet figured an explanation lay in the chemical properties of human emotion. As the air expanded, or contracted—it was definitely doing *something*—Violet said, "They wouldn't let me speak to you before the trial, Mr. Daigle. Or after. I would have. I wanted to. But your daughter said no."

"I figured that," Frank said. "Thank you for accepting." He hoisted the other box and looked at Harriet. "I didn't realize I was holding the glass. I wouldn't have hurt her. Or you."

Everything in Harriet was telling her to follow Violet's lead, to take the moment in a spirit of compassion. But now that she'd made her stand, she found herself unable to backtrack. Her fear was not physical, after all; she just didn't want the complication. She could hear Corinne mocking her: *Stop thinking and take the damn gift!* But what good could come from twisting up with an unpredictable man?

"You can put them back in the box," Frank was saying to Violet. "I've got paper there, for protection."

"I'd rather hold them," Violet said, and Harriet wondered, not for the first time, how hard it must be to keep your things in prison.

"Oh, sure," Frank said. "Let me get this out of your way." He whisked the empty box away, along with Harriet's unaccepted box, and then, thankfully, the moment ended. He left them standing in Poetry, silent.

"It was me behind the wheel, Harriet," Violet said. Her voice was quivering. "I know you'd prefer it to be otherwise."

"Of course I would," Harriet said. "But that doesn't mean—"

"You want me to be a better person than I am. Someone like you, someone good like you."

"Oh, Violet."

"I left her there, Harriet. I left that man's wife right where she was, thinking only to save myself, and now he's saying sorry." She clutched her bookends ever tighter. "*He* is saying sorry to *me*." Then she rushed down the aisle and disappeared.

After a moment, hearing the urgent jingle of the front door, Harriet wished Corinne back to life for a sisterly tête-à-tête, some ruthless wisdom Corinne would impart. What came to her instead was a vision of herself as a young woman, too young for her task, standing at a bedside in the family farmhouse, looking into her father's ravaged face.

She is holding a syringe. He has days, or weeks, maybe months more of spoon feeding and bed changing, and she is twenty-two years old, she has already nursed her mother through the end, and now here is her father, same bruised eyes and yellowed fingers. For a minute she stands over him, holding the syringe, too much morphine, heart thudding, five minutes, maybe ten. Until he opens his rheumy eyes and reads her mind. Reads her heart. She drops the syringe, undone by shame, then gentles a pillow beneath his balding, bruised, beloved head. He knows; he will die knowing. His own daughter, his favorite.

He was dead within hours, and she married Lou not long after, believing she needed saving. But had she really? Couldn't she have saved herself?

She gathered her things and hurried through Poetry and past Puzzles and Games and into the front of the store, where through the windows she spotted Violet outside, on the same bench where she'd comforted her in the first blush of May, a terrified ex-con with few prospects. Now it was June. Violet had come so far, and how Harriet hated to see her once again diminished. Her hand went to her heart in vicarious pain.

All at once, appearing like a sheltering cloud in the blinding sun, there was Frank Daigle, bending to speak to Violet in a way that put Harriet in mind of Lou with the girls, that same branching concern. She became aware of Frank's hands, large and marked, the hands of a machinist for sure.

"I love Frank," said Marnie, materializing at her shoulder. A couple of the other clerks had also gathered.

"I feel bad for that girl," the tall one, Robin, murmured.

"Me too," said Jake, the cubbyhole fellow who rarely ventured onto the floor. "But I feel worse for Frank."

"Imagine if you took a life."

"I know, right?"

"Even if you didn't mean to."

"I feel bad for both of them, honestly."

"She's so *skinny*. I mean, is that what happens when you kill someone? Do you stop eating?"

"She's stronger than she looks," Harriet said, facing them. "We all are."

"Next," Baker called from the counter.

Harriet handed over a book of poems by Maya Angelou. "I'll need eleven more," she said, as Baker examined it, back and front. "I trust it meets with your approval?"

"I'd go with Claudia Rankine," Baker said, ringing it up. "But Maya's okay. You buying that one, too?"

"Yes," Harriet said, handing over the book of quotes. As she set it on the counter, it opened to what could not possibly—could it?—be a random page. *Forgive everyone.*

20

Violet

AT MY TRIAL, WHICH LASTED six and a half days, Mr. Daigle's daughter—her name is Kristine Streit—stared me down like a snake thinking hard about lunch. My own sister was doing more or less the same thing, sitting there with my mother, who couldn't look up from her lap, not once except at the end of each day when they were leading me out.

Not that I blame Kristine Streit, I don't. But Vicki? When I was two and Vicki was five, my mother tried night after night to return me to my big-girl bed, but I crawled back to Vicki every time. She lifted the covers and I dove.

You think things like this last a lifetime, but they don't. The stork dropped big-mouth party-girl Vicki into the wrong family, is what happened. My mother preferred me, the reader, which Vicki figured out around age twelve, and that was that. If our motorcycle-riding dad had lived, Vicki would've been *his* favorite, and maybe every single thing would've turned out different.

My mother called me a born reader. *She's a born reader, that one.* I tore through just about every book in the Abbott Falls Public Library. The head librarian, Mrs. McHale, high red wig that looked like a hedge on fire, she was my favorite person from childhood. *Good for you, Violet*, she said whenever I checked out the maximum. My mother worked at a desk behind Mrs. McHale's—research, acquisitions, and events—and she blush-smiled every time Mrs. McHale told me *good for you*.

Mama was thinking: *Good for us.*

One time Pastor Rick caught me with a copy of *The Catcher in the Rye* and rebuked my mother in front of the congregation. Rebuking was Pastor Rick's big talent. It was Mama's week to bring snacks—delicate shortbreads that took hours to make, and he knew it. The congregation wasn't much, about forty families total, but this was my mother's tribe. He waved his pale little creep-hands and called her heedless, and worse, for allowing me to read a "writer of filth." Mama just bowed her head and took it. Nobody spoke up, not even her own sisters, as I gripped her hand and prayed for Pastor Rick's haybale hair to catch fire. That night, my mother slipped the "filthy" book under my pillow. *I also read this at thirteen*, she whispered, her breath so sweet in my ear. If you read with pure intention, she believed, then Jesus does not judge.

This was news to me. One: Mama had the guts to defy Pastor Rick, if only in secret. Two: Mama knew something about Jesus that Pastor Rick didn't.

When I started seeing Troy, I checked out a copy of *Our Bodies, Ourselves*. Well, I stole it. I didn't want my mother or Mrs. McHale to draw correct conclusions. And boy did that book come in handy, because Troy was a moron about protection. He believed—I am not kidding—that "pulling out" was an A-one perfect form of birth control. How about plus a condom, I said, and you'd think I'd asked him to pluck his eyebrows. What about diseases, I said, and he said aren't you a virgin? I didn't push it because I could not believe a boy like Troy, a boy other girls wanted, wanted me.

Surely Mama found *Our Bodies, Ourselves* under my bed after my arrest. Imagine knowing that your daughter is a manslaughterer and now a library thief as well.

I never wanted a trial. I wanted to plead guilty, but Mama said no, begged and cried, and Vicki and Aunt Linda and Aunt Pammy and the uncles said I could be proved innocent, a wayward girl under a spell, nobody judges a family for its wayward girl. Turns out, the brutal shame of a trial is worse than getting sent straight up. Your friends, your coworkers, your neighbors, your teachers, your congregation, perfect strangers—everybody tracking the lurid plot of a wretched story. A trial is its own punishment, and I deserved that too.

On the day of my sentencing, I felt a heat at my back that didn't feel like Vicki and didn't feel like my mother and didn't feel like Pastor Rick and didn't feel like a reporter. I turned, whip-quick, just long enough to catch the forever burning vision of Mrs. McHale, her hedge wig and kind, jowly face and heart-punched disappointment. All those times she'd walked me through the stacks with her clickity heels and high creaky voice, fake nails tapping the spines as she picked this book or that. When they led me out that day, I glimpsed her again, whispering something to my mother, caressing her back. *She made a mistake*, is what I hope she said. *You raised a good girl, Eleanor*.

This was just after Mr. Daigle's daughter, Kristine, made a victim statement, pin-drop quiet in the courtroom. Hard as it was to face her wet and heaving self as she announced to God and everyone what I'd done to her family, I welcomed every syllable. This broken daughter was my true and necessary punishment, the thing I deserved more than prison. The gallery vibrated with pity, and I was glad.

Green was her favorite color.

She loved without condition.

Everything Kristine Streit said about her mother I could have said about my own.

This is where my thoughts have landed when Mr. Daigle finds me outside the bookstore. *You alone are enough*, goes that Maya Angelou quote, and she could not be more wrong. Ask anyone in my not-speaking-to-me family.

His big hand lights on my shoulder. "Are you all right, Miss Powell?"

Of course I'm crying—*again*, and on the same bench, too, snot on my sleeve. Mr. Daigle fishes one of those giant man-hankies from his pants pocket. "It's clean," he says.

I take it, wipe my eyes. "I'm the one who should be asking are you all right."

His resting hand feels like one of the birds, a lightly weighted warmth. It stays there as I mop my face with Mr. Daigle's man-hanky.

"Can I tell you something?" he asks.

He wants something of me. Whatever it is, I'll disappoint him. "Maybe not right this minute?" I say, still mopping my face.

Though it's hot and sunny, Mr. Daigle's wearing one of those cotton, old-guy zip-up jackets, which he takes off and shawls over me. He pats my shoulder again, and when he takes away his hand, it feels like a vast, epic loss. "Do you mind if I sit here, Miss Powell?"

"I don't mind." I don't know what to do with the hanky. "Call me Violet."

"Frank."

He gently takes the hanky and returns it to his pocket, which strikes me as the height of chivalry.

"I guess you can tell me now," I say, bracing myself. He's going to give me his sorrow, and it's going to be heavy, and it's going to be mine.

"You're young," is what he says instead. "You have time to make something good of your life."

"I hope so. I'm trying."

"I never intended to scare you, Violet," he says. He regards me for a long, painful moment. "I'm very sorry."

"I wasn't scared," I tell him. "I'm the manslaughterer, not you. I think you were trying to get away from me."

"Not you," he says. "The memories."

It strikes me that he, too, might have nightmares. How could I have been so selfish not to think of that until now?

"I'm not much of a drinker," he says. He adjusts the collar of his shirt, which is soft and plaid and reassuring. "I like a beer on a hot day, but that's about it."

"I'm not much of a drinker, either," I tell him. "Except for that one time."

I close my eyes, and Lorraine Daigle's car rises up to smack me in the face. I swerve in time, and she doesn't, and the world erupts anew.

"I think about her every night before going to sleep," I tell him. "Every night, Mr. Daigle. Please know that I won't ever forget her."

"What I'd like you to know, Violet," Mr. Daigle says, "is that I myself had a period of time, back along. First an extra beer, then two extra, then a whiskey chaser, then another before bed. It sneaks up on you."

He's one of those people who know how to keep eye contact without being weird. He's just kind of there, not pinning you in place but allowing you to exist without feeling judged.

"One night," he says, "I watched a Pats game—are you a football fan?"

"My ex-fiancé was a wide receiver."

"Well, this was a late game, a real barnburner against Miami that I watched in a bar where nobody knew me. Why the bartender didn't cut me off I can't say. Different era. I drove home from Brunswick seeing double."

Suddenly Harriet's here, a little throat-clearing, that soapy scent, store bag crinkling. I feel her standing there, watching the two of us. "I was telling Violet a little story," Mr. Daigle says.

"Don't let me stop you," Harriet says, clearly not going anywhere till she knows what's what.

"I dinged the mailbox pulling into the driveway," he says, "but other than that, no damage. Thirty-four miles drunk, and I didn't hit anything. Or anyone. I drove home, and nothing happened. Not because God loves me more than the next guy, not because I was gainfully employed, a good husband and father, an upstanding citizen and therefore not a 'real' drunk. Nothing happened only because I was lucky."

He places his hand on my shoulder again, over his own jacket; the weight reaches me under the cloth. I feel his forgiveness.

"I had no business driving, but I drove anyway," he says. "It's a finer line between any of us than we usually care to think."

Harriet sits on the other side of me, though she doesn't say anything.

"When the cops got there," I say, my head filling with needles, "we were getting ready to run."

"I know," Frank says. "I was at the trial."

"She was alive for at least a minute, Mr. Daigle," I confess. "They said instantly, but it wasn't, quite. I don't understand how you can even look at me." I loosen my grip on the bookends, ready to give them back. "I can accept your apology, which isn't necessary. But I honestly don't know how to accept your forgiveness."

"Apologies require acceptance, so I thank you," he says, nudging the bookends back into my lap. "But as I understand it, forgiveness flows in one direction only."

If you've never happened upon a man whose wife died because of you but finds a way to shine with mercy, I'm sorry. His face has bitty scars from hot metal chips, and even those bitty scars strike me as beautiful, and I know this will sound ridiculous, I mean, I know it's ridiculous, but right in this peculiar moment, I feel like I'm meeting my father. Not that I think Frank Daigle is my actual father-who-I-don't-remember. It's more a feeling like if I could have known my father, we would have had moments like this.

I look down at my bookends. "These must have taken a long time."

"Forty-four years," he says. "That's how long I plied my trade, and you never stop learning." He reaches out to pet one of them, leaving a print. "I never made a likeness before. Not much call for machine parts shaped like cats." He points out a copper-colored stripe along the cat's feet and tail, like the enchanting stripes on a real cat.

"Mr. Daigle?"

"It's Frank."

I bow my head, nearly to my knees, cradling the bookends in my lap. "Frank. If you were in my place, you wouldn't have run."

"We can't know these things," he says. "I don't know what I'd have done in your place, and thank God for that."

I stay bowed over, and they speak over me, Harriet murmuring something I don't quite catch, Frank murmuring back. I'm a sniveling mess in the hot cave of Frank's coat, but at least I've got him on one side and Harriet on the other, and though I can't hear what they're saying, I know it's not bad. It's about me, and it's not bad, which is how I screw up the guts to ask them to help me, to please please help me.

"Help you what, dear?" says Harriet.

"I need . . ." My head is thundering, and I speak into my knees. "I need . . ."

Right now Frank and Harriet feel exactly like guardian angels, which Pastor Rick said is not revealed in Scripture but fuck him.

"You need what, Violet?" Harriet asks. "What do you need?"

"I need my mother," is what comes out, and after a few small questions, a few mild words back and forth, Frank and Harriet agree that needing one's mother is a good and natural thing.

Frank will drive.

21

Frank

THE DRIVE TO ABBOTT FALLS took an hour and a half, a passage of time that, to Frank, felt edged with magic, plucked from the normal course of events, as if they were traveling not by car but by snow globe. Violet in the back with the bookends in her lap; Harriet next to Frank, her profile, when he chanced to peek, pleasant and reassuring. She, too, said little, and Frank didn't mind. He'd spent most of his life with talkers.

"Look at that pretty tree," Harriet said.

They all looked: an ancient oak in somebody's field, its intricate architecture reaching for an empty sky.

"There's another one," Violet said.

"Where?"

"Other side."

"Oh. Oh my gosh, yes."

He was reminded of car trips in his long past, playing Twenty Questions with Kristy while Lorraine wrote cheerful "travel notes" on their map. Those sweet times felt strangely nearby, relivable. He felt landed and at peace.

About an hour in, Violet came to life. He learned about the scientist she worked for, about the parrots and their charming ways. She began to remind him of a young Kristy: enthusiastic, curious, a tad gullible. He had little use for God these days, and yet a feeling came over him, so urgent and instructive as to be nearly a physical voice: *You belong exactly here, exactly now.* He hoped that Harriet, despite her reasonable distrust of him, felt the same.

The western part of the state—a series of factories along the Androscoggin River—arrived as a surprise. They descended into the bowl of a rural-industrial valley ringed by lush hills. In time they crested a long, upsloping stretch of road, and into their sights appeared a massive paper mill, its stacks heaving huge white clouds into an already billowing sky. A railroad track cut through the thickness of trees. Stretching the length of several football fields, the mill yard shone with grand pyramids of cut wood and other, neater stacks of slimmer, longer, de-branched trees.

"Turn here," Violet said. "Over the bridge."

Frank crossed the bridge over the Androscoggin, accosted by the smell of sulfur. He imagined a young Violet growing up here, a devout child walking to church with her mother and sister in the commanding shadow of industry. The mill seemed almost to breathe, and surely those who lived near such immensity often felt small.

"This is it," Violet said. "My hometown."

He glanced at Harriet and then into the rearview mirror. Violet was gawking at the river, the smokestacks, the little town hall, the clapboard library, the modest houses one after another, taking it in with such love and longing he had to look away. He continued another mile or so along the eastern bank of the river.

"Can you turn here first?" Violet asked. "And drive slow?"

He did as she asked, glancing alternately at Violet in the rearview and at Harriet beside him. He was keenly aware of her, though his blood went quiet. The drive north had righted something in him, calmed an unease that had been present since the trial.

Like Frank, Harriet kept an eye on the back seat, and when he felt the startling pressure of her hand on his arm, he slowed the car, creeping past a house that had riveted Violet's attention: a shabby two-story with a lopsided porch. It looked occupied but not loved.

"Can you stop?"

He did. Violet got out, considered the house for a few seconds, got back in. "Okay," she said, and that was all. "Take the next left and keep going for a while."

Frank obeyed, and within ten minutes they came upon a small cemetery built on a rise. The grass was thick and freshly mowed, the entrance paths neat and wide, heavily graveled. He wished the cemetery crew would show up so he could tell them: nice work.

"Here," Violet said.

Frank guided the car between two stone pillars, crackling along the path until Violet asked him, quietly, to stop.

He pulled over. No one spoke. The cemetery settled around them, green and silent. Violet stirred in the back seat, gathering up a bouquet of roses, richly red. It had been Frank's idea, a quick stop at a supermarket, and he was glad; he turned around and smiled. "Just wave us over if you need something."

She got out and headed across the grass, turning once to look at him. He wondered if she was thinking of the courtroom, how their eyes had met then. The stone she found was modest, a plain granite slab in a row of similar stones. He watched her kneel.

"I don't suppose your parents are still living?" Harriet said.

"My mother died when Kristy was a baby," he said, watching Violet lay the flowers down. "My father got early Alzheimer's not long after. Took his time, but he still died young." *You married a bully, son,* his father had blurted, pre-diagnosis, at Frank and Lorraine's tenth-anniversary party. This outburst in his taciturn father turned out to be the earliest sign.

"What about you?" he asked.

"Same," Harriet said. "Mother first, then my father not long after. I've outlived both their life spans now."

"Me too."

"I used to feel a little bit guilty about it."

"Me too."

Harriet said, "Our parents got so little time, and we got so much."

"So far," he said, and Harriet laughed.

"I'm sixty-four," she told him, "but I don't feel it."

"I thought you were younger."

"Then you'd be the first."

Her eyes crinkled in that way he liked. She knew he was fibbing, and that he knew she knew. This knowledge animated the space they shared.

"I'm glad you agreed to come along," he said. "I didn't think you would."

"You might've been planning to murder Violet with your tools and whatnot."

"You didn't think that," he said, alarmed.

"No." Her face changed. "Oh, look at that poor thing."

Violet was tracing her fingers over the letters on the stone.

"I'm glad to be here for her," Harriet said.

Again, that feeling of being in a foretold moment. He'd felt this way, he realized, since the first time he'd seen Harriet walk into the store, girlishly swinging her pocketbook from one finger.

Violet had arranged the roses on a patch of grass so dry it looked white. The contrast was startling and beautiful.

"Roses in the snow," Frank said.

"Aha," Harriet said. "Saint Juan Diego."

"You know the story?"

"It was Sister Esther's favorite."

"For me it was Sister Mary Philippa," he said. He'd been a second grader in need of magic, and the story thrilled him. The Blessed Mother filled the peasant-saint's cloak with roses, in December, to prove his story of apparition. Little Frank couldn't get over it—roses in winter! In a time long before flower shops! The way Violet laid the roses down reminded him that he'd once believed in miracles.

Harriet said, "Violet thinks her mother died of a broken heart. Imagine thinking that."

"My guess would be cancer," Frank said. "She looked ill at the trial."

At the mention of the trial, Lorraine elbowed into the space between them.

"Do you pray, Frank?" Harriet asked. Her hair, backlit by the sun, looked nearly golden.

"Lapsed," he said.

Harriet sighed. "Me too. I suppose most of us are by now."

"Well, it's hard to square a lot of it."

"I agree," she said, "but when my husband was sick, I rediscovered the rosary. It's immensely comforting even if you don't believe."

"Old Catholics die hard," Frank said.

She had a sweet laugh. "Lou was an atheist who found Catholic guilt quite alluring."

Just then, a freshly waxed Buick with a dealer plate rolled into the graveyard through the parallel entrance. The Powell headstone lay equidistant between the two paths, Violet in her lime-green shirt a bright blot on the solemn ground. Two women, one young and one not, got out of the car.

"My goodness," Harriet said. "Are they headed for the same grave?"

"The young one is Violet's sister," Frank said, on alert now. "I recognize her from the trial."

He observed the unfolding scene with a knifing pity: Violet rising to her feet, then a standoff of sorts, some gesturing on the part of the older woman—Violet's aunt, Frank supposed, a rickety blonde in a black tank top that exposed her sunburned arms. She clutched a small white purse that she used as punctuation. The sister, a redhead, stood with her arms dangling, ghostly pale and expressionless in a crisp blue top and a flowing, shroud-white skirt. The aunt appeared to be seething about sin and repentance, though from the car Frank caught the harangue only in mouthfuls.

"Should we—" Harriet began, and Frank didn't wait for the rest. He got out and hurried across the grass, thankful to hear the swishing of Harriet's slacks just behind him.

"Let me say goodbye, Aunt Pammy," Violet was pleading. "I don't want anything from you."

"If it's money you can forget it."

"I wasn't even going to stop by your house, how would I ask you for money?"

"I gave you money before," the aunt said, her eyes rabbit red and squinting. "Or did you forget? You turned it right over to Troy, didn't you, so Romeo could fix his chariot and elope with Juliet behind our backs."

"Aunt Pammy—"

"Quite the fairy tale," the aunt said. She had a hard, bony face and looked like a smoker. "Yessirree, it's one for the books."

The sister appeared to be holding her breath; Frank couldn't recall her name.

The aunt was on a roll. "I have asked Jesus to forgive me for my own hand in your sweet mother's death. If only I would of refused to give you money—" Her face puckered, but she managed to finish: "If only I would of refused, that shitbox car would be in a junkyard where it belongs, and my darlingest sister would be alive." She wiped her eyes with the knuckles of one fist.

Violet said, "Aunt Pammy, it's not your fault, you had nothing to do with it, nothing."

"Don't you tell *me* what's what. I know what's what." She bent to snatch up the flowers Violet had laid on the grave.

"Those are for Mama," Violet said.

"They're gonna die, Violet," the aunt snarled. "And turn black. And guess who's gonna have to pick up a bunch of dead black roses?"

Violet paused. "You, I guess."

"Darn straight." She handed the roses to the sister, who looked stricken.

"How did you know I was here?" Violet asked.

"Eddie takes me to visit Eleanor every single day," the aunt said. "When he's on day shift, your sister takes me. That's how it so *happened*." She jabbed her purse like a fencer. "Your mother was the type of person you love forever and no day feels right until I talk to her."

The sister, barely audible, said, "Becca Frye saw you stop by the house."

Violet had shrunk like a furled leaf, her shoulders up around her ears. He wanted to scoop her up and carry her to safety, but thought it best to let her stand her own ground.

"I pray for you every night, Violet," the aunt said. "That's the truth. I beg God for the strength to forgive you, I do. But no answer comes." She knuckled her eyes again. "No answer comes."

Vicki, that was the sister's name. She'd sat with the mother over the days of the trial, a contained vessel of rage, her hand curling around the mother's shoulder. The aunt must have been the other woman at the trial, the one in the hat. All these women; Frank knew to be careful.

"I have a right to be here, Aunt Pammy," Violet said.

"That's between you and God."

"Give me five minutes. Please."

Violet made the sound a person makes when trying not to cry. Frank consulted Harriet, who spoke with her eyes: *She's strong enough.*

"Pastor Rick says Jesus must forgive us before we forgive ourselves," the aunt informed one and all. "Maybe you should wait for Jesus, Violet, before you take it upon yourself."

"I did wait for Jesus," Violet said quietly. "He never showed up."

Frank watched in a kind of awe as Violet suddenly straightened her shoulders, facing her family like a forgiven person. She didn't have to wait for Jesus, or her aunt, or that snake of a pastor; she could do the job all by herself.

"Pastor Rick would say to wait some more." The aunt's voice sounded like turned milk.

"That's good advice," Violet said—quiet, steady—"from a man who sticks his fingers up ladies' privates."

The aunt's rabbit eyes flew open. "How dare you! How dare you tell stories on a man of God to take the spotlight off yourself!"

"It's not stories."

"It is, and you know it."

Frank felt a little sick over the turn this was taking, but also absurdly proud of Violet for not backing down.

"What I know," Violet said, "what I *know,* is that Pastor Rick said having sex with him would bring me closer to God."

The aunt gasped, mouth agape. The sister, Vicki, stared at the ground, her rosy mouth shut tight and trembling.

"Don't worry, Aunt Pammy, I didn't do it," Violet said. "Is that why God hates me?"

"You take that back, Violet Powell."

Violet shook her head. "You can't take back the truth."

Frank could sense Harriet nodding. They were a team now, the three of them united against God and Pastor Rick and Violet's stingy family.

Suddenly the aunt aimed her flaming attention on Frank. "Who the heck are you? The parole officer?"

"Maine doesn't have parole," he said, mightily controlling his anger. "Not that Violet would need it." Frank looked straight into the aunt's haunted face. "And I can't help but wonder what your pal Jesus would make of you right now."

"Ex*cuse* me?" The aunt's neck rose from the rack of her shoulders like a heron sensing prey. The sister shrank like a baby turtle the heron planned to eat.

"Whatever she may have done," Frank said, "surely this young lady deserves a moment with her mother."

"Who asked you?"

Then Harriet chimed in: "His name is Frank." To Frank, who was fast losing his already shaky faith in the essential goodness of the human species, her voice came as a balm.

"It's the husband, Aunt Pammy," the sister whispered, but in the empty graveyard, her words carried. "We should go."

"What husband—" the aunt began, and in a flash, all righteousness dropped from her face, her neck, her shoulders; Frank could see gravity at work, and how that gravity revealed the ravages of grief.

The aunt's tight lips parted, and she took two breaths: one thousand one, one thousand two. "You're the husband?"

"I am."

Thoroughly disarmed, the aunt just stood there, clearly at sea, unable to properly digest this information. "I didn't recognize you, Mr. Daigle."

"Understandable."

"You look well." She swallowed two or three times, squishing the purse as if defending it from marauders. "I'm very sorry for your loss."

"Thank you," Frank said. "I'm very sorry for yours."

The aunt made a tiny, mewling sound somewhere between a word and a not-word, then abruptly turned to stalk back to the car. The sister thrust the flowers into Violet's hands and scurried to catch her aunt.

"Vicki," Violet called.

The sister halted midstride, doubled back at triple speed, gripped Violet in a ferocious, nearly violent embrace. This was goodbye; Frank could see it in the sister's grief-beaten face. She had made her choice, and it would live as a nail in her gut for the rest of her days. He felt a gush of sympathy as she gulped and turned, the crushed flowers dropping, and tottered back to the car on her spindly shoes. The car backed out the way it had come in, made a two-point turn, and headed toward town.

"So," Violet said. "That's my family." She petted the top of her mother's stone. "We weren't always like this."

"Shall we leave you here with her?" Harriet asked.

Violet nodded, and Frank shepherded Harriet back to the car, moving slowly, eyeing the various monuments as he walked. It was a classic Maine immigrant mill town—Diconzos and Murphys and Vitkuses and Thibodeaus lying in great number beneath a variety of memorials, some blunt and emotionless, others ornate to the point of theatrical. Lorraine's headstone, at Kristy's request, had been richly filigreed with weeping angels. What did people do at their dead wives' graves? Make declarations? Deliver news? Frank had only one question: *What did I do wrong?*

"Good God," Harriet fumed, once they were back in the car. "I wanted to pull that woman's lungs out through her throat."

Frank turned to her. "I'd take five minutes in an alley with the pastor."

"No jury on earth," she said.

Violet had salvaged the crushed flowers, again dropped to her knees, and appeared to be conversing with her mother. And possibly her father, Michael, whose name appeared above Eleanor's.

"Oh, I could have punched her," Harriet said. Her cheeks pinked up irresistibly. "Really. I could have."

He glanced out the window, all those graves, all those lives with their chances used up. "She's more to be pitied, I suppose. The young one, too. Especially her."

"Well," Harriet said, softening. "Yes."

For a while all went quiet. Frank thought about turning on the radio, but in the end preferred the silence. Next to him, Harriet gave a little sigh. He caught the scent of hand cream or body lotion, something pleasing and feminine. He felt comfortable, and surprised to feel that way. She was unexpectedly easy to be near.

Then, as if they'd been conversing for hours, she said, "After Lou died, I ate tuna-fish sandwiches for a month." He turned to her; she was watching Violet at the grave. "I'm talking breakfast, lunch, and dinner, one tuna-fish sandwich after another, white bread, iceberg lettuce. And water. That's it. For a month. Grief is a strange beast."

Frank had mourned Lorraine despite her betrayal. They'd been married for so long, and they had Kristy between them. But to call it grief would be not quite right.

"At the same time," Harriet said, "I was undone for less time than I expected. A new life arrived after Lou."

For Frank, a new life had not arrived, and it had not occurred to him to seek one. What if this was it? This, today?

"It took some time," Harriet added, "years, honestly, for me to stop feeling bad about liking my life."

"I wouldn't have guessed that," he said. "Still waters."

"Quite the contrary, Frank. I'm an open book." She shifted to face him directly; her eyes were large and intelligent, and he felt seen through. "Will you do me a favor?"

"Yes." That sparrow in his chest woke right up. "Of course. Anything."

"If I ever have to face my spiteful family with the worst thing I've ever done, I would really, really like you to be there with me."

She was reading him, reappraising. He felt like the cat in the bookstore window. "Happy to," he said, and her smile warmed him.

Violet returned. She got into the car, wordless, and buckled up. Frank backed into the main road, headed again toward town. As they left the valley and drove south, he heard a meek "thank you" from the back seat.

"You're welcome," Frank said, and Harriet said it, too, and that was it for conversation. They made the return drive in silence. Frank didn't mind; that snow-globe feeling came back, for the silence did not feel charged or heavy but merely necessary.

"Where can I take you?" he offered as they arrived back in Portland. It was suppertime now, or past, daylight beginning its first fade, in that slow way of summer.

"Can you drop me at the university?" Violet asked.

He did. She picked up her bookends.

"Thank you for these," she said. "I've never owned anything this beautiful."

He hardly knew what to say. "They put together pretty good," he managed, and waited as she walked down the paved path to the old science building and let herself in.

Now they were alone and the silence changed. "Next stop?" he said.

"I live on Belmont, but I left my car downtown."

"I'm just over on Chenery. Funny we never ran into each other."

"Maybe we did and never noticed."

"I would have noticed," he said.

She laughed brightly.

They reached her car quicker than Frank wished. He pulled into an illegal spot just behind hers, engine idling. He thought about asking her to dinner—he was hungry, and so must she be—but this day had been fraught and strange, and he had no clear sense of his standing.

"Not that it's my business," he said, "but I'd like to know how Violet makes out."

Harriet thought it over. "Give me your phone."

"I don't carry it with me."

She dug into her purse, tore a page from a small notepad. He watched her write down a number—neat, even script. "Do you want mine?" he asked. Hoped.

"My phone's out of juice."

He jotted his own number and handed it over. "Aren't we the tech wizards," he said.

"Aren't we, though." She smiled, clicked shut her purse, retrieved her bags, and got out. Before shutting the door, she leaned in. "A lot of men in your situation wouldn't have done this today, Frank. I judged you quite harshly."

"I scared you," he said.

"Not really," she said. "Not in retrospect." She shrugged prettily. "The problem with retrospect is it never shows up beforehand."

He laughed with her, just a little, enough to match her.

"Anyway," Harriet said. "You were kind today."

"The girl needs elders, is how I look at it."

"That's exactly what I was thinking on the ride back," Harriet said. "Exactly that."

"Well," Frank said, unable to believe his own words, "maybe we could do something all together sometime. An outing."

"An outing, yes, how nice."

They made no further inroad on this hazy plan, though Harriet did linger a moment. "I'll take my apology after all," she said, glancing into the back seat.

"I'd be obliged." Frank got out, rounded the car, and retrieved her bookends. Handing over his apology at last, he felt like a boy, jangling with nerves.

"I had a good time," she said, "which sounds odd, I know."

"Not to me."

He watched her clip smartly away toward her own car, and the day was done.

Tomorrow, though: tomorrow was already a wonder-in-progress, a gift unwrapping, as if Frank, too, had just been released from prison.

22

Violet

PRISON AGES YOU. EVEN ONE night takes a toll, and I spent 668 nights there. After seeing Vicki and Aunt Pammy, I feel once again like prison me—the manslaughterer who took the life of a kindergarten teacher and then killed her own mother with grief.

The me who went to dinner at Harriet's, who bought undies with lace, who got a job at a bird lab and fell stupid-crazy in love with a scientist and met sociable parrots who didn't know the things I'd done and wouldn't care if they did—*that* me burned back to ash when Aunt Pammy said *no answer comes*. As if God, wherever he is, doesn't know my name. As if God, when Aunt Pammy begs him every night to guide her path to forgiveness, says to her, *Violet who?*

So I don't ask to be dropped at my apartment. I don't invite Frank and Harriet up for a pot of noodles with butter and salt, which doesn't sound like much, but I've kinda perfected it. Why don't I invite them? Because at this moment, being driven back home by two unreasonably nice people, I am prison me, and my name is No Answer Comes, and No Answer Comes does not invite people up for buttered noodles.

I ask to be dropped at the lab instead, hoping they'll think I have duties. Obligations. Like the birds might die without me. Without my lab coat, I try to look qualified: proper posture, even weighted down with my purse and the bookends. Behind me, Frank's car idles at the curb as he and Harriet wait to "see me in" safely. That's something people their age do and exactly how they say it. Which is kind of unbearable, if you want to know: after a whole day of showing nothing but kindness and then not being invited up for supper, they still insist on "seeing me in."

Frank would've liked the noodles. Harriet would've pretended to. I'm glad to know that much about them. That tiny fact.

The trick is not too much salt and not too little. Which takes intention. Maybe that's what people mean when they say they cook with love.

The building's unlocked, the muted back-and-forth of night courses wafting from the classrooms. There's a long bench by the elevator where students sit during class breaks, and who do I see there but Troy. Not a glimpse from a bus window but a here-and-now, gut-kicking meet-in-person. I feel like a train derailing.

"Hey," he says, getting up. He doesn't even look surprised.

"Have you been following me?"

He shrugs. "I know you work upstairs."

As I breeze past, he catches me by the sleeve. "Come on, Violet. I haven't seen you in three years."

I take a second to compose myself, to just stand here like a normal person, to pretend I'm not thinking of the hissing car, the gasping woman, the shock of Troy's grip on my arm. He looks good, I'm sorry to say. All that shiny hair. Still working out, tee shirt one size too small.

"You're taking summer classes?" I ask him.

"Yeah." I forgot about his eyes, the deep amber brown of a begging dog, thoroughly misleading. "The professors here suck," he informs me.

"I thought you were in your uncle's store."

"He wants to promote me to buyer, but first I need a degree."

"No you don't."

"It was my dad's idea. A trick to get me back in school."

"I guess it worked."

"Not really. I buy my term papers." He seems to think this is funny. He folds his arms high on his chest to show his idiotic biceps. Jacked-up guys were never really my thing, too much time in front of a mirror. I never told Troy this, but now I do.

He drops his arms, scowling. "Does your boss know you did time?"

"It's not a secret."

"Maybe he thinks it's hot." He shows his teeth, which look whitened, like he thinks he's a movie star now.

"Fuck you, Troy." Now I'm really moving, just short of a run. The hallway is empty, and I hate that my footsteps sound scared, because they're not.

He calls after me, trotting to keep up. "Come on, Violet, stop."

I stop. "What do you want?"

"Nothing." He lowers those fringed, girlish eyelashes. "I'm sorry, that's all."

"Sorry about what? Hooking up with Becca Frye the second I got sent up? Insulting me just now? Or being a rotten person in general?"

"Jesus, Violet. I just said I was sorry."

I shake my head, in no mood for this. "You were the first name on my visitor list, Troy. I put you ahead of my *mother*."

Of course he ignores this. "I hope prison didn't fuck you up," he says. "Really."

"What are you imagining? Lesbian rape in the shower?"

He smirks; that's exactly what he's imagining. "Prison," I tell him, "was boring and stupid and soul-crushing. It made me feel just as worthless and invisible as you made me feel. So I'd say it didn't fuck me up any worse than I already was."

Now his face does that familiar *baby, please, baby* thing, and I want to smash his mouth with my fist, straight through teeth and bone. "I thought we could be friends again," he says.

He actually I'm-not-kidding says this. I once thought his arms meant home, that his body was my haven. How could I have been so dumb, and for so long? Even now, he looks ready to receive love and comfort with zero consequences because his whole life prepared him for nothing but.

"You are the worst friend I ever had," I tell him. "There's plenty of competition, but you win. Not only did you not visit me even once, you didn't come to one single minute of my trial."

"I was advised not to by my lawyer," he whines, "who my dad spent thousands on."

"Guess she was worth it." In the end, the football star got charged with nothing: not leaving the scene of an accident, not furnishing alcohol to a minor, not a single contributing this or accessory that, and I said not a word against him despite my mother's pleas, Vicki's threats, my own lawyer's doomsday speeches.

I get up close to his face, catching a spicy whiff of him, and for a second I'm knocked off my game, inhaling him, my mind reeling backward, a sensory memory of smoky hair, sweat on sweat, tumbling sheets drenched with us.

I shake it off, speaking way too loud: "Do me a favor, *friend*. If you see me on campus, pretend I don't exist. After three years of practice it shouldn't be that hard."

"Hey," he says, louder still. "This was no fucking picnic for me, either."

I stare him down. "Please, Troy, tell me how not-a-picnic it was for you."

"You wrecked my life, Violet. That's for real."

I'm stunned speechless, but he means it. His face darkens. I check out the exits as he grabs my arm. Again.

"Ow. Let go."

"Why the fuck did you take the wheel?"

"You *told* me to."

"You knew better and you did it anyway."

He is correct. I knew better and I did it anyway. I wanted to please him, and Lorraine Daigle paid for my desire.

"You know what I never did, Troy?" I wrest my arm away as a knot of rage forms in my throat. "I never blamed you. My lawyer wanted me to have been *coerced*. My lawyer wanted me to be a pathetic little weakling under my boyfriend's control. He wanted the booze poured down my throat, the pills stuffed down my gullet against my will by a bad man."

"That's bullshit."

"That's what I told him."

"You were driving," he says. "It was you."

"It *was* me. Which doesn't make you innocent."

"Oh, I think it does, Violet."

"We left Lorraine Daigle in her wrecked car."

The doe eyes narrow. "She was dead."

"She wasn't. Face it."

"Well, aren't you something else, Saint Violet. Aren't you just a stellar human being."

"I paid for what I did."

"I *also* paid for what you did!" he fumes, teeth gritted. "My dad and uncle sent me here because they were sick of my face. I barely left the house for a year. If that's not prison, then what the fuck is?"

"Uh, let me think. Oh, wait, I know. *Actual* prison." I poke his sculpted chest. "Your mother didn't die of grief. Your uncle gave you a job. Becca Frye couldn't wait to bang you. Your dad hates your face, but he's still looking after you. And I'm gonna guess that people in town still high-five you for two state championships. All things considered, what you're calling 'prison' is in reality loving hearts that took you in again."

He squints. "What?"

"You got forgiven. Don't pretend you didn't."

"People looked up to me, and now they don't."

"You played football, Troy. It's not like you were out there saving orphans."

His eyes smolder now, a hint of his true nature. I saw this once or twice when we were together and put it in a category called Don't Look.

"Who the fuck do you think you are, Violet Powell? Answer me that."

I adjust my whole self now, as tall as I can be. "I am a person trying to face my mistakes." I gasp with the truth of this: the simple, liberating truth.

"You're a Bible-thumping bitch-whore from Stickney Street," he says. "I was a fucking *hero*." He grabs my arm again, nearly upsetting my bookends, and I realize that what I thought was cologne is booze. I might as well admit that the man I chose was an alcoholic when I met him, an alcoholic when we dated, an alcoholic when I said yes I'll marry you, an alcoholic when he said drive, and an alcoholic when he said what the fuck did you do. I chose him.

A woman with green eyeglasses opens a classroom door. "Everything okay out there?"

"No problem," I call, shaking him off again.

"Troy?" she says. "Break ended ten minutes ago."

I turn tail, and this time he doesn't follow. When I get to reception, I realize I'm breathless, not from taking the stairs by twos but from the fury and regret and also the confusion of seeing Troy again, a five-foot-eleven wideout from Class C who once believed he was headed for the pros. The part of me that doesn't hate him pities him, and the part of me that doesn't pity him loves him.

I did. I loved him.

I stow my purse and the bookends in my locker, where I've taped Mrs. Rocha's goodbye note: *YOU GOT THIS!!!* It's just words, dumb cheerful words, but the note cuts a bright gash in this awful day, and *no answer comes* dissolves into that brightness. I put on my spare lab coat even though I'm not technically working, and once I button it up, I'm capital-*V* Violet again, with a small-*v* violet inside me.

In the Bird Lounge I discover the third-shift student, a poetic type, hunched over his laptop, frowning at the screen, muttering to himself. The birds have been put down for the night. An hour and a half early. They start to rustle beneath their cage covers as they realize it's me.

"*Bada-bing bada-boom!*" Ollie shouts. He's such a little dope.

The student looks up for a second, registers my presence, finds it beneath his interest, and goes back to his screen.

"Why are they put down at six thirty?" I ask him.

The kid has the decency to look sorry. Sorry to see me, of course, but also sorry to have not done right by the birds. The supper-shift students, four-to-eight, are often here alone after five thirty and really we just have to trust them to do what they're told. The kid doesn't say anything, all mop-hair and dowel-bones and shadows beneath his large dark eyes.

"Don't tell Petrov, okay?" he says.

"They're supposed to be up till eight."

Now he looks annoyed. "It was just this once."

Why am I so mad? Oh, I'm so mad. "These *birds*," I announce, snapping off the cage covers one by one and opening the gates, emphasizing the word *birds* to bring home the truth that even the worst bird is better than the best human, "these *birds* have dedicated their lives—lives that are worthy, lives that are noble—to the advancement of human understanding." They're all staring at me, still behind bars except for Ollie, who has stepped out, ready to party. "Did they ask for this burden?" I add, for good measure.

It takes a second for the kid to get that I expect an answer.

"I guess not."

"You guess not?" I ask.

"No."

"No?"

"No, I guess not."

"I hope by 'no, I guess not,' you mean 'no, I guess they did not ask to live out their one and only life in a laboratory when they could be winging through bountiful rain forests eating mangoes and drinking dewdrops.'"

"I don't really think you can drink dewdrops." His face gives nothing away, but I know he's laughing.

"You're on thin ice, Buster." These kids make me feel like an old lady and also talk like one.

"It would take a lot of dewdrops to constitute an actual drink," he says, giving his moppy hair a toss. "Even one sip would take, like, a million dewdrops."

The kid's name is Mason. Mason Braun. Which sounds like a no-neck bouncer or a phys-ed teacher. But really someone should've named him Percy.

"If these birds are to fulfill their obligation to *us*—an obligation they did not ask for—then we in turn must fulfill our obligation to *them*: to keep them well, keep them fed, keep them intellectually engaged." These are Misha's exact words, coming in handy.

Mason glances guiltily at the birds, all four of them perched and judging. "They looked tired."

"Projecting much?"

"What?" he says.

"Looks like you're the one who could use forty winks." Forty winks. I sound like Ollie.

He gets defensive now, gesturing to the microwave. "I fed them exactly at five, and totally according to the recipe."

"It's your *job* to feed them at five and totally according to the recipe. It's also your job to interact with them until eight o'clock, which is their actual bedtime."

"*Heavens to Betsy!*" Ollie shouts, stepping onto my shoulder.

"Does this bird look tired to you?" I ask. "Did he tell you he was tired? Did he tell you 'I'm tired' while you were gaming on your laptop?"

"I wasn't gaming," he says, tapping the keyboard to prove it. An acre of unparagraphed prose appears.

"Paper due?"

"Tomorrow," he says.

"How long have you known about it?"

"About what?"

"About the paper."

"I don't know. Coupla weeks."

"And you started it when? Tonight?"

Now he looks genuinely hurt. (Because the truth hurts.) "Why are you being such a bitch?"

This is the second time within ten minutes I have been called a bitch. One thing I was looking forward to on the Outs was not being called a bitch, but clearly that was too much to hope for. "Not only are you neglecting the birds," I inform him, "you're wasting your education." Ollie is marching in place on my shoulder. *Kids these days*, he huffs through his feet. "Do you know how many other people would love to have a paper due tomorrow, Mason? Who would be checking it for errors of punctuation, structure, and clarity of thought?" This is pretty much verbatim from the speech my tenth-grade English teacher, Ms. Matthews, gave weekly, except she substituted "oppressed female children in Afghanistan" for "many other people."

Suddenly I want to strangle this kid, get my hands around that long, poetic neck of his, because he doesn't seem to want the education I would gladly take in his place.

"Get out," I tell him. "You're fired."

He laughs. Yes: laughs.

"Out," I order him again. Ollie's all for it, marching like crazy, but nobody else says a thing, they're all head-cocked and side-eyeing but not talking.

Mason flips the laptop closed. "You're nothing like the last one. Sophie was awesome."

"Sophie hated birds," I say, which feels like a betrayal, though it's true.

Now Mason gets up with great fanfare, gathers his stuff. "Petrov'll hear about this."

"Yes, Mason. He certainly will hear about this."

He doesn't look like a poet anymore; he looks like an obnoxious entitled headcase whose parents love him more than God. His soft, shapely lips, the type certain rich people are born with, curl in a hard-to-describe contempt that only somebody like him can confer on somebody like me.

"You can't fire me," he says. "You're a lab assistant."

A tingle of rage zips up my spine. I lift the lapel of my lab coat to show him the badge Mrs. Rocha gave me as a promotion present, VIOLET POWELL, LAB MANAGER, and I'm pretty sure nothing in my life so far has given me such pleasure.

Men's faces change weirdly, they do. A minute ago I was a fangless lab rat, and now I'm a threat to his résumé.

"Who's Petrov gonna believe?" he growls. "Me, or an ex-con?" I kind of wish he would hit me instead. "Everyone around here knows you were a pity hire," he says. Not true, but a well-aimed blow none-theless as he strolls away, door clanging behind him.

The birds go nuts, a big, whooping lollapalooza, lots of whistling and yodeling and other earsplitting jungle noises. Despite their toys and mist showers and nutritionally balanced mash and easily gotten nuts and fruits and the unnatural absence of predators, something in them remembers where they belong. And boy do they let you know it; it's not all smarts and cuteness in here.

"*We hold these truths to be self-evident!*" Ollie hollers into my ear.

"Oh, Ollie. You're my best boy."

With nobody else to finish the shift, I spend the next two hours chatting with the birds, skritching their necks, running them through half-hearted lessons just for fun.

"What toy, Charlotte?"

"*Cork.*"

"What color, Ollie?"

"*See you later, alligator!*"

At bedtime, I kiss the birds on their hard black beaks and sing them a little bit of "In the Garden" before covering their cages. When I stop, they ask for more. By which I mean they start whistling, a kind of woot-woot, like drunk people at a concert.

So I keep going:

He speaks and the sound of his voice
Is so sweet the birds hush their singing . . .
And the melody
That he gave to me
Within my heart is riii-inng-inggg . . .

"*Oh, he walks with meee,*" Charlotte sort-of sings. Then she quits, waiting for me, so I finish the song alone.

We had a singing group for a little while, a regular thing, a "wellness initiative" every Monday after Noon Chow, sixty minutes with Jenny Little, a skinny grandma who directed a church choir in Bar Harbor before she got sent up for selling drugs out of her barn. It started out okay, funny warm-ups and short tunes with simple harmonies, mainly folk songs and spirituals. But Renee ruined it. She didn't mean to; it's not her fault she sings like a tractor stuck in a ditch. I was the jerk for minding. It's just that I so badly wanted one thing to be beautiful. One thing to be not ruined. Book Club turned out to be that one thing.

Routine is vital to the birds' health and well-being, so I tuck them in at eight sharp, Bob and Alan cuddling up, Charlotte dipping her head to her shoulder. Ollie nods off almost instantly, little old man, so I cover him first. I hear Bob make this cute little *erk* sound, saying good night to Alan. I call them "the cowboys," and I believe they enjoy it.

As I finish up in the Bird Lounge, washing the dishes Mason left in the sink, I start to hope Frank and Harriet grabbed a bite after dropping me off, some boring older-folks restaurant where they don't turn the music up too loud. That would make this day end right.

Just as I'm finally ready, coming out of the locker room with my purse and bookends, Misha barges through the front door with a stack of folders. There's another grant deadline tomorrow, and he's doing it all himself.

It doesn't occur to him to ask why I'm here so late; he thinks everyone should work the way he does: relentlessly. "I can help you with that grant," I tell him. "Mrs. Rocha showed me."

He closes his eyes. "Too much, too soon," he says. "I cannot afford to lose you."

"You won't lose me."

He stops to "observe." He sets the folders on the reception desk, and we stand there in the dimming light, just breathing. Two humans with no words.

"I need you," he says at last. His lips part, baby-pink inside.

My instinct is to draw closer, his body a tidal pull, resistance futile, but then Ollie calls out from the Bird Lounge, and something in me—maybe the same something that will make me a good lab manager—takes a step back instead, bumping the desk. The folders go flying.

"No," he says, as I reach for them. "Let me." He bends to the floor, scoops them up. Then stays there, half kneeling, looking up at me, eyes warm, all that ice melting. His gaze strays to my bookends, which I'm holding, hard.

"A gift from a friend," I say, which is how the moment breaks, it does, the moment breaks, but not enough to save me.

"Good luck with the grant," I whisper, leaving him on his knees.

Down the stairs I go, holding my breath past Troy's classroom, and then I'm out, where night somehow has fallen, and as I hurry along, my body sparkling with desire, I resume the conversation I had today at my mother's grave. I didn't say goodbye to her, as I expected to. I said hello.

I said, *Hello, Mama. This is me now.*

23

Harriet

FULL SUMMER ARRIVED LATE, A sudden sweep of heat, the prison stuffy and overwarm.

"AC's fucked up," Renee said. "We're dying in here."

"Maybe somebody's crawling through the ductwork," Marielle suggested. "One of the guys trying to escape."

"Good luck," Jenny Big said. "Hey, Bookie, I like those shoes."

"Macy's," Harriet said. "Thirty bucks on sale."

The women approved of both the sale and the two-inch heel—bought on impulse, Harriet's first frivolous purchase in years. "My niece will love these," she said. "She'll swipe them next time she's home."

They had the Visitors' Room today, that well-lighted rectangle with a view of the field. Harriet unpacked her book bag: pens, loose leaves of paper, her copy of Yeats, and a stack of Maya Angelou to be handed around at the end.

"Shall we begin?" she asked.

"We shall," said Desiree, and everyone settled, reciting together: "I am a reader. I am intelligent. I have something worthy to contribute."

"We shall bid farewell to Yeats by writing love poems today," Harriet suggested. "We've learned from the master, after all."

"I'll miss him," Brittie sighed. "Best boyfriend ever."

Jacynta quoted, "*Tread softly because you tread on my dreams.*"

Yeats had softened them up. Despite their general willingness, the women had until now harbored a spiky insistence on their personal space, a natural result of confinement, worse when they met in the supply closet, better in the airy Visitors' Room. Weeks of Yeats and his lyricism had sanded their edges, though; today Harriet sensed thinner, freer-flowing air between one body and the next.

"I got no use for a love poem," said Dawna-Lynn. "Men are pigs." Her hearing had been twice postponed, making her edgy.

"It doesn't have to be to a man," Harriet told her. "Or a woman. You can write a love poem to a place. To an object. To a feeling."

Jenny Big: "To a dog?"

"Of course."

Dawna-Lynn groaned.

"Leave her alone," Renee said, but Jenny Big was already writing.

"Does it have to be iambic pentameter?" asked Aimee.

"Wouldn't kill you to try," said Shayna, who rarely wrote words but rather shut her eyes while everyone else wrote, then delivered something she'd written and memorized in the quiet of her mind.

"Do what you like," Harriet said. "This isn't an assignment, it's a celebration."

"Of what?"

"Of the fact that you liked an author I brought in."

This was met with general hilarity, except for Dawna-Lynn, drumming her fingers on the table, rabbity and distracted.

Summer light melted through the windows as they settled over their pages. Harriet listened for a moment to the thrilling shush of pen on paper, the sound of escape. Then she began to write along with them, as she sometimes did, and surprised herself with a sudden inspiration. Her pen joined the others, racing across the page.

One by one they set down their pens, then looked up at Harriet, faces confident, obliging, readable. This moment never failed to break her in half.

Dorothy, who worked in the kitchen, had taken to bringing in a pitcher of water and a stack of paper cups. Dorothy and Aimee poured the water now, as some were finishing up, others rereading. This touch of formality—a cross between a tea party and a cocktail hour—had become as necessary as their opening declaration.

"Vodka neat, with a twist?" Dorothy asked.

"I'll go with a latte today," Harriet said. "Double shot, extra foam."

"You got it." Dorothy daintily filled Harriet's cup.

"I'm done," said Jacynta, the final holdout.

The women took turns reading, the usual mix of fire and ice, the usual applause.

"I wrote a love poem to my old self," Jacynta said. "It's called 'Before.'" She ran a hand through her ill-cut hair, cleared her throat. "Aw, I don't know."

"Don't chicken out," Renee said.

Kitten: "Read it, Jacynta."

Dorothy: "Go ahead, honey."

"*Sweet good child,*" the poem began. Jacynta spoke quietly; everyone leaned in. The poem took place in a childhood bedroom filled with bears. It ended, "*Remember.*"

Nobody spoke for a time. Harriet said, "Thank you, Jacynta, that was beautiful." Then everyone clapped.

"Harriet, you read," Brittie said.

"No, no," Harriet said. "This is your show."

Desiree said, "You never read, Bookie."

Then Shayna: "We never ask her."

And Marielle: "Sorry we never ask, Bookie."

And Jenny Big: "We're asking now."

So Harriet read a few lines. She was no poet, though some poetic phrases had come to her today. She'd written about, of all things, buying shoes. In her poem a woman buys shoes from a man with a pleasing voice.

"*Like a cello with rain damage,*" she read.

"Oh, that's cool," said Renee.

Jenny Big: "Shhh. She's reading."

Harriet went on, heart thumping, to intricately describe the shoes, their "luscious shape" and "juicy shine."

She put her paper down, feeling suddenly shy. "That's it."

"Girl!" Shayna laughed.

Brittie said, "That's one sexy-ass poem, Bookie."

Then Jacynta: "Who knew she had it in her?"

And Marielle: "I think it's about Lou."

And Dorothy: "Is it about Lou?"

"I don't know," Harriet said. "It just came to me." Lou had a hundred splendid qualities, but his voice did not sound like a cello. Lou was a trumpet.

"Can I go?" Aimee asked. "Mine's about a baby."

"Enough with the fucking baby," Dawna-Lynn muttered.

"*Hey*," said Jenny Big.

"We agreed to grant each other our subject matter," Harriet reminded everyone.

"And you, Jenny Big," Dawna-Lynn said, voice eerily rising. "Haven't we heard enough about your famous fucking dog that's only dead because you burned him up in your house?"

"Watch your mouth," said Stoneface, startling everyone. How had he gotten in, and when?

Dawna-Lynn leapt to her feet. "Watch your own mouth, fuckwad."

It happened in seconds: a blur of motion, a scraped-back chair, Dawna-Lynn in a headlock, the women springing away from the fray, Harriet stranded between, shouting, *Please, oh, please*, another CO appearing out of nowhere, a screeching mudslide of obscenities, Dawna-Lynn snarling and gnashing as the COs muscled her out the door and down the hall to the Fishbowl.

It took no time at all for the women to catch their breath and retake their seats. Not Harriet, who sat slowly, adrenaline shooting through to her fingers and toes.

"Lugged for sure," said Marielle.

Harriet was panting and trying not to show it. It had all happened so fast. So slickly. And the women, so quiet in the chaos. They'd done nothing but get the hell out of the way. They hadn't even looked surprised.

"You okay, Bookie?" Kitten said.

"Yes, yes, of course." She realized she'd been swallowing hard.

"Her hearing got canceled," Jacynta said. "New lawyer fucked up."

"Plus her ex-husband's new wife just had twins," Jenny Big explained. "Some skank she knew in high school."

"Why'd she get her hopes all up?" Marielle asked. "She knew better than to think he'd take her back."

Renee: "Sucks."

Brittie: "Does."

Stoneface returned, fast-walking and clanging with equipment. "That's it for today, girls," he announced.

Harriet glanced at the clock. Only ten minutes to go anyway, not worth arguing. And in truth she was too shaken to argue. She posted herself at the door, trying to appear unaffected, handing out copies of Maya Angelou as the women filed out in silence. She'd forgotten to collect the pens, but there they were: someone, probably Kitten, had placed them in a neat row, capped, tips facing all the same way. There were moments in Book Club—she supposed she should call it Writing Club now—that made Harriet want to flee to 2-Walk, find a cell, weep in private.

She stashed everything in her book bag under the unreadable watch of Stoneface. When she glanced up, she found him smirking. He snapped a quick look at her shoes.

He'd heard her poem.

Harriet wasn't a blusher, but her face burned. She felt half-dressed, exposed to the elements, utterly powerless, her privacy shredded. Is this how the women felt, not just sometimes but all the time? She shouldered past him and hurried down the corridor toward the exit, where Mr. Flinders was waiting. "Security check," he said, grabbing her bag and placing it on the table near the first of the exit doors. Harriet watched him paw through her things, his bony fingers counting out the pens, flicking through her copy of Yeats and Angelou. He felt under the seams that connected the straps to the bag. This post-class check had not happened, not ever, not even after her first session over a year and a half ago.

"You look clean," he said.

"I am clean."

He reached past her—she recoiled—and punched the buzzer to let her out. After an especially long wait came the metallic scrape of the door unlocking, a sound she couldn't get used to. Mr. Flinders opened the door for her, eyes still on the bag.

When at last she burst into daylight, she rushed to her car and sat for a while, trying to shake the stomach-churning image of Dawna-Lynn being dragged away. She longed to charge back inside and upbraid Mr. Flinders and anyone else who did not know grief when it spit in their faces. The women knew; they had not lashed back, had not told Dawna-Lynn to shut the fuck up, not even Jenny Big or Aimee, the targets of her venom. They knew exactly how it felt to be Dawna-Lynn today.

Eventually she put the car into gear and drove slowly past the field, where a chittering flock of birds swooped its length, dipping into and out of sun and shadow. She opened all the windows, listening to a high-pitched din not unlike the ambient sound of the prison. She took in the scents and colors, the celebrating birds, the alternating pleasures of stillness and motion. Clumps of daisies erupted here and there, cutting drunken paths through the waving grass.

She would not keep her poem. Not because Stoneface had ruined it, though he had, but because she never kept what she wrote in Book Club. At home she would read the poem once more, then tear it in half and toss it. How could she let her poem breathe on the Outs while the women's poems remained trapped inside with their authors?

She slowed to a stop, took a last lingering look at the field, and breathed it in: once for herself, once for them.

24

Violet

SINCE THE DUSTUP WITH MASON the jackwad, I've worn my lab coat with more confidence. Of course Misha took my word over his, and the students regard me now with caution. My full-time status, not to mention a raise, means I'm a person to be reckoned with.

Frank insists that any promotion is a good thing, but Harriet keeps chirping about "stepping-stone jobs." Truth is, after three months I want to stay till the end of time.

Tonight Frank picks me up after work, and the three of us—me, Frank, Harriet—go to a lobster shack across the bridge in Cape Elizabeth, Frank's treat. We eat at picnic tables on a low bluff and admire the crashing waves. When we circle back to the window for ice cream, Harriet turns to me and says, "The usual?"

Those two words, wow.

Harriet gets pistachio; Frank, too. They might be dating, or trying to, taking me on "outings" as a way to be together. It must be strange to date when you're old—strange enough when you're young. After ice cream Frank drives us a little farther down the point, where we walk the beach for an hour, nothing but us and a few tourists, a few small birds skittering ahead of the tide, and a man with a big dopey dog who takes a shine to Frank. The sky turns a shocking shade of lilac just before the daylight dims all the way.

I grew up on a river, and the ocean scares me, to be honest, but with Harriet and Frank I feel safe. With Misha I feel the opposite of safe, and both ways make me oppositely happy.

Frank is in my phone now. Contact #5, after Harriet, Sophie, Misha, and Mrs. Rocha. Harriet believes the employee shouldn't be at the employer's beck and call, but I like being needed and Frank says you can't argue with that.

Frank drops me off first. I wave goodbye, the two of them now shadows in the front seat of Frank's car, and a vision seizes me, a flash of my mother and father driving away, on a date, I think, their heads inclined toward each other as they talk. It's not so much a memory as a knowledge that precedes memory, the knowledge that I had a mother and a father, and they were in love.

I drift to sleep on that knowledge, a quiet, easy sleep, until my phone clangs in the dead of night.

"Violet," Misha says, "you must check on the birds."

"Now?"

I struggle awake, rattled, caught between dreamland and here-land.

"Do you think I call at this hour because I wish you to check on them next week?"

I snap on my bedside lamp, and Mrs. Rocha's afghan bursts into color. "Did something happen?"

"I have a feeling," he insists. "You live near enough, please check."

He's in Falmouth Foreside, a ten-minute drive at this time of night, a fact I fail to point out. I get up, wash my face, and head down the hill to the university. I'm not afraid of Portland anymore, but I can't say I love walking the streets at this hour. Misha says go, so I go, which doesn't yet strike me as even a little bit troubling because whenever he draws near, my body fills with diamonds that sparkle when I move. Also, obviously, he turns me into a helpless ditz who makes corny analogies to diamonds.

There's this thing in science called Mutual Exclusivity, which is when babies learning to talk can't assign two labels to one thing. A kitty is a kitty but not a cat. A rock is a rock but not a pebble. Troy once brought a friend of his, a metalhead parasite also named Troy, to his baby cousin's house and she threw a class-A, thunder-and-lightning cat-fit. "No Troy!" she growled at the second Troy, her pointy elf face pink with outrage. Little kids figure it out eventually and so do some birds, but not Ollie, who refuses to learn that you call a red block either "red" or "block," depending on the question.

In other words, I love poor, lowly, regular-smart Ollie the best; he knows what he knows and won't be swayed. He won't solve Mutual Exclusivity no matter how long he lives, but he sweet-talks me all day and often makes me laugh out loud. Even though he's Einstein compared to, say, a Chihuahua, he lives in the shadow of two Extra-smarts and a Superstar. When a local TV personality came to the lab last week—I arranged it myself—Misha left poor Ollie in the Bird Lounge, never even introduced him.

"You hurt Ollie's feelings, Misha," I told him after the TV personality left in her short skirt and crimson lipstick. We were alone in the Ob Room, and Misha gave me one of those stop-time looks he's been throwing my way—smoldering, focused, intensely confusing.

"Do not become a scientist, Violet," he said, "unless you want to work with bacteria. Bacteria have little personality. Even you would agree." This could have been an insult, a velvety insult to a high school graduate with nothing but affinity to recommend her. On the other hand, it could mean he appreciates a soft heart.

I keep reminding myself that he prefers me to Sophie, who's going for her master's.

"And don't call him Ollie," he said.

"He likes it."

"How do you know?"

"I just do."

"Have you made careful observations, formed a hypothesis, designed an experiment, analyzed the results?"

"No."

"Then how do you know?"

"Same way I know Ollie's your favorite."

"Oliver is useless."

"And your favorite."

"Intuition is the opposite of science," he said, but before he turned to leave, he studied me just long enough to show he might think it over.

The birds were done for the day, having performed charmingly for the TV personality. Misha, too, performed charmingly, possibly because the TV personality had a smoke-and-whiskey voice that even a tree stump would find enchanting.

As I unlock the outside door to a darkened Huntington Hall, I make a mental note to pay myself for an extra hour—regular time, not overtime; I'm practical but not greedy. Inside, the long corridor tremors with that otherworldly nighttime gleam you see a lot in slasher movies. Troy loved slasher movies, loved it when I mashed my face into his chest as we sat on his mother's huge white slasher-movie sofa. It's always the girls who get killed the worst, always the girls' bodies you see half-dressed and sticky with blood except for their boobs, which remain shapely and untouched, and you're supposed to laugh, Troy always said you're supposed to laugh, because the girl asked for it, she opened the door or lifted the veil or peeled back the shower curtain, and what did she expect, but sometimes Troy's laughing bothered me. If his parents weren't home we'd do it right there on his mother's matching white rug as the credits rolled and at those times the sex wasn't fun at all. I mean, I loved sex when I believed I was giving Troy a beautiful gift that only I could bestow, but after the slasher movies I didn't feel like me and he didn't feel like him and honestly the last thing I wanted after seeing girls my age chainsawed to death was to make love. Not that he asked my opinion, and nothing about post-slasher sex felt even a little bit like a gift only I could bestow. Dawna-Lynn told us once that it's a thing now to ask permission, and nobody believed her. *I swear to you bitches*, she said, *it's the twenty-first century, and the guy's supposed to ask.*

A building at night makes sounds—the plumbing system or the boiler or a loose latch or a psychopath on the prowl. My steps fall loud and wrong, and in this low, creepy light, the EXIT signs appear to be floating free of the doorways. I don't dare watch the elevator open, so I take the stairs, which is almost worse. My breathing sounds overloud, jouncing with each step, and when I get to the door my key makes a chilly scratching sound as I muscle it into the lock.

These are prison sounds.

But soon I'm in the good quiet of the Bird Lounge, where I belong, and I'm glad to be here in the night, even though I have to rise again at seven. In prison you have to be up and standing at six for head count so I got used to waking early even after restless nights.

Ollie's already rustling inside his covered cage. The others sleep like rocks, but Ollie's always the first one to snap awake. My Ollie. I flip on a small lamp, hoping not to disturb the others.

"*Hello, dear*," Ollie rasps. The other birds have a slight Russian accent, mostly in the meaty *L* sounds, but Ollie sounds like a geriatric potato farmer from northern Maine. I lift the sheet and see that, of course, he's fine.

"*Hello, dear.*"

He's picked this up from Bob and Alan, his label now for humans, all humans. Imagine if all the humans who ever lived had been called nothing but "dear"—Saddam Hussein, Mussolini, Attila the Hun. Makes you wonder about the course of history.

"Beddy-bye, Ollie," I whisper, covering him again.

I take a peek at Charlotte and the cowboys to get a full head count, feeling suddenly like a CO checking the inmates. Everybody's fine.

Misha picks up on the first ring.

"All's well in bird land," I tell him. "Just like last time."

"Which bird?" he asks. I can hear something in the background, somebody running water, clinking a glass.

"All of them."

"How listless?"

"What?" I can hear a low, female murmur now, the glass again, water again.

"Violet," Misha says. His exasperated-boss voice. "Did you take her out of the cage?"

"Who? Charlotte?"

"All right. Don't move her."

"She's asleep," I say, confused. "Why would I move her?"

"Yes, all right, yes," he says, and hangs up.

"*Heavens to Betsy!*" Ollie calls from his cage.

"Your trainer's gone insane," I tell him, lifting the sheet. I open the gate, and he steps onto my shoulder.

"Daddy says don't move you," I whisper, "but Mommy says okay." I kiss him on the beak, then take him into the Ob Room so we won't disturb the others. I'm up anyway, and so is Ollie, who doesn't get enough attention in my opinion, so here we are.

"Pretty here at night, Ollie-boy," I say, looking out the glass windows at the empty campus. A full moon makes long, eerie shadows of the trees. The campus forms the heart of a mishmash neighborhood, triple-deckers squeezed between hoggish Victorians with wraparound porches. The campus buildings look dropped here by aliens.

"*I'm a birdbrain!*" Ollie says.

A student taught him this as a joke, and Misha fired her for disrespecting the birds. I place Ollie on a perch so we can converse eye to eye. He cocks his head to see me better. "You're no birdbrain," I tell him. "You're my smartest, sweetest boy."

"*You said it!*" Ollie calls. "*You said it!*"

My laughter echoes in the empty room, but I can't help it. Four months ago I was just getting sprung from prison, and now it's August, the nights already sharpening. I'm wide awake and I have a job and Harriet is my friend and Frank is my friend and I know what Mutual Exclusivity means.

I sit on the floor, eyes closed, and sing "In the Garden" to Ollie, all the verses. He tries to join in, then decides to just listen. I can't remember ever being happier.

But he bids me go
Through the voice of woe
His voice to me is ca-all-linng—

"Violet."

I lurch to awareness, thinking Charlotte got out and somehow opened the door—I wouldn't put it past her—but it's Misha. It's Misha who comes to me, reaches out, gently lifts Ollie, and takes him back to the Bird Lounge.

I follow him out there, but I don't know what to say. Have I done something wrong? Or right? I think I know what's happening and I think his wife is the reason he made no sense on the phone and I think he called me in the middle of the night not to check the birds but to summon us here, but I say nothing in case I'm wrong.

"I'm sorry I took Ollie out," I whisper.

He turns to me, a pouring attention. "You're still here."

"I am." Time feels like a tolling bell.

"Stay," he says.

He has a wife. I know he has a wife. Misha has a wife who murmured in the background and ran some water, a glass of middle-of-the night water for her supposedly worried husband, who is here now, and I am here now, and oh my God I am aching.

"*Aaand he walks with meee,*" Ollie sings, loud and comical, "*and he talks with meee . . .*"

"You've been teaching him," Misha says, retucking Ollie's sheet.

"He's smarter than you think, Misha."

Misha moves to the door and turns off the lamp, a quiet, suggestive click. He opens the door to the hallway and waits. In my entire time here, he has not touched me except to shake my hand and mend Alan's bite on that first day, but I feel "ravished," to borrow a word from Jenny Big's romance novels. Thoroughly ravished.

"Come here," he says. So I do. How can I not? Is this what sleepwalking feels like? I follow him out to the hallway and into his office, where he settles on that elephant of a couch. I sit next to him, aware of my stuttering breaths.

"You love me," he murmurs.

It's just a kiss at first, lips to lips, nothing slutty or dirty or raw, and oh my God I never knew what a sloppy kisser Troy was until now. Troy was a bloodhound and Misha's a cat, and not just any cat, I mean the kind of regal, elegant cat you might find in a pharaoh's tomb. Or on handmade bookends. His lips meet mine in a shock of warmth, not-wet-not-dry, and his hands, too, so warm, pulling me in, and then I'm in, inside that teetering madness. I guess the word is *surrender*.

Misha is by turns tender and fiery, patient and hungry, and we mirror each other the way we do with the birds, do this, good birdie, do that, good birdie, each in turn, teaching and being taught, first him, then me, like a dance, awkward at first, then fluid and easy. I'm vaguely aware of Ollie's restless muttering, audible through two shut doors, and the creak of pipes somewhere in the building, and the sigh of suede against thrumming skin.

Misha is a person of many labels—man, trainer, scientist, colleague, employer—but only one arrives in this stopped moment: *mine.* When he whispers *my violet, my violet,* the world goes both dark and light, and the laws of physics die a gorgeous death, and I will never hear my name the same way again.

When it's over, not soon, he reaches across me, a whiff of sex and spice and man-odor—and pulls his crumpled pants from the floor. I hear a soft rattle as he rifles the pockets. When he brings his fingers to my mouth, my lips part willingly.

It's a shelled walnut, sweet and meaty, my reward.

25

Harriet

HARRIET MISSED VIOLET'S PRESENCE IN Book Club. Her insights. Her attention to language. Her ease in accepting fictional characters as fellow creatures. The others, Jenny Big and Dawna-Lynn and Jacynta especially, enjoyed turning characters into defendants, themselves into jurors, indulging in the pleasure of umbrage—catnip to the powerless.

From the outset, their righteousness had seemed therapeutic and probably necessary, so Harriet resolved not to temper it, maintaining her hope that the next book, or the next, would finally crack the ice. Frank Daigle's suggestion of poetry had done just that, but the women's passion for Yeats-the-sexist could hardly compare to the torch they now carried for Maya Angelou. Harriet had always considered Angelou a tad pious, but her voice, and its ferocious calls for freedom, its evocation of "caged birds," spoke to them like no other.

In fact, Book Club had taken a mystifying turn. While reading a poem called "Phenomenal Woman," Harriet expected some eyerolls. Instead, the women pronounced Maya the greatest poet of all time, living or dead, without caveat. She hardly knew what to do with this level of enthusiasm.

They were back in the Visitors' Room, sans Dawna-Lynn, who was stuck in the Pod for one more day. Stoneface opened the door and poked his head in, square and chalky, Mount Rushmore minus the gravitas. Instinctively, Harriet tucked her feet beneath the chair; she had not worn the poem-shoes today, might never wear them again.

"Flinders wants to see you after class," he said to her.

"Hey, Roberts," Renee called. "Fix the friggin' AC." Today the temperature had plummeted, an over-repair that had everyone in goose bumps. Harriet had removed her cardigan in solidarity.

Stoneface eyed the room. "I'll get right on that, Thibodeau. Your wish is my command."

"Would you like to stay and hear a 'phenomenal woman' poem?" Harriet asked. Sometimes the COs showed some humor, even Stoneface, but not today.

"I'd rather be boiled in oil," he said. "Flinders. Don't forget." Then, mercifully, he shut the door.

"I know how we can bust outta here," Shayna shouted over the laughter. "Open the gates or we tase you with a poem."

"You in trouble, Bookie?" asked Kitten.

"I can't imagine why I would be," Harriet said, though she could. "Maybe there's a new protocol for book orders."

A murmur of disgust. Since the Big Balls visit, a pall had lingered, pervasive as an odor: color-coded badges still mandatory; moratorium on library donations reinstated.

"Did you forget to submit in triplicate?" Marielle asked.

Brittie said, "Bet she used the wrong color ink."

Then Renee: "Or picked a book like *100 Tips for Bustin' Outta the Slammer*."

And Jacynta: "*Wire-Cutting Made Easy*."

And Desiree: "*Tunnel-Digging for Dummies*."

They were laughing again, but Harriet had her eye on the corridor. Outside the windows, Mr. Fingers had collared Stoneface, with whom he was in deep conversation.

"Okay," Harriet said. "Who wants to read?"

Everyone.

Jacynta went first, a sizzling sixteen lines that ended

I am a phenomenal woman
boom-boomin' my phenomenal ass
down 2-Walk
like a queen.

"So good, Jacynta!" said Dorothy.

Then Marielle: "Queen Jacynta!"

And Kitten: "That was super awesome, J."

Jenny Big raised her beefy hand. "I'll go next."

Stoneface watched from the corridor. Harriet sensed a change, as if air itself understood malice; she felt the itch of surveillance and didn't like it one bit.

"Go," she said.

Jenny Big's poem—largely about her deceased dog, Elmo—ended

I am a phenomenal dog woman
I see through phenomenal dog eyes
I hear through phenomenal dog ears
And I bite
And I bite
And I bite.

"Powerful use of repetition," Harriet said.

Aimee said, "Wow, Jenny Big!"

Then Shayna: "That's badass."

"I'm next," Dorothy said. She unfolded her paper. "I am a phenomenal woman," she read.

Big thighs
hairy chin
heart of molten steel.

Applause all around. "That's got muscle," Harriet said, thrilled, imagining the next few weeks, a blizzard of poems, maybe a publication of some sort, or a reading at Town Meeting. The remaining poems celebrated small boobs, gray hairs, monthly miseries, all manner of female complaint turned inside out, and quitting time approached in a rare moment of all-for-one agreement, in this case, that "phenomenal women" lived everywhere, even here. Especially here.

Kitten said, "What did you write, Bookie?"

Harriet glanced down at the two words on her page: *Thank you.* "I couldn't quite get going today."

Marielle, sitting next to Harriet, leaned over and asked, "Who you thanking?"

"Nobody," she said, suddenly ablaze. Was this a late-in-the-game hot flash?

"Holy shit," Desiree said, "Bookie met a boy!"

A clatter of laughter, some oohs and ahhs.

"Let's not be ridiculous," Harriet said, as Frank Daigle barreled into her thoughts unbidden: his height and leanness, his cello voice. Her new shoes with heels. What on earth?

"Bookie did meet a boy!" said Brittie.

"I did no such thing."

"Did so!"

"Come on, Bookie, spill it."

"You know you're dying to."

"Ladies," she said, "whether or not I have met a 'man' is nobody's business."

"Ooh, a *man*!"

Shayna sang, "*Ain't messin' with no toy, I don't need no baby boy . . .* ," a song Harriet did not know, but of course it was all about sex. Most songs were.

"All right, now," Harriet said. "Who's next?"

"You are, Bookie!"

They were all grinning at her, awaiting news of Bookie's grand love affair.

"There is absolutely nothing to tell."

"Ha!" Kitten crowed. "That means there *is* something!"

"What if I did happen to meet a man?"

"I knew it!"

Harriet glanced around the table. Everyone leaned in; they wanted a story. Of course they did. All humans want stories, all the time. But this story involved Violet. "Let's just say our earliest encounters were inauspicious."

"You don't get a second chance to make a first impression," said Brittie, who had once taken a Dale Carnegie course.

Harriet laughed. "Turns out you do." For a startling second, she imagined telling all. The great irony of coming into a prison once a week was how unguarded she felt with guards all around. She clasped her hands demurely, smiling at them. "The rest is none of your beeswax."

Shayna asked, "Was the poem you didn't write for *Mr.* Beeswax?"

"Oh, good grief."

"Was it, Bookie?"

She gave in. "Possibly." As soon as she said it, she knew the truth: she'd put pen to paper, and Frank Daigle appeared.

Marielle said, "What's his name?"

"Yeah, Bookie, tell us his name."

Harriet straightened her papers, tapped them on the table. "I believe we're out of time."

"Bookie . . . !"

"Oh, all right," Harriet said. "His name . . ."

"Is . . . ?"

Harriet took her sweet time, collecting the pens, restuffing her book bag, putting on her sweater. Packing up pained her, leaving them inside as she left to gulp the fresh air. "His name," she said, "is Ethan Frome."

And so Book Club broke apart that day in a torrent of laughter that Harriet hoped might carry them through Noon Chow.

Moments later, she was seething under the clammy interest of Mr. Flinders, a middle-aged tweed who scrutinized her from behind his pristine desk in the unit office. He picked up a letter opener from his desk, put it back. Picked up the matching magnifying glass, set it down. Then he asked to see her bag, which he inspected for several minutes.

"It has come. To my attention," he said. He did this a lot. Broke sentences. Into fragments. Giving you time. To figure out. What you did wrong.

"If this is about last week, Dawna-Lynn was upset over a family matter."

"Well aware," he said. "That's not. What's come. To my attention."

What *had* come to his attention:

ACCEPT NOTHING FROM INMATES; GIVE NOTHING TO INMATES.

DO NOT SHARE PERSONAL INFORMATION WITH INMATES.

DO NOT INITIATE OR ACCEPT PHYSICAL CONTACT WITH INMATES.

DO NOT RELAY INFORMATION FROM AN INMATE TO ANY OUTSIDE PERSON.

DO NOT RELAY INFORMATION TO AN INMATE FROM ANY OUTSIDE PERSON.

Harriet had broken each of these rules to one degree or another. She brought in clippings related to the books. She brought postcards with vibrant images to spark the imagination. Once, she'd brought in a "hi" *from* Violet and delivered a "hi back" *to* Violet. And, every week, she brought herself—her full, unfettered self.

Mr. Flinders returned her bag. "I believe. You were warned. Previously," he said, speaking not only in his customary chop, but also in his customary ass-covering passive voice. "The rules were put into place. For the safety and well-being. Of the volunteers. As for the inmates, their period of incarceration is designed. To be valuable. And orderly. And conducive to the ongoing discipline. And cohesiveness. Of the unit."

"I'm sorry, Mr. Fingers. *Flinders*."

Oh, God. Harriet's bag slipped off her lap and she bent to pick it up, scalded by his blistering regard. Righting herself, she faced him squarely. "Mr. Flinders," she said. "Are you letting me go?"

"You tell me, Mrs. Larceny. Larson, sorry. You tell me. What you would do. In my place."

"I would give me a warning and hope for the best, because what these women get from Book Club every Friday *is* valuable, and orderly, and conducive to the ongoing discipline and cohesiveness of the unit."

"A little bird told me different." He pursed his lipless mouth. "A little knitted bird. An item of contraband. That should not have been taken. From this building."

"It was a gift, Mr. Flinders. A token," she said. "The women enjoy Book Club and wished to say thank you."

"Myriad freedoms. Are given up. After incarceration," he said. "Choosing one's means of gratitude. Is one of them."

For God's sake, speak English, Harriet thought, but he'd telegraphed his meaning well enough: Giving the women something they loved did not comport with his notion of rehabilitation. He didn't like the sound of laughter wafting down the hall. He didn't like to see heads bent over good books. He didn't like that the women got to escape the daily drudge and he didn't.

"The safety. Of our volunteers. Is taken seriously here," Mr. Flinders went on. "In particular our older volunteers. Of more advanced age." He smiled sourly. "Our younger volunteers are more wily."

By great effort—by titanic, herculean, superhuman effort—Harriet did not snatch the letter opener and stab Mr. Flinders in the throat.

In Book Club she'd let down her guard, yes; she'd allowed herself to forget where she was. She had done this not because her aging brain was on the fritz but because the women needed her to be willing, not wily. They gathered each Friday in a reality of their own making; that was their tacit agreement, and it worked. This did not strike her as a fireable offense.

"We're not running a coffee house. Where poetry is read." He sat back, pleased with his metaphors. "Acts of unspeakable depravity. Have been committed. By these girls. The details of which would unravel your cashmere cardigan."

Ah, Harriet thought. *There it is, you bastard. I'm the rattlebrained, cashmere-wearing Junior Leaguer; the gull, the goose, the witless do-gooder; the bleeding-heart innocent who hasn't known a day's hardship; the monocle-wearing one-percenter dripping with noblesse oblige.* She swallowed back a retort—*fuck you* came to mind—and settled instead for flattery.

"Mr. Flinders, are you a poet yourself? Your syntax is always such a surprise."

Amazingly, he lost his footing. "I've been known to dabble," he said. "Life gets in the way."

"Oh, it does indeed," Harriet agreed. "Which is why it's so important to stay engaged in the creative arts. Even for women who—"

"You're done here." Like a horror-movie shapeshifter, he reverted in an instant. "You had your chances. To follow the rules. You chose not to."

"But I have another book order arriving next week. If I could just—"

"No."

Hatefully, she imagined his poetry: *How do I. Love thee. Let the ways. Be counted.* She rose with as much dignity as she could manage, not much. "I bought this sweater at Renys, forty percent off," she said, knowing exactly how she sounded—a woman of means pretending otherwise—but she couldn't stop herself.

Mr. Flinders had hit a bullseye, reminding Harriet of her life of ease. Lou had petaled her path with love and money. In the current world, being a well-to-do white lady felt dimly shameful, her yearning to "help out" close to pitiable. She wondered now if she'd chosen prison because her work there would be hidden. She'd told almost no one. She could do-good as she wished, be as laughable and cliché as she had to, without exposing herself to ridicule or scorn. The women, who had themselves been exposed to all manner of ridicule and scorn, did not judge her. They reserved their judgment for fictional characters, who could not be damaged. In the women's presence Harriet felt perfectly, unapologetically herself.

She buttoned the offending sweater all the way up, vibrating with rage but unwilling to fully burn the bridge. "Mr. Flinders," she said pleasantly, "if you would please tell the women I didn't leave by choice."

"I'll be sure," he said, lips pruning. "To do that."

As she left the unit office, she caught sight of Jenny Big and Kitten in the dayroom, working together on a jigsaw puzzle. Kitten looked up, then Jenny Big. "See ya next week, Bookie!" Jenny Big hollered. "Don't be late!" This was what she always said; Harriet was never late.

She waved back, holding her breath, then pressed the button to exit, aware of the dayroom at her back, the circles of seated women, the idle chatter, the yarn and fabric. From a great distance—from Jupiter, say—the dayroom could be mistaken for a quilting bee.

Sometimes whoever controlled the lock made her wait a long time. She glared up at the camera, feeling self-conscious in her pretty sweater, which felt like a neon sign. Finally the lock gave—that concussive jolt—and she stepped into the next chamber, where she pressed another button, waited again, then entered the long central hallway, a grimy quarter-mile straight to Security, where one of the friendlier COs gave her bag a quick peek and returned her keys.

"See you next time, ma'am," he said. He had the clean, rosy face of a cherub.

Harriet could not bring herself to speak. She made her way down the metal stairs, waited for yet another steel door to open, then walked the ten yards of asphalt to the outside gate, where the lock opened instantly and she was out, on the Outs for good.

She sat in her car, taking one sip of air after another, rocked by grief, feeling old and irrelevant. Retired people were often thought to be lonely, but it wasn't that. It was the feeling of uselessness, of being done with it all.

The air felt sticky, nearly chewable. Harriet peeled off her forever-tainted sweater, dried her eyes, and drove out of the parking lot. The prison receded in her rearview, along with the sun-shimmering field in which the prison social worker had once spotted a meadowlark.

Sophie was a big believer in "telling your feelings," but a twenty-four-year-old on the cusp of a mistake was not the confidante Harriet required. She knew only one person who might know what it was like to be her right now, who might know what was like to be made useless. To be thought old. To be kept from your heart's desire.

26

Violet

OLLIE'S DANCING UP A STORM, dying for breakfast. He loves his bird mash, which you have to microwave for ten seconds exactly—fifteen and you can just forget it. If Ollie were human he'd be one of those chefs who throw flaming sauté pans at the line cooks.

He's like this only at breakfast time; otherwise he's a doll. Right now he's stomping a demented foxtrot on the top of my head and giving useless instructions—"*Rock around the clock! Rock around the clock!*"—as Charlotte and the cowboys wait politely, like guests at a queen's tea.

I got here an hour early to redo the weekly schedule, which took forever, a shitshow of cancellations and switch-ups because summer session's coming to a close and students are supposedly studying for finals. (At the beach.) One of them quit altogether because I didn't "show empathy" when Bob bit her. One, Bob barely drew blood, and two, she knew better than to nudge Bob away from Alan. Not everyone can be jolly old Ollie.

Tell that to the psych students. Every single one of them believes God gave them a special gift with animals. Well, he didn't. I made the same mistake myself and have the scar to prove it. Parrots don't "read your aura." What they read is affinity, which is another word for respect. So I'm short another student and doing a lot of my old job, but I'm also trying to do my new job as well as Mrs. Rocha expects me to. Even though she's not here anymore. It makes for long days, but again, except for an occasional outing with Harriet and Frank, it's not like I've got a calendar full of dinner parties. It's not like *I'm* invited to a queen's tea.

So here I am, serving warm mash with a mango side. Two seconds after I get everybody fed and showered, first-shift arrives in a flurry of apology, and before I can convey my firm-yet-courteous lab-manager disapproval, Misha barges in, waving the same abstract he ranted about all day yesterday.

An abstract is a concise summary of an endless scientific paper, in case you didn't know.

"This Danish woman," he splutters, "is a menace." He means Dr. Frida Sondergaard, who recently announced her "breakthrough" teaching African greys the concept of same/different. I already knew about these birds, Bjorn and Helga, because on YouTube they sing the Danish national anthem together. In harmony. Wearing little Danish hats. I'm talking thousands of hits, with a donation link to her lab. Dr. Sondergaard recognizes that modern science is ninety-five percent showbiz. Misha does not, because he has never once looked at YouTube.

He rattles the pages, and I realize it's not the abstract he's got in his fist; it's a copy of a related article from the *New York Times*, featuring Bjorn and Helga and their gloriously pretty trainer. "Don't Call Them 'Birdbrains': Groundbreaking Study Shows Parrots Know Sticks from Stones." You wouldn't believe how many news outlets pounce on smart-animal stories. Especially talking animals. Extra-especially talking animals with pretty trainers.

Unfortunately, Misha's not what you'd call photogenic. Or telegenic. I don't mean his face, which is beautiful. I mean he comes off aloof and arrogant, even in photos, and he's not a smiler. You wouldn't be a smiler, either, if you were a former four-year-old who watched the KGB haul your father off to parts unknown and punched your mother in her already broken teeth for good measure. The point is, interviewers get thrown off their game, and Misha gets irritable and condescending, and then the birds, catching a drop in temperature, go quiet exactly when we most want them to talk. Mrs. Rocha could make Misha behave, but then, she was fifty-eight years old. Misha won't do an interview, not even in print, unless he's one hundred percent sure it'll result in money for the lab.

Mrs. Rocha warned me that Misha can be usefully competitive, so I decide to take advantage. "I heard Dr. Sondergaard's getting a brand-new lab, courtesy of the Danish government," I say, total lie, very lah-di-dah, giving Alan a final squirt with the mister.

"New lab for breakthrough that is not breakthrough?" he growls, speaking like a cartoon Russian, which he does when greatly agitated.

"Yup," I say. "I'm pretty sure I read that."

"Idiots!" Misha's in a lather not because Dr. Sondergaard's birds got a new lab and a piece in the *Times* but because our birds have been same/differenting for years. He crushes the insulting pages and tosses them to Alan, who happily obliterates them.

"Couldn't agree more," I say, still super casual.

The first-shift, a theater major who wears her grandma's hippie dresses from the sixties, is hovering at the play table, starting Ollie's physical therapy and pretending to not listen. To Misha, she's invisible anyway; everyone is. She clucks sweetly as Ollie agrees to be gently shooed over his sponge balls, gripping his dodgy feet without complaint.

"Danish birds know stick from stone," Misha mutters. "Stick from stone! Why is this news?"

It's best to treat his rhetorical questions as actual questions. (I learned this from Mrs. Rocha.) Very calmly, I look up at him—a long way up, the man is *tall*. I try to give him a look—a lover's look, a you-and-me look—but he has a stunning ability to stow his gigantic life into tiny boxes. Capital-*V* Violet in this box; small-*v* violet in that one. Where his wife goes, I don't know. Or care. Love can blind you to everything but your own rapture.

"It's news, Misha," I inform him, "because people find animal intelligence fascinating."

"People find old news fascinating?" His cheeks redden adorably. "Oh, yes, my-my, how fascinating! Beautiful Danish woman teaches parrots same/different! Birds know this stick same as that stick! How fascinating and breakthrough!"

You can't really blame him. It's one thing for a bird to say "same" when shown two sticks, or "different" when shown a stick and a stone. Charlotte can do that any old time, won't even demand a nut for her trouble. But if you show her a red stick and a blue stick and ask "what same?" she'll tell you "stick." If you ask "what else same?" she'll say "wood." If you ask "what different?" she'll tell you "color." Our Superstar knows not only *that* two objects are same/different, but *how* two objects are same/different.

Misha is waving his arms now, like an elm in a windstorm. "Treat birds like baby children," he rants. "Praise every silly word! And too much kiss-kiss!"

"Misha," I insist, very coolly, channeling Mrs. Rocha and skipping the fact that he himself is a bird-kisser. "Misha, listen. Until people get to see Charlotte do her thing, then Dr. Sondergaard's parrots *aren't* old news, they're *new* news."

He stops waving then; he does listen to me on occasion. Another reason to love him, I guess. Probably Mrs. Rocha felt the same way. Well, not the exact same way. No earthly creature could feel what I feel.

"The first time I realized that Charlotte was *thinking*, I nearly fainted," I tell him. "And so will people watching YouTube."

"YouTube," he mutters. "Circus for unemployed simpletons."

"Not enough people know your work, Misha. You publish a paper once every three years. You treat reporters like imbeciles. You intimidate visitors. Mrs. Rocha told me the *60 Minutes* guy was so offended he never ran the story."

"Do birds fall in love! Stupid, silly man."

"Bob and Alan are in love."

"Violet. You try my patience."

"Charlotte and the cowboys should strut their stuff once in a while, Misha. It'll be good for the lab."

"Is very silly, to call birds cowboys."

"Sillier than Bob and Alan?"

"Did I name them Bob and Alan?"

"No, but that's what you call them."

"Because their names are Bob and Alan." He's calmer now, his English returning to normal.

"What would you have named them?"

"Bird One and Bird Two."

"Dr. Petrov," I say. An air shift, and now we have each other's eyes. "That's just sad."

"Do I look sad?" he asks. "Do I look like a sad man?"

This is foreplay, and only we know this.

"We do not run a circus here," he says. Nothing in his expression remotely matches the words coming out of his tender mouth.

I stand my ground, still looking up at him, smiling. We have a secret—a too-much-kiss-kiss secret—and whenever he recalls it, that certain luscious look, my body catches fire anew. I've come to love his moods. They bring him closer to me, not farther away, because I believe he does not love his wife, that his wife does not love him, that I am the only one who understands him. Even now, this part is hard to admit.

The hippie girl is suddenly watching us openly.

"You mock me," Misha says to me.

"Yes, Dr. Petrov," I answer, super-serious. "I mock you."

He calms completely then, which he does when I call his bluff. He fires off another eye-glint of just-us, and time stops.

I'm sorry; I know, but it does. The moment lengthens and contracts and recalibrates, and we find ourselves again. When this happens—often enough that I look for these moments, dream of them, live for them—he'll say something all-business, like: "Back to work for us." Or: "You win." But today, even though the hippie girl is exercising Ollie and pretending not to see, Misha reaches out with one finger and traces my jaw, an electrical charge that feels like the trail of a falling star. It lasts not a second before he drops his hand.

"No makeup," he says.

"What?" My ears are sort of ringing from all that voltage.

"Do not hide this face."

"I'm not hiding." But in fact I put on a little something this morning, hoping to look older, more professional and serious. More like a woman.

"Do not age yourself. You are young one time only."

He observes me in that way of his for a long, loaded moment, then touches my face again, as lightly as it is possible to touch anything, as if he's just walked into a museum with DO NOT TOUCH signs all over the place but a certain painting has bewitched him so thoroughly that he has to, he just has to.

"Set up the channel, and I'll think about it," he says, in perfect English, and the moment vanishes. He gives Ollie a kiss, then scoops Charlotte from atop her cage, and heads for the Ob Room. "Bring the others," he says to me, which means the cowboys but not Ollie.

As the cowboys step onto my arm, side by side, he adds, "Don't forget the logs," and closes the door behind him.

I fetch the logs—pages and pages of questions and responses in three-ring binders. So I've got one arm full of binders and the other full of birds. "Can you open the door?" I ask the hippie girl.

She says, "You can report that."

"Report what?"

"Uh . . . harassment?" She holds my gaze for as long as she dares—I'm giving off my best don't-fuck-with-a-felon vibe, my best I'll-decide-what's-harassment—then she lowers her eyes and opens the Ob Room door.

Charlotte's in a grand mood. The cowboys, too, seem pretty stoked. Have they caught the electricity? Do they feel my swoony, feather-girl, cloud-hopping pleasure? They sidle up and down my arm, and for creatures that weigh a pound each, they sure know how to make themselves known.

"*Want nut*," Charlotte says, getting ahead of herself.

"Not yet, my honeybee," Misha warns her, then gives her one anyway.

I open Charlotte's logbook to Object Permanence, a study that employs a version of an old boardwalk shell game. Hide a treat under one of three cups, switch the cups, and the bird keeps track of the treat. Ollie can do this. A common seagull can do this. A below-average collie. Dr. Sondergaard's birds do this all day long—on YouTube.

Our version, though, makes the Danish birds look like dopes. Four cups, a pompom in four different colors hidden under each cup, multiple switches. Charlotte can track four colors and sometimes five. Try it yourself; good luck.

Charlotte watches, engrossed, as Misha sets up the cups, showing her each colored pompom before hiding it. He makes the first switch. "Where is yellow?" he asks.

Her beak makes a little *boop* sound as she taps a cup. He lifts it: yellow.

Second switch. "Where is blue?" *Boop*. Blue.

"Misha," I plead, "you have to let me record this."

"No recording."

He's protective, maybe even paranoid, about revealing his work until it enters the world as a peer-reviewed scientific paper. Also, it has to do with the birds themselves—he resists anything that smacks of indignity. Our birds, who belong in the wild, are martyrs for science, even Ollie, and we're morally bound to accord them every due respect. If there were a Medal of Freedom for animals, Misha would put their names in.

Third switch. "Where is green?" *Boop*. Green.

Bob and Alan perch nearby, rapt. They adore the shell game, though they're only two-color trackers so far. This is my favorite part, watching them learn from her. Their bright, inquiring eyes, irises the color of clean straw. Their cocked heads. Those tiny, sparkling brains at full throttle.

I make a note in the log. "This would be an enormous hit on YouTube."

Misha grunts, gives Charlotte a pompom—that's the treat, a biggie—and she joyfully shreds it to smithereens. Then he invites the cowboys to the table.

"Are we logging this?" I ask.

"Just practice," he says, scattering some pompoms, minus the cups. "Look, Alan. How many red?"

Only three, but poor Alan's counting is pitiful.

"Come on, Alan. How many red?"

"*Three!*" Charlotte squawks, Alan flapping in a huff because she's forever stealing his answers. When Misha laughs, a rarity, it comes to me: this is a rehearsal. He's testing the birds' knack for razzle-dazzle, aiming to crush his peacocking Danish rival. He *wants* Charlotte to butt in, a plot twist of the sort Dr. Sondergaard couldn't pull off even if she thought of it first.

Mission accomplished. I'm already framing the video in my head.

"Bad birdie," Misha fake-scolds Charlotte. No idea he's been played. His face gives me nothing, but I know the wheels are turning. I give a walnut to Alan, another to Charlotte, and one to Bob just because.

I'm happy. That's all.

"Good good birdies," I croon.

"Don't call them birdies."

"*You* do."

"I certainly do not."

"You call Charlotte your honeybee, your heartbeat, your best girl." I smile; at certain times, he whispers these words to me.

The Ob Room goes quiet. Nothing but a gravelly munching from Charlotte and the cowboys, and faint sweetie-pie sounds from the hippie girl, who's playing with Ollie on the other side of the door.

"That Danish woman," he says. "No integrity, Violet. Methods: inconsistent. Birds: stupid."

He doesn't mean the last part, but clearly the *Times* piece has gotten to him, not to mention my fib about the new lab. For the rest of the day, he smolders in his office, brooding over the full-length version of Dr. Sondergaard's paper. I spend that same time registering a YouTube channel called Petrov's Parrots, which Misha will change to Avian Cognition Studies and cost us thousands of views.

After that I post the schedule and order the week's supplies. I leave a message at the *New York Times* that we have a way better bird story, with *actual* breakthrough research. I also score an interview with a behavioral-psychology website and one with *Living with Parrots* magazine, which Misha will deem far beneath him.

But he'll do all of it, because he's feeling a tad bloodthirsty. Because he got an article in the mail.

Sent by me.

Just before five, as I'm prepping supper with Ollie yelling "*Yummy!*" into my ear, I hear Misha leave. I'm taking third shift, here till eight; he knows this. And what I know about him floods me with power.

As the birds chow down, I fetch my copy of *Spoon River Anthology* from my locker and bring it back to the Bird Lounge. Harriet and I are still discussing it, and even Frank is getting into it. Last weekend, as we slid into our booth at Frank's favorite pizza joint, Harriet gave him a copy. He couldn't have been more surprised if she'd presented him with a six-shooter, but now we're a book club of three. Spy novels are more Frank's cup of tea, but he agreed to give it a go.

I open the book and start reading aloud, as I often do when stuck on third shift. This is family time. I'm the mom, and they're the kids. "Listen to this," I tell them.

Passer-by,
To love is to find your own soul
Through the soul of the beloved one.

"What do you think, guys? Discuss."

I used to race through books one after another, but in Book Club Harriet taught us that when you slow down, you notice more, and when you notice more, you feel more. Reading one book makes it part of all the books you've ever read, Harriet said, so she was forever dragging other books into our discussions.

QUESTION: If Gatsby had a brother like Ethan Frome, would he have made the same mistakes?
QUESTION: If Franny and Zooey could speak from the Spoon River graveyard, which one would tell the story, which the "meanwhile"?

The questions were never simple. In *Franny and Zooey*, Harriet thought, the meanwhile is this monster unspoken grief over a dead brother, and the story is everybody in the family having witty conversations and going to college football games and having nervous breakdowns and saying things like, "Don't you know who that Fat Lady really is? . . . Ah, buddy. Ah, buddy. It's Christ Himself. Christ Himself, buddy."

But we disagreed, all of us: me, Kitten, Jenny Big, Brittie, Marielle, Dawna-Lynn, Renee, Dorothy, Jacynta, Aimee, Shayna, and Desiree, the charter members of Book Club. We thought the monster-unspoken-brother-grief was the story. The meanwhile was everyone pretending nobody died. Harriet called that an astute observation.

Unless you slow down, you don't see these things.

"*More*," Charlotte says, so I flip through the pages, looking for an epitaph she might like. In this book it's hard to find a person who liked living and didn't mind dying, but here he is, Fiddler Jones, and I read it slow:

I ended up with a broken fiddle—
And a broken laugh, and a thousand memories,
And not a single regret.

The kind of guy, in other words, whose story and meanwhile are one and the same.

The birds prefer singing to reading, though, which is what I'm doing when Misha returns at eight, as I knew he would.

"Hello, my birdies," he says, meaning all of us.

The cowboys commence singing like a couple of drunks, Charlotte screaming at them to shut the fuck up (not in those exact words), while Ollie flies straight to Misha's shoulder to claim him. Despite his bad people skills and general crabbiness, Misha is the parrot version of the Second Coming, and no matter how often he claims otherwise, he flat-out loves it.

"I came back to apologize," he says, helping me resettle the birds. "You were not the true target of my irritation today."

I kiss Ollie good night, then Charlotte and the cowboys. "That's not why you came back, Misha."

"Don't kiss the birds."

"They like to be kissed." I turn to him. "So I kiss them."

"Tell me, my violet," he says, "who would not like to be kissed by a woman named for a flower?"

With these words he tethers me in place, another sizzling body-shock, his hands nowhere near me. They're folded, in fact, one over the other, as if he intends to sing me a hymn.

He does this on purpose, makes me come to him. Asks me to decide. Makes me complicit. He tells me I have power over him, he is helpless under my spell, he is weak, I am strong, he cannot but succumb. That's how he says it: "I cannot but succumb," like a character from *Wuthering Heights*.

Then why am I the one who feels helpless? It's Friday evening; I'm sentenced to two days without him. Monday feels like a faraway mountain ringed with clouds. So I do decide. I open his folded hands.

By the time I wake on the Buckingham Palace couch, it's well past ten, a weak moon offering little illumination. Misha stirs a little, kisses a spot I love just below my ear. "I must go," he whispers.

"Oh, don't," I whisper back. "Let me tell you something first."

His breath is wet and warm on my neck; I feel him nod. He will stay.

I want him to know about the day in Book Club when Harriet explained that stories have a meanwhile. As I talk and talk, his eyelashes flutter against my skin.

"'Ah, buddy,' I quote. 'It's Christ Himself. Christ Himself, buddy.'"

"My violet." I feel him smile, a sweet pressure against my neck. "What nonsense are you speaking?"

"I'm teaching you how to read."

"The great Harriet woman told you that literate adults must be taught how to read?"

He doesn't mean this as a real question, but I decide to take it that way. "Yes, Misha. As a matter of fact, she did." I sit up—with some effort given the tangle of our bodies—to make sure he can see me. "The writer writes the words. The given reader reads the words. And the book, the unique and unrepeatable book, doesn't exist until the given reader meets the writer on the page."

Misha opens his icy eyes, which do not look icy to me.

"*We* are the given reader," I tell him. "*We* decide what's the story and what's the meanwhile."

He breathes out, a relaxed, after-sex sigh. "This great Harriet woman, she was your schoolteacher?"

"Not exactly."

He slides down, his head on my lap. His eyes flutter closed. He's half smiling. I amuse him, which is okay. But I really want him to hear this. I want him to name what I am to him.

I've never spoken to him about my time inside, but I tell him this: At the end of Book Club that day, Aimee—meek little Aimee—raised her hand. *Once upon a time,* she said, *a baby-thrower roamed the land.*

Meanwhile, his ex-wife rotted in prison. The end. Aimee's ex *was* in fact roaming the land at the time in a brand-new RV with his pregnant girlfriend.

Then Dawna-Lynn said, *If prison is the meanwhile then where's my fucking story?* and we all kind of thought the same thing, stuck in our meanwhile of fish sticks and scratchy towels, but then Renee said, *I think my story is here, honestly, I'm clean and sober, all those drugs were the meanwhile,* and Marielle said, *I hope my story hasn't started yet,* and Aimee said, *May I go again?* and we all said yes, go, and she said, *Once upon a time Aimee kicked a baby-thrower out of her story. Meanwhile, the baby-thrower roamed the land and her friends said good riddance.*

So we all said *good riddance.*

"I do not read novels, Violet," Misha said. "Why do you tell me this?"

"Because life is the same as books, Misha. There's a story and a meanwhile, and we get to say which is which."

"Ah, my violet," he says. "You are young." He pulls me down, enfolds me. "Life is not the same as books."

I say nothing more, though I know I'm right. As my eyes adjust to the low light, I catch the length of our entwined bodies glimmering in shadow, and I see what he means about my power. It's a dazzling thing, visible in this dreamy half-light.

A feeling comes over me, an odd, hovering feeling, and I imagine I suddenly see and know and understand everything, like the people in Spoon River speaking from their graves. Some of them lived long lives, some short, but after it was over, they chose at last: *this* was my story. I believe that Misha, whose history emerges in little chapters whispered in the aftermath of our lovemaking, has already chosen. The KGB man who took his father; his journey to America; his work, his papers, his lectures; his house and whoever lives in it; everything that is not us on the Buckingham Palace couch—that's his meanwhile.

His story is here, twined with mine, gleaming.

And as for me—twenty-two years old; punished and returned; motherless and guilt-stained; wrapped in the arms of a brilliant man, quenched and happy—I am Fiddler Jones, living in the now, without regret.

27

Frank

He scrambled four eggs and apologized because eggs were all he had. Hot sauce helped, though not much. He did have parsley, so he garnished their plates.

"Don't apologize," Harriet said. "You weren't ready for company, and I certainly didn't expect to be fed."

"Well, it's late. You must have been starving."

She checked her watch. "Eight o'clock, good grief. I should be the one apologizing."

She didn't, though. She simply ate with gusto—the woman could eat—because when he said he enjoyed cooking, she took him at his word.

"A man of many talents," she said, popping the sprig of parsley into her mouth.

"Not *many*," he said. "Some."

After a beat, she said, "I like your humor, Frank. You have to look for it."

"Not too far, I hope." He cleared the plates, his body buzzing, revived by the glow of a woman in his house. He shouldn't have apologized; apologies had always irked Lorraine. *For God's sake, Frank, it's like you're sorry for existing.* For decades he'd sensed a whiff of wrong in everything he aimed for, but Harriet seemed to accept his good intentions. Or, more precisely, to accept his intentions as good.

"I didn't expect to bend your ear this long," she said.

"I don't mind." He didn't. "I'm sorry you lost your place."

"I stewed about it all day. Then I mustered the courage to come here."

"I'm glad, Harriet."

The evening seemed to be closing. He should have offered wine with dinner; they could be lingering right now over a second glass. *Don't go,* he thought. *Please, don't go.*

"The living room might be more comfortable," he said, though it wasn't: upright furniture, bare wood floors, all Lorraine.

To his surprise, she accepted, gliding into the living room and choosing a seat on the wingback sofa. The thing could accommodate a family of elephants; he sat next to her, not overly near.

"The women will think I deserted them without notice," she said, settling in as far as the sofa allowed. "What kind of volunteer would do that?"

"Probably some do," he said. "Doesn't sound like the easiest work."

"It is, though." She looked at him. "As a girl I spent my time with old people and ended up with a foot in two centuries. Three, now." She clasped and unclasped her hands, and again he wished he'd thought of wine. "I came late to teaching and wasn't one to take chances. I didn't have that modern knack for panache."

He thought she looked quite modern, though, her natural colors adding plenty of panache to what he now saw was an ugly, stolid piece of furniture he'd never liked. It wasn't worthy of her right now.

"Anyway," she said. "They do make it easy. Even when they're trashing a book, from prologue to acknowledgments, there's a willingness to engage. *Was*, I guess I should say. *Was* a willingness." She dabbed at her eyes. "And all I had to do was show up when I said I would. That's all they expected. The worst teacher in the world can do that."

"You're selling yourself awfully short," he said. He wanted very badly to hold her hand.

"Oh, I'm not, really. And now I'm being thrown out like a moth-eaten coat."

"It's the prison's loss."

"Flinders is a vindictive little troll," she said. "He didn't want them to have those two hours of pleasure. There are people like that, Frank. They go into corrections with no 'correction' in mind, only punishment." She sat up as if hearing an alarm. "Frank, what if they don't replace me? How will the women feel if I leave without a fare-thee-well and nobody comes to fill the gap?"

How worried she looked, how at sea, and yet even her distress sparkled. He'd never spent time with a woman who could so generously fill a moment.

"You know what?" she said now, bunching her fist. "I'd like to march right back there and bust Mr. Fingers smack in that prissy pink face."

"I'll bust him," he said. "You hold him down."

She looked startled, thinking he meant it, and all at once, in a surge of desire, he did mean it: he would bust a man's chops for this woman, he would tear a man limb from limb.

Then Harriet laughed, a bright, bubbling laugh that stirred the dormant house, and Frank joined her, and it felt natural and familiar, a recognition in his body, as if he'd known Harriet in a previous life and heard her laugh exactly this way. He did not believe in such things, but maybe she did.

"Harriet," he said, "would you care for glass of wine?"

"Oh, Jesus God, yes."

"I didn't ask before because I thought it might be, uh, inappropriate to the occasion."

"I can think of no occasion," Harriet said, "including funerals, nuclear summits, and parent-teacher meetings, that could not be vastly improved by a full-bodied red."

Frank selected a bottle from his stash in the kitchen cupboard and nervously returned with a pinot noir, a corkscrew, and two stemmed glasses. "My son-in-law brings me wine when they visit," he said, presenting the bottle, which featured a cocker spaniel on the label. "It might be expensive."

"Goody."

"I should've served it with the so-called dinner."

"Oh, but it'd be gone by now," Harriet said, sprightly as a wren. "And we wouldn't have this deliciousness to look forward to."

Frank had seen a movie once in which the leading man, a filthy-rich art thief, swanned into his study holding a bottle and a goblet in one elegant hand. He wished for a world in which he could pull off such a trick. Instead, he set the bottle down with an unstylish clunk.

"Violet might be in over her head with the bird scientist," Harriet said suddenly. Violet was often on their minds.

"I was thinking the same thing." The cork came out straight and easy—was that good or bad? "She talks of nothing else."

"He must be well into his forties. Married, I suspect."

"I hope he's not the type to take advantage," Frank said, sideswiped by a fatherly protectiveness. "She seems so young, despite all."

"Oh, I know." Harriet lifted her glass. "To Violet."

They nodded, sipped.

"Dear God," Harriet squeaked. "Dear God Almighty."

"Is it turned, do you think?" Frank spit his back into the glass.

"Frank, the look on your face!"

They were laughing again—when had he ever laughed like this?—as he trotted into the kitchen for a replacement. "I've got a dozen bottles in here," he called to her. "My son-in-law thinks I sit alone and drink all night."

"Don't you?" Harriet called back. "I certainly do."

He peered out from the kitchen door and saw that she was joking, and that she knew he knew she was joking, and that the joke had layers visible only to retirees living alone.

When he returned with a new bottle, Harriet's prettiness arrested him anew. Like a mature tree in autumn, he thought, full and flaming. Delicate lines crisscrossed her rosy face. She had a sweet mouth. "Frank," she said, as he poured two fresh glasses. "Do you ever feel invisible?"

"Yes," he said, "but not at the moment."

Harriet smiled, then picked up her glass. "I'll go first in case it's fatal; my kids don't need me anymore."

The glass looked expensive in Harriet's hand. Lorraine had bought twelve of them—fancy, with beaded stems, a German glass company—after completing a wine-tasting class at Adult Ed. He hadn't touched the glasses in over three years. When would he have found an occasion? Maybe it was dust they'd tasted.

Harriet took a sip, swallowed, and set down the glass with a little *plink*. "Don't shoot the messenger," she said, "but your son-in-law is trying to kill you."

"No!" he said, and took a cautious sip. "I never trusted that boy."

Harriet was frowning at the label, a crow wearing a World War I helmet. "Maybe he chooses them for the pictures."

"Third time's the charm," Frank said, heading back to the kitchen, and it was: a robust red they both pronounced worth the wait. The label, a reproduction of a lurid French painting, featured Parisian streetwalkers in a dance club.

They'd killed most of the bottle when the phone rang—a designated ringtone that Kristy had programmed years ago: "Dancing Queen" by ABBA. "That'll be my daughter," he said. The phone jounced perilously along the edge of the mantel as it spewed a staticky version of that awful song, coming to rest just short of a plunge to the floor. He turned to Harriet, who looked—well, she looked like a lot of things, all of them beyond his powers of description, but the word that came to him just then was *trustworthy*.

"She's calling to remind me we're not speaking," he confessed.

"You're not speaking?" She set down her glass. "Why not?"

He told her, and it took some time.

Her eyes brimmed. "Frank, that's awful. That's—To make you the villain, well, it's just awful."

"I don't know why I told you."

"A story like that," she said, "you have to tell someone."

The phone rang again. *You can daaance, you can jiiive . . .*

Frank sighed, braced himself.

Harriet said, "Shall I leave?"

"No," he said. "Please stay." He got up, rescuing the phone before it fell. "Hello, sweetheart."

"Dad, I just this second realized we haven't done a thing about Thanksgiving and we should be figuring this out, like, *yesterday*."

"Thanksgiving's three months away, Kristy."

"I know, but Tom's sister wants to stay in New Hampshire, his mom doesn't know up from down right now, and it could be her last

Thanksgiving in her own home, or *anywhere* for that matter, but she's two hours in the other direction, and we certainly don't want *you* on the road, so it's gonna take a little finagling to do both trips on the same—"

"No, no, you stay with Tom's people, sweetheart," Frank said, hatching his own Thanksgiving-day plan, which involved a roasted bird, baked yams, and a bottle or two of the Paris-streetwalkers wine.

"That's not what I *meant*, oh my God," Kristy said. "We'll do *both*, Daddy, of *course*, what I'm saying is we don't know how many Thanksgivings we have left, do we, and I can't go another day not speaking to you."

"Well, that's good news, sweetheart."

"Even though I'm really, really mad at you, Dad. Like, spitting-nails mad."

Harriet was listening—Kristy was a loud talker who made not-listening impossible. He smiled at her, and she smiled back. Never had Frank been more grateful for the presence of another human being.

"You've no call to be mad," he said gently, "and that's the last I'll say about it."

"Fine. We'll be one of those families who don't say the essential thing."

"Good, then. We agree."

"Good?" she said. "*That's* how you want it?"

"Saying the essential thing might be overrated."

He waited, not long, while Kristy recalibrated. Harriet watched him, nodding sympathetically.

"All right," Kristy said, and charged ahead. "The thing is, the boys don't want to do both trips, they have *friends*, which is good, I mean it's good they have *friends*, but it's *not* good they won't cooperate on the most thankful day of the year . . ."

As Kristy nattered on, Frank moved to the couch, seized by a need to be nearer Harriet, whose expression offered him instant solidarity. He clinked glasses with her, and she whispered, "Lou and I raised two of those."

"What are you laughing at, Dad?" Kristy said.

"I'm not laughing."

"It sounded like laughing."

"It wasn't, sweetheart."

Harriet was writing furiously on a notepad she'd grabbed from her purse. *I'll miss you madly, but it's the way of the world to make choices.*

Frank read it, thoroughly confused, until Harriet pointed to the phone.

"I'll miss you madly," he said, "but it's the way of the world to make choices."

"What?"

"I'll miss you madly, but it's the way—"

"You'll miss me madly? What does that mean?"

"It means, well, it means it's all right that you can't come for Thanksgiving."

She went suddenly frosty. "Is this your way of saying you have plans with someone else?"

"No, sweetheart. It's my way of saying . . ." He glanced up at Harriet, who handed him another note in her hurried scrawl. He recited as he read: "I feel very lately to be your father."

"What?"

"Lucky. I feel *lucky* to be your father, and I believe that forgiveness is a gift from God."

Harriet gave him a thumbs-up.

"Dad, that's . . . Well, that's beautiful, what you just said."

Harriet put her notepad away, watching him with a bemused approval. Frank enjoyed this immensely.

"I love you, Dad."

"I love you, too," he said. "Don't forget that, now."

It took a few more minutes to finally disconnect, and when he did, Harriet said, "Your daughter makes my girls look like amateurs."

He let out his breath. "At least she agreed to skip the essential thing. Small mercies."

"She didn't skip it, Frank," Harriet said. "Quite the contrary. Her essential thing is you."

Her words entered his awareness as the bone truth, and he decided then that he was in love with Harriet Larson. As the wine relaxed him, the house itself relaxed, an ease it had not known in quite some time; so when Harriet said, "I suppose I should go," he said, "Oh, don't."

She got up anyway. "You were kind to listen to my tale of woe, Frank."

"It wasn't kindness."

"I knew you'd understand," she said, collecting her purse. "Thank you for offering to help me kill Mr. Fingers."

"Say the word."

He walked her to her car, and as she fumbled for her keys, she stopped. "What am I doing?" she said. "I just drank half a bottle of wine." She looked at the sky. "It's a beautiful night, four blocks, I'll walk."

"I'll walk with you," Frank said.

He did, and it was indeed a beautiful night, the air cool and snappish, autumn not far off. A sliver of moon hung high in a starless sky. At one point Harriet slipped a little on a loose brick; when she took Frank's arm to right herself, she kept it there, linked with his, and he felt as if he'd won a prize.

Her house was a rambling Queen Anne with a wraparound porch. Well kept, with a sizable flower garden past its summer glory, anchored by a massive hydrangea tree in full bloom. She'd left some lights on, and there was her cat silhouetted in the window.

"Now, that's a pretty picture," Frank said, and meant it.

They stood together at her gate, like people at the end of an old-fashioned date.

As if reading his mind, Harriet said, "A few years after Lou died, my niece decided I was drowning in solitude, so she sneaked me onto a dating site."

"How'd it go?"

"Oh, merciful lord, he collected golf pencils." Her laughter was bright and girlish, and it made him laugh with her. He, too, had been set up once—with Mr. Pierce's cousin, about a year after the accident. The cousin turned out to be forty-three, a fact Frank didn't discern until after they'd ordered wine. The cousin had never heard of Bill Monroe; Frank mistook Alice in Chains for a slasher movie. Worse, her terrifying eyelashes, which could not have been real, reminded him queasily of whiskbrooms.

As Harriet's laughter subsided, the air between them went melancholy. "Marriage is no stay against loneliness," she said. "Wouldn't you agree?"

"I would," Frank said, thinking of Lorraine and her volunteer awards. "I would definitely say that." He opened the gate and walked her to the front steps. "Lorraine was a good woman."

Harriet nodded. "Lou was a good man."

The presence of their absent spouses did not feel awkward to Frank, or maudlin, or wrong. He and Harriet had each lived one life already; no point in pretending otherwise. They lingered at her steps, small talk gone dry, and Frank found the silence between them deeply consoling.

Harriet was gazing at her house, which had handsome gables and well-kept trim. Frank thought it had an air of having been happily occupied. Again reading his thoughts, she said, "I made a good life with a man I did not deeply love."

Frank took her hand. He said, "I made a good life with a woman who did not deeply love me."

A dog down the street barked, once. They remained in this magical silence for a little while, as their separate pasts floated harmlessly between them. Lorraine came to him in a memory he'd forgotten till now, smiling with her whole face, picking her way over stones and tree roots and yoo-hooing toward friends gathered at the shore of a lake up north. For all her bristly ways, Lorraine knew how to enjoy herself.

That lake would be sheeted with ice before long, the water beneath it still and sleeping, like those good times, like those erstwhile friends, like Lorraine herself. He thanked Harriet for hauling this memory from the deep, for reminding him that his marital loneliness had been broken, more often than he sometimes remembered, by gladness.

Harriet asked, "Do you miss her?"

Frank considered this. "I think about her."

"I think about Lou." He still had her hand, which felt natural and right. "Frank," she said, "would you like to come in?"

He would, yes. Indeed he would. He met the cat, and waited in the parlor while Harriet made tea. She set the cups on a glass table that looked brand-new in a house that smelled of old wood.

"We should let it cool a little," she said, sitting next to him. "Oh, what a day. I must look a fright."

"Harriet, you're as pretty as a block of milled aluminum."

"As a what?" Her dimples about toppled him clean over.

"Shiny and perfect."

She waited a moment, then leaned in to kiss him.

"Oh, my," he said.

"If this turns out to be our first official date, Frank Daigle," she said, "I give it an A." Her lips were sweet and generous, her body a tender weight against his. She stood, bringing him with her, and again they kissed, longer and deeper, in the low light of this house filled with memories that had nothing to do with him. They whispered little things as they ascended the stairs, kissing as they went, and at the landing Frank stopped, mainly to believe his own eyes.

She delivered a low laugh that he felt as an exquisite ache in his body. "You know Violet's been conspiring for just this outcome, Frank."

"I was miles ahead of her," he whispered.

Yes he was, and oh this fine woman, sweet lord Jesus, guiding him toward a bedroom, where she nestled with him on a bed with a frilly white spread and throw pillows printed with images of cats and apples. They lay there together, face to face, no light but what the slender moon allowed them, and he felt like a boy again, a boy who had been called home many times and had finally surrendered to that call.

They held each other, smiling, kissed some more, ran their hands over each other. As he unbuttoned her blouse—blue cotton dotted with tiny cherries—he found he could barely breathe, overthrown by her willingness, her warmth, her beauty.

"Are you okay?" she asked.

"I don't want to seem overly grateful, Harriet," he said, sliding his hand down her shoulder and bringing the blue cotton with it, "but I'm overly grateful."

"Don't get your hopes up," she whispered. "Underneath all this razzmatazz, I'm a sixty-four-year-old lady who loves ice cream."

"Nothing wrong with ice cream," he said as her blouse came open, revealing a sturdy white brassiere with thick straps. The practical brassiere, surprisingly, was the kind that hooked in the front. A tiny pink bow covered the hook. He had never, not in his entire life, beheld a sight more entrancing.

"You are beautiful," he said. "Harriet, you are as beautiful as a . . ." And there his powers of speech came to a full stop, for he was wholly undone.

She held his face. "Beautiful as a what?"

"I'm no good at metaphors, Harriet."

"That was a simile, Frank."

Again they laughed, and they kissed, and she gave up her whole self, and he gave up his whole self, and the world felt like a block of milled aluminum, it really did, glowing and durable and without flaw.

28

Violet

Harriet and Frank are a thing now, whatever that might mean to people their age. He fixes little things around her house: hinges de-squeaked, wonky floorboards righted, kitchen knives honed enough to thrill a Hun. Car ardently waxed, motor oil refreshed, tires pumped to perfection. Harriet hasn't slipped a word about this all summer except to whisper, "I feel like a girl," one time as we stood in line for ice cream.

Yesterday Frank drove us to the beach for a late-September, last-hurrah ocean walk. As I trailed them in a frisky breeze, picking up shells I thought Ollie might like, they tossed their shoes and waded in, holding hands, the two of them laughing, Harriet shock-squealing at the cold. How I wanted Misha to see this, to imagine the two of us later in life, splashing into freezing water and getting nothing but warmth in return.

We're in love, too; our lustrous secret. *Sorceress*, he calls me. Our YouTube channel has ten thousand subscribers, and Charlotte's the cover girl for this week's *Boston Globe* Sunday magazine. *Magic*, he says. *You are magic.* I call him "darling," like an heiress from one of Jenny Big's paperbacks. I hear passion in his every syllable, because passion fills every syllable of mine.

I tell myself the usual stories: they're separated; they're estranged; the marriage is loveless; the marriage is crumbling; the marriage is convenient; the marriage is over but he loves her parents. In these scenarios I don't think of her as an actual person. She is Wife, a label I might learn for the price of a walnut. The moat of bliss that surrounds me is far too wide for the truth to cross over.

Frank and Harriet are coming today to meet the birds, but Misha's in a mood, waiting for peer reviews on his latest paper, a second-stage analysis of the object-permanence study. There's widespread interest since I posted a video of Charlotte competing in a shell game with the hippie girl. Charlotte thrashed her, to put it politely, tracking four pompoms through five switches, and the hippie girl thought it was hilarious to get spanked so bad by a parrot, which is why I picked her. Some people get mad. But the hippie girl laughed, a loud, infectious chortle, and so Charlotte laughed (exactly like Mrs. Rocha, which made me miss her), and the video went viral. We raked in four thousand bucks in thirty hours. It doesn't hurt that the hippie girl is cute. Not to mention Charlotte.

I peer into Misha's office, where he's scowling into his laptop. Mrs. Rocha's afghan is still here, smothering one of the classy leather chairs. He senses me, looks up briefly, then resumes reading.

"Misha? My friends are due here any minute."

He grunts at the screen. "How is this my concern?"

"I need you to be charming and helpful."

He looks up again, his reading glasses sliding down his nose. "When am I not charming and helpful?" Again, he resumes reading—or I should say rereading. It's Dr. Sondergaard's newest publication, a short paper on object labeling, a study so lame I don't know why he bothered reading it even once.

"Misha."

"What?"

I wait. Not an hour ago we were tangled on the Buckingham Palace couch inhaling each other's breath. Finally, he looks up again.

"It's important," I tell him. "To me."

He frowns. "These are special friends?"

"If I had parents, it would be them."

He closes his laptop. "You have no parents?"

I'm a little stunned, and maybe he is too, to realize that he does not know this essential fact of my life. He, too, was orphaned early. I believe he turned Mrs. Rocha into the mother he had long pined for, but then I could be projecting. My theory is that all humans secretly long for the mother they always wanted. This longing turns half of us into resentful babies who didn't get properly mothered, and the second half into surrogate mothers for the first half. After Mrs. Rocha quit, Misha was left without guidance, and I was the next logical choice.

I am, in Misha's words, "delectable," so I'm not the mother exactly. And yet, despite the fever he creates in me, he often makes me feel motherly. I soothe him; I pet his hair; once he laid his head on my breast and cried. On the other hand, I sometimes wake on the Buckingham Palace couch with his arms twined around me and believe, in that first waking moment, that it's my mother's arms holding me fast.

He hikes up the sleeves of his lab coat, showing his pale forearms. "What do you wish me to do, Violet?"

"I wish you to welcome my friends and introduce them to the birds."

He wants to say no. I see that. He looks me over, chin resting on his clasped fists, elbows planted on the desk. It's five thirty and he's had a fraught day, not counting our late-afternoon interlude.

"We're going over to Harriet's for supper afterward."

I consider inviting him, but he stops me with a look of alarm.

"If you could just say hi, Misha. Show them a few things."

"Yes, yes," he mutters. "I will do as you wish." Then he rethinks his snippy tone, as he often does. He has to shake himself, literally, into a different place, the place where I'm waiting. He unclasps his fists, taps the desk with both palms. Yes, yes. "I will be charming and helpful," he says sweetly. He gets up, comes to me, kisses me slow. "Whatever you ask, my violet."

Is there anything like a lover's arms? That blanketing gladness? That muffling care? No there is not. It makes you deaf, it makes you blind, it makes you stupid.

"Orphan," he says, holding me fast. "I'm sorry. My honeybee, my heartbeat, my best girl." He is so warm, like the birds. I love being wrapped in him. "Poor little birdies," he murmurs. "Two orphans."

"Poor little birdies," I repeat. "Two orphans."

"Harder," he whispers, and I squeeze him around the waist, holding in this warmth for as long as he wants, both comforting and being comforted. In other words, I feel like both Misha's mother and Misha's child, so how do I not double-believe when he speaks of love?

When Frank and Harriet arrive I sign them in, show them around reception and my office and even the locker room, feeling proud. As for them, they're beaming. I stand there and bask.

"Good evening," Misha says, emerging from the inner sanctum. He holds the door open. "Welcome, Violet's friends."

After introductions, Misha leads us to the Bird Lounge, where Jamal is washing bird dishes after supper. Misha tells him to take a break.

"An hour should do it," I say.

"Fifteen minutes," Misha says, then Jamal's out the door and gone. We collect Charlotte and the cowboys and head into the Ob Room.

"Can Ollie come, too?" I ask.

Misha opens his hands—Mr. Charming-and-Helpful. So Ollie gets to join us.

"Well, isn't this fascinating," Harriet says, looking around as I set up the session table.

"This one should run for office," Frank chuckles, already beguiled by Ollie, who's made haste climbing the front of Frank's shirt, button to button, all the way to his shoulder, where he now stands like a sea captain scouting for whales.

"Ollie loves people," I say. "Don't you, little boo?"

"*Bada-bing bada-boom!*" Ollie calls, and everybody laughs except Misha, the schoolmarm declining to encourage the class clown.

Harriet keeps some distance. "Do they bite?"

"Only if you deserve it," I tell her. "But you won't deserve it."

"I've never met a parrot before," she says. "Not in person."

"Oliver is not the exemplar," Misha reminds her. "He is our charity case."

"He's a lovey-boy, is what he is," I inform one and all. "Not to mention an excellent dancer."

Misha gives me the eye; we've had our discussions about how we refer to the birds, not to mention how much time Ollie gets to spend in the Ob Room. But he lets me take the lead, sensing that I want to impress Frank and Harriet. I flash him a flirty smile—*Darling, I'll reward you for this*—but really I'm thinking it's time to tell him about Mama. We are orphans, we two, we are poor little birdies, and I can hardly wait to share not just love but sorrow.

"Ollie has talent," I tell Frank and Harriet. I figure we'll start with him and work up to Charlotte, who will blow their minds. I put Ollie on the session table, where he sings "In the Garden" with me, the whole chorus with only a few prompts.

Frank and Harriet applaud mightily, surprised and delighted. Ollie bows the way I've taught him to. Misha clucks his disapproval—we are not running a circus here, et cetera—but honestly, it's adorable, and Ollie has no role in the research, so why not let him be a pet and enjoy it? I give Harriet a walnut, which she offers to Ollie with exceptional care.

"*Yummy*," Ollie says. "*Yummy yummy*."

"My goodness," Harriet coos, "he's so cute."

This is why Misha hates visitors. He's tolerating this for me.

For me.

"I've heard a lot about you, Ollie," Harriet says. She runs her finger along his back, already succumbing. People can't help it.

Now it's showtime. Alan goes first, but he answers "yellow" to every question, which he does when in a snit. What color—*yellow*. What toy—*yellow*. What shape—*yellow*. He's miffed that I've taken him from Bob, and that he's being asked to work after supper. Also, he doesn't like to be smiled at, and Harriet's smiling like crazy. Frank's not sure it's okay to laugh—and it isn't; Misha doesn't want wrong answers encouraged, even in the most casual setting, another reason he hates visitors.

I invite Bob to the session table, where he promptly names "wool" and "rock" and "key" and correctly identifies red, blue, yellow, and green.

"Well, I'll be damned," Frank says.

Harriet softly claps her hands. "Unbelievable."

I'm so happy to have this to show them. So amazed and grateful.

"Why did Sophie not tell me this part?" Harriet asks. Misha looks up, and she adds, "My niece, Sophie Martin. She worked here."

"Oh, yes," Misha says. "No affinity."

If Harriet is offended she doesn't say so, and I suddenly feel for Sophie. Working for Misha would be dismal if you weren't in love with him. Even then it's no cakewalk.

This time I let Frank give the treat. "Here you go, Mr. Bird," Frank says, which makes Harriet smile all over again.

Now it's Charlotte's turn, and Misha takes over, arranging a jumble of objects in various colors. "You will enjoy this," he says to Frank and Harriet, and I realize that he's getting into the spirit of things, figuring out how good it feels to show off once in a while. Not everything has to be work. The atmosphere turns light and jovial, like an impromptu family picnic. I want to throw my arms around Harriet and Frank, thank them for their visit, their interest, their show of friendship.

It's at this point I hear a faint knocking, thinking it's the pipes, which frequently tick and tock in this old building.

"Charlotte, look," Misha says. "How many block?"

"*Six*."

"How many paper?"

"*Five*."

Again, I hear the knocking: a light *rap-rap-rap*, and I recognize it now as someone tapping on the outside door. We get so few visitors, the sound is foreign. Maybe Jamal's back early and forgot his key; but Misha's drilling Charlotte, suddenly enjoying himself, so I let Jamal wait. This isn't a session; Charlotte's answers won't go into the logbook; this is nothing but fun. Dr. Mikhail Petrov is having fun, and I am the one making it happen. I wouldn't interrupt this for anything.

"How many red?"

"*Three*."

"How many wool?"

"*Two*."

Frank whistles his astonishment, and Harriet's mouth drops open. "I don't believe it. I really don't." She looks at me. "I thought you might be exaggerating, Violet. I'm sorry."

"That's okay. It's pretty hard to believe."

"It *is*," she gushes.

Harriet and Frank can't get enough of this, and their wonder is contagious. Charlotte breezes through her exercises, glad to be so roundly appreciated, rising to her best behavior. Even Misha seems pleased.

"Don't ask if it's a trick," I warn them, "because it isn't."

"We do not run a circus here," Misha says, because even though he's having fun, he's still Misha and can't help himself.

"Oh, my, no," Harriet agrees. "This is scientific research. To think that such humble pets can . . ." She shakes her head, incredulous. "Not pets. Colleagues."

Which is, of course, exactly the right thing to say. Good ol' Bookie.

The Ob Room door opens, and a woman appears. Behind her, near the cages, I glimpse Jamal, back from his break. We all turn to the woman as Misha abruptly stands. He looks surprised. Shocked, you could say. He is shocked to see this woman.

"Am I interrupting?" she asks Misha, smiling timidly. Frank and Harriet and I smile back, because who wouldn't? She's tall and pretty and dressed in a vivid shade of blue and hugely pregnant, a cliché of mother-to-be radiance.

"Not at all." Misha blinks like a man in sudden sunlight. To us he says, "This is Katya," but his eyes remain on her.

For a second or two we all just stand there, all of us and the birds. The moment gains momentum, and meaning, and the clouds part, and the woman's ring matches Misha's, and she is a real woman, a woman with a name, Katya, and there is a child in her womb, and I am a stupid, stupid, stupid girl.

"You are Mrs. Rocha?" Katya asks Harriet.

"I'm just visiting."

"Mrs. Rocha left in June," I say. My voice sounds weak and far away.

"Mrs. Rocha is gone?" Her accent is like Misha's, mild and charming.

"I took her place. I'm the lab manager."

I suppose my face tells the story. And his face. There must be a study somewhere about how certain knowledge between humans bursts from seemingly nothing, an instant and full communication without words, like a flock of birds changing direction midair. Each bird, at the exact same moment, knows.

Harriet and Frank: what they must think of me. I try to catch their eyes, determined to face them, but they're busy leveling the great Dr. Petrov with a look that could blister paint off a car.

"Mishka?" Katya says. Her elegant face drains of color. "May we speak in private?"

She leaves the room with a dignity that must be inborn, her shoulders and back straight and true despite the weight of the baby.

"Excuse me," Misha says. He brushes past me and follows her out, shutting the door behind him. I hear first the Bird Lounge door open and shut, then the door to his office.

Now it's just me and Frank and Harriet and the birds and my monumental shame. I collapse at the session table and bury my face in my hands.

"What can we do?" Harriet asks, very quietly.

"Oh my God," I mutter. "Oh my God, I am a terrible person."

Ollie lands on my shoulder, pressing his feet consolingly into the divot between my neck and collarbone. I can't look up; now I know what it means to "hang your head."

Harriet says, "You're not a terrible person, Violet. You're a good person learning a terrible lesson."

"Listen to Harriet," Frank says.

At my ear, Ollie is muttering creakily, "*There-there.*"

I take a deep, shuddering breath. "I chose not to think about her at all." I look straight at Frank, into the limitless sky of his kindness. "I crashed into her life like I was drunk at the wheel." I cover my face to hide again. "I talked myself into making her invisible."

"He also made her invisible," Harriet said. "Whatever mistake you made, you didn't make it alone."

"The woman deserves better," Frank says. His pinky finger finds Harriet's and twines there. "This might be her chance to believe it."

It will be a long time before I understand all of what he means.

"You deserve better, too," Frank says. "Let's get you out of here."

I wipe my eyes. "I want to say goodbye to the birds."

"All righty," Frank says, "we'll be downstairs," and I hang my head again.

I slip into the Bird Lounge, where Jamal is pretending to read. But of course he knows. Her weeping floats from Misha's office through two doors—Katya, her name is Katya—the sound high and fragile and disbelieving, a rainfall of Russian pleas punctuated by Misha's rumbling reassurances. He's in his sumptuous office, probably sitting with her on the Buckingham Palace couch.

He declares, low and sure, the same phrase, over and over. Finally, I make it out:

She is nothing.

In perfect English.

I back into the Ob Room and shut the door to mute the sound. The birds say nothing, not so much as a whistle, cowed by the change in routine, the altered atmosphere, the perception that something's amiss. I kiss Charlotte, then the cowboys, my goodbyes taking longer than I expect. Maybe I'm hoping that Harriet and Frank will give up waiting and go on back to Harriet's without me and have a glass of wine together in Harriet's parlor, where Tabsy will be waiting on the sill.

I hear Misha's office door slam shut, and a moment later the outside door, so I move to the window, Ollie quiet on my shoulder, and in a few minutes there she is, striding across the parking lot, straight and queenly even with the burden of her belly. *I'm so sorry*, I tell her in my mind, resting my forehead against the window, awash in sadness, drowning in it, longing to reverse time, to scroll backward through September, through August, through July, through June, through May, where I can hear Misha say "you look like a violet" and quit on the spot. I would unlive all of it, the best months of my life, for her, for the wife, for Katya, because I know how it feels to believe you are loved when you're not.

"Time to go, little boo," I whisper, placing Ollie on a perch.

"*I love you*," he says.

I love you is new, and he learned it from me. It strikes me then that Misha never gave him enough credit, because Ollie's old, even in people years. Ollie simply required more time, more patience, and I know without a scrap of doubt that when Ollie tells me he loves me, he means it. I pick him up, squish him a little, and he doesn't protest.

In time I leave the Ob Room and enter the Bird Lounge. "The birds are resting," I tell Jamal, snatching a few things and stashing them into plastic bags. "Leave them in the Ob Room for ten more minutes."

"Okay," he says, watching me. "Where are you taking that stuff?"

"Ten minutes," I repeat, slipping out of the Bird Lounge into the hallway, where Misha's door is shut. I take a breath, pass his office, enter reception and grab my purse and jacket from the locker room. I leave the spare lab coat but keep the one I've got on. Badge, too. At the last second I decide to keep Mrs. Rocha's note.

YOU GOT THIS!!!

"Come on, come on," I whisper, approaching the outside door, so close, when I hear him behind me.

"She never comes here, Violet," he says. "There was a problem with her mother—"

"Don't speak to me, please." I do not, cannot, turn around.

"It does not have to end, my violet."

"Misha."

"Yes."

"You will write a letter of recommendation," I tell him, making my voice blunt and cold, exactly the opposite of how I feel. "I am efficient, innovative, and reliable. I can be trusted. I have affinity. You are very sorry to lose me."

"I *am* very sorry to lose you," he says, drawing nearer. "Don't tell me this."

"You will give me a month's severance. And with the exception of my final check, which will include overtime hours you'll find in the reception log, you will not contact me in any way, ever again."

"Please, my violet."

"I don't belong to you." I let out a breath. "You will give me these things, Misha, and in return, I will say nothing about the unprofessional, selfish, and inhumane behavior we both engaged in, under the nose of your greatly pregnant wife."

I can hear him breathing, but he draws no closer.

"Say you will give me these things, Misha."

"Violet—"

"Say it, Dr. Petrov."

He waits, not long. "I will give you these things."

Then he opens the door for me, such chivalry, and solemnly lets me go. I take the stairs for the final time, hurry down the long ground-floor corridor for the final time, nudge open the heavy double doors for the final time, and when I stumble into the crisp, darkening evening, Harriet and Frank are waiting, illegally parked, engine idling.

As I get into the back seat, I realize that Misha has given me one last gift—the chance to refuse him.

"Step on it," I tell them, shutting the door.

Frank and Harriet turn around to show their kindly faces.

"*Heavens to Betsy!*" Ollie says, and I open my jacket to show them.

29

Frank

FRANK HAD MET A PARROT only once before, when he was a kid. A green-cheeked conure, petite and colorful, whistling from the lower branches of a poplar in the neighbor's yard as a clump of children begged it to *c'mere c'mere c'mere*. He was Frankie then, ten years old; he laid down his bike and looked up, whereupon the bird fluttered to his shoulder, its talons leaving imprints that he did not discover till evening.

He hadn't thought of this odd event in decades, but now he recalled the bird's voice, that sandpaper rasp: *I love you I love you I love you*. Until the bird spoke into his ear, he'd had no occasion to know how starved he was for love. One of the neighborhood mothers swept the bird into a towel, and the rest of the story wisped out of memory.

At the edge of this memory, Harriet was saying, "Violet, we have to return him, right now."

Of course they had to return him. But Frank kept driving, because the bird liked him. At the moment it was leaning against his neck, surprisingly warm. Was it purring? Was that what it was doing?

"I can't," Violet sniffled. "He needs me."

"But you could land back in prison," Harriet said. "The bird is university property."

"Ollie doesn't belong to the university," Violet said. "He belongs to Misha, who won't come after me, because he won't want one single other person to know he's a lying cheating faithless deadbeat lowlife fake-hearted fraud."

Frank glanced into the rearview. Tears sheeted down her cheeks. "Oh, now sweetheart," he crooned.

Harriet laid her hand on his arm, and he turned to her. The light was failing fast in the way of autumn, and he loved how she looked in it. She whispered, "We have to bring him back."

The word *we* socked him with joy. He plowed straight through a yellow light, feeling anointed, full of purpose, recklessly in love, exactly the way Violet must have felt before the crash.

"Oh, boy," Harriet said, though her tone betrayed her. She was trying to be the grown-up, the dreary upholder of rules, he could hear that, but a teetering whimsy skated in between the beats. She turned around. "Violet," she said, "how do you plan to take care of him?"

"I have affinity," she said, loud and clear.

Violet was heartbroken, not broken; he could see that. She would not be broken, and he liked that about her, had known it from the moment he'd spotted her in the courtroom, something about the way she held herself, a steely blend of contrition and resolve. For days he'd watched her; he'd been drawn to her, drawn to the mistake she'd made, the mistake of loving someone for whom she'd given everything in return for so little. He saw himself in that shipwrecked girl, so willing to take what she had coming.

"You said yourself parrots need lots of attention," Harriet was saying. "You'll have another job—yes you will, a better one, mark my words—but you can't care for him if you're at work all day. Isn't that right, Frank? Don't you agree?" She finger-ruffled the bird's head and made a cooing noise of the sort she'd so recently aimed at him.

"I'll take him," Frank announced, shocking himself, pulling into Harriet's driveway now, a little too fast. "Ollie can live with me."

"Well now, that sounds awfully . . . rash," Harriet said, weakening by the syllable.

He wanted to laugh out loud. He'd been alone for decades; he understood this now. These two marvelous women, and this exceptional bird, were snapping a lid on that solitude. Or blowing the lid clean off. Right now, this minute. Sometimes, rarely, we understand a moment in the moment. Frank understood this moment.

"He'll have to see me every day, though," Violet said. "His routine will be all screwed up, and he'll need me as his anchor." She was still crying a little.

"Sounds good," he agreed. And, amazingly, it did. Aside from the berserk spaniel from Lorraine's dog breeder, he'd never had a pet.

"We'll make a plan over dinner," Harriet said, relenting. "Frank and I spent the afternoon preparing a delicious paella, and I think what you need more than anything right now, Violet, is a hot meal and people who care about you."

Ollie hopped into Violet's lap and scrambled inside her jacket, a tattered denim thing with rivets. As Harriet helped her out of the back seat, careful not to disturb the bird, Frank collected the bags, crammed with toys and bird food. As he followed them up the walk, he felt grateful and infused, all these splendid creatures commended to his care. He felt like the man of the family.

Kristy would have to understand. He would, as her father, help her to understand. *Depth of mercy, can there be, mercy still reserved for me.* His daughter had never been kind enough; that was a fact. He would teach her, and she would learn. He was her father.

All at once, Harriet began to laugh. "Oh my God, Frank, is this a caper?" Her face took on a childlike glow. "Have we just pulled off a *caper*?" He knew that over dinner she'd list a hundred reasons to take Ollie back—she was still Harriet, after all—but for now she brimmed with mischief. If not for Violet's broken heart, he'd have proclaimed his love then and there.

The porch light was on, illuminating the season's first scatter of leaves. From inside Violet's jacket, Ollie muttered, "*Whew, that was close!*" and everyone, even Violet, laughed. Frank could not remember ever, not even once in his life, feeling this right in his skin.

As they entered the house, Ollie poked his head out from the collar of Violet's jacket, scrambled down her arm, hopped straight to Frank and into *his* jacket, where he nestled there, warm and quiet.

"He loves you, Frank," Violet said. "I don't blame him."

What came to him was the mother who'd swept the green-cheeked conure into the towel: Mrs. Flynn. Little Frankie had trailed her over the course of his tenth summer when his mother once again fell ill, when again his only job was to make himself scarce. Mrs. Flynn became his imagined mother, Mr. Flynn his imagined father, the five Flynn girls his imagined sisters. Clara, Cindy, Cathy, Chrissie, Claire. They'd been his unwitting salvation then, and though he could barely conjure their faces now, their names had never left him.

"Oh, the cat," Harriet said. "I just remembered."

Violet flicked on the foyer light. "I don't think Ollie's ever met a cat."

Ollie felt still and warm inside Frank's jacket; sound asleep, he realized, a surrender that put him in mind of Kristy as a newborn. Back then he'd felt awed and grateful that, somehow, this was his life; he felt exactly that way now.

"I'll go round up Tabsy," Harriet said. "Hang on to the bird."

She took a step, then stopped, chin lifted. Frank sensed it, too: something awry. Harriet raised her hand as if testing the air, and Frank detected an off-ness in the house, the faintest whiff of something swampy and organic that did not belong in Harriet's clean, well-kept rooms.

"Someone's here," Harriet whispered.

Frank motioned for the women to stay put as he inched his way through the foyer and down the short hall, following his senses. He peered into the quiet of the parlor.

It was a woman. She was sitting in Lou's recliner, staring at him in the lamplight. She blinked a few times but said nothing. Her unwashed hair hung flatly from her scalp, wilted and weedy. Her shirt hung loose, too long, and the cuffs of her water-darkened pants pooled on her muddy sneakers. Her hands rested peacefully on the cat, who slumbered in her lap, unawares.

Harriet stepped into the room behind him. "What on earth?"

The woman lifted one hand. "Hi, Bookie. I fucked up big-time."

30

Harriet

What came to Harriet first was Dawna-Lynn's "phenomenal woman" poem, its fangs and claws, and a vision of her scuffle with the guards, kicking as they dragged her to the Fishbowl.

But the creature sitting in Lou's chair appeared spent. Declawed, defanged. Clothes inside out, damp and mud-streaked. Hands badly scratched, gouged in spots.

"You left us, Bookie," Dawna-Lynn said. "They all do." Her speech slurred with fatigue.

"It was Flinders," Violet said, suddenly at Harriet's elbow. "He fired her for taking the knitted bird."

Dawna-Lynn frowned vaguely toward Violet. Ten extra pounds, well cut hair, clothes that fit. And something else: a mightiness born of scaling the cliff and not giving up on the way back down. Of course she looked like a different person.

"Violet?" Dawna-Lynn said. "What the fuck?"

"Hi." Violet lifted her hand. "Really. It was Flinders."

"Asshole."

"Yup."

Harriet checked briefly, silently, with Frank. They agreed: slow and steady, no sudden moves.

"Is that Ethan Frome?" Dawna-Lynn asked.

Harriet nodded. "His real name is Frank."

Frank tipped an imaginary hat; he looked perfectly calm, willing to wait.

"We pictured a geezer with a gut, Bookie. He's cute." Her eyes were lidded with fatigue. "I found this nice, quiet place to sit. Nice and quiet."

Harriet edged a little farther into the room. "Shall we talk?"

Dawna-Lynn said, "We shall."

Harriet claimed her usual chair. One thing at a time. First: sit. At her elbow, a stack of prison volumes, possibly a good omen. Violet took the sofa. Frank remained at the door, his expression neutral, his eyes doing all the figuring. *Easy does it*, he telegraphed to her.

"I don't know how you got here, Dawna-Lynn," Harriet began, "and I don't need to know."

"Your house is just how I pictured it, Bookie." She gestured hazily.

Again, Harriet nodded. "Now that you *are* here, though."

"You shouldn't leave your doors unlocked, Bookie." Dawna-Lynn squeezed her eyes shut, then popped them open. "Tabsy, too, he's exactly how I thought. He came right to me. I said, 'Here, Tabsy,' and he came right to me."

At the sound of his name, Tabsy lifted his head, stood up, stretched, thumped down from Dawna-Lynn's lap, and strolled out of the room. Dawna-Lynn didn't appear to notice. "Your house is peaceful," she said. "Just exactly how I pictured it." She looked at Violet. "Good to see you, Cindy-Lou Who."

"You too, Showtime," Violet said, her eyes welling, whether from her fresh heartbreak or the draggly sight of Dawna-Lynn, Harriet couldn't tell.

How strange to have them both here, in her parlor. One so clearly on the Outs, the other so clearly not. To think of all the times she'd wished them here, all of them, sitting right here in their blues.

"Dawna-Lynn?" Harriet said, very gently. "We'll have to decide what to do here."

"My daughter's coming to get me."

"When?"

"I borrowed your phone, that's all I touched. She's gonna drive me to Canada."

"Your daughter?"

"She's seventeen, old enough. I didn't touch anything else. Just the phone."

"Your daughter is coming here?" This did not sound true.

"I used the phone, but then I came in here and turned on a light and sat here in the quiet."

Frank had yet to say a word, though Harriet sensed a coiled readiness. She met his eyes again; he gave a slight nod. She saw now what he was doing, declining to add a male voice to this female negotiation, or whatever it was. Frank Daigle understood women, she realized. He understood how to not make things worse for as long as that remained an option.

"Is this Lou's chair?" Dawna-Lynn asked.

"It is," Harriet said. Lou would have had the cops here already.

"I thought so. It's so quiet."

"When is your daughter coming?"

"Couple hours. I'm not sure. It wasn't the greatest conversation."

Harriet checked with Frank again. He made no move, which felt right.

"How about you, Violet," Dawna-Lynn asked. "How's life on the Outs?"

"It's okay," Violet said, her face crumpling.

"Aw, honey." Dawna-Lynn rose to her feet, squelched across the room, and plopped down next to Violet, who was trying not to cry.

"Is this about a boy?" She slung one arm over Violet's shoulder. "It's always about a boy."

"Yeah," Violet whispered, then melted into Dawna-Lynn's arms and wept.

Harriet glanced at Frank. He looked stricken.

"Men are pigs," Dawna-Lynn said. "Not you, Ethan."

Harriet tried to stretch the moment, tried to simply be here. Time felt both long and short. Violet dried her eyes, and then, somehow, it was her arm around Dawna-Lynn's shoulder, a reversal that reminded Harriet of the way the women in Book Club praised each other's poems.

"We missed you, Cindy-Lou Who," Dawna-Lynn said, wiping her own eyes. "You were always so fucking nice to everybody." She regarded everyone with a curious resignation. "Did you know you can walk around this city soaking wet, with your blues on inside out, and nobody gives a shit? What the hell is wrong with people?" She got up with effort, returned to Lou's chair, closed her eyes. "I love your house, Bookie. It's the quiet, you know?"

More time passed; how much, Harriet could not say. Frank's presence calmed her. She felt no alarm, no special urgency. Everything that awaited them seemed far away, irrelevant.

The cat sauntered into the room and jumped back into Dawna-Lynn's lap. The parlor filled with the restful sound of purring. All right, then; they would listen to this purring.

"Maybe I could live here," Dawna-Lynn said at last. "I could help you around the house. I could live here and have a cat and everything. And help with the cooking maybe. And sing."

"Honey, you're bleeding," Violet said.

"Oh." Dawna-Lynn peered down. Some of the cuts had opened, beads of blood crisscrossing the back of her hands; palms, too. Brambles, maybe; barbed wire. "It's okay, it doesn't hurt."

"Dawna-Lynn?"

"I know, Bookie," Dawna-Lynn said, staring at the ceiling. "But I'm so tired. Oh my God, Bookie, I'm so fucking tired."

More silence then, more long-short time. Harriet kept looking at Frank just to remind herself of him. He was thinking. She could feel him thinking.

"When I Get Out First Thing I Do," Dawna-Lynn murmured, "I call my daughter, who hits the fucking roof."

A moment or two passed.

"When I Get Out First Thing I Do," Harriet said, "I get supper out of the warmer before the house burns down."

Dawna-Lynn smiled a little. "Your turn, Ethan."

Frank said, "I don't know what this is." He spoke softly.

"You pick something sort of out of reach," Dawna-Lynn instructed him, coming back to life a little. "But at the same time it's still possible in your dreams."

"I see," Frank said.

Dawna-Lynn was studying him, and just as Harriet wondered if she was connecting his voice to the poem she'd written about shoes, Ollie shot from the cave of Frank's jacket and took flight.

"What the fuck!" Dawna-Lynn shrieked, cowering, hands clapped over her head as the cat vaulted away. Ollie zigzagged the room and plummeted straight into her lap. Terrified, she froze in place, fists tucked beneath her chin as Ollie tromped back and forth across her knees.

"What *is* that?" she asked through gritted teeth. "What the fuck *is* that?"

"That's Ollie," Violet said. "My colleague."

Dawna-Lynn frowned down at Ollie, then sized up the six inches of lab coat that hung beneath Violet's jacket.

"I work for a bird scientist," Violet said.

"Wow."

"Till today, anyway."

"Aww, Violet. Was it him?"

Violet nodded.

"Well, fuck him," Dawna-Lynn said. "Does this thing bite?"

"He's a sweetheart," Violet assured her, getting up to fetch Ollie. As she gentled him from Dawna-Lynn's lap, she said, "You saved me, you know. I thought I was gonna die when I got sent up, but then you sang those funny songs at Town Meeting."

Dawna-Lynn gave a little snort. "Good times."

"Yup."

Ollie settled with Violet for a moment, then flapped back to Frank, who remained where he was, waiting. Waiting for the women. Harriet watched him watching Dawna-Lynn and saw what he saw: a bedraggled, doomed, powerless woman at their mercy.

Dawna-Lynn leaned forward as if to get up but did not get up. Maybe she couldn't. She'd begun to shiver, whether from relief, or shock, or the elements, hard to tell. She looked cold, long exposed, feverish.

Frank spoke from the doorway—again, quiet, unassuming. "Could we have a word in the kitchen?"

"Don't call the cops, Bookie," Dawna-Lynn pleaded.

"They won't,"Violet said.

"Promise."

Violet looked to Harriet, who suddenly felt like the Book Lady, responsible for creating order out of chaos. Peace out of calamity. "For now," she said. "I promise."

Dawna-Lynn leaned back in Lou's chair and closed her eyes.

Harriet followed Frank and Ollie out to the brightly lit kitchen, a feeling not unlike emerging from a darkened movie theater: real life hit her smack in the face. "What do we do, Frank?" she said, grabbing a pair of oven mitts. "She's a fugitive."

"It's a sticky wicket, I'll admit." Again he was calm, and calmed her in turn. By now Lou would be giving a full report to the remaining cop, a curt, accurate step-by-step of the night's events. They'd go to bed with all the strings tied up.

Violet appeared now, her eyes still damp. "No way her daughter's coming."

"*I love you,*" Ollie said, and hopped from Frank's shoulder to hers.

Harriet rescued the paella from the oven warmer. "Look, we have to call someone."

"The poor thing's in terrible shape," Frank said. "I hate to send her back like that."

"I could bring her to my place for a while,"Violet offered, glancing back toward the parlor.

"You'll do no such thing," Harriet said, setting the pan atop the stove. "Let me remind you that the three of us, right this very minute, are committing a crime."

Violet consulted Frank, who said, "Maybe not technically."

"*Yes*, technically," she said, coming fully to herself. "We're aiding, or abetting, or harboring, or *something*. Something criminal." She was still wearing the oven mitts, which undermined her authority, so she tore them off and tossed them on the counter. "This evening began with a bird heist, in case you forgot."

Frank thought it over. "It's your house. If there's any harboring going on, you and I will take the blame. Violet's clean, she doesn't even live in the neighborhood." He crossed his arms, shoulders squared; he had wonderful shoulders. Every facet of his bearing telegraphed certainty.

"Frank," Harriet said, "you're not suggesting we harbor her indefinitely."

He cupped her face in his huge hands. "I'm suggesting we give the woman a meal."

"Yes," she said, putting her own hands over his. "All right, good, yes." One thing at a time.

"And a hot shower," he added. "Maybe a peaceful nap on a good bed. That's a few hours of harboring, tops. Then we call."

Violet said, "I vote for that."

Harriet stepped away. Cahoots: right here in her kitchen. Frank opened his arms, and she walked straight in, resting her head on his chest. "Frank Daigle," she said, "there will be no I-told-you-so's left in the English language once Sophie gets wind of this."

They returned to the parlor as a single unit, cahoots all around. Dawna-Lynn looked up. "I know you have to call."

"We do," Harriet admitted. "But not right now."

"We're sorry," Frank said.

"It's okay, Ethan. Not your fault."

"*Oh, he walks with meee*," Ollie sang.

"It talks?"

"I taught him that," Violet said. Her expression held both pride and grief. She'd lost so much tonight, Harriet realized; Ollie seemed a fair trade after all. To hell with Dr. Parrot.

"*Whew, that was close!*"

"You said it, birdie." Dawna-Lynn covered her face. "When I Get Out First Thing I Do I go straight back inside, where they add to my time." Her hands muffled her words. "Oh my God, Bookie, this house is so pretty. I miss my kids. I'm so hungry." She dragged her fingers through her stringy hair. "I'm just really fucking hungry."

Harriet bent toward Dawna-Lynn, ignoring the odor. "Would you like some paella?"

"My grandmother used to make that," she murmured. "I had a good childhood, Bookie. Everybody loved me."

Frank ferried the food from the kitchen to the parlor, which became a harbor indeed, a pause in time, a bubble reminiscent of Book Club. He served Dawna-Lynn first. Harriet watched him do this, and waited for her turn, feeling cared for in a way she had never before experienced. She watched as Frank settled Ollie on a dish towel with a nectarine and a bowl of nuts from Violet's stash. He brought water, both for Ollie and for the women. After that he served a heaping portion of paella to himself.

He was a man who waited. They ate where they sat, in silence. Dawna-Lynn kept an eye on Ollie, fascinated.

"Let's get you showered," Harriet said when they finished. "I'll find you some dry clothes."

Once on her feet, Dawna-Lynn seemed almost too tired to walk and Frank's idea to offer her a nap seemed the only decent gesture. Violet led her to the upstairs bathroom, taking Ollie with them in case the cat got ideas. From the hallway Harriet could hear weeping; she heard Violet helping Dawna-Lynn off with her clothes, murmuring encouragement, starting the water. "*That's the ticket!*" Ollie rasped.

"All I did was drive the car," came Dawna-Lynn's voice, small now, resigned. "Fifteen years, and all I did was drive the car." Harriet heard the linen closet open and close. "I drove the car for an asshole who used me up."

"It's okay, honey," Violet said, "we've all been there."

Harriet slipped into her bedroom, where she rooted around for clothes that might fit. She was all in now, determined to send Dawna-Lynn back in a halo of scented shampoo and the rustle of fresh clothing. After a nap, as long as she needed. And another helping of paella, to see her off with a memory of her grandma.

As she inspected her closet, she felt Frank's hands on her shoulders. She leaned back, let him hold her up. "Wow," she said.

He enfolded her from behind, crossing his arms over her chest. "Wow."

"We make a good team, Frank Daigle." She turned around, nestling into him. "I knew just what you were thinking."

"Do you know what I'm thinking now?" He drew her a little closer.

She laughed. "I hope so."

He said, "When I Get Out First Thing I Do I ask Harriet Larson to be my wife."

Harriet Larson had said yes all her life. To her parents. To her teachers. To Lou and the girls. To Corinne and Sophie. She'd said yes to shopkeepers, to doctors, to car salesmen, to Girl Scout leaders, to Mormons on rounds, to hairdressers who wouldn't let her go gray. She'd been raised to say yes, to agree and approve and adapt and accommodate, to step aside as the architect of her own happiness. After Lou's death she vowed to say yes only when that yes belonged to her, solely to her. And so: Yes to college. Yes to teaching. Yes to retirement. Yes without being asked; yes *before* being asked. Yes to Book Club. Yes to Violet. Yes to the filthy and broken Dawna-Lynn, for whom she was searching out a bright, becoming color from a closet too full of beige. These yesses felt like power, like gateways, like love.

"Frank." She laid her cheek on his chest. "Yes."

31

Violet

Of all the books we read, over the year and a half of Book Club, *Spoon River Anthology* stayed with me the longest. I liked that the ordinary dead spoke for themselves at last, even if someone else had engraved different words on their stone. I liked that they told stories about each other. And I liked that so many recalled not how they died, but how they lived.

Lydia Puckett was the real reason Knowlt Hoheimer died a soldier.

Herbert Marshall broke an engagement, forsaking Louise for Annabelle.

Elmer Karr gave thanks to the loving hearts that took him in again.

I'm guessing that Lydia and Herbert and Elmer lived acceptably long, acceptably happy lives, but when the time came to wrap it up, they reached back through the decades for a story that most defined them. One that would forever speak for them.

Just as I reached back to find the one that spoke for me.

It might seem odd, or at least inelegant, that in the telling I told Frank and Harriet's story too. Or that the story I chose ends with me in Harriet's bathroom, helping Dawna-Lynn off with her clothes. But we never see the shape until the end. Dawna-Lynn stoops, head down, briar-whipped and razor-cut and naked, then raises her arms and hangs on to me, weeping. I hold her there, choosing to be the loving heart that takes her in again. It makes my own heart feel better. Easing her into the tub, I recall a song she once sang at Town Meeting. She hums it with me, then quietly sings the words. I fill a pitcher with warm water, humming along, soothing Dawna-Lynn with her memory of brightening a grim place with the best thing she had. Ollie watches from the sink, copying us, whistling a bit, trying to follow along.

This moment, pouring water over the grimy hair of a woman in despair, will forever mark the end of this shimmering time. I am doing for Dawna-Lynn what Frank and Harriet and Ollie did for me.

I suppose how I lived *after* this moment is my real story: a short first marriage to a good man, a long and gratifying second try, three beloved children, a career as a research librarian. I forged a fraught but cordial relationship with Kristy; I made a genuine friendship with Sophie, who spoke at my funeral; I outlived Frank and Harriet and deeply grieved them. After Vicki died, her son found me and befriended not only me but also my children. And I outlived Ollie, who died at the astonishing age of seventy-four. My children adored him. We kept track of Misha's work, though I never revealed my connection. I learned to play the piano; I read thousands of books. My life unfolded as most lives do, day upon day of doing my best and occasionally my worst, that human continuum. My passing arrived softly, in the company of my firstborn, and her firstborn, and Dawna-Lynn, who served her extra time and never went back.

Even the least eventful life holds an avalanche of stories. Any one of mine would give you a fair impression of who I was and how I lived. But the one I chose—the one that now composes this epitaph—isn't a story at all. It's what Harriet would call the meanwhile, the important thing that was happening while the rest of the story moved along.

My name was Violet Powell.

I took a life. I lived and died.

Meanwhile, I was loved.

A Note on the Parrots

I based the animal-intelligence research in this novel on the groundbreaking work of Dr. Irene Pepperberg. She has conducted studies with African grey parrots for decades, beginning with Alex, whom she bought from a pet store in 1977. Though Alex's brilliant career as a research colleague ended with his premature death at age thirty-one, he left a rich legacy for future researchers exploring avian cognition. Unlike the fictional Dr. Mikhail Petrov, Dr. Pepperberg is a warm, delightful person who invited me to her lab in 2019 to visit Alex's successors. (Actually, I invited myself, twice, and she finally agreed.) There I met Athena, an eight-year-old party girl who loves her leisure time; and Griffin, age twenty-four, an A student who once thrashed twenty-one Harvard students in twelve of fourteen trials of the old boardwalk "shell game." These birds are truly astonishing, and their contribution to scientific research cannot be overestimated. To read more about the work of Dr. Pepperberg, or to make a donation to her foundation, go to alexfoundation.org. I thank her for her inspiring research with these radiant creatures.

Acknowledgments

I love an acknowledgments page that gives me a sense of how a book came to be, whom the author relies on, and what vulnerabilities the author unwittingly reveals. Alas, what I often find instead is a boring list of strangers' names. So I'd like to not only thank a few people, but tell you specifically who they are and what they mean to me.

Huge thanks, as always, to Gail Hochman, who makes everything I write better. Gail reads faster and more deeply than anyone I know. She can read a 350-page manuscript over a weekend (along with lord knows how many others in those bursting tote bags) and retains the smallest details of character and every turn of plot. It's quite the parlor trick, and a tribute to the care with which she embraces her clients' work. For the first time in our long association, Gail visited me in Maine last summer, and I now have a forever memory of watching the stars with her on an evening cruise in my husband's motorboat on Casco Bay. Gail has a huge personality and gigantic mind, but on the ocean that night, she seemed endearingly small, marveling at the view with childlike glee. That's what makes her a good reader; she doesn't miss a thing.

Marianne Merola, the reigning queen of foreign rights, has been the other fixture in my professional life. For many years she was a voice on the phone: reassuring, calm, kind. I'm sensitive to voices and often make assumptions based on them. When we finally met in person, I found that she matched her voice perfectly. She is also really, really funny.

She and my husband have a ridiculous email rivalry that is too convoluted to recount here, but it has been a source of much entertainment. Thanks, Marianne, for that and everything else.

After a publishing shuffle with my former publishing company—an increasingly common source of anxiety for writers—I wound up with a new editor. She is young and I am not, so I entered into this crucial new relationship with a twinge of trepidation. To my relief, I found in Jessica Vestuto a smart, insightful, and generous editorial guide. Huge thanks to Deanne Urmy, my former editor, for putting us together. Like Deanne before her, Jessica does not try to bend the work to her will, but rather asks all the right questions at all the right times to bend the work to its *own* will, making it a better version of itself. This is a thousand times harder than it sounds. I'm deeply grateful, Jessica, and honored to be your first.

I also owe many thanks to the teachers and students in the Precision Machining and Manufacturing department at Southern Maine Community College. During the fall semester of 2019, I attended class once a week and learned to run the machines as a way to get closer to my character Frank. The young men in my class, most of them around age nineteen, could not have been sweeter or more patient (writing, not machining, is my jam). I would like you to imagine me, a smallish, sixty-something woman, wearing safety goggles and moving a block of aluminum through a monster milling machine all morning. In the afternoon, I took a related print-reading class from my husband, whose prodigious skills could not, alas, redress my terrible, inborn lack of spatial perception. He has long forgiven me our first orthographic-projection assignment, when I drew a cartoon Snoopy in lieu of the side view of a stop-block.

Machinists make the world go round, they really do, so if you know someone even remotely thinking of this as a profession, please encourage them!

I write in a backyard studio built by my aforementioned husband, and I feel lucky to have it. However, whenever I'm stuck, I hie to other havens in the hope of a jump-start. Susan and Bill Nevins loan me their camp on Moosehead Lake every year, a retreat that I share with my childhood best friend, Denise Vaillancourt, whom some of you may remember from my memoir, *When We Were the Kennedys*. Denise and I adore that place, where chipmunks, if you ply them with sunflower seeds, will allow you to stroke their silky fur. Once, we saw a bull moose amble across the yard while we were drinking our morning coffee on the deck. Needless to say, it's a place where I always write well. Thank you, Susan and Bill.

I flee more often to the Birdhouse—the screened-in deck of my dear friend and surrogate daughter, Jessica Roy, who lives about four blocks from me. The aptly named Birdhouse sits high up, treetop level, and Jess's partner, Bill Seidel, brings me tea and cookies as I work. The Birdhouse bonus is Moxie, their petite, affable black Labrador retriever, who keeps me company out there, mainly because Labs live for treats and I am a pushover. Bill owns a rental condo in Edgecomb, Maine, on the Sheepscot River—a gorgeous estuary that fills with buffleheads and loons in winter. He offers the condo for free whenever I'm *really* stuck, or when I need a few uninterrupted days to solve an especially knotty narrative problem.

I also make a yearly retreat to my friend Amy MacDonald's family camp on Bearcamp Pond in New Hampshire. Every fall, five women gather there for a few days. Amy and I write, Lindsay Hancock and Jenny Scheu paint, and Deborah Luhrs cooks and knits and keeps our annual book discussion on track. They are dear old friends all, and have fed my creative life more than they know. Lindsay's stunning painting of Bearcamp Pond hangs above my desk.

Patrick Clary, an old friend and lifelong correspondent, read the first full draft with loving attention that helped the second full draft emerge. Moreover, he did it *by hand*. When I first saw all that ink, I thought, *Uh-oh*. But every note was right on point and saved my eventual editor a lot of headache. I'm grateful, Pat, for your letters, your reliable moral support, and your long friendship. Sorry about the title.

To the band—my beloved writing group—I owe more than I can ever express, except to dedicate the book to you. Which I have, in gratitude for our unique and necessary bond. I can't imagine writing one more sentence without you.

To the bookstores we writers rely on: thank you. I feel unbelievably lucky to live in Portland, Maine, a city of 65,000 that somehow can sustain five independent bookstores. (Not to mention the used-book venues, and Nonesuch Books across the bridge in SoPo.) It's an embarrassment of riches in my town, from plucky little Letterpress Books in the north end, to the sleek and friendly Print on Munjoy Hill, to the gifty Sherman's on Exchange, to the brand-new Back Cove Books on Woodfords Corner, to the warhorse Longfellow Books on Monument Square, which is the model for Wadsworth Books in *How to Read a Book*. If you're coming to Portland for a visit (everyone is, these days), please fit some book-buying time between the ferry cruises and brewery tours.

My sisters, Anne and Cathe (and their menschy husbands), steady the ground beneath my feet in so many ways. They are tiny women with big opinions about many things, including my books, which they apparently find flawless. Anne is always willing to read a draft, Cathe likes to wait until publication, so applause comes both sooner *and* later.

Dan Abbott, my tall, bald, handsome, adorably affable husband who reads every draft with love and ruthlessness, sincerely considers me the best writer in the Western world. (He hasn't read many in the Eastern world.) My career would not be possible without him, and that's the truth.

Last, a word to my readers. Thank you for writing to me, for choosing my books for your book clubs, for coming to my talks and readings, for gently pointing out mistakes of local geography, for recommending my books to your kids and your parents and your friends and your booksellers, for noting them on your blogs and social-media pages. It's always a pleasure to meet you, sometimes in person, more lately on Zoom, occasionally in an airport or a coffee shop or on the street. Every one of these encounters makes me glad to have chosen this vocation.

This all sounds misleadingly farewell-ish. At the moment I don't have another novel cooking, and as a writer in the autumn of my career, this could well be it. But that's what I said after the last novel, and then this one plinked into my head in the wee hours of an August night. I got up, opened a notebook, wrote down what Violet was saying, and by the following August I had a full first draft, the fastest writing I've ever done. I hope that happens again, when I least expect it.